PERFECT HAPPINESS

PERFECT HAPPINESS

YOU-JEONG JEONG

Creature Publishing
Charlottesville, VA

This is a work of fiction. Names, characters, places, and incidents either are the products of the author's imagination or are used fictitiously. Any resemblance to actual persons, living or dead, events, or locales is entirely coincidental.

Originally published in Korean by EunHaeng NaMu Publishing Co., Ltd.

Published with the support of the Literature Translation Institute of Korea (LTI Korea)

ISBN 9781951971335
LCCN 2025935831

Cover design and spine illustration by Rachel Kelli
Author photo © Hong Jinwhan

CREATUREHORROR.COM
@creaturepublishing

CONTENTS

PART I: MOTHER'S DUCKS

CHAPTER 1

Mother was good at making duck feed, and Jiyoo knew exactly how she did it.

First, Mother bought pork. She preferred stuff that still had the bones in it—pig head, pork ribs, hind legs. She got these at the wholesale market. The meat they sold at the supermarket was too expensive. Of course, Mother never used the word "expensive." It wasn't polite to talk openly about money. Instead, Mother said it was because the ducks needed strong bones.

Next, Mother prepared the meat. She needed a few tools for this. The first was a cleaver to cut through the bone. Her cleaver had the look and weight of a small axe. She needed both hands to raise it above her head. When cleaving, it was important never to hesitate. "You have to bring it down decisively, with no emotion." That's what Mother said.

Her second tool was a boning knife. It was long and sharp, perfect for slicing through meat. Actually, it was so sharp that it made slicing meat off the bone as easy as peeling wrapping paper off a present. Mother also used a carving knife for severing tendon and cartilage. The last of her tools was a sashimi knife, used for making thin strips of meat. Jiyoo wasn't sure exactly why Mother needed to slice the meat so thin. Weren't large chunks enough? But Jiyoo never got the chance to ask her. She wasn't allowed to talk to Mother when she used the sashimi knife—Mother might cut her hand if she lost focus.

Once the meat was prepared, Mother put everything—bones and all—into two large pots to boil. She cooked it until any remaining meat fell cleanly off the bone. The boiled meat then went into a grinder designed for making sausages. Mother needed to be careful not to let her hand get caught in the blades. She said the grinder didn't know the difference between pork rib and human hand. Everything went into the grinder, even the bones. Mother would mix the fine white powder into the meat, and then she would pack the meat into plastic bags.

The first time Mother made duck feed was one day last spring. That was also the first time she had taken Jiyoo to the cabin in the country. Since then, they had come four more times: once in May, twice in the summer, and once last month.

And every time they stayed at the cabin, Mother would make duck feed. At first, she wasn't particularly good at handling the knife, but now she was a pro. She cleaved, chopped, and carved with accuracy and speed. And thanks to her teachings, Jiyoo could talk like a butcher.

Jiyoo's job was to fetch the wheelbarrow from the shed in the front yard when Mother was done cooking. It was the same one Great-Grandmother used many years ago for working in the vegetable garden. Now, they used it for moving duck feed to the reedy wetlands, located on the property just a short walk down the path across from the front gate. Thankfully, Mother was good at pushing the wheelbarrow.

The Half Moon Marsh was no bigger than the YMCA pool where Jiyoo took swimming lessons. It was maintained by two sources of water: one was the stream trickling down from the nearby mountain, and the other was a natural spring located deep beneath the wetlands. Even though the marsh was shallow, Jiyoo wasn't allowed to play in the water because of the thick mud that lay at the bottom. Nor was she allowed to wander off the trail that circled the marsh. There was a deep gorge just beyond the wetlands, a fall from which would "shatter every bone in her body." Jiyoo went to see the gorge just once. Behind Mother's back, of course.

The wetlands were on Mother's land. Grandma had willed it to her along with the countryside cabin. The Half Moon Marsh was located at the far end of the wetlands, where all sorts of birds gathered. Most of the birds came here during the winter and left again in the spring. The few ducks that stayed never left the marsh. They lived here until they died. To them, the swamp was a "happy duck house," as Mother liked to call it.

Mallards were the most common duck in the happy duck house. There were a few mandarin ducks, too. The drakes of that species were like beautifully crafted dolls. Mother called the drakes "scoundrels" because they were always cheating on their mates. There were also moorhens, queer little birds that hung around the other ducks for scraps. Even stranger were the loons, who liked to hide in the reeds or underwater. At dusk, the loons would cry out from the wetlands as dense fog settled on its waters. And sometimes, they would cry out from Jiyoo's dreams.

On the path circling the Half Moon Marsh was the feeding rock, which was wide and flat and steep, like a slide. Mother would push the wheelbarrow up that rock to throw feed to the ducks. She didn't need to call the ducks. Dumping the feed from the wheelbarrow into the water was enough. The ducks knew exactly what to do. Flying, paddling, diving—they all swarmed to the feed. They loved Mother's cooking.

Jiyoo's kindergarten teacher once asked the class a question:

"So, what do ducks like to eat?" she asked.

Everyone raised their hand but Jiyoo. "Worms." "Slugs." "Loaches." They had a lot to say for knowing nothing about ducks.

Jiyoo's teacher had a peculiar habit of only ever picking on kids who weren't raising their hand.

"How about you, Jiyoo?"

Jiyoo didn't like talking in front of the other kids. Her stomach started to grumble whenever that sea of eyes locked onto her. It made her feel like a giant serpent was wriggling beneath her belly button. But Jiyoo didn't have the courage to stay silent when someone called on her to speak. What she managed to get out of her mouth was closer to a wad of spit than a sensible answer.

"Pork," Jiyoo said.

The children all giggled. Some slapped their desk as they laughed. A few even called out, "Dummy!"

The teacher asked again, as if to give Jiyoo a second chance. "Perhaps you meant woodlice?"

Jiyoo kept her lips shut. She was furious. Furious for being laughed at even though she gave the right answer. Furious because there was no way she could prove to them that she was right. Furious because her teacher thought she didn't know the difference between mammals and bugs. Jiyoo told Mother about this.

"They reacted that way because they don't know," Mother said. "It's a well-kept secret of the Half Moon Marsh."

Aha, it was a secret. Hearing her mother's explanation, Jiyoo felt her anger withdraw. Suddenly, she understood everything. Indeed, she was smart. And it wasn't just Jiyoo who thought this. Auntie and Grandma also said so. Jiyoo was especially good with words and finding their hidden meaning.

"And what did Mother say about secrets?" Mother asked, as though she were drilling Jiyoo.

"You can't tell anyone about them," Jiyoo answered.

"And?" Mother said, hinting that Jiyoo hadn't given a full answer.

"And if you tell someone, you get punished."

Yesterday afternoon Jiyoo came to the countryside cabin in Mother's car. They came the same way they always came, but this time they didn't stop at the wholesale market. They did stop, however, to pick up Father off the side of the road.

This was his first time coming to the countryside cabin. It was also Jiyoo's first time seeing him since he left. She didn't know why it was Father had left. All she remembered from that day were a few dream-like fragments of foggy memory. But Jiyoo's mother *did* tell Jiyoo why they were getting a divorce: because Father was a "scoundrel."

Last night before Jiyoo fell asleep, Father whispered something in her ear.

"Daddy's not going today. I'll be sleeping downstairs." In a sleepy voice he added, "Let's go to the Half Moon Marsh at dawn."

Jiyoo fell asleep quickly. She had thought she would have a hard time falling asleep because of her excitement, but she didn't. Jiyoo could hear a loon cry in her dreams. It sounded like it was coming from the attic. But when she went to the attic, the sound moved downstairs. And when she went downstairs, it moved to the bathroom. Jiyoo ran to the bathroom, but as soon as she opened the door, the floor beneath her feet collapsed and she fell into an endless pit of darkness.

Jiyoo woke, her legs straight and stiff. Looking out the window, she could see a full moon. The large crimson ball hung in the sky just above the Half Moon Marsh.

"It's okay. It was just a dream. A dream that'll disappear when you wake up in the morning."

Jiyoo thought she could hear Mother's voice coming from somewhere.

"Just close your eyes."

Jiyoo closed her eyes. To wake up, she first needed to fall asleep again.

When she opened her eyes again, dawn was just breaking. Amidst the faint blue light of the early morning sky, there was the fishy smell of meat—faint, but unmistakable to Jiyoo. Mother must be preparing duck feed, she thought to herself. She must be teaching Father her secret recipe. If that was true, they must have made up last night. *That's definitely what happened.*

Jiyoo hopped out of bed. She ran out of her room without changing out of her long underwear and without making her bed—two things Mother wouldn't approve of. But Jiyoo was in such a hurry she forgot about this. She wanted to make sure that last night's dream had disappeared.

*

When Jiyoo reached the landing, her feet refused to move any further. Now that she was halfway down the stairs, things had gotten so dark that she couldn't see any farther down the stairs. It felt like a deep ravine was lurking beneath her next step. The air was cold, and Jiyoo could hear the whirring of a machine coming from deep in the darkness. Jiyoo looked back up the stairs at the faint blue light shining out of the wide-open door she had just sprinted out of.

Should I go back to my room? Should I be a good girl and lie in bed until Mother calls me?

Shaking violently in the darkness, Jiyoo tried to figure out what was happening downstairs.

The kitchen was directly at the base of the stairs. Because it didn't have any windows, the kitchen turned pitch black if you turned off the lights, even during the day. The fact that the lights were off told Jiyoo that Mother was not in the kitchen. It also meant that the door between the kitchen and the living room would be locked. The whirring sound was probably the sound of the overhead fan. Mother always turned on the overhead fan when boiling meat. She and Father must be in the living room. All Jiyoo needed to do was check. All she needed to do was make sure her dream wasn't real.

Jiyoo descended the stairs feeling the edges of each step with her toes. As expected, the gas stove was on. Jiyoo could make out the faint image of two pots placed atop blue flames. She walked toward the door to the living room, which was also shut, as she thought it would be. It was exactly ten steps from the bottom of the stairs.

The countryside cabin was a house of twos. Two stories, two bedrooms and bathrooms split between the first and second floors, and two doors in and out of the house, one next to the bathroom, and one near the kitchen.

The layout of the house was a bit different from most. Coming in through the front door, you were immediately met with a long and narrow island-turned-dining table, in front of which was the kitchen. Across from that was the door to the living room. In the living room was the door to the bedroom, which was placed directly opposite the door from the kitchen. Inside the bedroom, again placed directly opposite the door, was a large window. Seen from this perspective, the house was like a tunnel, running through the center of which was a series of three doors and one window.

Most days, Mother left both interior doors open. Jiyoo would sit on the kitchen-side of the table, where she would stare directly at the window in the bedroom. She liked looking into the kitchen from outside the bedroom window. From there, she could spy on what Mother was doing without her knowing.

On the other hand, when all the doors were shut, Jiyoo felt uneasy. She felt both sad and ashamed, like Mother had locked her out. Sometimes, Jiyoo would hover in front of the living room door, trying to figure out what she'd done wrong. Right now, as she stood outside the living room, was one of those times. All she could do was dither in front of that closed door.

I could knock or call out to Mother or open the door slightly. But wouldn't that anger her?

Jiyoo brought her ear close to the door. She could hear the whirring coming from the other side. It was like the overhead fan, but louder and harsher. Perhaps a vacuum cleaner? If it was, it had to mean Mother was cleaning. And that would mean she and Father were both awake. But this didn't necessarily mean it was okay for Jiyoo to go in.

There were many rules to follow when Jiyoo was with Mother. It was against the rules to open a closed door without permission. That was true whether Father was around or not. But despite knowing this, Jiyoo still wanted to open the door. She wanted to know that last night's dream was over. She wanted to see with her own eyes that nothing was wrong, that nothing had changed from yesterday.

Jiyoo first tried knocking. When there was no answer, she opened the door slightly and put her eye up to the crack. Her heart dropped suddenly. The living room was pitch black. The whirring seemed to be coming from the direction of the sofa. But Jiyoo couldn't hear anyone. She whispered into the dark.

"Mother?"

Jiyoo's voice was swallowed up by the loud whirring. She couldn't even hear her own voice. It felt like she was only moving her lips. She called out again, this time in a louder voice.

"May I come in?"

Jiyoo thought she heard someone say, "Come in," but it could have been her imagination. She placed one foot in the living room, then called out again.

"Should I turn on the light?"

Again, she thought she heard a yes, but she couldn't be sure. The whirring continued. Jiyoo flipped the switch on the wall. The lights came on and showered the room in white light. She couldn't help but shield her eyes. When she opened her eyes again, she almost screamed. She was so startled that she forgot how to breathe for a moment.

Sitting on the couch was a person—a woman, naked and hunched over with long black hair draped over her face. The whirring sound Jiyoo had heard wasn't from a vacuum. It was a hair dryer, which the woman held in her pale white hand and slowly swung back and forth. Jiyoo could feel her throat finally start to open as the words she had been holding back came out.

"Mother!"

The whirring stopped. The hand holding the dryer paused. The woman tilted her head to the side and looked out at Jiyoo through dangling locks of hair. Jiyoo felt her stiff knees begin to loosen. It was Mother. Jiyoo hadn't called out "Mother" because she thought the woman was her mother. "Mother!" was just what she screamed when she was frightened.

"Mother—"

It took some time for Jiyoo to accept this unfamiliar-looking woman as her mother. Mother explained that she had just taken a shower and was drying her hair, but it took time for Jiyoo to accept this. Eventually, Jiyoo realized Father was missing, as were his bag and padded jacket, which had been draped over the sofa armrest.

Jiyoo looked back at the front door. Father's sneakers were also missing. It wasn't the dream that had disappeared, but Father and all his stuff. It was as if he had never been here at all.

Father had left. Jiyoo turned her eyes to the patio, trying not to show disappointment. A thick blackout curtain was covering the glass sliding door.

"Why are you glancing around like that?" Mother asked.

Startled, Jiyoo turned to look at Mother. When their eyes met, Jiyoo shook her head.

"Didn't I tell you not to speak with your head? You're not some neanderthal."

Mother's voice was high and thin, like the chirping of a bird. It was so quiet that Jiyoo almost had to lean in with her ear to catch it. When Mother's voice was high-pitched and shook nervously like this, Jiyoo had to be quick on her feet. It was a sign that Jiyoo was annoying Mother. Just like she was right now.

Jiyoo went over to Mother. She brought her toes flush with the front of the sofa:

"Good morning, Mother."

Mother brushed the left side of her hair to the side and tucked it behind her ear.

"Did you sleep well?" Mother asked.

"I don't know."

"What do you mean you don't know?"

The corners of Mother's mouth were quivering, just like her voice. Jiyoo could feel herself withering. She wouldn't have come into the living room had she known Mother was in a bad mood.

"Because my dream didn't disappear."

Jiyoo felt her body tremble as she said this. A scene from her dream was replaying itself in her head. Why hadn't the dream disappeared after waking up? Jiyoo wanted to ask Mother, but she resisted the urge. She didn't think it would be wise to ask. But she didn't know why she felt this way. It was just a feeling.

"What do you remember?" Mother asked.

Jiyoo didn't answer. She was suddenly distracted by Mother's right hand, which was still holding the hair dryer. Bandages were wrapped around her wrist all the way to the first joint of each finger. And blood was staining the parts on her thumb and the edge of her hand. No, "staining" wasn't the right word. The bandages were completely soaked, as though droplets of blood would fall from the bandages at any moment. Mother seemed to be unaware of this, and Jiyoo thought she should tell her immediately. Without warning, she grabbed Mother's hand and yelled out, "Mother! Your hand is bleeding—"

"Eek!" Mother shrieked in pain. Her shriek was so piercing and terrifying that Jiyoo went rigid, Mother's hand still in hers.

"Go away." Mother brandished her elbow and shoved Jiyoo aside. As she did this, the hair dryer hit Jiyoo on the chin and fell to the ground with a crash. The nozzle on the hair dryer broke off and skidded across the floor. Jiyoo stumbled back two steps but caught herself before falling.

"Why would you do that?" Mother said.

Jiyoo cupped her chin in her palm and stepped back. Her chin was throbbing from being hit with the hair dryer. And her cheeks were blushing from being scolded. Jiyoo's vision became watery as something hot started to well up in the back of her throat.

Jiyoo dropped her head. Afraid that she might start to cry, she clenched her jaw and swallowed hard. A terrifying long silence followed. The only thing that could be heard was Mother's irregular breathing.

"Jiyoo," she finally said, "come here."

Jiyoo batted her eyes as she finally let the tears flow. She wasn't sure if she believed her ears. Had Mother really just said, "Come here"? At times like this, "Come here" was more terrifying than "Go away."

"Jiyoo Cha," Mother said again.

Jiyoo was still not used to this name. Father's last name was Seo. So, naturally, everyone, Grandma, Auntie, even her stepfather, called her "Jiyoo Seo."

But recently Mother would refer to Jiyoo using stepfather's last name. She told Jiyoo she would go by this name next year when she entered elementary school. Jiyoo needed to practice, Mother explained. She needed to practice answering when Mother called her by what would soon become her new name. Jiyoo walked over to Mother and stood in front of her.

"Jiyoo Cha," Mother said again.

"Yes?" Jiyoo said reluctantly.

"Look at Mommy." Her voice was now somewhat softer. Jiyoo raised her head.

"Why did Mommy get angry?"

Jiyoo knew the answer. How could she not? Mother always pointed it out to her. "Because I startled you."

Mother extended her hand and touched the left side of Jiyoo's jaw. It was Jiyoo's right side that had been struck with the hair dryer.

"Does it hurt?"

"A little," Jiyoo said before quickly adding, "But I'm fine now."

Mother opened her arms toward Jiyoo. "Come here, my daughter."

Jiyoo reluctantly entered Mother's embrace. She could feel the sensation of Mother's round, subtle, exposed breasts on her shoulder. She could also hear a heart pounding loudly, the way a rabid dog would bark. But she couldn't tell if it was hers or Mother's.

"Forget about dreams," Mother muttered as she rubbed Jiyoo's back with the tips of her fingers. "What's important is that I love you more than anything else in the world."

It sounded like Mother was talking to herself. Her words were as cold and distant as the wind that swept across the wetlands every day. Tears started to flow from Jiyoo's eyes again, tickling her eyelashes.

"Do you understand?" Mother said as she held Jiyoo in front of her and looked her in the eye. At times like this, "Do you understand?" wasn't really a question. It was Mother's way of sending a message—a message that it was time to apologize.

"I'm sorry, Mother," Jiyoo said. "I'll be more careful from now on."

Mother collected her hair behind her shoulders and sat up. Her breasts were tight and puffed out, like a pair of cocked pistols. Jiyoo glanced furtively to the side of the sofa. She was thinking about whether she should bring Mother her clothes or keep pretending she hadn't noticed.

"I have something to tell you," Mother said. She seemed like she was done talking about her hand. "Your father left yesterday."

Mother's eyes looked glazed over as she said this. Her eyes were directed at Jiyoo, but her attention was elsewhere. Jiyoo knew this look well.

"He told me to tell you he's sorry he couldn't keep his promise."

Jiyoo had already figured this out. She also had a hunch about why Mother wasn't in a good mood. She must have had a fight with Father last night. Like they always did when they used to live together. Mother believed that Jiyoo didn't remember those times. She was only half right. Although Jiyoo didn't remember everything, there were a few fragments of memories that remained. Like the vivid images from that night Mother cut her wrist with a kitchen knife.

That night, Mother and Father were having another fight. She wailed and screamed and threw things at him. Jiyoo hid under the kitchen table. She covered both ears to block out the screaming and closed her eyes so she wouldn't see this person she didn't recognize, all the while wishing desperately for the fight to be over.

Ever since then, the images from that day would from time to time find Jiyoo in her dreams. Mother sprawled out on the kitchen floor, her hand covered in blood, the kitchen knife at Jiyoo's feet, Father's hands as he wrapped Mother's wrist in a towel, and the blood vessels popping out of his forehead. Most vivid of all was the memory of waiting for Mother in the emergency room with Father.

Jiyoo figured something similar had happened last night. But something seemed different. Of course, Mother had bandages on her hand again. But this time, Father hadn't taken her to the emergency room. He had left even though Mother was bleeding. Or was that really what happened? There was a whispering voice somewhere deep inside Jiyoo's head that said otherwise, but Jiyoo didn't want to hear it. Instead, she waited for Mother to explain.

"Father won't be coming back anymore."

Jiyoo felt the tips of her dangling fingers twitch slightly. *Anymore?* She wanted to ask what Mother meant by this, but she resisted the urge. Mother had said so, and that was that. Asking wasn't going to bring Father back. Nor did Jiyoo have the courage to ask why he left. After all, more important than Father's absence was Mother's feelings—at least to Jiyoo they were.

"I don't mind," Jiyoo said, finding a safe thing to say. "I can play with you, Mother."

"No. Mommy has something to do. You go play in your room."

"You want me to play in my room?" Jiyoo asked, not sure if she understood.

Jiyoo's mother only stared back at her. This meant yes. It also meant not to come back down until she gave Jiyoo permission. In other words, she wouldn't be going to the Half Moon Marsh today. Jiyoo wanted to go, even if she had to go by herself. She wanted to know why the loons had been so noisy last night.

"All day?"

"You can handle it, can't you?" Mother asked.

Good daughters never say no to their mother. That was Mother's Rule Number One.

"Yes," Jiyoo replied.

"Do you have anything else you want to ask?"

Jiyoo could hear a voice in her ear saying, *It's better not to.* So Jiyoo said no.

"Good. Then you know what you need to do now, right?"

"Go upstairs, get dressed, wash my face, and make my bed."

Jiyoo gave an answer she knew her mother would like.

"Good. I will bring you breakfast in thirty."

Breakfast? In my room? Jiyoo was about to ask Mother before shutting her mouth. Mother had never brought breakfast up to Jiyoo's room before. Jiyoo thought this strange, but she tried not to let it bother her. All she wanted to do right now was escape Mother's gaze as soon as possible.

"Okay. I'll finish everything before you come upstairs."

Jiyoo turned toward the living room door. Mother bent over and picked up the hair dryer that had dropped to the floor. The whirring started up again.

When Jiyoo reached the threshold, her toe hit something. It was the nozzle to the hair dryer.

Jiyoo ever so slightly turned her chin to look back over her shoulder. The hair dryer was by itself blowing hot air across the floor. Mother, on the other hand, was on her knees, apparently looking for something underneath the sofa. Jiyoo slid the hair dryer nozzle across the floor, which might have been the thing Mother was looking for. But Jiyoo didn't slide it toward Mother. She slid it toward the kitchen table. The nozzle slid under the table like a speeding bullet. It let out a scratching sound as it skidded across the floor, but it seemed like Mother hadn't heard it. If she had, she would have asked about it.

Jiyoo left the living room. She tiptoed up the stairs like a ballerina and then disappeared into her room.

*

That day was unbearably long. Jiyoo felt like she was trapped, not on the second floor, but in time. Only after eating, going to the bathroom, perching on the windowsill and staring down at the wetlands, reading all of *Frozen II: A New Destiny* which Stepfather had bought for her, and glancing at her Snow White clock more than one hundred times did the sun finally set. Even though she couldn't make out the hands of the clock in the dark room, she knew it had just turned ten because the train of dwarves inside the clock made ten passes.

Jiyoo sat up in her bed. She leaned up against the headboard and listened to the sounds of night coming in through the window—branches from the maple tree in the front yard bumping up against one another, a faint breeze caressing the reeds, the barking of the dog from the neighbors down the road. The night was placid, boring, and bright.

Lying on the moonlit windowsill was a tray with a bowl of goulash on rice, silverware, and a cup of water. Mother had brought it up an hour ago. It felt like she had barely remembered Jiyoo's dinner.

When she brought the food, Jiyoo was lying on her bed pretending to be asleep. Without turning on the lights, Mother came into the room, laid down the tray, and then left. Jiyoo didn't touch the goulash. But it wasn't because it tasted bad.

Mother was as good at making goulash as she was making duck feed. And Jiyoo knew exactly how she made it. Mother would stir-fry large chunks of beef with onion, add water and bring it to a boil, add goulash seasoning, paprika powder, and potatoes, then boil it all down until the meat was tender. One pot was enough to last days. Just like seaweed soup, the longer you boiled it, the richer the flavor. At least, that's what Mother said.

Apparently, Mother learned how to make goulash from her Hungarian roommate while studying in Russia. Stepfather's opinion was that, of the dishes Mother cooked, this was one of the "acceptable" ones.

Jiyoo agreed with her stepfather. But she didn't want to eat any more of Mother's goulash. It wasn't that she was being picky. No one would want goulash three meals in a row, especially after being locked in their room all day. Unfortunately, because Mother cooked a full pot of goulash last night, it might be on the menu for the rest of their stay.

Downstairs was now quiet. The whirring of the vacuum cleaner and the grinder had ceased. And Jiyoo hadn't heard a sound out of Mother since she brought up dinner. It seemed like she went to sleep as soon as she went back downstairs. But that was understandable. She had spent all day tirelessly doing "chores"—Who wouldn't be tired? And if Mother was really asleep, she wasn't going to wake up suddenly and bring Jiyoo another bowl of goulash.

Jiyoo looked over at the bedroom door.

You want to go to the attic, don't you?

Jiyoo could hear a voice in her head. Mother had named the voice "Mischievous Mouse."

When Jiyoo didn't answer, the mouse in her head goaded her on.

Go if you want. You can play up there if you clean up and don't leave any traces.

Are you sure? Jiyoo thought of the box of puppets in the attic and the day she discovered it.

The second floor had three doors: the bedroom door that faced the stairs, the door to the left which led to the bathroom, and the door to the right which had a lock on it, all connected by a long hallway. Whenever they stayed at the cabin, Jiyoo's curiosity about what was behind the locked door became unbearable. And when she found the keys hidden in the drawer of the hallway dresser one day, she felt like she had dug up lost treasure; one of the three keys on the chain fit the lock to the attic perfectly.

Jiyoo didn't hesitate before opening the door. She was immediately met with complete darkness. There wasn't a single window. Jiyoo flipped the switch on the wall, but even with the lights on, the room wasn't as bright as a normal room. Indeed, the only light in the room was a single dim lightbulb attached to the wall. The first thing that her eyes locked onto was the ceiling of the room, which matched the one in the second-floor bathroom. It followed the slope of the roof.

Stepping into the room, Jiyoo was struck by a musty smell. Stacked on the long, narrow wood floor were all kinds of objects. A rolled-up carpet that had been stood upright, a blanket wrapped in a plastic cover, a curtain stuffed in a plastic bag, old comic books, plastic baskets filled with unrecognizable junk, and an assortment of paper boxes.

And among all these objects was a box full of hand puppets. Overwhelmed by excitement, Jiyoo ran downstairs. She wanted to ask Mother if she could play with the hand puppets.

"Mother."

Mother, who was chopping meat on the counter when Jiyoo called her, turned around. When her eyes met Jiyoo's, she smiled. Jiyoo loved Mother's smile. Or rather, she loved the moments when Mother smiled. Those moments when the corners of Mother's eyes curled up as she beamed at Jiyoo with her beautifully straight teeth. Her sparkling eyes were asking, *Yes, my daughter?*

"Can I play in the attic?"

"The attic? You mean the storage room upstairs?"

"Yes, that one," Jiyoo said, barely able to hold back her excitement. She had almost revealed the fact that she found the key. She had wanted to ask if she could play with the things in the attic. The puppets were one of the things in the attic.

Mother turned back to face the counter and threw down the cleaver she'd been holding. When she turned back to look at Jiyoo, the smile had disappeared from her face. Her lips had turned thin, her cheeks hollow, even the sparkle in her eyes had disappeared. So icy was her expression that Jiyoo felt like she shouldn't breathe. Breathless, Jiyoo waited for Mother's response.

"No, you may not."

If Mother said no, that meant no. She had never changed her mind once she said no. In other words, there was no point in Jiyoo's going downstairs, waking up her sleeping mother, and asking again if she could play with the puppets. It was enough that she had cried her eyes out that one day.

Jiyoo stepped down from her bed. The walk to the attic felt so extremely long. She could reach the room in ten seconds normally, but she had to be careful. She had to lift her heels as she walked, stop several times to listen to the sounds downstairs, and open the attic door in a way that didn't make a rattling sound.

Only after entering the attic and closing the door could she finally relax. The attic was located directly above the first-floor bathroom. There was little chance the sound of her footsteps would cross the living room to reach the ears of her sleeping mother. She could now let her heels touch the ground.

Jiyoo turned on the light and started to move around the room. Being careful not to touch any of the boxes, she worked her way into the forest of cardboard. The box of puppets was in the corner of the room where she had left it. She removed the lid and found what she was looking for: Four hand puppets, four chairs with stakes to seat the puppets, a roundtable, a set of teacups, plates, and other things for playing house.

Jiyoo had originally planned on bringing the box to her room to play with. But now that she saw it, she gave up on that idea. It was much heavier than she'd imagined. It wasn't too heavy to lift, but it *was* too heavy to both lift and move. It was probably so heavy because of all the wood, which, except for the puppets themselves, comprised everything in the box. With difficulty, she could probably drag the box across the floor, but there were too many obstacles to navigate. And the room was too cold to play in. She had only been standing here for a few moments, but the cold wooden floor had made her feet into icicles. There was also a draft seeping in through the ceiling, causing her to shiver.

Just take the puppets. Jiyoo had made up her mind, but there was one problem. What if mother woke up and came upstairs? Jiyoo gave Mischievous Mouse a quiz. If Mother suddenly opened the door to her room, how many puppets could she hide before Mother saw?

One, the mouse answered.

Just one? Jiyoo asked in protest.

Just one, the mouse said again. *You act as if that's a small thing. It's Mother we're talking about.*

Mother decided the rules. And she also gave punishment when the rules were broken. Excuses didn't work on Mother. She never forgave anyone, even if they begged. She showed no mercy, not even to Jiyoo. In fact, she had made Jiyoo an orphan once.

Mother and Stepfather lived in Cheongyeon together. Mother's work was in Incheon, and Jiyoo lived at her grandmother's house in Hagik-dong. She attended the kindergarten near Mother's work. On weekdays, Mother would stop by Grandmother's house to drop Jiyoo off at kindergarten on her way to work. She would do the same thing on her way home from work, but in reverse. Jiyoo spent the weekends at her stepfather's house.

Jiyoo didn't complain about living apart from Mother. After all, she was able to see her every day, so she never forgot she had a mother.

But when Mother made Jiyoo an orphan, this wasn't possible. Mother wouldn't come to take her to school. She wouldn't call either. Jiyoo would have to take the school bus and spend the weekends at Grandmother's. Most times it only lasted for a week. But it could last as long as a month when mother was really angry. Whenever this happened, Grandmother would hold Jiyoo tight, her eyes filled with tears. Then she would mutter something Jiyoo didn't quite understand. "My child, it's my fault you suffer."

When Grandmother cried like this, Auntie would always erupt in anger: "Oh, would you stop it."

Sometimes Auntie would drive Jiyoo to and from kindergarten. She would even take Jiyoo to the toy store or cat café to cheer her up. Jiyoo liked Auntie almost as much as Grandma, but these acts of kindness just weren't enough. Auntie wasn't Mother. So, it was best not to get in trouble in the first place, even if it meant having less fun.

Jiyoo took out the first puppet. It was wearing a plaid shirt and jeans and on its chest was the word "Dad." The second puppet had short hair and was named "Mom." "Baby Brother" was wearing a red hat. And then there was a princess with long braided hair and a crown: "Yuna."

Reading this name, Jiyoo realized whom these puppets belonged to. They were Mother's. Or to be more exact, Mother when she was a little girl, back when she lived with Grandma and Grandpa in this cabin. It was hard for Jiyoo to imagine that Mother had ever been little.

Jiyoo calmly drew a family tree in her head. Grandmother, Grandpa, who had passed away, and Auntie, Mother's older sister. "Baby Brother" had to refer to Jiyoo's uncle. The only problem was that Jiyoo didn't have an uncle, at least not on her mother's side. Another problem was that there was no older sister in the puppet family. In other words, someone who shouldn't be there was, and someone who should be there wasn't.

Then who were these puppets? Mother's imaginary family? When Mother was alone, had she also played with her imaginary family in this attic? What stories did she tell them? And why had she acted so scary when Jiyoo brought up the attic?

Jiyoo's mind was whirling with questions. But she had no answers. The longer she thought, the more confused she became. It felt as if she were trespassing in Mother's secret world. Suddenly, she thought she could hear Mother's angry voice.

Quick, put everything back!

A loud thud came from somewhere. But Jiyoo couldn't tell if it came from inside the house or outside. It sounded both like the front door being closed or the wind knocking something over. Jiyoo listened closely. But she couldn't hear any sounds coming from downstairs.

Jiyoo could feel a sense of unease returning to her. She needed to go back to her room as quickly as possible. Remembering that she shouldn't leave any traces behind, she placed the puppets back in their original positions. The mom in the mom's seat, and the baby brother in his. But in Yuna's seat was something strange. She hadn't noticed it when she took the puppets out. It was a severed puppet leg. It didn't belong to t a human puppet. The leg was covered in light-yellow fuzz and connected to a webbed foot.

A duck's foot, Jiyoo guessed. She wondered where the rest of the duck was but decided she wouldn't go looking for it. Nor did she have time. She sat Yuna on her chair and closed the lid to the box. She was planning on only taking Dad Puppet back to the room with her. If he were Mother's imaginary father, perhaps he could also be Jiyoo's imaginary father.

Jiyoo returned to her room. When she lifted her legs onto the windowsill, she realized she was in the clear. The downstairs was still silent. She felt relieved. The attic was locked again, Mother was fast asleep, the night was still young, and Jiyoo had slept plenty during the day. Not even Mother would be able to figure out what she had been up to—as long as she returned the puppet before morning.

Jiyoo put the puppet in her hand and brought it to eye level. It was so strange. In the moonlight, the puppet looked just like her real father. The glasses, the clothes, even the sneakers. She mimicked her father's deep voice as she talked to herself:

"Jiyoo, what did you do today?"

"I read a book," Jiyoo said in her normal voice. "It's called *Frozen II*. It's my third time reading it. After that, I took a nap."

"Wasn't that what you were reading in the car?"

"Yes, that one. I do like it. But I wanted to go to the Half Moon Marsh. I wanted to know if the loons were okay."

"Are loons your favorite?"

"Yes."

"Why?"

"Because they're strange. Sometimes they howl like ghosts, and other times they scream like children. You heard them last night, didn't you Father?"

"Strangely enough, tonight I haven't heard them."

He was right. Tonight, they had been silent. Jiyoo looked out the window.

"I guess they're asleep. They must have hoarse voices after last night."

The moon, which was hanging from the maple tree in the front yard, drifted through the sky toward the wetlands. Unlike last night, the moon wasn't crimson in color. It was large, white, and even rounder than before. The moonlight was so bright that Jiyoo felt like she could see individual reeds in the Half Moon Marsh if she opened her eyes wide enough. The fog suspended above the field of reeds was following the movements of the wind and dancing like waves of mercury. The night was still silent and bright, but it was not boring anymore.

"Father, why did you leave?" Jiyoo finally asked the question she had been dying to ask.

"I'm sorry. Something came up. I bet you were disappointed?"

Jiyoo batted her eyes as if to say yes.

"Just a little. But, Father, are you really not coming back?"

"No. I'm coming back. What, did you forget the promise we made at the Half Moon Marsh last night?"

Jiyoo hadn't forgotten. How could she forget that promise? Her father's movements, his words, his expressions, his voice—from the moment he got into the car to the moment Jiyoo fell asleep, she remembered everything.

Yesterday, Mother showed up unexpectedly at Jiyoo's school and had her dismissed early. It was just before lunch time. Seating Jiyoo in the back seat, which was not where she usually sat, Mother said something Jiyoo could hardly believe.

"We're going to meet up with your father in a bit."

Jiyoo was so excited she stopped breathing for a moment. Did she mean Father and not Stepfather?

"There are two secrets you must keep from your father."

First, Mother told Jiyoo that she mustn't tell father that she was living with Grandma. And second, she mustn't mention anything about Stepfather. Jiyoo didn't ask why. There were a lot of secrets she had to keep. The exact secret depended on whom she was talking to. But regardless of who it was, Mother never explained to Jiyoo why she had to keep each secret a secret. But perhaps she would make an exception for Father. Actually, Jiyoo was most curious about whether the father Mother was referring to was her real father or stepfather.

And it turned out to be her real father. There he was, standing at the lonesome bus stop in the middle of nowhere. Slung over his shoulder was a bag, and in his hand was a McDonald's Happy Meal. He got into the back seat as soon as Mother brought the car to a stop.

"My daughter," he said as he sat down. He was out of breath, as if he had run here. He looked at Jiyoo, placed the Happy Meal by his feet, and spread his arms as wide as he could. Jiyoo knew he was trying to initiate a hug, but even so, she didn't move. She just gave Father a blank stare. Something was off. Was this really her father? He seemed like a mirage, one that would disappear as soon as she reached out to touch it.

"Jiyoo, did you forget Daddy?"

His eyes were begging her to hug him while there was still time. Jiyoo glanced at the rearview mirror. Mother's icy stare was locked onto her.

Mother couldn't bear to see Jiyoo acting close with other people. Holding hands, hugging, maintaining eye contact for too long—all of these were things Mother hated to see Jiyoo do with other people. Jiyoo wasn't even free to do these things with Grandma. Jiyoo was the only one who could recognize that icy glimmer in Mother's eye's when Jiyoo showed another person affection. She knew what Mother was going to say the moment the two of them were alone. *I guess you love Grandma more than me. I guess you'd be happier living with Grandma from now on.*

"Hello, Father."

Jiyoo decided to go with a greeting instead of a hug. She placed both hands on her lap and politely bowed her head. This would usually win her compliments, but not this time. Father dropped his arms, his eyes moist. And his lips, which had been wearing a smile, puckered into a strange shape. It took several seconds before he finally spoke.

"Hi, Babe."

Babe . . . Jiyoo had almost forgotten. That's what Father used to call her.

"Look at you. You're all grown up."

His voice was trembling slightly. Jiyoo could feel her chest pounding. Her breathing was becoming irregular and her throat tight. She wanted to say something, but nothing was coming out of her throat. She didn't know what to say. She felt like she had been too harsh on him.

"Honey, put on your seat belt," Mother said.

The eyes staring at Jiyoo disappeared from the rearview mirror. Her father placed his bag on the car seat and fastened his seatbelt. As he did this, she couldn't help but stare at the strap on his bag, hanging from which was a fist-sized keychain of a bumblebee. The keychain was grubby and had multiple stains on it. Jiyoo had a hard time believing this could belong to her father.

"Ready?"

Mother turned on her left turn signal and stepped on the gas. As the car exited the curb, the sound of music started playing from Father's coat pocket. Mother's eyes appeared in the rearview mirror again. Father hurriedly stuck his hand in his pocket and took out his cellphone. As soon as he pressed accept, a girl's voice started talking on the other end.

"Joon-young, where are you?"

"Kyochon."

This time it was Father who glanced furtively at the eyes in the rearview mirror.

"Min-young, I'll call you back later."

The girl was beginning to say something when Father abruptly ended the call.

"You haven't changed at all," Mother said.

"I won't answer the phone from now on," Father said as he shook his head.

Mother was smiling gently through the rearview mirror.

"You must have forgotten about what you did at Lotte World on Jiyoo's birthday."

"That was an emergen—"

"You better not make any mistakes today," Mother said, cutting Father off. "Only then will I believe you and let you look after Jiyoo. You said you wanted to see Jiyoo alone next time, didn't you?"

Father made eye contact with Mother as he gave her a nervous smile. His expression looked as though he still hadn't figured out what it was that Mother wanted. Jiyoo was beginning to feel uncomfortable. She was afraid that Mother and Father were about to fight again, only moments after reuniting. Jiyoo didn't know who Min-young was, but she wished Father would turn off his cellphone already. After all, wasn't that what Mother was asking?

"*I* don't answer phone calls when I'm with Jiyoo."

Mother had decided to teach Father a lesson. She took her phone from the cellphone mount and showed it to Father.

"I just turn the thing completely off. Because I want to have a good time with my daughter, distraction-free."

Father turned off his phone. When Mother extended her hand backward, he meekly put the phone in her hand. The two didn't speak to each other after that. Jiyoo took *Frozen II* from her school bag and pretended to read it. When Father spoke to Jiyoo, she only gave him short answers. And instead of looking at him, she would stare at the bumblebee hanging from his bag and shake or nod her head. She did this when he offered her the Happy Meal, too. She hadn't eaten lunch and was hungry, but she just shook her head at his bag. Saying no required a powerful imagination.

The French fries must be salty and mushy by now. And the bulgogi burger is probably too sweet and greasy. I bet the coke is flat, too. I'll definitely throw up if I eat it in the car.

Father ate the Happy Meal all by himself. He leaned his flushed face against the car window and stuffed the fast food into his mouth as he stared out the window.

"Jiyoo, do you want to show your father the Half Moon Marsh?" said Mother when they arrived at the countryside cabin. Jiyoo was walking up the stairs with her school bag and turned around to look at Mother. *Just the two of us? Was that allowed? Isn't it going to be dark soon?* After asking these questions to Mother, she asked one more question, "What about you, Mother?"

"Mommy needs to prepare dinner. You can just leave your bag on the stairs. I will put it in the room for you."

Jiyoo stood side by side with Father at the front door. Mother followed them out as she said to Jiyoo, "The ground will be soggy from the rain last night. You should change into your boots."

Jiyoo took her father to the shed. Next to a large ladder were three pairs of boots arranged in a row. A pair of yellow boots for Jiyoo, a pair of blue boots for Mother, and a large pair of large black boots that had never been worn before. Mother had bought these boots at the wholesale market the first time they came down to the country. Jiyoo thought it was strange at the time.

"Why are you buying three pairs?" Jiyoo asked.

"You'll find out when the time's right," Mother said with a grin on her face.

It appeared the time was finally right. Mother was always prepared.

Jiyoo handed Father the unworn pair of boots and put on the yellow boots for herself. When they came out of the shed, Mother was there waiting for them.

"Come back before dark," she said. "Don't make me come looking for you again."

But Jiyoo had never made Mother come looking for her. She had snuck out once before, but that was only once, and in secret. She thought Mother was being unfair, but she didn't complain. She didn't really have the time to. In her mind, she was already holding Father's hand and running down to the wetlands. If only Mother hadn't been watching from the front door, she would have really done it, too.

Jiyoo's legs were twitching, and she had to suppress the urge to run. Because of this, she could already feel a cramp in her calves; she hadn't even crossed the road yet.

"So," Father began after they crossed the road, "what's at the Half Moon Marsh?"

Jiyoo answered as they entered the side path. "You'll see when we get there."

The side path extended in a straight line toward the Half Moon Marsh. It was the only piece of solid ground in the entire wetlands. The path was apparently built by Jiyoo's great-grandmother who had hired workers to place gravel and sand on the loose soil. Jiyoo's great-grandfather, who had many aches and pains, used it for walks. His walking partner was Mother when she was a little girl. As an ornithologist, Jiyoo's great-grandfather would take Jiyoo's mother to the Half Moon Marsh and tell her stories about the ducks. Come to think of it, all the stories Jiyoo heard from Mother must have been from her great-grandfather.

"You mustn't leave the trail," Jiyoo warned Father who was walking on the edge of the path. He looked down at her. When their eyes met, he mouthed to her, *Why not?*

"The reeds grow in thick mud. The ground is so soggy that only weeds and reeds can grow in it. You can't farm on it, or build houses on it, or make golf courses."

Father's gaze scanned the field of reeds once, then returned to Jiyoo. She felt awkward, so she said something to break the silence.

"That's why the countryside house and wetlands aren't worth anything. No one has offered to buy them."

"Where'd you hear that? Was it Mother?"

Jiyoo said yes and shrugged. She felt a bit embarrassed about getting excited and talking so much.

"Do you guys come down here often?" he asked.

Jiyoo thought for a moment before answering. It was a secret that she and Mother came down to the countryside cabin sometimes. No one knew, not her stepfather, not her auntie, not even her grandmother. So, was it a secret to Father, too? No. If it were, why would he be here?

"Sometimes. Mother used to live here when she was young. It's Great-grandmother's house."

Aha. Father nodded his head. "I think I've heard about this place from your mother. That village we saw on our way in: Woo—"

"Woohyeri Village."

Jiyoo felt relieved that Father knew about Woohyeri. Now she didn't need to worry about whether she could tell him or not.

"We don't go down to the village. So we don't know anyone."

The late-afternoon sun suddenly hid behind a dark cloud. The field of reeds became dark, the wind a notch colder. Jiyoo quickened her pace. She was nervous that the sun would set before she could show Father the "happy ducks" of the Half Moon Marsh. Father widened his strides to keep up with Jiyoo.

Soon, the Half Moon Marsh came into view. The sun hadn't set yet, but there was already a thick fog floating on the water. Jiyoo stopped in front of the feeding area.

"We're here."

There was a lot more water in the Half Moon Marsh than last summer. The water level was right up to the edge of the feeding area. Only the very tips of the reeds and cordgrass were sticking out of the water, the air above it swarming with red dragonflies. Jiyoo took a running start, then jumped up onto the feeding rock. Father followed and stood behind her.

"Mother and I come here and give the ducks their feed," Jiyoo said as she looked down from the feeding rock.

"Do you buy the feed?" Father asked.

"Mother makes it."

"Your mother? How does she make it?"

Jiyoo told father how to make duck feed. As he listened, he would sometimes nod his head. He looked surprised that ducks ate pig meat.

"But where are all the ducks hiding?" Father asked. "I haven't seen one yet."

Jiyoo turned to look at the water beneath her feet. Just as she anticipated, there was a dark shadow moving beneath the murky water. Jiyoo tried to scream, but it was already too late. As soon as she opened her mouth, a jet-black shadow sprung up from beneath her feet. Startled, Jiyoo twisted her body and lost her balance. Her foot slipped, her legs shot up into the air, and her shoulders and head fell backwards. She instinctively closed her eyes.

The impact of the fall wasn't as bad as she thought it was going to be. She didn't even get pricked by the reeds. Nor did it seem like she had fallen into the thick mud. It took a few moments for Jiyoo to realize a pair of arms had safely caught her. There was a sturdy body supporting her back, and a voice whispering in her ear.

"Are you okay, Babe?"

Jiyoo waited before answering. She was listening to the pounding of her father's chest on her back. Suddenly, unchained memories began to flow in her mind. A long time ago, her father's hands and arms were always waiting nearby. Whether she tripped or missed her step, they were always there, like magic. She now remembered just how much she missed this safe and warm sensation. The sound of his voice every night in her dreams.

"Knock-knock. Earth to Jiyoo. You're not asleep, are you?" Father asked.

"No," Jiyoo said, trying to stifle the smile that was trying to form on her lips. "I'm awake."

Father lifted Jiyoo up and sat down on the ground. Jiyoo was now seated on her father's lap, in his embrace. After a while, Jiyoo noticed the loon. It waddled up onto the rock, craned its neck, and started to cry. An eerie wolf-like howl filled the sky.

Wa-oooooo.

"That's a loon. They're not afraid of people," Jiyoo said.

Jiyoo lifted her body and stood up. She gathered herself and extended her hand out to her father who was still sitting on the ground. Father took her hand and got up with a grunt.

"That little guy is called a loon, you say?" Jiyoo's father asked.

He wore a big smile as he asked this.

"Should we get back at it for scaring us?" he asked.

It was all Jiyoo could do to nod her head without cheering.

"On the count of three. One, two…"

Three. Jiyoo jumped onto the rock. She shouted as she landed next to her father. The loon screamed out in surprise, jumped a meter into the air, then flapped its wings as it fell into the water with a splash.

"Go away, you bully! And don't mess with me again!"

Jiyoo took her thumb and stuck her nose up at the loon. This and the words she had just said were two things she would never say in front of Mother.

Mother always pointed out when she did something vulgar.

"And where did you learn that one?" Father asked as he laughed heartily.

"Auntie taunt me."

"Jane taught you that?" A bittersweet smile appeared on his face.

"Well, there's this kid at school who picks on me. When the teacher's not looking, he pulls at my hair, lifts up my skirt, and sticks out his foot to trip me. Auntie says I shouldn't be scared of kids like that. 'Next time he's mean to you, slap him across the face and say this,' she said."

Father laughed again, this time even louder than the last. But Jiyoo didn't know what was so funny.

"So, *did* you do it?"

"No."

Jiyoo cast her eyes downward.

"Auntie said I can do it. She says I have 'determination' . . ."

Auntie Jane had taught Jiyoo that determination was the courage to see something to the end. But as far as Jiyoo saw it, this was something she didn't have. She practiced endlessly in her mind, but whenever the time came, her heart would race and she would start to feel dizzy and nauseous. And in the end, she never stood up to the bully.

"But I'm too shy. I get embarrassed and act stupid when I get excited. If I don't want to be treated like a dummy, I should just keep my mouth shut, like I'm not even there."

Father's laughing stopped, and the cheer on his face disappeared.

"Did your mother tell you that?"

Jiyoo suddenly felt uneasy. Seeing the look on Father's face, she realized she said something she shouldn't have. At times like this, the best thing was not answering. Thankfully, Father didn't press her. He only added one more thing:

"Your Auntie Jane is right."

Father studied Jiyoo's face for a moment. His gaze was cautious and gentle. A few seconds later, the smile returned to his face. He seemed to be telling Jiyoo that he wasn't scolding her. It was the flapping of wings that finally broke the silence.

"That's a coot," Jiyoo said.

Aha, Jiyoo's father mouthed. "You know your stuff."

Jiyoo shrugged her shoulders. "They're a bit grumpy. That's why they race around on the surface of the water."

Jiyoo's father again mouthed the words *Aha*. Behind his glasses, his eyeballs were spinning round and round like giant Ferris wheels. Jiyoo had seen this look many times. It meant that Father was impressed by how much she knew.

"Should we go to look at the other ducks?" Jiyoo asked.

As soon as she asked, Jiyoo's father took her hand. Jiyoo took her father to the trail circling the Half Moon Marsh. It was by the time they arrived at the end of the trail that she saw another duck she knew. The little rascal was sitting in a dip in the grass and silently staring up at Jiyoo as though it were going to the bathroom. Afraid that it would fly away, Jiyoo quickly turned to her father to show him.

"It's a mandarin drake."

She didn't tell Father that its other name was scoundrel. She thought this would upset him. But she didn't have any time to tell him because in the grass near the water was a nest. It was made of grass and reeds and had several light-brown eggs inside it. Jiyoo counted the eggs. *One, two* . . .

"I see five eggs."

Father put his fingers to his lips. *Shhh.*

"Let's see what duck these belong to."

Father wrapped his arm around Jiyoo's shoulder and squatted in the reeds. They didn't have to wait long. A loon swam over and gently perched itself atop the eggs. In the distance, another loon called out. *Wa-ooo.*

"Mother told me that when the daddy loon is far away, he'll call out to his young. Like this."

Jiyoo stuck out her lips and made them into the shape of a duck bill.

"*Wa-ooo*. I'm coming. *Wa-ooo*. I'm cominggg . . ."

Jiyoo's voice trailed off. Talking about ducks was fun, but not what she wanted to talk about. She wanted to ask Father where he had been and why he was here now. Jiyoo's father seemed to know what Jiyoo was thinking. He then made a promise, one Jiyoo would never have imagined.

"From now on, Daddy will come more often."

Jiyoo wanted to ask Father how often was often. But she couldn't. If this was a promise he was making on the spot, she wouldn't want to put him in an awkward position. If he hesitated while answering, she would start to doubt his promise. So, Jiyoo decided to ask Auntie Jane how often "often" was the next time she was at Grandmother's house.

"Promise?"

Father extended his pinky toward Jiyoo. She took her pinky and curled it around his. Then after hesitating for a moment, Jiyoo asked another question.

"But what if you forget your promise?"

"I won't forget. Never."

"What if you forget your promise to not forget?"

Father gave Jiyoo a big smile. But for some reason, his smile seemed somewhat melancholic. Jiyoo turned toward the direction of the valley and looked at the space beneath her feet. Her eyes were seized by a dizzying landscape. The valley, which was gnarled with pines and large boulders, was dark and deep. Across the valley, the evening sun was descending on the mountain, painting everything in the wetlands in bright red. Wind rushed in and out of the valley. Jiyoo looked back at her father.

"Let's go home. Mother will be mad if we're late."

By the time they arrived home, Mother had just finished preparing dinner. The atmosphere was more like a party than supper. On the table were candles and a vase with three roses. In the middle of the table was a chocolate cake with a single candle, next to which was a bowl with salad and a breadbasket, as well as cheese, butter, and a bottle of wine. There was a wine glass and a juice glass set at the place closest to the living room, and a single wine glass set at the place closest to the kitchen.

Father looked a bit surprised. He took off his shoes and was about to step into the cabin but hesitated for a moment as he looked at Mother, who pointed toward the bathroom with her thumb.

"Wash your hands first. The both of you."

Jiyoo washed her hands with Father. Or to be more exact, Father stood behind Jiyoo and washed her hands for her. As he lathered her hands, he asked her:

"I used to wash your hands like this all the time. Do you remember?"

Jiyoo nodded. One by one, the memories returned to her. Father's getting into the bathtub with her and bathing her. Playing games with the bubbles floating on the water. And Mother's coming home, seeing her and Father in the bathtub together, and exploding with anger. "Honey, what are you doing with the baby?"

Jiyoo returned to the table, walking side by side with her father. Mother handed Father the corkscrew, then lit the candle on the cake.

"It's your first father-daughter reunion. Don't you want a picture?" Mother asked as she poured wine into Father's glass. He nodded, and Mother took her phone from inside the sink drawer and turned it on.

"Okay. Hold your glasses up and put your cheeks together. Say cheese."

Jiyoo and Father did as Mother said. Mother stood with her back against the kitchen counter and pressed the shutter button.

"This is a really beautiful picture."

Mother returned to the table with the phone. Father took the phone as she handed it to him. Jiyoo, too, looked at the picture on the phone screen. The two of them were smiling happily. They looked so cozy, as though they had never been apart, not once. But the background was eerily dark. Behind them, the doors to the rest of the house were all open. The unlit living room and bedroom both looked like dark caverns threatening to devour Jiyoo and her father.

"I'll send it to you," Mother said as she tossed her phone aside.

Jiyoo thought how nice it would be to have her own cellphone so that she could look at the picture whenever she missed Father. Of course, she would never say this out loud. It wasn't something Mother would like.

The goulash was surprisingly good. Mother was more talkative than usual. And Father also looked like he was in a good mood. He finished the bottle of wine all on his own. He was drunk even before they finished dinner.

"Jiyoo, I think it's time for you to go to bed," Mother said.

Jiyoo got up obediently. She also thought it was best to go to bed early. If she wanted to get up early tomorrow, that was. Father had said they would go to the Half Moon Marsh again together. And Mother had said it was okay.

"But then why did you go?" Jiyoo asked as she touched the face of the Dad Puppet with her fingers.

Everything from that day felt like a dream now—her walk with Father to the Half Moon Marsh, the family of loons they saw, Father's promise to come more often. Perhaps Mother was right; perhaps Father wasn't going to come anymore. That must be why he left without saying goodbye, right?

Right? Jiyoo asked Mischievous Mouse.

What came was an answer with no emotion: *Right.*

Jiyoo took her hand from the puppet and placed him near her toes. She rested her chin on her knees as she stared out the window. A full moon was descending on the wetlands. As the marsh received the light from the moon, it sparkled like a gigantic lake. But there was something moving inside the dark-blue field of swaying reeds: a single orange light.

Was it a firefly? But it wasn't summer. Jiyoo craned her neck and squinted her eyes to get a better look. The light was slowly moving along the side path. It was moving away from the cabin, toward the Half Moon Marsh.

CHAPTER 2

Eun-ho spent the night with his eyes wide open. But this wasn't the first sleepless night he'd had recently. His insomnia had started the day his Wife left for her mother's house. Today was the fifth day of her absence.

When morning came, Eun-ho could feel his brain starting to short circuit. Nanoscopic errors littered his memory. *Why did I come to the kitchen again?* Only when he reached the study did he remember he wanted to brew a cup of coffee. But now he had a new problem. *Why did I come to the study?*

Eun-ho's absentmindedness continued to the bathroom. By accident, he ended up washing his hair with shaving cream and brushing his teeth with face wash. When the toothbrush, which ejected from his shocked mouth, fell into the toilet bowl, Eun-ho's subconsciousness did something very uncharacteristic: it swore. *Goddamnit!*

No sooner did he swear inside his head than he thought he could hear Wife's voice:

Why are you always so irritable? It's your fault, after all.

Irritability was, as Wife put it, Eun-ho's "congenital disease." And yet, despite ostensibly having it since birth, Eun-ho only became aware of his condition *after* marrying Wife. According to her, irritability was just one of three defects of his that threatened their marriage. She pointed out his irritability so often that now he questioned everything he did. *Am I just being irritable? Am I expressing my emotions like an adult?*

But not this morning. Today, Eun-ho didn't care if he was being irritable. Or rather, he felt his irritability was well justified.

Indeed, all it would take was a neighbor's staring too long at his flower garden for Eun-ho to run out of his house and pick a fight with them.

After fishing his toothbrush out of the toilet bowel, Eun-ho went to his study to put his laptop and books in his bag. It was the weekend, but he would rather be at the office right now than at home. He could busy himself with writing the final exam for his students and hopefully quiet his thoughts, which were squawking like a murder of crows.

Eun-ho paused for a moment as he put on his shoes to leave the house. *Shoot*, he said as he went back to the study. He had forgotten that he'd hid the phone in his desk drawer last night. Eun-ho returned the phone to the living room and plugged it into the wall. Then he checked one more time to make sure he hadn't forgotten anything. He did this slowly so that he wouldn't have to come back to the study for a fourth time.

I think that's it.

Until yesterday, despite it being early winter, the weather had been warm and sunny, as though it were still early fall. But it had taken a sudden turn. Outside a cast-iron sky was hanging low. Cold, damp, vicious wind was battering the trees in the front yard, pushing dead leaves into the street. The weather was as foul as Eun-ho's mood.

Eun-ho considered going back inside for a coat. As he stood at the front door and weighed his options, two vehicles passed by the house. The first was a delivery truck. The second was a tailgating slate-blue jeep. By the time the two vehicles disappeared, so had Eun-ho's desire for a coat. It wasn't worth going back to his study for a fifth time. Besides, it wasn't like he was going to freeze to death on his way from the school parking lot to his office.

Eun-ho buttoned up his jacket before walking down the stairs toward the driveway. Just as he was opening the car door, the jeep appeared again. Its hazard lights were blinking as it backed up. It slid backwards in one smooth motion before stopping in front of Eun-ho's driveway. Had this street been a shopping mart parking lot, Eun-ho would have marveled at their handling. But if this jeep thought it could park illegally on the street in front of *his* house, it had another thing coming.

A woman hopped down from the driver's side of the jeep. A bob cut just below the earlobes, no makeup, an oversized hoodie, black leggings, and sneakers: she looked like she had just been chased out of the gym. She looked lean, too, like a cheetah.

The woman crossed the street. Without hesitating or looking around, she came straight toward Eun-ho. Some women drove their husbands crazy spending half an hour deciding what to wear: this woman wasn't one of them.

Eun-ho couldn't tell if she was really walking toward him. But by the time he realized she was, she was already speaking to him.

"Do you live at #111 by any chance?"

She had a deep, earthy voice. Had Eun-ho had his eyes closed, he might not have known it belonged to a woman.

"Can I help you?" Eun-ho knew his tone wasn't friendly, but he didn't feel like being friendly today, especially not to someone illegally parking in front of his house.

"Is your name Eun-ho Cha by any chance?" she asked.

Eun-ho didn't answer immediately. Before that, he needed to figure out who this woman was, how she knew his name, and how she knew where he lived. She didn't seem like an angry parent wanting to complain about their child's grade, but he couldn't tell if this was good news or bad news.

"Are you?" the woman pressed him.

Eun-ho's eyes floated upward to the woman's windblown hair which looked like a chestnut burr. She definitely wasn't a parent. She looked too young to be the mother of a high school student.

"I am, but who are—"

"I'm Jane Shin."

It took a few seconds for Eun-ho to recognize the name. Jane was Wife's older sister, someone whom he knew existed but had never actually met until now. He thought of the family photo hung in the living room of Wife's mother's house. Was this woman the person smiling next to his late father-in-law? In some ways she resembled her, but in some ways she didn't.

"I see—"

Eun-ho looked down at his feet. He didn't know how to react. Should he welcome her with open arms and invite her in? That would be the right thing to do, but not what he wanted to do. Eun-ho thought about why his sister-in-law would come to see him. Soon, he realized that his shameless wife must have sent Jane here to do her bidding.

This wasn't the first time Wife had run away to her Mother's house without warning. But she didn't do this as some form of impulsive, enraged protest. No, this was for leverage. It was something she did when she wanted him to get on his hands and knees. Eun-ho was usually notified of Wife's sojourn after she had left, via text message.

—I'm spending some time with the kid.

By "the kid" she meant Jiyoo, the daughter she'd had with her ex-husband. Because Jiyoo lived at her mother's house after the divorce, "I'm spending some time with the kid" was synonymous with "I'm spending some time at my mother's." And "some time" really meant "until things change." And things would only change when Eun-ho got on his hands and knees and begged for her to come back.

Usually, "some time" was over in a day or two. Actually, it had never taken Eun-ho more than forty-eight hours to produce a written apology or to reaffirm his vows. Technically, he could let his temper flare or try to get back at her by giving her the silent treatment, but he knew that he didn't *really* have a choice. Eventually one of them would have to bend to the other one's will. And that person was invariably Eun-ho. Not only did Eun-ho always take the easy way out, but he was also afraid. Afraid of ruining his second marriage and establishing a pattern of failure in his life.

The problem was that Wife did this too often. This was already her fifth time, and it had only been a year since they got married. Roughly extrapolating, this meant that this routine would repeat itself fifty times over the next ten years, and one hundred times over the next twenty. Considering his Wife's personality as a woman who vacillated between extremes of fire and ice and always found ways to take things to new extremes, the probability that this routine was going to continue, if not get worse, was very high. For the rest of his life, it seemed Eun-ho was destined to live in hell.

Right now, he was desperately fighting the urge to beg. Despite not being a "real man," he wasn't foolish enough to be dragged to hell. But there's always a price to defiance. The first price that Eun-ho had to pay was his health. Every night he lay in bed sleepless, fluctuating between the extremes of wanting to teach Wife a lesson and wanting to run to her like a scolded puppy.

His night would always start with anger directed at Wife's bullying. Next came regret for acting like an idiot and upsetting Wife. Then there was fear about the looming possibility of divorce, which made him anxiously consider getting in his car and driving to his mother-in-law's house before it was too late.

When morning came, Eun-ho would sit on the toilet pulling at his hair, desperately trying to regain the will to fight.

He knew that there was no way Wife hadn't recognized his slow reaction. The fact that she sent her sister Jane was proof that she was anxious now, too. She must have coerced Jane to come here and scout Eun-ho out, to see what he was thinking. Or, she might have been sent here as a sort of vanguard meant to pressure him into folding so that Wife wouldn't have to hurt her pride by coming back before he begged her to.

The appearance of his sister-in-law in the batting line-up ignited a fire in him. It disgusted Eun-ho to see how Wife's family always received her with open arms, to see how blood bonds trumped everything, even right versus wrong. But his conviction hadn't just been reignited; it was blazing stronger than ever. Now, it was *she* who was going to have to beg to come back home.

"I'm here to see Yuna," Jane finally said. "Can you call her for me?" Her tone was unbearably arrogant.

"She's not home," Eun-ho said. "You should know that."

Jane lifted her chin and stared at him. The expression on her face was like that of a difficult chess opponent, stubborn and hard to read.

"And why should I know that?" Jane paused as she pursed her lips. Her mind seemed to be hard at work searching for her next words. Eun-ho could wait.

"Then deliver this message to Yuna," Jane continued. "Our mother is out of the country now, so don't bring Jiyoo over to the house. I'm *not* going to look after her."

Eun-ho cracked a smile. Who would be dumb enough to believe that she came all the way to Cheongyeon from Incheon to deliver this short message. It wasn't the 19th century anymore; telephones were a thing. It seemed Jane wasn't as smart as the rumors made her out to be.

"I'm not sure what you're talking about, but if that's all you came here for, a phone call would have—"

"Yuna's not answering her phone." This was the second time she had cut him off. "Her office told me she was on vacation since this Tuesday." Despite Jane's apparent composure, each word was dripping with anger.

But something else was bothering Eun-ho now, causing the smile to disappear from his face. Vacation? What vacation?

"Your landline says it's disconnected, and I tried calling your cellphone, but I couldn't get through."

Eun-ho remembered that he had only reconnected the landline to the wall just moments ago. His cellphone, too, would still be in the drawer of his desk at the office. He'd left it there intentionally on Tuesday, early that week, afraid that his will might falter as he spent the long night by himself, afraid that he would end up calling his wife as he lay in bed missing her. For similar reasons, he had unplugged the landline and hid it from view.

"Please give her my message."

Jane left without waiting for Eun-ho's response or for him to say goodbye. She turned around and jogged across the street with her long grasshopper-like legs. After getting into the Jeep and starting the engine, she backed up at high speed toward the gate to the neighborhood. When she reached the forked road past the gate, she spun her car around and disappeared. Her reckless driving matched her short-tempered personality.

Eun-ho got into his car and sat in the driver's seat as he went over the conversation with Jane. At the time, he had been too preoccupied with her hostility to pay much attention to the content of what she was saying. But nothing that she said had made sense to him. What bothered him the most was her message to Wife: *Don't bring Jiyoo over to the house.*

Eun-ho and Wife got the children together on the weekends. Eun-ho's son from his first marriage, Noah, would come from his grandmother's apartment in Hanam, and Wife's daughter from her first marriage, Jiyoo, would come from her grandmother's house in Incheon. This weekend, however, Jiyoo would not be coming because Noah's grandmother was going to be there. Eun-ho had hoped that the five of them could spend a happy weekend together, but Wife rejected the idea. Jiyoo, apparently, felt uncomfortable with Noah's grandmother. Thus, it was decided that Jiyoo would stay at her grandmother's house.

Eun-ho couldn't just dismiss what Jane said as nonsense. If she really needed an excuse to come here, she would have come up with a better story. Eventually, Eun-ho decided to take her words at face value. According to what she said, three things had to be true: Jiyoo's grandmother was out of the country, Jiyoo was with Wife, and Wife wasn't at her mother's house. But if she wasn't at her mother's house, then where was she?

Eun-ho's mind went blank for a second. This last question hit him like a golf club to the head. As he drove to school, the same question was bouncing around in his head non-stop. *Where was Wife?*

Eun-ho had no answers. It felt like he was trying to squeeze water out of the air. Just before he arrived at school, he realized the focus of his questioning was all wrong. He shouldn't be asking about his missing wife. He should have been asking about Jane. That's where he would find answers.

The mere appearance of Jane was beyond suspicious. He had never met Jane before, and that was because Wife and her were not on good terms. As far as Eun-ho knew, Jane would never show up at his door as Yuna's relief pitcher.

In fact, Jane hadn't even come to their wedding. And whenever Eun-ho and Wife went to her mother's house, Jane was always absent, even though he knew she lived with her mom. She was never around, not even for holidays or family events. The explanation he usually got was that Jane had to work overtime or was on a business trip. But after a year of her coincidentally always being out of the house when they showed up, he started to wonder if she even existed.

Of course, he had heard a few things from his mother-in-law—mainly that Jane was single, worked as a journalist, and had moved back in with her mother after their father passed away. But that was about it. Everything else he knew about Jane was from things Wife had told him. The point of all those conversations, however, was about how much they hated each other as sisters.

Even stranger was that Wife never used the familial term *Unnie* to refer to her big sister. She only referred to her by name, which was very odd, like calling one's parent by their first name. Jane *this*, Jane *that*. And sometimes when she was emotional, she would forego the name and just call her "that bitch."

The feelings had to be mutual. Even if they weren't, Eun-ho doubted Jane could be fond enough of Yuna to make this trip for her. Based on these observations, Eun-ho edited his original assumptions:

Jane really had come to see Wife. Which meant Wife wasn't at her mother's house.

But this only led him right back to where he started: *Where was Wife?*

Eun-ho carefully retraced his memory. Had Wife actually said she was going to her mother's place? She hadn't. He'd just assumed that was where she went because she took Jiyoo with her. Now that he thought about it, he realized that whenever Wife left the house like this, he never actually went to Incheon to make sure she was where she said she was. Only once had he asked her where she disappeared to.

Wife's answer: "I went home." He didn't ask any more. He didn't want to look paranoid because, according to Wife, only neurotic people were paranoid. Instead, he asked his question again, but this time to Jiyoo.

"Jiyoo, where were you and Mom?"

Jiyoo answered without much hesitation.

"Home."

Would Jiyoo lie? Or perhaps this was a clever white lie. Home could mean many things. It didn't necessarily have to refer to her grandma's house. Eun-ho thought about what other homes could exist. There were three that came to mind. The first was Jiyoo's grandmother's home in Incheon. The second was Eun-ho and Wife's home in Cheongyeon. And the third was her biological father's home, whose location Eun-ho didn't know.

A bolt of lightning struck Eun-ho's skull, starting a fire inside his consciousness. Jiyoo had to be at her biological father's home.

Eun-ho glared at the red traffic light above the intersection when another question popped into his head. But was this just the first time?

*

Eun-ho hung up the phone after hearing it ring for the twentieth time.

Since arriving at school, he had been calling home at one-hour intervals. It was already six in the afternoon, and no one had answered. This meant that his wife hadn't come home yet. It also meant he had to move on to Plan B.

Their original schedule had been to go to Hanam early on Saturday morning to pick up Noah and his grandmother and head to the Yangpyeong camping site. There they would play soccer with Noah and have a barbeque before coming back to Cheongyeon Sunday morning.

Noah's grandmother didn't usually accompany Noah to their home in Cheongyeon. The reason they both were coming this weekend was because her apartment in Hanam was undergoing renovation. It would take several days before she could move back in. The renovation was scheduled to start Monday, so Noah and his grandmother were planning to stay until Wednesday.

Eun-ho had kept the camping plans a secret from Noah and his grandmother. He was planning on surprising the two of them, especially Noah. He wasn't good with surprises, but he was hoping to change that.

But as things turned out, it was lucky that he hadn't told them. He wasn't prepared to be scolded by his mother for ruining such a perfect weekend. It would be like giving Noah a bad check for his birthday.

Noah believed Eun-ho was coming today. Noah lived for the weekends when he could see his dad. Despite knowing this, Eun-ho hadn't gone to pick up Noah. He couldn't bring his mother to his house in Cheongyeon, not while

Wife was AWOL.

Eun-ho's mother was unaware of Wife's sudden and frequent sojourns away from home. And he was trying to keep it that way. The effort it took to keep her out of the know was less than the effort it would take to clean up the mess once she found out. This was a lesson he had learned from his first (albeit short) marriage. Eun-ho was hours away from being checkmated, but he wasn't ready to give up. He couldn't let his mother get involved in their problems.

That morning, Eun-ho had called his mother as his first step of damage control. He told her that Wife's mother was sick and had gone to the hospital to get tests, that Wife might have to stay by her side at the hospital. He used this as cause to delay picking up Noah and her until later that night. This was the best excuse he could think of. It had the benefit of allowing him to sneak in the caveat "*If Yuna comes home, that is.*"

And now that he had confirmed that Wife wasn't home, there were two steps he could take. First, he could try calling Wife on her cellphone. She might not be taking Jane's calls, but she might take his. If he could convince her to come home—that is, if he raised the white flag—they could go to Hanam together to pick up Noah and his grandmother. This was the easiest and most reasonable solution. Although, it was also the thing he wanted to do the least.

It wasn't just because of his pride. His original goal of fixing Wife's frequent sojourns away from home had been completely thrown out the window by this visit from Jane. He was less afraid of calling her than he was of what that call would confirm: the creeping suspicion growing in his mind, the suspicion that his wife was using her daughter as a shield to meet her ex-husband, the suspicion that his wife was at her ex-husband's house. He was afraid that when he asked her where she was, she would answer him truthfully.

Please, be anywhere but his *place.*

Although he had lived in voluntary obedience to her until now, he wasn't going to allow her to step outside of the ring and shoot him in the back of the head with a gun.

The way things were going, there was a good chance that he would give up on Wife, which was the thing he feared the most, more than even her cheating.

But that couldn't happen, not now. If it needed to happen, it needed to wait until after Monday.

Eun-ho chose the second solution. He called his mother and recited the speech he'd prepared. His Wife's mother had been admitted to the hospital;

Wife needed to stay by her side; he had something to do at school; it would be difficult for him to pick them up from Hanam today.

"What, doesn't Yuna have a sister?"

Eun-ho's mother's voice was dry and hoarse. It wasn't difficult for him to imagine his mother on the other end of the line, sitting up straight, contorting the corners of her mouth into a scowl.

"Her sister is out of the country on a business trip," Eun-ho said.

"But why does that mean *you* can't come?"

Eun-ho began desperately thinking of another excuse.

"I need to be somewhere tomorrow morning. I have a meeting with my advisor to talk about an issue with my master's thesis."

"Is that so?" Eun-ho's mother's voice dropped two octaves. "That professor of yours is really something. Meeting with pupils on a Sunday morning . . ."

Shit. Eun-ho couldn't believe he had forgotten that tomorrow was Sunday. Immediately, Eun-ho started making whatever excuse he could think of: how his professor called people to meet on the weekends because he was strict and had nothing better to do; how if he didn't go when his professor called him, everything he had done up till now would be for nothing; how it was a long drive to his professor's home in Anseong.

"I wouldn't be able to get to Hanam until after five."

"Five!"

Eun-ho's mother was furious. She began giving Eun-ho a long diatribe.

"After five? What do you expect us to do after five on a Sunday night? Do you know how disappointed Noah was when he found out you weren't coming today? Do you even care? Can't you act like a father for just one weekend? How long do I have to raise *your* son?"

Eun-ho closed his eyes. His cheek felt wet, as though the spit of his incensed mother was being teleported through the receiver.

"Do you remember the promise you made to me the day you married Yuna? Didn't you say you would take Noah in and raise him yourself?"

Eun-ho's mother had opened her usual playbook of attacks. This would take at least an hour.

"Mom, just hold on for a second."

Eun-ho quickly cut off his mother.

"Mom, Jinu is waiting for me. I told him I'd take him out for a bite." This was the card Eun-ho always played to get out of difficult conversations with his mother. "I'll call you back later." And with that, he hung up the phone.

Eun-ho placed his cellphone on the desk. His ears were ringing. He was seeing two and three of the laptop sitting on his desk.

"What are you doing? I've been waiting."

Startled, Eun-ho turned around to find Jinu with his butt perched on the side of the desk, glaring down at him. Eun-ho became red in the face. He hadn't known someone was eavesdropping.

"Did I just hear you say you're going to take me out for a bite?"

Jinu was tossing his car keys up and down as he snickered. Eun-ho was about to ask him what he was doing at school on the weekend, but instead just looked down at his cellphone. *How much did Jinu hear? Did he hear me making elaborate excuses to my mother?* The only way to know was to ask Jinu directly.

"How long have you been here?"

"Just long enough to hear you use me as an excuse. I dropped by to pick something up."

Jinu waved a Nintendo Switch in the air to show Eun-ho. Jinu took it with him everywhere he went. Students gossiped about how Jinu, or "Mr. Kim," as they called him, spent his nights and weekends at home alone, playing *Animal Crossing: New Horizons*. They teased him for being the only male teacher at Cheongyeon High School who was single.

"So, what's on the menu?" Jinu asked.

"Let's get out of here first." Eun-ho put his notebook in his bag as he answered. After thinking for three more seconds, he also put his cellphone in his jacket pocket. He would need it tomorrow.

It was already dark out. Eun-ho thought of his house, which would be completely empty right now. He asked himself the same question that he had asked every day for the last four days when heading home from work: *Will Wife be there when I get home tonight?* If she was, there was no avoiding the emotional collision that would ensue. And if she wasn't, Eun-ho's head might explode. Either way, Eun-ho didn't want to be sober when he got home.

"How about drinks instead of dinner?" Eun-ho asked.

Jinu agreed immediately, not even pretending to think about it. Thirty minutes later, they were seated in an izakaya located on a busy street in Jeongin-dong. It was just the right amount of noise and commotion to distract Eun-ho. Plus, he was with an old friend, someone with whom he could sit down and enjoy a drink in silence.

Despite having finished two bottles of soju, Eun-ho didn't feel drunk enough. He felt more like he had been sipping on shots of beer. It was only enough to dull the pain of his headache.

"It's been what, more than two years?" Jinu asked with no pretext or follow up.

Since what? Eun-ho asked with just his eyes, a glass of soju resting on his lips.

"Drinking together!"

Eun-ho felt his face become hot. His ears were burning from embarrassment, as though they had been stung by a hive of bees. Eun-ho emptied the rest of his glass into his mouth.

Jinu and Eun-ho had been friends since high school. It was pure chance that they were hired by the same school in the same year. They had gone their separate ways in college, but working together at the school had rekindled their friendship. They went to the gym together, went to baseball games together, went to see Noah together—they even sometimes took Noah to the coast together.

But that all changed once Eun-ho started dating Yuna. She didn't like him associating with Jinu. She had three reasons for disliking him: he was a bragger whose only gift was a large frame; he lacked social awareness; and he slept like a bear whenever he got drunk.

"Let's have one more before we go," Eun-ho said as he pressed the service bell.

Jinu stole a glance at his watch before asking, "You sure? I know how Yuna can be."

"Yeah."

"But shouldn't you at least call and tell her you're going to be late?"

Eun-ho moved his cellphone from the table to his bag. He meant it as a sign to stop asking, but Jinu was doggedly persistent.

"It's the weekend. Isn't she waiting for you at home?"

Which home? Eun-ho clenched his jaw to stop himself from saying something he would regret. His whole body was getting warm, probably from the delayed effects of the alcohol. And his vision was starting to go cross.

"Did you guys have a fight or something?"

Eun-ho could sense a disingenuous sense of anticipation in Jinu's tone. He sounded like he wanted to hear a juicy story about marital fighting. Eun-ho shook the empty bottle of soju to show the waiter who was approaching their table.

"If you're not careful, you might go in your sleep."

Jinu said this and began snickering to himself. Eun-ho didn't understand what Jinu meant, but these words none-the-less irked Eun-ho. Jinu had said the same thing last year at their wedding. Right now, Eun-ho was in a shitty mood, and this sounded like a mean joke. He glared at Jinu without responding.

"I'm just worried, that's all."

Jinu stopped snickering and looked Eun-ho in the eyes. He was studying Eun-ho's face.

"After all, I'm the one who introduced you two, aren't I?"

While it was true that Eun-ho and Yuna never would have met without Jinu, to say that he "introduced" them was an exaggeration.

"You don't need to worry," Eun-ho said, ending the conversation.

Jinu and Eun-ho left the bar two hours later. Eun-ho called a surrogate driver for Jinu and helped him into his car. After Jinu left, Eun-ho called his own surrogate driver and stood by his car as he waited. Snow began to fall. Although, being early winter, the snow was closer to sleet than anything else. The wind made it feel like ten degrees below zero. With every breath, the tip of his nose stung as a droplet of moisture dripped from it. At the same time, his face was burning red. His stomach was rumbling, too. And inside his mind, a pointless question was spinning around like a song stuck in his head.

If I had known it would be like this, would I still have married her?

The answer was probably yes. He used to be crazy for her. Actually, he was still crazy for her. And not just a little.

It was three years ago, around this time of year. Eun-ho had just heard the news that Yoon-hee, his new ex-wife who had gone abroad to study as soon as they got divorced, had eloped with a redneck from Texas as soon as she arrived in the U.S. Apparently, she had met him when she used to work as a corporate interpreter. While it almost sounded like a rumor, Eun-ho knew it wasn't because he had heard it from Yoon-hee's mother when he and Noah bumped into her at the department store. Yoon-hee's mother started crying in the middle of the store, lamenting the fact that Noah would have to be raised by a single father—or worse, a *stepmother*.

This happened two years after Yoon-hee had suddenly left Noah with Eun-ho, saying "He's your son. *You* raise him." It was all so fresh that the ink on the divorce papers was still wet. Eun-ho couldn't say he felt happy for Yoon-hee. If anything, it angered him to hear that she'd remarried so soon. He was convinced that she had been seeing that man while they were still married. The affair must have been why she asked for a divorce. She'd said she wanted "freedom." He never imagined that by "freedom" what she'd meant was a redneck from Texas.

The voice of reason inside Eun-ho's head was telling him to stop imagining things, like a doctor telling a patient with rhinitis to stop blowing their nose. And just like a sickly patient, he needed medicine, something to stop his imagination from growing and ruining his life, a miracle drug that would allow him to forget his ex-wife and start anew.

So, Eun-ho decided to take a trip to Lake Baikal in Russia. It wasn't a decision he made after a lot of deliberation, but one made while drinking soju by himself and watching a movie.

The movie was *The Way Back*, a drama about escapees from a Siberian Gulag who traveled 6,500 kilometers by foot through a blizzard in minus-fifty-degree weather. Coincidentally, the escapees were searching for the same damned thing his ex-wife was: freedom. Seeing beautiful Lake Baikal on the screen of his TV, Eun-ho got the idea of going on a trip. But he needed a friend. So he asked Jinu to join him.

"Lake Baikal? That's a bit random, don't you think?" Jinu asked.

From the look on Jinu's face, Eun-ho could tell he wasn't particularly interested. But Eun-ho didn't want to admit that he was doing this because he needed to get over his ex-wife. Instead, he told Jinu that he had seen the lake in a movie. Jinu changed his mind after watching the movie. He suggested they go as soon as winter break started. Jinu even actively helped plan the trip. But the more plans he made, the worse his "as long as we're there, we might as well . . ." obsession became—an obsession that all tourists suffered from.

Jinu reasoned that "as long as we're going to Russia," they might as well start in Vladivostok, which was located in the southern-most region of Russia. From there, they could take a four-day-three-night ride on the Trans-Siberian Railway to a city called Irkutsk, which was said to be close to Lake Baikal. Jinu also reasoned that "as long as we're on the Trans-Siberian Railway," they might as well go the whole distance. So, from Irkutsk, they could go to Mongol, which was right next door from Lake Baikal and on one of the railway's detours. Jinu even convinced Eun-ho to go to the Gobi Desert. He was trying, it seemed, to reenact the entire journey from the movie. Eun-ho put a thumbtack on Moscow, marking it as their final stop.

"Moscow is as far as we go."

They agreed on an eighteen-day trip. They would spend eight days alone on just the train. Jinu took care of the small things: researching, scheduling, booking train tickets and hotels. Eun-ho, on the other hand, had the difficult task of being the one who had to pump the brakes on Jinu's over-ambitious plans.

When January came, Eun-ho and Jinu got on a plane bound for Vladivostok. When they finally arrived in Russia, the sun had already set. Despite being the size of a small bus terminal, Vladivostok International Airport had as many travelers as any other international airport. And perhaps because arrivals, departures, baggage claim, and the duty-free shopping area were all squeezed into the same place, the airport felt even more crowded than normal. Once they got their luggage, Jinu ran to the restroom.

"Wait here."

Eun-ho sat on a bench guarding their two 26-liter backpacks. The whole time he waited for Jinu, Eun-ho was being tortured by a woman across from him who was trying to replace her SIM card. He knew immediately that she was Korean. Everything about her—her hat, her knitted gloves, the muffler around her neck, and the green passport on her knees—was Korean.

But he couldn't see her face because she was staring down at her SIM card and her straight black hair was blocking her face like a curtain. What Eun-ho could see, however, was her long, padded black jacket, jeans, boots, and a bandaged right hand. Looking closer, he realized her index finger was in a splint.

Eun-ho concluded that the woman must be right-handed. If she were left-handed, she would have used her left hand. But instead, she was stubbornly using her right middle finger and thumb to pinch the SIM card and place it flat onto the SIM tray. Her hands were trembling, as though she had been drinking. She even dropped the chip several times.

But Eun-ho was more interested in the woman's left hand. It's white skin, the slender fingers, the softness of her fingernails. It looked like the hand of a fairy. Eun-ho couldn't help himself from imagining what it would be like to touch a hand like that. Was it as soft as it looked?

Having nothing better to look at, Eun-ho continued to stare at the woman as she struggled. He rooted for the right hand while secretly gawking at the left. But her repeated failures made him feel frustrated. The longer he watched her struggle, the harder it was to watch. Of course, he could have stopped watching if he wanted to, but he didn't want to. He was unable to take his eyes off her hands, determined to see her succeed. And when the SIM card eventually flew out of her hand, he almost cried out in disappointment.

To Eun-ho's surprise, the woman didn't lose her composure. She put aside the items on her knees, crouched down on the floor, and stuck her head under the bench to look for the chip as she held her hair up with her injured hand. Had Jinu not come back from the bathroom at that very moment, Eun-ho might have gotten up to hold her hair for her.

"What's so interesting?"

Jinu followed Eun-ho's gaze as he turned his head toward the woman. When he finally found her, the woman was sticking her butt up into the air. Jinu shook his head from side to side as he slung his backpack over his shoulder.

"You perv."

Jinu started walking toward the exit. Eun-ho followed him, but his mind stayed behind with the woman. He was dying to know if the woman had found the SIM card. And just before walking through the exit, Eun-ho stole a glance back at the woman, whose torso was now all the way under the bench. The muscles in his throat suddenly contracted.

When they stepped outside of the airport, they were confronted with a scene from Disney's *Frozen*. The falling snow was so thick that they could barely see the street or the sign outside the airport that read -24°C.

They headed straight to the train station, and by the time they boarded, the temperature had dropped another three degrees. And as they crossed vast snowy plains, endless forests of birch trees, wide frozen lakes on their way to Khabarovsk Station, the temperature only continued to drop, reaching as low as -32°C.

It was 8:30 a.m. local time when they arrived in Khabarovsk. The sun was just starting to rise outside the cabin window. Factory chimney stacks near the station were pumping smoke into the sky, and beyond that was a desolate landscape of buildings. Khabarovsk must have been the biggest city in the area because they had cell service for the first time in days. From outside the train, they could hear a loud thumping noise. It was the noise of crews stripping ice from the train with crowbars. The train was scheduled to stay in Khabarovsk for fifty minutes.

Jinu was sleeping like a hibernating bear. He had been unconscious since drinking that bottle of vodka last night. Eun-ho put on his jacket and left the cabin. He didn't have a particular destination in mind; he just wanted some fresh air. An old Russian lady, whom he had bumped into several times already, was standing by the window in the hallway. She was glued to the window, as if staring at something outside. Eun-ho walked up beside the grandma, curious to see what she was looking at.

On the platform was a woman. She was bundled up in a mask, muffler, and woolen hat. She was using a disposable camera, not a cell phone, to take pictures of the snowy landscape. She turned her body clockwise as she took pictures of the chimney stacks, railroad tracks, and station. Finally, she turned toward the train window that Eun-ho was looking out from.

When Eun-ho saw the woman's right hand, which was covered in bandages, he realized she was the woman from the airport. She must be a passenger on this train, too.

Eun-ho wondered if she had found her SIM card before leaving the airport. He felt excited, like he had bumped into a minor celebrity in a public bathroom. Eun-ho began observing her carefully, just as he had at the airport. He didn't feel guilty. After all, stalking was what our hunter ancestors did on the savannah.

After what could have been several minutes, an older lady with a hefty bag approached the woman. They stood facing each other and exchanged a few words. The older lady took out a transparent plastic bag containing what looked like bread. The woman with the camera put her left hand inside her jacket pocket and pulled out a handful of coins.

Soon, Eun-ho experienced another torturous struggle, second only to the SIM card incident at the airport. With the disposable camera in her right hand, the woman used her right middle finger to slide coins from her left palm one by one into the hand of the older lady. Her movements were so tediously slow that Eun-ho wanted to scream out in frustration. It would be faster if she let the lady count the coins for her.

"What's so interesting?" Jinu said, appearing behind Eun-ho.

Eun-ho turned around to find Jinu standing at the door to their cabin, his eyes bleary as though he had just woken up. Eun-ho was unable to answer him.

Jinu walked toward Eun-ho, but by the time he arrived at the window, the woman had already disappeared. Eun-ho hadn't seen the end of the transaction and was worried something might have happened to the woman. What if human traffickers had appeared and kidnapped her?

From that day on, Eun-ho ran to the window every time the train made a stop. But the woman never appeared again. All he ever saw were empty platforms at night being blanketed with snow.

Eventually they arrived at Irkutsk Station, just west of Lake Baikal. They spent the night there and departed for Lake Baikal the following morning. The hotel staff assured Eun-ho that the lake was "very close." But Eun-ho slowly realized that the Russians had a different concept of "very close." After riding for several hours through snowy plains on a bus whose heater was cranked so high it nearly baked them to death, they boarded a boat—aptly named the Hover Craft—to cross the frozen Lake Baikal. When they reached the Olkhon Island, there was an old truck that must have belonged to the Russian military waiting to drive them to their final destination: Khuzir. The red sun was just beginning to set when they reached the inn.

Jinu opened Google Maps as soon as they checked in and finished unpacking. Apparently, there was a sacred rock called the Shaman Rock near their inn. As Jinu explained, the spirit of the rock would grant any wish made when the setting sun touched the mountain ridge across the lake. Not only that, but the rock was a sacred site for many of the world's shamanic traditions, or so the travel guides claimed.

After such a long journey, the last thing Eun-ho wanted to do was leave the inn. But Jinu persuaded him to come by telling him it was just a "short walk."

Jinu must have been using the Russian definition of "short" because it felt like they were on an Arctic expedition, scaling steep, slippery hills of ice and snow and jumping over gaping crevasses.

They barely met anyone on the trail, not surprising because it was already dusk. Eun-ho was starting to doubt they would get back before it turned dark. He also wasn't sure if they should rely on Google Maps in such a foreign and remote part of the world. There was a not-so-insignificant chance that they wouldn't be able to find their way back. But just as these doubts started to creep into Eun-ho's head, large pillars wrapped in colorful strips of cloth appeared in the distance.

"That must be it!"

Jinu pointed to a towering structure of black rock located on a tombolo just behind the pillars. The tombolo was a cluster of large, jagged boulders that formed two large humps. And at the base of the rock were what looked like piles of stones that people had stacked. Eun-ho approached what he thought was a tall stack of rocks. Only after getting close to it did he realize it wasn't a rock, but a person—or to be more precise, a woman with her arms crossed, staring up at the Shaman Rock.

Everything she had on was black—her muffler, her long padded jacket, her boots, her fur hat that looked like it belonged to Lara from Doctor Zhivago, even her hair was black.

She was standing in front of two piles of rocks, each composed of four flat black stones. Stuck in the ground between the two piles of rocks was a freshly cut branch and burned incense, as though someone had been mourning the death of a loved one. Despite the strong wind, the faint scent of incense was able to reach Eun-ho's nose.

Eun-ho paused as he approached the woman. He didn't want to scare her by getting too close without warning. If this were a busy city street, he could pass by her without a second thought. But they were the only people in the area. Eun-ho tried to act ambivalent toward her by turning away and looking out at the lake.

As the blood-red sun made its descent toward the horizon, the sky glowed purple. Everything else—the lake, the mountain ridge across the lake, the hills they had just crossed—was bathed in the blood of the sun. In the distance in the shadow of the mountain, a black Jeep was racing along the shore, kicking up a cloud of icy dust.

Eun-ho imagined what could be lurking under the frozen surface of this vast, primal lake. What would it be like to be trapped under the ice, in that deep, blue water? The power of this image sent a shudder through Eun-ho's entire body. Suddenly, Eun-ho heard the sound of a camera. He turned around to find Jinu standing next to the woman taking pictures of the Shaman Rock.

The woman turned to look at Jinu.

Jinu stared back at her for a while before asking, "Do I know you?" He took a step closer. "I think I've seen you somewhere before."

Eun-ho couldn't believe Jinu. They hadn't come all the way to Siberia just so he could hit on women. The woman turned away without replying. She immediately came face to face with Eun-ho, who was just two steps away from her. In walking over to Jinu to stop him from bothering the poor woman, he had accidentally blocked her escape.

The woman looked up into Eun-ho's eyes. As she did this, the wind suddenly changed direction, blowing the hair out of her face. The light from the sunset refracted in her pupils, bringing out hazel flecks. Her eyes were asking him who he was. They looked scared, perhaps irritated, and were suspiciously studying every feature of his face.

There are two kinds of beauty in the world: universal beauty that all humankind agrees on, and exclusive beauty that only a few captive individuals can see. This woman's beauty belonged to the latter. All Eun-ho could hear was his heart pounding out of his chest.

The woman blinked once, as if to ask him to step aside. He respectfully lowered his gaze and made way for her. As he looked down, he caught a glimpse of the bandages on her right hand. This was the third time he had bumped into this woman from the airport. What were the chances?

"Excuse me, you didn't go to Dong-a University in Seoul by any chance?" Jinu asked from behind the woman's shoulder. "Yuna Shin? Class of 2009? Majored in Russian literature?"

This caught Eun-ho off guard. So earlier, his asking her if they had met before wasn't just a cheap pick-up line.

The woman slowly turned her gaze toward Jinu. Her captivating hazel pupils were so good at expressing emotion. Her eyes were clearly asking, *How the hell do you know me?*

"It is you. I knew I recognized you."

Jinu gave the woman a friendly smile, but she wasn't putting her guard down. Eun-ho could sense her back tensing up, even through her thick, padded jacket.

"Don't you remember me? We've met before."

The woman simply stared at Jinu waiting for him to explain.

"You made me coffee one time. At your apartment, when Jiwoon moved out."

Her eyes began darting across Jinu's face. A million emotions appeared and disappeared in her sunset-illuminated pupils. Eun-ho couldn't decipher every emotion, but the last facial expression was clear as day:

Aha . . .

"Yes, I think I remember now," she finally said.

Her voice was so quiet that Eun-ho felt like he needed to pull his eardrum out of his ear just to hear her. The end of her sentence even trembled slightly, conveying a sense of unease.

"You were a biology major. Your last name is Kim, and your first name is—"

"Jinu."

Jinu saluted with one finger placed at the edge of his eyebrow.

Everything that happened after that depressed Eun-ho. The two reunited college friends were awkward at first, but before long, the two of them were on their way to a bar to catch up. Eun-ho tagged along. As he trailed behind them, he was able to overhear parts of their conversation.

Apparently, the woman, or Yuna as Jinu called her, had arrived at Olkhon Island that afternoon. She was travelling alone. She worked for her father's company. And the pile of rocks that looked like gravestones wasn't hers. In college, she had made Jinu and a man named Jiwoon a cup of coffee at her apartment.

Jinu and she were the same age and had graduated the same year from the same college. That meant she was also the same age as Eun-ho.

The two of them entered a pub near the inn with Eun-ho still third-wheeling. The place had only a few things on the menu, there were too many people, and the music was too loud.

After being seated near the entrance, the woman said to Jinu: "By the way, you haven't introduced me to your friend?"

Jinu opened his eyes wide, as if he'd just remembered something important. In a reluctant tone of voice, he introduced Eun-ho as "A once promising writer turned divorced high school Korean teacher." While Jinu said it like a joke, Eun-ho knew what Jinu was doing. Jinu was trying to pick off Eun-ho before he could steal a base. Or better yet, he was intentionally trying to peg Eun-ho before he even had a chance to swing.

Eun-ho's mind went blank for about five seconds after Jinu's unnecessary attack.

With her gaze still locked on Eun-ho, Yuna asked Jinu a question: "And what about you, Jinu? What would you describe yourself as?"

"Me? I'm a wild lion who's always ready to mate."

Yuna raised her eyebrows but didn't say anything.

"And what about you, Yuna?"

Yuna gave him a smile as her eyes turned into half-moons. "I'm divorced. As of last week."

Jinu was speechless as though he had accidentally swallowed his own tongue. But was he more shocked by the fact she was divorced or that she had only gotten divorced last week?

Eun-ho, on the other hand, was hopeful because that meant the goalie box was empty. Whether it was a week ago or a year ago, it didn't matter. What was important was that she was single.

"I never would have guessed!"

Yuna laughed at Jinu's delayed answer. Her teeth shined brightly as she burst out in laughter.

Eun-ho held his breath as he watched her. Her laugh was so light and smooth that it tickled his stomach, as though he had swallowed a feather. This sensation spread through to the back of his neck, causing the hair there to stand up. Thankfully, the waiter came before the rest of the hair on his body stood up.

"What are you going to drink?" Jinu asked Eun-ho.

But Eun-ho was unable to respond; his mind was focusing on keeping his composure in front of Yuna.

"I'll have vodka," Yuna said once Eun-ho didn't reply.

They all agreed on vodka. As Yuna conveyed their order to the waiter, Eun-ho was once against surprised. First was the fact that she spoke Russian. Second was her ability to talk through the pub's noise without needing to raise her voice. The waiter naturally lent her his left ear as though she had commanded it.

"I guess the rumors that you went to Moscow to study were true," Jinu said after the waiter disappeared. "You sound like a native!"

She took this as a joke. "You mean people were spreading rumors about me?"

The conversation continued, but the one-sidedness of their small talk didn't really make it a proper conversation. For every three things that Jinu said, Yuna only said one thing. She often omitted important details or didn't finish her sentences. She would say, "Would you . . . " and point at a napkin with her eyes to indicate what she wanted. From what Eun-ho could tell, this was her natural way of talking.

Eun-ho silently listened to them talk. Not only was there no way to include himself in their conversation, but he was also too busy extracting information from everything she said or stealing glances at her between sips of vodka.

Every once in a while, they would make eye contact. Whenever this happened, she would show him a smile with those half-moon eyes. Instead of smiling back at her, Eun-ho would divert his attention to his shot glass. Eun-ho was a thirty-four-year-old divorced man, and yet he was behaving like a teenage boy with a crush on the girl next door. Robert Frost was right: "A mother takes twenty years to make a man of her boy, and another woman makes a fool of him in twenty minutes."

Eun-ho noticed Jinu starting to become less talkative after just a few shots of vodka. He was probably tired from the long trek in the cold back from the Shaman Rock or famished from not having a proper meal all day. Eun-ho went to the bathroom, and when he came back, he found Jinu with his head resting on the table. Eun-ho shook Jinu's shoulder, but he was fast asleep. Eun-ho looked at Yuna. She offered what was her attempt at an explanation:

"I swear it wasn't me."

Eun-ho slung Jinu's arm over his shoulder and used Jinu's belt to help hoist him up. Yuna collected their belongings.

It took less than five minutes to walk back to their room. Jinu felt lighter than usual, despite being fifty percent heavier than Eun-ho. Perhaps it was that Eun-ho was simply too preoccupied with Yuna to notice.

Eun-ho couldn't tell if Jinu had intentionally given him this opportunity to be alone with Yuna, but either way, he wasn't going to miss it. He couldn't remember the last time a woman could make him feel this way just by laughing.

Eun-ho laid Jinu down on the bed. He took Jinu's socks off and pulled the bedsheets over Jinu so that he would be warm. Yuna put the belongings she had brought from the pub on the sofa. Eun-ho took his padded jacket and put it on, then held his scarf and hat in his hand.

"Where are you staying?"

She smiled. "So, you do know how to talk."

Come to think of it, this was the first time he had spoken that day. This wasn't unusual nor was it intentional. Most of the time, he was happy to let Jinu do the talking. Eun-ho didn't hate talking; it was just that he was more comfortable listening. The only exception to this was when he was talking to his mother.

"Nikita House," she finally answered.

He took out his cell phone and opened Google Maps. It was a ten-minute walk. Too bad it wasn't farther, he thought.

Google guided them through the main road in town. It was still early in the evening, but almost every store was closed and the only thing roaming the dark, empty streets was a pack of stray dogs. In the distance, Eun-ho could also hear what he thought was the howling of wolves in the forest.

The brightest lights were coming from the night sky. Shooting stars fell like rain from space, and the Milky Way looked like an archipelago of stars in a dark blue ocean. With every step they took, the sky sparkled with the vapor trails of falling meteors. The constellations were so bright that they looked close enough to bathe his face in blue starlight.

Eun-ho took slow steps so as not to walk ahead of Yuna. Silently, to savor the sound of snow crunching beneath their feet. Eun-ho hadn't spoken a word since leaving the inn. And he kept looking at his watch anxiously. Six minutes had already passed in vain. Only when the main gate of Nikita House came into view did he find an excuse to spend more time with her.

"Can we stop there?" Eun-ho said as he pointed to one of the only stores remaining open on the street. Eun-ho didn't have anything to buy, but that didn't matter.

"Only if you buy me a Nuga Bar," she replied.

A Nuga Bar? He'd buy her a hundred. Eun-ho desperately hoped that this quaint store located in a remote pocket of Siberia had the same ice cream they had in Korea.

Despite being a small shop attached to a guesthouse, the store sold everything from souvenirs to ice cream. Eun-ho examined the selection of snacks before picking out a bag of peanuts for himself. Despite being small, the bag was densely packed with nuts, making it as heavy as a brick. Yuna took an item out of an ice cream freezer and waved it in the air.

"Nuga Bar."

Despite only being inside for less than ten minutes, the weather had changed for the worse. Eun-ho was attacked by a flurry of snow as soon as he set foot outside. And when he breathed in, a sharp pain shot up his sinuses, making it feel like his head was inside the mouth of a crocodile. The tears that formed in his eyes turned to icicles and hung from his eyelashes.

Eun-ho stopped walking and covered his eyes with his palms.

"Is there ice in your eyes?" Yuna's voice asked from the darkness. It sounded like she was standing directly beneath his chin. "Don't rub your eyes. That'll make it worse."

Eun-ho uncovered his eyes to find that Yuna's face was just beneath his. She was looking up at him and studying him, her breath close enough to tickle his Adam's apple.

"I think I'm okay now."

Nodding, she stepped back. Half her face was covered in snow, and her long hair, which stuck out from her fur hat, was flowing in the wind like a lion's mane.

"Shall we get going?" she asked. Her face looked like it was blue with frostbite, and yet the cold didn't seem to bother her. She adjusted her scarf and marched into the blizzard.

As they walked, Yuna peeled back the wrapping on the Nuga Bar and started nibbling on it. Eun-ho took out his phone to check the temperature. -41°C.

"Isn't it too cold to be eating ice cream? Your teeth must be freezing?"

Instead of answering, Yuna offered Eun-ho a bite as if to ask, *You want to find out?* Eun-ho took the ice cream bar, not wanting to shy away from a challenge. Yuna had already eaten away all the chocolate coating, leaving only a bar of milky white ice cream. Eun-ho stared at the ice cream for a moment. He was pretty sure ice cream became frozen solid at -41°C.

Eun-ho took a bit of the ice cream, but before his teeth could make contact, his lips became stuck to its white surface. Eun-ho frantically pulled his lips away, tearing the thin skin on his lips and filling his mouth with the taste of blood. Tears formed in his eyes again.

"You should have let your saliva dissolve the ice before pulling away."

Eun-ho could detect enjoyment in Yuna's voice as she said this. Yuna offered Eun-ho a tissue, which he exchanged for the ice cream. Yuna immediately began nibbling away at the Nuga Bar again with her front teeth, as if to show him how it was done. The way the ice cream crumbled in her mouth sounded like crunching snow.

"Can I ask you three questions?" Eun-ho asked.

Yuna nodded, the Nuga Bar still between her teeth.

"Did you find your SIM card?"

Immediately, the crunching sound stopped. He shot off the second question.

"Was the bread from Khabarovsk good?"

Now she seemed to understand where these questions were coming from. Yuna took the Nuga Bar from her mouth and looked at him. The way the reflection of light hanging from a streetlamp was swaying in her pupils reminded him of a swinging bell. The image was so intense that he could almost hear the sound of church bells.

Did she think these questions funny or creepy? Eun-ho realized it would be best to put out the fire in her mind before it spread.

"I'm not a stalker. I just happened to see you."

Her answer to the first question was no. She had lost her original SIM card, too, so her cellphone was useless. The answer to the second question was also no.

"I have a question for you, too, Eun-ho."

The way she called Eun-ho by name seemed significant, as though it were a fortuitous sign of her interest in him. Eun-ho decided not to ask his third question, which was about how she had hurt her hand. He just nodded and tried not to grin. *Shoot away. I'll answer your questions all night.*

"Why did you get divorced?"

Eun-ho flinched slightly. This question was neither expected nor very polite. But Eun-ho liked Yuna too much to be offended. He thought for a moment about this simple yet deep question. When he couldn't think of something witty to say, he decided to tell her the embarrassing truth:

"She told me to get out of her life."

Yuna burst out laughing. This was the second time he had heard her laugh, and he was even more captivated than the first time. Last time, her laugh had made the hair on his entire body stand up. But this time, it aroused something deeper inside him. For a moment, he forgot about the cold because his body was on fire. From head to toe, his whole body was radiating heat.

"That's unfortunate," Yuna finally said, releasing Eun-ho from her torturous spell.

Eun-ho was just about to agree with her when he stopped. He had been too mesmerized by her to notice they were being surrounded by a pack of dogs.

Black dogs, yellow dogs, gray dogs, spotted dogs, huskies—but just from their size, you'd think they were wolves. Not only that, but they seemed to understand teamwork, too. The dogs had made a perfect circle around them and were slowly closing the distance. Some of the dogs were licking their chops, others were pulling their noses back and baring their teeth with a growl, and in the back of the pack, a few dogs were howling.

These dogs probably worked as cattle dogs by day and neighborhood thugs by night. They had their eye on the Nuga Bar in Yuna's hand. Eun-ho put Yuna behind him, and Yuna hid the Nuga Bar behind her back. But the dogs continued to come closer, their paws crunching on the snow.

"Go away!" she said in a loud whisper.

But the dogs were going nowhere.

"Don't come any closer," Yuna said again in a futile whisper.

Yuna turned around and stood back to back with Eun-ho. She moved the ice cream bar from her left hand to her right. The dogs shifted to move the focal point of their circle. Yuna switched hands again, and the dogs followed.

Eun-ho realized this wasn't a fight they could win. They were both outnumbered and outclassed. Judging from their numbers, they probably made a living by robbing tourists at night. With his finger, Eun-ho gently tapped Yuna on the leg.

"The ice cream bar. Give it to me."

Understanding immediately, Yuna gave it to him without protest. Eun-ho took the ice cream and threw it in the direction of the store. He then took his bag of peanuts, and threw that, too. A few moments later, they heard the bag of peanuts pop. The dogs rushed toward the sound, barking and howling. Eun-ho grabbed Yuna's hand and ran toward Nikita House.

"They're chasing after us," Yuna shouted as she struggled to keep up with him.

Eun-ho wrapped his arms around Yuna's shoulders as they burst through the front gate of Nikita House. Once inside, he used his back to push the heavy wooden door shut. Just as the door shut, they could hear dogs ramming up against the door. From their barking, Eun-ho could guess at least four dogs had followed them here.

It took a while for the dogs to quiet down. As they waited for the dogs to retreat, Eun-ho held Yuna's shoulders as he leaned against the door, even though there was no reason for them to wait like this, with their bodies glued to each other for so long.

"There goes my Nuga Bar, I guess," Yuna said as she freed herself from Eun-ho's embrace.

Eun-ho dropped his arms in an awkward, delayed manner. "There go my peanuts."

Nikita House was less a hotel than it was a collection of bungalows. The administration office was located at the entrance to the hotel, and guest rooms were located in independent huts. Judging from the way the paths diverged, it looked like a large resort.

"Where's your room?" Eun-ho asked.

Yuna led him along a path to the right of the office. Her hut was opposite a café. Eun-ho stopped in front of her door. This was his moment to say something—something that could connect them. He needed to ask her for her number or make an excuse to see her tomorrow.

"I bet they sell ice cream at that café. But I doubt they'll carry Nuga Bars."

Eun-ho pointed to the café which was still open.

Yuna let out a slight laugh. "I don't know. You don't think we'll run into another pack of dogs, do you?"

Unfortunately, they were chased out of the café as soon as they stepped inside. The café was closing, the employee said.

Now there was no reason for them to stay together anymore, no place for them to be together. They couldn't huddle together in a flurry of snow, and yet he couldn't suggest they cuddle up in her warm room together. Eun-ho decided it was time for him to go. It was better to gain her trust than it was to scratch an itch.

"I was thinking of going on a northern tour tomorrow," Eun-ho said. "Do you want to come with?"

"Only if you buy me a Nuga Bar," she replied as soon as he asked.

The next day, Jinu suffered from a bad hangover that included headaches and vomiting and was incapable of joining Eun-ho and Yuna, let alone leaving the hotel.

On his way to Nikita House by himself, Eun-ho brought Yuna another Nuga Bar. He practically danced down the sunny street, which was now free of hungry dogs.

There are times when everything just seems to work out. Times when it seems like the heavens have big plans for you. This was one of those times. Eun-ho felt like the universe was sending him a sign. Fate had helped him last night by sending him vodka, a Nuga Bar, and a pack of hungry dogs.

*

"Dad!"

Noah opened the front door and ran out to see Eun-ho, who was just getting out of the elevator.

"Noah."

Eun-ho caught Noah and lifted him into the air. Noah's five-year-old body lifted into the air as if gravity had momentarily been turned off. Noah's arms and legs, which were constricting Eun-ho's neck and waist, were as thin as the stem of a cosmos flower. His heart was racing like a small rabbit's heart, and his breathing was irregular, as though he had just run for gold at the Olympics.

Eun-ho had been lost in thought the entire drive over, but now he was abruptly brought back to reality. He had almost forgotten that his son had asthma, that he was a shitty father who was incapable of raising his own son.

"Did you miss Daddy?" Eun-ho asked with his face pressed up against Noah's cheek.

"Yes," Noah said before immediately launching into a question. "Dad, in forty days, I can join a soccer team, right?"

Eun-ho didn't know what he meant. Noah leaned back to look Eun-ho in the eye. There was a shadow of apprehension pulled over his clear, black pupils.

"Forty, right? Or forty-one? You said I could go when I turned six!"

Had he said that? Eun-ho frantically searched his memory. He had no recollection of making such a promise.

"That's what the doctor said last time."

Pity wrinkled Eun-ho's brow. Like all boys his age, Noah loved soccer. But he wanted to *play* soccer, not just watch from the sidelines. His dream was to kick the ball with the other kids at daycare. Unfortunately, this dream only filled Noah with disappointment.

Noah couldn't run for long because of his asthma. After just a few meters, he would be out of breath and his lips would be purple. Noah was also undersized. If one of the other kids elbowed him, he would fall right over. And when he played too hard at school, he would pay the price later that night. So, Noah wasn't allowed to play with the other kids. The thing Noah wanted most in the world was to learn how to play soccer, but what he really needed to learn was the hard truth that he wouldn't always be able to do what he wanted.

Noah satisfied his desire for playing soccer by dribbling couch cushions around his grandma's living room. But recently, he couldn't even do that because several neighbors had filed noise complaints. So, Noah could only play pretend soccer on the weekends when he came to Eun-ho's place. And every time he came, Noah would beg Eun-ho to enroll him in a soccer academy.

It appeared that the family doctor's estimate that Noah would be able to join a soccer team in the near future when his asthma improved had been a revelation to Noah. To his young brain, "in the near future" must have been interpreted as "when he turns six." The only problem was Noah's birthday wasn't any time soon.

"What are you talking about? You've got a lot more time than that before you turn six."

"But Grandma says that in Korea everyone gets one year older on New Year's."

Eun-ho could hear Grandma's voice from inside the apartment: "Are you going to stay out there all night or what?" This spared Eun-ho the pain of having to burst Noah's bubble.

Eun-ho quickly entered the apartment. With Noah still in his arms, Eun-ho took off his shoes and stepped into the living room.

"Your timing couldn't have been any better." Noah's grandma was standing in front of the sofa with her arms crossed. "Why are you so late?"

The wall clock was pointing to 4:30. He was thirty minutes early.

"Noah has gone to the veranda window a hundred times today to see if you'd arrived."

Eun-ho put Noah down. Dressed in a sweater, a pair of jeans, and socks, Noah looked ready to go. Eun-ho could picture Noah getting up early that morning to put on his clothes. According to her, Noah did this every Saturday when Eun-ho came to pick him up.

Lying on the sofa were Noah's jacket and his grandma's coat, and beneath that on the floor was Noah's favorite soccer ball and two bags. One bag was Noah's, inside of which would be his inhaler and other belongings, and the other was his grandma's. Eun-ho slung the bags over his shoulder and turned to her.

"Mom, Let's go."

Noah's grandma got in the back of the car with Noah. For a while, she didn't say anything to Eun-ho. But this wasn't done voluntarily; she didn't have the chance to because Noah was chirping like a sparrow. Only when Noah tired himself out did she finally have a chance to speak.

"Is your wife back from the hospital?"

Eun-ho said yes despite knowing the more accurate answer was "probably." After all, he hadn't been able to confirm that she had come back yet. All he had to go off was the text message he got from Wife a few hours ago.

—I'm out grocery shopping. I'll see you when you come back from Hanam with Noah and your mother.

At the time, Eun-ho was brewing coffee. After the whirlwind of emotions from earlier that morning, Eun-ho had finally come back to Earth. He'd just succeeded in taking his mind off Wife's return and was thinking about what to do next. He used the tried-and-true method he used to use when he was a college student majoring in literature: What would Jinu do?

First, Eun-ho thought about the possibility of an extramarital affair. What if she was at her ex-husband's house? But he had yet to find anything he could accept as solid evidence. Everything he had was circumstantial. There was no need to get wrapped up in a sense of betrayal just yet.

Eventually, Eun-ho decided it was something he would have to look more into after Noah and Mom went back to Hanam. He had options. He could find a private detective, or he could investigate himself.

More important right now was Noah. Eun-ho couldn't let his son down again—even if that meant letting Mom finding out about Wife's leaving the house. Eun-ho decided to go to Hanam once he had his cup of coffee.

It was just as he put his key in the ignition that Eun-ho received the text message from Wife. His head flooded with questions again. It was as if she had anticipated his every move, anticipated that he would delay picking up Noah until Sunday, anticipated that he would lie to his own mother to buy time, anticipated how long he would wait and how he would react once he saw her message. There was no way this was a coincidence. She had planned it all out.

—I'm out grocery shopping. I'll see you when you come back from Hanam with Noah and your mother.

The tone of her message infuriated him. She acted as if she were simply stopping by the grocery store on her way home from work. Between the lines, Eun-ho could read a mocking and condescending message: *I'll save you. Just this once.* Eun-ho could almost hear her arrogant voice: *I have an excuse that will explain where I've been. And you have no choice but to accept it.*

Eun-ho felt pathetic, but he had no choice but to follow her orders. He sent her a reply:

—My mom thinks your mom's at the hospital.

—K

This angered Eun-ho even more. Not "Okay." Not "OK." Just "K." *She must think me a complete pushover.*

Eun-ho could hear a derisive voice in his head telling him, *She doesn't just* think *you're a pushover, you* are *a pushover.*

Eun-ho left the house fuming at the ears. He only started to calm down after he got onto the freeway. By the time he arrived outside Mother's apartment, he had found enough composure to function like a normal human being.

"But why is her mother in the hospital?" Eun-ho's mom asked.

"We haven't gotten the results back yet."

"What hospital is she at?"

"Why? Are you going to visit her or something?"

Eun-ho's mom looked at him through the rearview mirror. Her eyes were telling him she knew he was lying.

"Why not? She's not some stranger. She's my daughter-in-law's mother."

A bicycle flashed across the street, just barely avoiding crashing into the hood of Eun-ho's car. Eun-ho slammed on the breaks. The car lurched forward as his mom let out a scream. The car only stopped once it was halfway through the crosswalk. Eun-ho looked and saw that the crosswalk sign was green. People glared at him as they walked around the front of his car.

"Watch where you're going!" Eun-ho's mom said as she held Noah in her arms, her eyeballs bulging out of her eye sockets. Her tone was as shocked as it was scathing.

Eun-ho let out a long sigh as a wave of fatigue washed over his body.

"Where's your head, Eun-ho?"

The answer was obvious. It was focusing on her nagging. But Eun-ho was unable to argue with her and just swallowed his words.

"You should slow down when you see a crosswalk. Don't you know you have a child in the car? What if you had hit someone? Don't you remember last time? You got distracted and almost hit that delivery bike."

Eun-ho just took it in silence. He knew that his mom wouldn't stop even if he told her to. Eun-ho had experienced this often as a child. The only difference was that it was Eun-ho's dad who was driving and not him. His mom would make all sorts of nasty remarks, if something happened, she would blame his dad's poor driving skills, and if his dad asked her to stop, she would bring up the past and continue to attack him until they got out of the car.

After his dad left the company, he "graduated from marriage," as he put it, and left Eun-ho and his mom for Jeju Island. Eun-ho only saw him two times after that. Once was on his wedding day with Yoon-hee, and the second time was on his wedding day with Yuna. Eun-ho didn't blame his dad for the way things turned out. In fact, he sympathized with him. Although, the same couldn't be said for her. Even after all these years, Eun-ho's mom still wouldn't admit that she was the one who drove Dad away.

But unlike him, Eun-ho couldn't run away. It would be a lie to say that he stayed out of some sense of duty to her. The truth was that he needed her to raise Noah. Eun-ho harbored no expectations that she would change. After sixty-five years on Earth, humans were more like mathematical constants than variables.

"Well, are we just going to sit here? Or are you going to go?"

Her shrill voice woke Eun-ho up from his deep thought. The light had turned green. Eun-ho stepped on the gas. Eun-ho listened to her nagging all the way to the house, by which time he was sure his eardrums had holes in them. "Slow down, you're going to hit the car in front of you." "Go faster, the person behind you is honking." "What's the rush?" "Stop passing everyone." "Why are you following this truck so closely?" "Pass him already!"

Only when they parked in the driveway did his mom stop her backseat driving. Eun-ho looked for signs that Wife was home. The lights were on, and Wife's car was parked in the garage. A thought was wiggling in the back of his mind, as tenacious and filthy as a cockroach. It was relief about Wife's return, a willingness to forgive her for everything if things would just go back to normal.

Eun-ho looked back at his mom.

"Take Noah and go inside. I'll get the bags."

After they got out, Eun-ho drove the car into the garage. Parking next to Wife's car, he took a second to steady his breathing. He had to go inside like it was just another day. He had to face Wife like nothing was wrong. He had to be a good enough actor to fool his mom. But could he do it?

Eun-ho got out of the car with the bags. He walked out to the driveway and headed to the front door. He opened the door feeling like he was going to the dentist. Wife was standing in the middle of the second doorway just beyond the place to remove shoes. Eun-ho looked at her with uncertainty as she beamed at him.

"Fewer bags than I expected," she said as her eyes moved down to his hands. "I cleared out Jiyoo's room."

Eun-ho knew immediately what she meant by this. This was the second time that Mother had come to spend the night. The first time, she had slept with Noah in his room. Jiyoo had slept by herself in her room, and Eun-ho and Wife slept together in the master bedroom. Peaceful times. But things had changed. It was this change that Wife was informing Eun-ho of. She would be sleeping in the master bedroom with Jiyoo, Grandma would be sleeping in Jiyoo's room, and Eun-ho would be sleeping with Noah.

"Put the bags upstairs and hurry back down. I'm making your favorite."

Eun-ho's lungs seized up. Her smile was as bright as a summer afternoon, and her voice was trickling gently into his ears like a mountain spring. But her eyes—Her eyes were cold, like a desolate gust of autumnal wind from the north. Eun-ho's senses were spinning from the dissonance of fire and ice on her beautiful trim face.

"My favorite?" Eun-ho asked with his jaw unhinged.

He asked this question despite knowing the answer, which had been given to him by the smell of goulash filling the house.

Suddenly, a loud noise could be heard coming from the living room. Eun-ho guessed it was the sound of Noah's soccer ball banging against the glass door to the balcony. Eun-ho took off his shoes and stepped inside. Wife turned sideways to let him pass, revealing a small shadowy figure behind her.

"Hello."

Jiyoo brought her hands together in front of her and bowed to him. Eun-ho's lungs seized up again as he remembered how Jane had told him not to bring Jiyoo over to their house. He couldn't figure out what Jiyoo's being here meant. Was it evidence that Wife and her sister Jane were on good terms? Or was it evidence that Wife and Jiyoo hadn't been at her mother's house? Or was it evidence for something else completely?

Eun-ho needed to respond to Jiyoo's greeting, but his mouth was clamped shut. He was afraid of his own mouth. He was afraid he might ask which "home" she had come from.

"Eun-ho, Jiyoo said hello."

Her voice still trickled like a mountain spring, but Eun-ho could sense the icepick lurking beneath the surface of the water. It was then that Eun-ho finally realized what he was doing. He was just staring at Jiyoo like she was a leper, ignoring her greeting. Although he couldn't see his own face, it probably wasn't very welcoming. The intensity and duration of his stare might even be scaring her.

"Jiyoo, you made it."

"Yes."

Eun-ho passed Jiyoo and continued to the living room. He could feel Wife's eyes burrowing into the back of his head, but he didn't want to make an attempt at redemption. Instead, he felt a sense of rebelliousness. Ignoring Jiyoo's greeting was an accident, but what Wife did to him was intentional. She didn't have the right to be angry with him.

Noah was taking penalty kicks between the sofa and the table. As the ball left Noah's foot, it pinballed around, hitting everything from the table and sofa to the flowerpots and the glass door to the balcony. The living room floor looked like someone had died there. The telephone was face down on the ground, there was dirt from the flowerpot on the floor, one of the branches on the Bengal rubber tree was broken, and the remote-control holder was on the other side of the room. It couldn't have been more than ten minutes since they arrived.

"Noah, you should sit down," Mother said as she chased Noah around the room. "Don't overdo it. You'll have an asthma attack."

Eun-ho went up to the second floor. The second floor was built like a loft with a high ceiling and was about half the size of the first floor. Two bedrooms faced each other with the living room, which was used as a playroom, between them. One room was Jiyoo's, and the other was Noah's. The bathroom was adjacent to Noah's room.

Eun-ho opened the door to Jiyoo's room but didn't turn on the light. He didn't even look inside. He pushed his mom's bag in through the doorway and closed the door immediately. Eun-ho didn't usually go into Jiyoo's room. In fact, he'd never once gone into her room by himself. He had no reason to go inside when Jiyoo wasn't there, and had every reason not to go inside when she was there.

According to Wife, Jiyoo's biological father had "sneakily" molested Jiyoo behind her back. But Eun-ho never learned what exactly she meant by "sneakily." All he knew was that it was the main reason for Jiyoo's father losing parental rights. But once he knew this, Eun-ho found it hard to interact with Jiyoo. He always had to be careful around her to avoid doing anything that might be misconstrued. Because of this, he could never imagine hugging her or rough housing with her like he did with Noah. He also felt too guilty to ever discipline her.

Jiyoo's personality was another reason their relationship lacked intimacy. Jiyoo was an independent and precocious kid who liked to keep to herself. She also had this calmness and spunkiness to her that Noah didn't share. She was too smart for her age, and beautiful, too, making Eun-ho that much more uncomfortable around her. The combination of these things made the distance between him and his stepdaughter like the distance between Earth and Pluto.

But if he had molested her . . . Eun-ho paused as he opened Noah's door. He had been too focused on the possibility that Wife was having an affair to notice the contradictory nature of it. Wife had tried so hard to keep her ex-husband from seeing Jiyoo. She didn't even accept the visiting rights that the court granted him. She said it was to protect Jiyoo from him. So, it made no sense for her to take Jiyoo to her ex's house—although, it might make sense if she was lying about why they had gotten a divorce.

Standing at the doorway, Eun-ho looked down at the bed. Noah's favorite stuffed animal, a large penguin with beady eyes named Pengsoo, was lying on the right side of the bed. Eun-ho stared at Pengsoo's open yellow beak for a moment before he heard a voice in his head: *You can think about this again on Thursday after Noah and Mom are gone.*

Eun-ho went back downstairs to find Noah and his grandma standing face to face with Wife and Jiyoo. Noah was hugging his grandma's waist, and Jiyoo had her eyes cast down toward the floor, her shoulders slightly angled toward her mom. Yuna and Eun-ho's mom looked like two team captains confronting each other on the pitch before a match. And between them was Noah's soccer ball.

"Obviously he didn't do it on purpose," Eun-ho's mom said. "And it's not like she's hurt."

Wife didn't even look at Eun-ho's mom. Her gaze was fixed on Noah.

"Noah," she said in a stern voice. "Say sorry to your big sister."

Eun-ho put himself between the two teams. No sooner did he ask what was going on than his mom came forward to explain. Jiyoo had been hit by one of Noah's penalty kicks. But to her eyes, the ball had only slightly tapped Jiyoo on the chest.

Wife explained the incident from her point of view. According to her, Jiyoo wasn't just "tapped." She had been hit so hard that it knocked her on her butt when she caught the ball. Then Noah came running over and pushed Jiyoo as he took the ball from her. This caused Jiyoo to fall backwards. The problem was that Noah wasn't apologizing.

"I doubt he pushed her on purpose. He just wanted the ball back."

"Is that how you taught him? To push other people over to get what they want?"

"I would never!" Eun-ho's mom, whose voice was already a notch higher than everyone else's, raised her voice another octave. "And Noah is barely six."

Wife responded to Eun-ho's mom raising her voice by lowering her own voice a notch: "Jiyoo and Noah are only eleven months apart."

"He has asthma, for heaven's sake."

"That doesn't mean he can hit Jiyoo."

Every time these two women exchanged blows, Eun-ho felt like he was being forced to swallow a quarter. Yuna wasn't the first woman who had butted heads with his mom. His ex-wife, Yoon-hee, also hadn't gotten along with his mom. Other than their names, not much had changed.

Eun-ho could feel something sour working its way up his throat. He wanted to take care of this before he vomited. It was because of this that he decided without much deliberation to take Wife's side and scold Noah.

"Noah, say you're sorry to your big sister."

Noah's face turned bright red. He looked at his grandma. There was clear betrayal in his eyes. He had trusted his dad to take his side. Noah's grandma answered Noah's plea for help and quickly went on the counterattack.

"You, too, Eun-ho? It's not like she has a broken bone."

Eun-ho put his hand on Noah's shoulder and pulled him away from his grandma.

"Are you not going to say you're sorry?"

Noah hugged his ball even tighter. His mouth wasn't opening. His stubborn eyes were making his intention clear to Eun-ho. *No.*

Eun-ho felt his Adam's apple swelling to the size of a soccer ball. This wasn't the first time this had happened. In fact, this happened every weekend Noah and Jiyoo got together. Usually, it was just small skirmishes. But according to Wife's analysis, Noah was just as irritable and sensitive as his father, so it was Noah's fault. But it was really Eun-ho's fault. He was the one who spoiled Noah. His son's condition made it impossible for Eun-ho to discipline Noah. And Eun-ho was always trying to make it up to Noah for not being able to be a good father and raising Noah himself.

And yet, Noah had never been as misbehaved as he was right now. He usually accepted his wrongdoing and apologized. His current behavior had to be related to the fact he had the support of an unconditionally loyal teammate. Eun-ho needed to separate Noah from his grandma if he wanted to handle this.

"Noah, Daddy needs to have a talk with you." Eun-ho grabbed Noah's hand. "No one come in." Eun-ho said this to prevent his mother from coming along as back up. But all the way to the study, Noah dragged his feet and glanced back at his grandma.

"Why are you scaring him like that?" Eun-ho's mother called from behind.

Eun-ho closed the door, shutting everyone out, and locked the door so no one would interfere.

Eun-ho sat Noah down on his chair and kneeled in front of him. He explained to Noah why he was wrong and why he needed to apologize. But Noah wasn't listening to what Eun-ho told him. He just glanced toward the door as he fiddled with his soccer ball.

"Noah, do you understand what I'm telling you?"

Noah shook his head. Eun-ho couldn't tell if this meant that he didn't understand or that he understood but disagreed.

"Should I say it again?"

This time, Noah shook his head again.

"Then are you going to say you're sorry to your big sister?"

Noah shook his head even harder this time. In fact, his denial was so strong that he had to hold onto the armrests of the chair so that he could twist his whole body in refusal.

"She's not my big sister," Noah finally said. "Tell her to go back to her home."

What did I just hear? Eun-ho couldn't believe his ears.

"Why does she always come to our house? Like a homeless person."

Something snapped inside Eun-ho's stomach. He stood up suddenly and grabbed Noah by the shoulders.

"Noah Cha! I think you need a time out."

"No. I don't want to. Don't let her come here."

Noah burst into tears. This started what was an uncontrollable wave of emotions. First Noah started screaming. Then he began contorting his body and thrashing his legs so violently that he rocked the chair back and forth. Eun-ho had never seen Noah act like this; he didn't know what to do. He risked hurting Noah if he grabbed him and tried to restrain him, and he risked Noah hurting himself if he did nothing.

"Noah Cha. Stop this right now."

Eun-ho decided to hug Noah and pushed him back into the chair. But Noah didn't stop thrashing. Eun-ho's heart plummeted as a realization hit him: Noah was having an asthma attack. His lips were blue, his breathing was a wheezy whistle, sweat was dripping from his forehead, his eyes were full of tears and half-closed, and his body was beginning to go limp.

Noah had had asthma attacks before, but that never made it any less traumatic for Eun-ho or Noah.

Eun-ho threw open the study door and called out to his mom to bring the emergency inhaler.

The minute it took for her to find and bring it to him felt like an eternal hell. They forced the inhalant down Noah's throat, and immediately Noah started coughing as he gasped for air. When Noah finally was able to breathe again, Eun-ho almost dropped to his knees, which would have been a mistake. He wanted to prostrate himself and beg for forgiveness. Had Eun-ho's mom not snatched Noah from Eun-ho's arms, he really would have done it, too.

"What kind of father are you?" As Eun-ho's mom held Noah and left the study, she took one more jab at Eun-ho. "You can't discipline him without almost killing him."

Eun-ho followed her into the living room. She laid Noah on the sofa, propped him up with a cushion, and started massaging his hands and feet. Then, she started barking commands. "Fetch water." "Turn up the boiler." "Turn on the dehumidifier." "Bring out the air purifier." "Get him a blanket."

All the while, she gave Eun-ho the stink eye as she talked to herself in a loud, rumbling voice. 'He almost killed my poor baby." "Look, your lips are still purple." "And you're ice cold." "He was so mean to you that you fainted." "And we're so close to curing you of your asthma. This will set us back months." "I've heard stories about fathers killing children from previous marriages. I can't believe my Noah almost became one of them."

No one else was talking. Eun-ho walked all over the house obeying her commands. Wife's eyes, which were following Eun-ho around as he did this, were saying, "Shut that woman up." Eun-ho just ignored Wife. His mom wasn't the kind of person to shut up just because you told her to. Nor did Eun-ho have any intention of stopping her. He was in a daze from the shock of almost killing Noah.

Noah stayed sprawled out on the sofa for a while. The wheezing in his breathing slowly disappeared, but it would take a bit longer for him to return completely to normal. For the rest of today, at least, he would be out of commission.

And yet, Eun-ho was worried. What if Noah's condition suddenly got worse? Should he take him to the emergency room?

"I'll prepare dinner."

Wife turned to the kitchen.

"How can you think about food at a time like this?" Eun-ho's mom asked to Wife's back.

Wife went into the kitchen without answering. Eun-ho's mom's eyes shifted targets from Wife to Jiyoo. Jiyoo put both hands in front of her and stood there awkwardly by the sofa. Her face looked as if she were waiting for her punishment. She had read the meaning in Mother's eyes. *Noah almost died because of you. Are you happy now?*

Despite being in the kitchen, Wife knew what look Eun-ho's mom was giving Jiyoo. She retaliated by intentionally being loud. She turned on the water full blast and noisily washed dishes. She dropped the utensil holder on the ground, put down heavy bowls too suddenly, and slammed the refrigerator door hard enough to break it.

By now, Eun-ho had come to his senses enough to think about other people. He turned to Jiyoo who desperately needed his help.

"Jiyoo, why don't you go into the kitchen and help your mother?"

Jiyoo let out a strange sound that was neither "Yes" or "Okay." It sounded like a sob caught in her throat. Only now did Eun-ho realize the whites of Jiyoo's eyes were red. As Jiyoo turned around, her shoulders trembled as though she were crying. She looked like she might fall over as she walked to the kitchen.

Eun-ho turned to Noah. But it was his mom's eyes he met, not Noah's. Her eyes were spitting at him: *You idiot.*

The back of Eun-ho's head was burning, too. Wife's eyes, which had locked on to the back of his head, were saying, *Mama's boy.*

In fact, it was his being a mama's boy that was Eun-ho's second marriage-threatening flaw.

Around nine, Noah's breathing returned to normal. What hadn't returned to normal was the mood. The only ones talking were Eun-ho's mom and Noah. No one touched Wife's goulash. Noah ate yogurt, and Eun-ho's mom had plain white rice with soup. Jiyoo counted grains of rice, and Eun-ho twice put his spoon in the goulash only to put it back down.

Wife didn't even sit at the dinner table. She was too busy providing Noah and his grandma with alternative menu items. When Eun-ho tried to get up from the table to help, she would sit him back down with her eyes. And when she was done getting Noah and his grandma their food, Wife started idling her time away by doing chores that could have waited until later. By putting away the unused bowls and wiping down the kitchen sink and gas stove, she was telling them, *I'm not eating with you people.*

"Are you not eating?" Eun-ho's mom asked as she took a bite of rice soaked in soup.

This wasn't something she said out of courtesy. Nor was it something she said to let everyone take a deep breath. She knew what Eun-ho's wife was doing. She said this to pick a fight.

"I will."

Wife took off her rubber gloves, hung them over the kitchen sink, and sat down. Only then did Eun-ho notice the bandages on Wife's right hand.

"What's wrong with your hand?" Eun-ho's mom asked.

Wife picked up her utensils with her knuckles as she answered, "I cut my hand while slicing meat."

This answer gave Eun-ho a sense of déjà vu. Two years ago on Lake Baikal, on the day the two of them left Jinu behind and went on a tour of the north side of Olkhon Island by themselves, Wife had given Eun-ho a similar answer when he asked the third question he had for her. *My knife slipped while I was slicing meat.*

At the time, Eun-ho had just accepted this answer. Back then, making eye contact with Yuna was enough to make his brain short circuit. But not anymore. As Eun-ho made eye contact with Wife, a completely logical question crossed his mind. Wouldn't a right-handed person cut their left hand while cooking, not their right? Of course, it wasn't impossible for a right-handed person to cut their right hand while cooking. But what were the chances of it happening twice? Had she grabbed hold of the blade instead of the handle?

"When did you cut yourself?" Eun-ho's mom asked.

"A few days ago," Wife answered as she looked down and pushed the goulash around her plate.

"Did you go to the hospital?"

"I got several stiches."

Eun-ho's mom nodded her head. She started making sarcastic remarks disguised as words of concern: "Cutting one's hand is no small matter." "What if she had bled out?" "Perhaps she should take cooking lessons."

Eventually, Eun-ho's mom changed the subject to something she really wanted to talk about.

"There's something I've been wanting to tell you."

"Please."

Wife's eyes were still cast downward. Her voice and tone had found their usual calmness. The only thing that wasn't back to normal was her countenance, which was as opaque as a window with its shutters closed and was making everyone at the table invisible. Back when they were dating, she would from time to time make this face and push Eun-ho away. When that happened, despite being together, it felt like they were miles apart. It always seemed to appear just as Eun-ho thought he had finally figured her out.

"I want you to take Noah back this month."

Wife looked up at Eun-ho. And Eun-ho looked at his mom. This was an unexpected and bewildering notice. She said this month, but really there were only ten days left in November.

"I just don't think I can wait until next March. I've been watching the way you two acted today and—"

"Before you say anymore—" Wife interrupted her in a quiet voice. "Why don't we talk about this in the living room over some hot tea."

"Yeah, Grandma," Noah said. "Talk about it in the living room. I'm sleepy."

Eun-ho's mom chewed on her lips as Noah dragged her to the living room.

Wife turned to Jiyoo.

"Jiyoo, don't you have something to do before bed?"

Jiyoo put down her chopsticks and got up. And then Eun-ho got his orders, too.

"Eun-ho, go to the living room and watch the kids. I'll clean up and be right out."

Eun-ho went out to the living room as he was told, but there wasn't much to watch. Noah was lying with his head on his grandma's lap, and Jiyoo was just standing there.

"Noah, you shouldn't lie down after eating."

Noah looked like he hadn't heard Eun-ho. When Eun-ho walked over to him, Noah turned his body and buried his face in his grandma's belly. Feeling embarrassed, Eun-ho turned to Jiyoo.

"Jiyoo, is there anything you need?"

"No. I'm going to do my homework."

Jiyoo bowed her head and said goodnight, once to Eun-ho and once to Eun-ho's mom.

"Goodnight."

Eun-ho's mom watched quietly as Jiyoo disappeared into the master bedroom.

"She's just like her mother."

No, she wasn't. She was too lanky, and her features too delicate. She probably looked more like her playwright father.

"I don't like her at all."

"That's just because you don't see her often."

Eun-ho's mom opened her eyes like tall triangles.

"Do I have to see her often to like her? Just look at how she acts. Who could like a child like that? Just today—"

"Mom—" Eun-ho raised his voice. "Would you quit it? Noah's here."

What Eun-ho really wanted to say was: *It's because of you that Noah's like this.* But Eun-ho didn't want to waste his energy; the real fight was yet to begin. Besides, it wasn't like he was going to make his mom like Jiyoo by arguing with her.

Eun-ho's mom hadn't liked Jiyoo from the outset. Or perhaps it would be more accurate to say that she didn't like that Jiyoo existed. In her own words, when both parents were divorcees with kids, one child had to disappear for the other to receive devotion. "You really believe Noah won't become the other child?" In her opinion, Noah was being sacrificed for Jiyoo.

Wife could only be half blamed for Noah's living with his grandma. The other half of the blame resided with an idiot who acted like a slave to his new wife. Eun-ho recalled last summer, the day he proposed to her.

Yuna spent that weekend at Eun-ho's place. They'd been seeing each other for over a year by then. He knew everything he could know about her, at least, that's what he thought. They got along so well that he wondered sometimes if they would ever fight. He believed she believed he was her soulmate. He was positive Yuna would say yes without hesitation.

But Yuna's reaction was unexpectedly lukewarm. Dating was fine, but marriage? She said marriage was only possible if the other person wanted what she wanted.

"And what do you want?" Eun-ho asked.

Her answer was so banal that he thought it ridiculous.

"Happiness."

Was there a human alive who didn't want this? Eun-ho said that he wanted the same thing she did. He added that happiness was precisely the reason he was proposing to her.

"Tell me, Eun-ho, what do you think happiness is? And be specific."

This caught Eun-ho off guard, like he had been sucker punched. He hadn't expected his proposal to lead to such a philosophical conversation. Honestly, he had never thought much about what happiness was. Overthinking happiness never made anyone happier. Eun-ho hesitated for a while before answering.

"I think you will eventually become happy if you slowly collect happy moments over a lifetime."

"Wrong. Happiness isn't addition." Yuna stared out the balcony window, as though she were searching for a distant horizon. Although he doubted she could see much more than the reflection of their apartment in the glass pane. "Happiness is subtraction. It's getting rid of the possibility of unhappiness until life becomes perfect."

Eun-ho couldn't agree with this, but he didn't have anything really to say. He waited quietly for her to continue.

"I've lived my whole life striving for that perfect happiness."

Yuna's eyes turned back to Eun-ho and regained their focus.

"A married couple is a team. Your effort needs to match my effort."

"I can do it," Eun-ho replied without hesitation.

She was asking him to strive for happiness, so what was there to object to? And he sincerely wanted to be happy. He thought marrying her would make him that.

"Promise?"

"Promise."

Eun-ho shouldn't have taken this promise so lightly. Only when they started preparing for the wedding did Eun-ho get an idea of what she really meant by "effort."

That day was the first time he had taken Yuna to Hanam. His mom asked Yuna if she was going to take Noah in when they got married.

"I will when we have a house for four."

This answer was the promise she made when they got married that Mother brought up day in and day out. The problem was that the two women had interpreted that promise differently. Mother thought the important part was "when you get married" and Yuna thought the important part was "when we have a house for four."

At the time, Eun-ho was living out of an apartment near school. Only having one bedroom, one bathroom, and a living room, it would be difficult to live with two kids there. Yuna's apartment was located in a high-rise apartment in Seogyo-dong. It was big enough to raise two children, but too far from Eun-ho's school. They either would have to live apart during the weekdays or he would have to commute more than an hour to work every day.

Yuna suggested a house as an alternative. She told him that they were building houses on the outskirts of Cheongyeon, and that there were still lots available. Most importantly, she convinced Eun-ho that it would be good for Noah. It would have lots of fresh air from all the trees in the area, and they wouldn't have to worry about inter-floor noise.

"Didn't you say Noah likes soccer?"

When they went to the open house, Eun-ho fell in love with the place immediately. It was a proper stand-alone house with plenty of space between neighboring plots. It also had its own garage and a small backyard. The house itself was built like a rambler with a loft. Not to mention the fact that it had four bedrooms and a large walk-in closet. They would be able to give Jiyoo and Noah their own rooms and still have one to spare. Yuna told Eun-ho he could use the remaining room as his study. He was thankful as he had just started his master's program.

"This is just the kind of house I wanted."

Yuna looked like she had already made up her mind. Eun-ho shook his head. He liked it, but there were still a lot of problems. First, the house was absurdly expensive. Eun-ho would have to sell his place and they would have to use up all their savings and take out a loan just to pay the down deposit. Not to mention the fact that they wouldn't be able to move in right away. They would have to wait until next June, more than six months away. Where were Eun-ho and Noah going to live in the meantime? Eun-ho thought they would have to settle for a three-room apartment.

But Yuna suggested a different plan. She would sell her apartment instead so that she and Eun-ho could live in his apartment close to work. Noah and Jiyoo would live at their grandparents' places. And then, when the townhouse was finally built, they would all move in together. If Eun-ho didn't like that, they could simply postpone the wedding. That way they could continue living separately until the house was finished.

Instead of postponing the wedding, Eun-ho decided to postpone his reunion with his son. He'd lived apart from Noah for almost five years, what was a few more months? Even though Eun-ho's mom didn't like the plan, she agreed to look after Noah for a bit longer.

It was relatively smooth sailing after that. At least until after they moved in because even after moving into the townhouse, Eun-ho was unable to bring Noah to live with him. Wife had wanted to bring the two kids together, on the same day. But she argued that they needed to have the same last name when that happened. Sending a brother and sister to the same daycare with different names was like advertising to the world that their parents were both divorcees. She didn't want the kids to have to go through that if they didn't need to. To her, such wounds were like the seeds of unhappiness just waiting to sprout.

This time, as well, Wife had a plan. She told Eun-ho all he had to do was adopt Jiyoo and change her last name. This was a clear solution to their problem, but there was only one major issue. Adoption papers by a stepparent were only accepted one year after filing for marriage. So, they would need to wait five more months.

Eun-ho rejected Wife's plan. It wasn't that he didn't want to adopt Jiyoo, nor was it because he was that upset about not being reunited with Noah. He simply rejected Wife's premise as invalid. Their second marriage wasn't some secret that needed to be hidden from the world. While it was true theirs wasn't your typical marriage, it wasn't the kind of flaw that warranted changing a child's last name or should prevent them from raising their own children.

Humans live in their own universe governed by their own beliefs. Wife's universe was one of perfection—flawless, faultless, spotless perfection. And she believed that perfect happiness started with filial perfection. This belief of hers was borderline religious. There was no room for compromise. Wife rejected his rejection.

This difference in opinion exploded into a fight in just a matter of minutes. They exchanged hurtful words without hesitation. Wife called him a selfish prick who only cared about his own child. In fact, selfishness was his third marriage-threatening flaw. And then, she accused him of going back on his word like a liar and slapped him. Once with a forehand, once with a backhand.

He was so shocked that he couldn't retaliate nor defend himself. He just stood there and took it as her slapping turned into punching. They had had bad fights before, but never had it turned physical. That night, Eun-ho finally understood how men who allowed themselves to be abused came to be.

Wife stormed out of the apartment as though she were the victim. The next day, Eun-ho received a message asking for a divorce, as though he had been the aggressor.

Eun-ho threw away his pride. He also gave up on his plans to bring Noah into the house as soon as they moved in. He didn't want to threaten their marriage anymore. Losing was better than ruining his marriage, he thought. That was the principle that ruled his universe. Even though he'd never said this out loud, she knew it as though she were some psychic. This was the reason he lost every fight.

When Wife finally came back home, Eun-ho went looking for his mom. He convinced her to look after Noah for yet a few more months. He didn't mention adoption. She would find out eventually; there was no reason to pay up front for a scolding by running his mouth. Instead, he used Wife as the excuse. He said Wife hurt her back and needed to receive treatment for a few months. His mom didn't look like she believed this, but she didn't protest, under the condition that he pay all her living expenses for the remainder of Noah's stay.

Last Monday was their first-year anniversary. Eun-ho met Wife in Songdo, where they had dinner and watched the classic *Before Sunset* at a car-park movie theatre before returning to her house in Cheongyeon to share a bottle of wine and make love.

Married life for Eun-ho was a mixture of bliss and agony. That night belonged to the former. It was a peaceful, satisfying night. The kind of night that made Eun-ho think they could grow old together if they could just do this more often. The kind of night that made him want to believe that they were normal. But that all changed when Wife dropped a new bomb on Eun-ho's chest.

Wife asked Eun-ho to fully adopt Jiyoo as his own child. Under regular adoption, the law would still recognize the father-daughter relationship between Jiyoo and her biological father. But under full adoption, those bonds of kinship would be severed. Jiyoo would be added to Eun-ho's family register as his rightful child, and her last name would automatically be changed. In other words, Wife was asking Eun-ho to uproot and replant Jiyoo in his family tree.

Eun-ho, who had been blissfully dozing off after making love, sat right up in bed. He would have been less shocked had someone started strangling him in his sleep. Why was this the first time he was hearing about this? This was probably her plan all along; he just had been too stupid to notice. They had already been married for an entire year, and he was still this bad at reading his own wife. Or rather, he was wholly incapable of reading her. Even a brainless sea cucumber could become a master of reading minds with a bit of training.

"I'll take care of all the paperwork." Wife got up and sat across from him on the bed. "All you have to do is agree." Her tone suggested that she didn't doubt for a second that he would agree. "You'll do this for me, won't you?"

Up till this moment, Wife still had a sweetish smile on her face. Eun-ho didn't want to betray her expectations, he didn't want to ruin the mood, but he had to speak his mind.

"No, I can't do it."

The smile disappeared from her face, as though someone had flipped the circuit breaker, *POP.*

"Why not?"

She wasn't really asking why not. What she was really asking was, *What's wrong with adopting Jiyoo?* This was the kind of cross-examination that someone did when they were so sure of themselves that they didn't believe the person they were talking to had a mouth that could think for itself. Eun-ho answered as though he felt he had to defend himself.

"It's not that simple."

"Why not? We've always talked about this. The process is basically the same. It's not like we're bringing the kids in any later."

"As far as I'm aware, you need the signed consent of both biological parents to do full adoption. Think about it from your ex-husband's point of view. He's basically relinquishing all blood ties to his daughter. You really think he'd be willing to do that? He's not crazy. You're asking him to hand over his only daughter. He's not just going to say, 'Yes, yes, of course.' "

The color was draining out of Wife's face. Daggers appeared in her pupils. These were signs that she was losing her cool.

"What if I get him to sign?" Wife paused for a moment before continuing. "Will you sign then?"

Eun-ho wavered slightly, but he had no intention of changing his mind.

"No."

"No?"

"This won't end with my agreeing to it. The fundamental problem is Jiyoo. Haven't you thought of the possibility that Jiyoo might grow up to resent us? How do you think she'll feel when she finds out that we cut her off from her biological father, who may I remind you is still alive? Haven't you thought about how much it will hurt her? Why do you have to have everything your way? Jiyoo might be your daughter, but she's not your property. She has her own life."

"You're such an asshole."

Wife twisted her lips as she smirked. Her glare was darting back and forth between his right and left eye, carving lines into his cornea with a razor blade. Eun-ho could feel her breathing starting to tremble. He could even smell the sour odor of perspiration on her pale skin.

Eun-ho couldn't help but admire her. Her entire body was perfectly coordinated in expressing her emotions. When that emotion was love, her body gave him bliss, and when it was rage, her body dragged him into the fiery pits of hell. Even though Eun-ho knew this, he couldn't stop.

"If I were Jiyoo, I wouldn't forgive you. Never."

Wife got down from the bed. She started a series of rage-filled verbal attacks.

"Don't pretend you're thinking of Jiyoo. I know you don't accept Jiyoo as your daughter. You shower your son with affection, but you treat my daughter like the neighbor's kid. You think I wouldn't know? I've never seen you affectionately hold her hand. You don't even smile when you look her in the eye. You're exactly like your mom. I'm sick and tired of you and your mother's hypocrisy."

Eun-ho walked around Wife and went into the living room. He locked the door so she couldn't come in. He thought they would start fighting in hand-to-hand combat if she hit him again. The next day, Wife left the house. That was her fifth time doing so. If her sister Jane hadn't come to see Eun-ho, he would have just assumed she was at her mother's house.

Yuna, where on Earth did you go?

This question, which Eun-ho had asked himself dozens of times over the past week, appeared again in Eun-ho's mind. He turned to look at the kitchen. Wife was just coming out of the kitchen with a tray of tea. Perhaps she went to her ex-husband's place to have him sign the adoption papers. Would she really have spent five nights there holding out until he signed? And even if that was true, Eun-ho wasn't sure what it would change.

"Is Noah asleep already?"

Wife put the tray down on the living room coffee table. Eun-ho examined the cookies and three cups of tea. Each cup was a different color: red, blue, yellow.

"Have some tea."

Wife offered the yellow cup to Eun-ho's mom and the red one to Eun-ho. It smelled tart yet sweet. Probably quince tea. Eun-ho's mom took a sip then looked at Wife.

"Did you make this?"

"If you like it, I can pack some for you when you leave."

Wife picked up the blue cup and sat down next to Eun-ho. A sudden silence fell over the living room. It was a long and awkward silence. The only sound in the room was the offbeat rhythm of people blowing on hot tea.

Eun-ho's mom was the first to put down her cup. She was also the one to break the silence.

"It's late, so let's finish what we were talking about earlier. Noah. What are you going to do about him?"

With her teacup nestled between two hands, Wife smiled at Eun-ho's mom. This was her characteristic smile: toothy with crescent-shaped eyes. She looked calm and relaxed. Even her voice as she answered had regained its usual softness.

"I always do as Eun-ho says."

Eun-ho almost choked on his tea. The hot liquid burned his airway. Wife had simultaneously thrown two balls at him from opposite directions. One ball was the claim that Noah's stay at his grandma's was Eun-ho's decision, and the other was a warning to Eun-ho to behave himself.

"Is that so?"

Mother turned to Eun-ho. Wife was looking down at her blue cup, as if to take a step back from the action. Eun-ho decided not to behave himself.

"You're going to take Noah by the end of this month, right?" Eun-ho's mom asked him.

Eun-ho sucked up the last drops of tea in his cup. A bittersweet aftertaste lingered on his tongue.

"Yes."

Wife raised one eyebrow and glanced at Eun-ho out of the corner of her eye. And that was it. She didn't add to what he said, nor did she refute it. Eun-ho put the cup down on the tray. He was bothered by the brown color of the tea, which reminded him of dried blood. Eun-ho knew almost nothing about China, but there was one thing he was sure of: Wife would never use teacups painted with primary colors like this.

"Good. Then I'll expect him gone by the end of the month." She stroked Noah on the head and then clicked her tongue. "Poor child. Who'll stand up for you now?"

"More tea?" Wife asked.

"No. It's almost eleven. I should sleep."

"I've made a place for you to sleep in Jiyoo's room on the second floor,"

Wife said as she put down her teacup and stood up. "Goodnight. Noah will sleep with Eun-ho."

Eun-ho picked up Noah with both arms and headed upstairs. He slid Peng-soo toward the side of the bed and laid Noah down. He undressed Noah and peeled away the hair stuck to his forehead. His face was a bit grubby from not being washed before bed. There were long furrow-like tracks of tears extending from his cheeks to his chin. Eun-ho's guilt resurfaced in his mind like grass perking up in the early morning. He was so ashamed of his heavy-handed discipline that it hurt. And he was afraid of the conflicts that would start in earnest just nine days from now. He had absolutely no idea how to raise a kid. He, a high school teacher, didn't know how to raise a kid.

"Eun-ho Cha—" his mom called out from the playroom. "I'm going to use the bathroom first."

By the time Eun-ho opened the door and looked out, his mom was already inside the bathroom. Eun-ho closed the window's curtains and lay down next to Noah. He took off his clothes and threw them onto the floor. He was intending on lying there until the bathroom was free, but immediately his body started to relax. The lights became dim, and his vision started to blur. And then, as if the sandman had hit him over the head, everything went black.

*

Eun-ho was wading through deep, blue water. At times he was being swept along by a swift undercurrent, and at others he was being pulled down into a dark ravine. When he reached the bottom, he was shot back up toward the water's frozen surface. It was dark and cold, and he couldn't breathe. This terrified him.

Eun-ho knew it was a dream, but he couldn't escape its pull. He was aware of his body as it moved through the water, but he couldn't move. His eyes were closed. And yet he could sense a white light moving across the surface of the water. He knew he was on a collision course for the ice, but he couldn't adjust his trajectory.

He hit the ice with great force. An explosion of light ignited before his eyelids. White, hot, searing rays of light blinded his senses.

Just as he felt something coming, he was sucked back into the darkness as though a rock were tied to his ankle. He had to still be dreaming. A thin crack formed between his eyelids allowing him to see a moving light just above them. It moved like a search light from his left eye to his right eye, to his ear, to his throat and chest, and through his body down to his legs. And then, suddenly, it disappeared as if someone had pulled the plug. The moment the light disappeared, Eun-ho saw something—something appearing from the darkness. Something small and white.

A hand. Eun-ho heard a voice from inside his head. And then his consciousness went blank, as though someone had pulled the shutters over his brain. Complete blackness.

*

When Eun-ho opened his eyes, he was lying face down on the bed. The room was mostly dark, but birds were chirping outside. Faint sunlight was leaking into the room through the curtains. It was morning. He had finally escaped the dream.

Eun-ho was about to turn his body to lie down on his back when he paused. There was something soft pinned under his ribs. At first, he thought it had to be Pengsoo. But his memory immediately reminded him it couldn't be Pengsoo. Last night, he had placed Pengsoo to Noah's side.

Eun-ho's body agreed with his memory. This didn't feel like Pengsoo, who was large and fat. This thing beneath him was small and thin, like the branch of a fledgling tree. It was so frail that it felt like it would snap if he took so much as a deep breath. It smelled familiar, too.

A horrifying realization seized Eun-ho. A voice whispered in his ear. *Don't move. Don't look.*

An unbearable amount of time passed. *Tick . . . tock . . .* Blood was rushing through his neck. His heart was letting out a frighteningly grating sound. A murder of crows was flying circles inside his mind. He couldn't take it anymore. Wanting to end the agony, Eun-ho turned over and got up in one single motion. He looked down and confirmed what it was.

It was Noah. He was face down with his face buried in Pengsoo's belly. Noah's limbs were limp.

Noah didn't answer when called to. Noah wasn't breathing. Noah had no pulse. Noah's head dropped lifeless when shook.

The world disappeared like a candle being blown out. Eun-ho's mind went dark. And from inside the darkness, he could hear his own screams exploding like a nuclear bomb in his chest.

"Noaaaaaah!"

CHAPTER 3

When Jane entered Elroy café from the company lobby, Min-young was sitting in the back near the window, her eyes cast downward and both hands resting atop her knees. She looked like a laptop in sleep mode, waiting for input from the world.

Jane was trying her best not to run back outside. Why had she agreed to meet this girl?

Min-young insisted that it was urgent and concerned Jane. But what could it be?

Jane vacillated near the entrance for a while before finally walking over to Min-young.

"Have you been waiting long?"

Min-young turned her head. She looked up at Jane as though she had just awoken from a deep slumber.

She parted her dry lips and spoke: "There are a lot of people here." Hardly an answer to Jane's question.

"It's lunchtime. There's always a lot of people."

Jane sat down across from Min-young. Jane thought about saying something like *It's nice to see you* but didn't because that would be a lie.

"How long has it been?" Min-young asked. "Seven years?"

Jane nodded. This was probably right. The last time they'd seen each other was at Yuna and Joon-young's wedding.

"Have you eaten?" Jane asked as she held up the menu.

"I only need this," Min-young said as she pointed to the cup of coffee on the table. "I can't be away from the office for too long."

To Jane's ears, Min-young's last sentence sounded more like: *You should order coffee, too, so this doesn't take any longer than it needs to.* Jane lifted her head to look at Min-young, who was looking at her in disbelief, as if she couldn't believe Jane wanted to eat at a time like this. Her gaze hadn't the slightest hint of respect for Jane's empty stomach. Had Min-young forgotten that it was she who asked to meet in the first place? When the server came, Jane accepted Min-young's reduced menu and ordered coffee as she tried to tell herself to think of it as a diet.

After the server left, silence fell between the two of them. Min-young looked down at her coffee, and Jane leaned against the back of the chair. Sitting patiently with her lips zipped was what Jane did best. Empty silence like this never bothered her, no matter whom she was with. She never felt the need to speak first or fill awkward pauses. In fact, she hadn't even asked Min-young what she came here to tell her.

"Jane," Min-young finally said. "Have you seen my big brother?"

The server came with Jane's coffee. He had perfect timing. This way, Jane wouldn't have to answer immediately. She looked down to hide her facial expression. *I should have known this was what she wanted to talk to me about.* Min-young's entire world had, and always would, revolve around her "big brother."

Many years ago, Joon-young had asked Jane to take his little sister Min-young to a rock concert. Kyung-ho Kim was performing that night, as Jane remembered it. Jane had gotten herself and Min-young front-row tickets. As soon as the concert started, the audience lit up like a fireball. Thousands of people screamed, danced, and sang along. But not Min-young; she was just standing there, eyes glued to her phone. With everyone dancing around her, she looked like Namsan tower, an immobile giant in the heart of bustling Seoul. Jane glanced at Min-young's phone to discover that she was texting Joon-young:

—*Big brother, where are you?*

Jane took a sip of her coffee. The hot liquid washed away the annoyance that was lurking just beneath her neck. Thanks to this, she finally felt like talking.

"Is that all you wanted to ask me?"

Jane wanted to ask a follow up question to this—*And why couldn't you just ask me that over the phone?*—but held herself back.

Min-young straightened her back. Tucking in her chin and peeling back her eyelids, she leered at Jane.

"This is important."

For a moment, Jane imagined herself sitting in front of not a twenty-nine-year-old woman, but an eleven-year-old girl. The look on Min-young's face was the same one from all those years ago, the face of an elementary school girl who believed her brother would always take her side no matter what. The first time Jane had seen this face was eighteen years ago on her way to Joon-young's apartment.

Jane and Joon-young were hanging out with four friends from drama club that day. They were just exiting Sillim station and heading for Joon-young's apartment to eat ramen when they heard the shriek of a young girl.

"Big brother!"

Jane turned around to see a young girl running toward them from across the street. Based on her size, she looked like she had to be in first or second grade. Joon-young shouted back to the girl.

"Min-young! Stay right there! I'll come to you—"

But the girl had already run into traffic. There was no crosswalk near her, and she didn't even look left or right. She had only one goal, and that was Joon-young. The oncoming traffic braked, swerved, and blared their horns. But the girl didn't care. Joon-young stepped down from the sidewalk with a dazed look on his face.

"Big brother!"

The girl flung her body into the air and latched herself onto Joon-young's neck, simultaneously locking her legs around his waist. Joon-young's face was ghost-white as he brought his arms under her for support. To put it into movie terms, they looked like vampire siblings who hadn't seen each other in centuries.

They stood there for a while, looking like the last survivors on Earth. Joon-young started saying something to her, but it wasn't clear if he was pleading with her or scolding her. "Why did you run out into the street like that?" "I said I was coming to you." "How many times have I told you not to do that?" "I almost had a heart attack." Every sentence was punctuated with eye-contact, back stroking, and hugging. Only when their long reunion ended did the girl turn to Jane and the other drama club members.

"And who are they?"

"My friends."

Joon-young introduced each of them to Min-young, whom he was still holding in his arms. But Min-young didn't look at any of the "friends," focusing her entire attention on the only girl in the group. Her rude, aggressive gaze made Jane feel uncomfortable, even ashamed. She was making Jane feel like an invader from Mars. If she weren't Joon-young's younger sister, Jane would have told her to be less rude.

Min-young, it turned out, was actually in fifth grade, making her eight years younger than Joon-young. They were originally from Geoje Island, but their parents had sent them to live together in Seoul. Even considering this, their sibling love was uncommonly intense. Jane figured it had to be the age gap.

To Min-young, Joon-young was at once a brother, a father, and her king. Joon-young likewise worshipped Min-young like she was an Egyptian princess. Whenever Joon-young looked at Min-young, Jane swore she could hear "Twinkle, Twinkle, Little Star" playing in the background. Joon-young was still doting upon Min-young like this the last time Jane saw him at his wedding.

Min-young hadn't changed one bit. The way she peeled her eyelids back into her head as she questioned Jane was more than enough to prove this.

"Why do you ask?" Jane asked.

"Joon-young is missing." The way she blurted this out was as if she'd been waiting for Jane to ask. "I can't reach him, he's not at home, and there's no one who's seen him recently."

"How recently?"

"Since last Tuesday."

Tuesday. Jane put down her coffee. *She* had seen Joon-young last Tuesday morning.

"I talked with him on the phone last Tuesday around 2 p.m.," Min-young said. "When I asked him where he was, he said he was in Kyochon."

2 p.m. was well after Jane saw him. Jane didn't want to mention her meeting with Joon-young. But even had she wanted to, Min-young didn't give her the chance.

"He said he would call me back and then hung up suddenly. Since then, I haven't been able to contact him. I've sent him text messages, but they're still marked unread. And when I call, it says his phone is turned off. Something has happened to him."

Min-young's hand was trembling as she touched her hair. Jane thought about what Min-young said. A thirty-seven-year-old man disappearing for six days was suspicious, but there were all sorts of explanations for someone not answering phone calls or text messages.

"Your brother is self-employed, and he has two legs. He could be anywhere doing God knows what. Perhaps he's just under your radar. Maybe he went to do research for a play. Or maybe he's on vacation. Or maybe he just wanted to go off the grid for a while."

Min-young stuck out her lips and let out a quiet smirk. Her response was akin to sending a single "lol" after receiving a long text message. She was mocking Jane's opinion without coming out and saying it to her face.

"You talk as if you don't know his situation."

Jane looked at her with exhaustion. When would this girl learn? Not everyone in the world knew or cared about her older brother's "situation."

"Actually, I don't."

Min-young jutted out her jaw and twisted it in a "You've got to be kidding me" manner. Jane loathed games of keep away like this. And if Min-young really wanted her help, she could try being politer. Jane wanted to tell her that she wasn't the least bit interested in her brother's "situation."

"Joon-young hasn't written any plays since the divorce. He does whatever work he can get. Deliveryman, chauffeur, construction worker." Min-young's voice was becoming more agitated. "He's been working two, sometimes three jobs just to send money to Yuna. Sometimes, he doesn't even sleep. And he doesn't have time to go see a doctor when he's sick. And yet you think he's gone on vacation?"

In contrast to Min-young, the voltage on Jane's emotions was quickly dropping. She wasn't the one who divorced Joon-young. *Yuna* was. Nor was she the reason he had to pay child support. Jane hadn't heard any details about their divorce. She didn't want to know, and she never asked. Nor did her mother provide her with any details aside from that Joon-young was found to be the guilty party, and that it was his responsibility to pay child support. Jane could care less that he was having a hard time making payments.

"I didn't come here to be yelled—."

"Aren't you worried?" Min-young said, cutting Jane off. "I said Joon-young is missing. You used to be friends. Why don't you seem to care?"

She was right about one thing. They used to be friends. But she couldn't be certain he was really missing. And it wasn't true that she wasn't worried. Of course she was. After all, he disappeared last Tuesday after they met. This worried her *very* much.

Jane contemplated telling Min-young about that morning. She didn't have anything to hide, but neither was she obligated to disclose this piece of information. She also didn't think that it would be much help. And if Jane was the last person, aside from Min-young herself, to be in contact with Joon-young, then revealing this would get her caught up in Joon-young's problems. The last thing Jane wanted was for Min-young to become suspicious of her. If that happened, Min-young would act like a stalker until her older brother was found; she would call Jane every waking minute and show up at her door without warning looking for him. After all, proper social etiquette, other people's privacy, none of it mattered when it came to her big brother.

Jane shuddered as she took a sip of coffee. Her intuition was whispering to her that Min-young had other motives for coming here. After all, Min-young had asked Jane if she met Joon-young, but she never pressed her for an answer. If she really expected an answer, she would have pursued it more—that was her personality. Jane decided to ask Min-young her true motives. After she heard Min-young's answer, *then* she could decide if she wanted to tell her about Tuesday morning. It still wouldn't be too late.

"What exactly do you want from me?"

As Jane suspected, Min-young had been waiting for this question.

"I want you to let me meet Yuna."

This caught Jane off guard. Let her meet Yuna? Did she not know phones existed?

"You can get in contact with her yourself. Why do you need me?"

Min-young opened her eyes wide and in a naïve manner responded to Jane's question with a question of her own:

"How?"

"You don't have her contact information?"

Min-young let out a loud scoff. "Not even my brother had her contact information. Why would *I* have it?"

According to Min-young, Yuna changed her phone number after the divorce. And she ignored the court's orders to allow Joon-young to see Jiyoo once a month. She even moved apartments. With no way to contact Yuna, Joon-young had made a formal request to enforce the court order.

Jane tried putting her memories in chronological order. When had their mother called Jane to tell her that Yuna's phone number had changed? And was her move to Seogyo-dong around that time? Jane wasn't certain, but both events seemed to have happened around the time of the divorce. If that was the case, then she couldn't tell her Yuna's new phone number. After all, Yuna had her own reasons.

"Have you tried calling her workplace?" Jane said, reminding Min-young that there was another way. By now, Yuna's vacation would be over, and she should have returned to work—assuming of course that she wasn't lying about having a job.

"Workplace?" Min-young then added something cautiously, as if to remind Jane of something she should already be aware of. "You don't mean your parents' business, do you?"

"Yes, that one."

"She stopped working there two years ago, didn't she?"

This time it was Jane who was confused. Min-young had to be mistaken. After coming back from Russia, Yuna had worked under their father. When he died, Yuna was the natural choice to inherit the business. She was the only one who had learned the family trade.

Jane had no interest in business. She didn't fight with Yuna over the inheritance. It wasn't like there was much to fight over, anyway. The five-story building that was the company headquarters and the house their parents lived in still belonged to their mother. Yuna's inheritance amounted to little but the land for the storage facilities. Jane happily agreed to Yuna's succession as head of the company, under the condition that Yuna pay their mother's living expenses.

And ever since then, Yuna had been running the business without any problems. She had shown no intention of quitting. At least, that was what their mother said. Jane answered Min-young as honestly as she could.

"I don't think so."

Min-young's face suddenly turned pale. Jane could see the blood in her face draining down through her neck.

"You mean she wasn't fired from the company?"

"Fired? She owns the company. Who would fire her?"

"Oh—"

Min-young closed her mouth and dropped her gaze. She looked like she was organizing her thoughts.

"You mean to say," she finally said, "Yuna was in charge of the company before the divorce?"

Jane could sense that Min-young was desperately trying to suppress her emotions. Feeling uneasy, Jane retracted her previous answer, afraid that she might have said something wrong.

"I'm not sure. All I know is that it was right after our father died."

This seemed to go in one ear and out the other. Min-young asked an unrelated question: "Do you know why my big brother quit his job as a writer and started doing a bunch of random side jobs?"

Didn't she say it was because of child support payments? Could there be another reason? Was this a rhetorical question?

"If what you say is true, that woman is a fraud."

Jane's emotions suddenly jumped from unease to uncomfortable. She instinctually resisted Min-young's accusation. Even though Yuna was Jane's estranged sister, Jane wasn't just going to sit here and allow this girl to call Yuna names. And besides, her dad's business was a small-scale distributor of industrial-grade lubricants and had less than ten employees, even including their deliverymen. Could inheriting such a business really make someone a fraud? If it was, then the ROK should be renamed the ROC—Republic of Con-artists. From large corporations to self-employed businesses, there wasn't a business in Korea that didn't engage in nepotism.

"Please watch your tongue. That's my younger sister you're talking about."

"Oh, that's right," Min-young's voice jumped an entire octave. "I forgot she was your sister."

Min-young's voice was loud enough to garner the attention of everyone in the café.

"I forgot that you're the sister of the fraud who screwed over my big brother."

Jane could feel the back of her skull become cold. She had nothing to do with her sister's divorce, and yet here she was, taking flack about it from a third party. Min-young's rage didn't look intentional. But when Min-young got angry, it was impossible to talk to her. In this respect, Min-young and Yuna were two of a kind. Once they were triggered, the only way for things to end was in disaster.

"I'm so stupid. I completely forgot that you and that woman are on the same team. There's nothing more despicable than blood ties."

Jane didn't respond to any of this. Anything she said would only make things worse.

"I was so stupid for coming here thinking that you were my big brother's friend. I really believed you would help me."

Min-young cursed under her breath. Jane could see flames igniting in Min-young's trembling pupils. Jane was no longer interested in what Min-young wanted from her. The most important thing for her right now was getting as far away from this fire as possible. Jane got up from her seat.

"I think I should go back to work now."

"Who said you could leave?"

Min-young suddenly pushed the table forward as she jumped to her feet. This caused the cups of coffee to come crashing to the floor. The eyes of the people sitting around them started flashing like paparazzi cameras. Just glancing around the café, Jane found no less than four people she knew. The server rushed over to their table. Min-young didn't pay him or anyone else any attention. Min-young shoved her bulging forehead in front of Jane's chin and started threatening her.

"You and your sister think you can get away with stripping my brother of everything?"

Jane's anger was reaching a boiling point. She put both hands in her pockets, afraid that she would resort to petty violence if this continued. Min-young stuck out one finger and prodded Jane's shoulder.

"Leave, I dare you. See what happens. You'll never work as a journalist again—"

Jane's head was starting to spin. There was a ringing in her ears, and she couldn't hear what Min-young said next. Jane turned around and walked as fast as she could without running toward the cash register. As the cashier rang her up, Jane looked back over her shoulder. Min-young was screaming as the server tried to restrain her. Jane couldn't understand what she was saying. All she could hear was the last thing Min-young said, which pierced the back of her head like an arrow.

"You're not leaving!"

But Jane had no intention of staying. She left the café and fled to the first-floor bathroom. The blood rushing through her head was making her dizzy and blurring her vision, so much so that she had to stand with her hand against the wall for several seconds. She was so angry that it felt like she could cook a steak on her cheeks. She could feel her own pulse through the middle of her forehead. Jane felt humiliated. She didn't remember reading in today's horoscope that she'd be struck by lightning.

Jane's phone started ringing inside her jacket pocket. It was Min-young. Jane turned off her phone and went inside an empty stall. She practically fell onto the toilet seat. With her shoulders hunched over, she didn't move. Someone entered the bathroom, and Jane held her breath, afraid that it was Min-young looking for her.

At the same time, she was embarrassed of herself—but only half as much as she was astonished. She felt like she'd be less shocked had a stranger attacked her on the street. She had absolutely no idea why Min-young and Joon-young were doing this to her, appearing one after the other, suddenly after seven years.

Joon-young was but a distant memory to Jane, both in practice and emotionally. So, when Jane got the phone call from him, it felt surreal. He called around 8 a.m. last Tuesday.

"You haven't changed your number."

This was the first thing Joon-young said to her. Jane was flustered. If she had known it was Joon-young, she wouldn't have answered. She picked up because she didn't recognize the number. His number wasn't saved to her cellphone because she had deleted it after he and Yuna got married. Apparently, he hadn't done the same.

"Can we meet for a minute? I'm going to be in Gwanghwamun around lunchtime today."

Jane didn't want to meet him. It didn't matter the reason. It didn't matter if it was just this once. Even if she wanted to meet him, she didn't have time. She had to go to Chungju to do research for her article series "Jane Shin's Guide to Literature Museums."

"I have to go to Chungju for work today."

Joon-young asked where she was. She answered that she was just leaving the house.

"Are you going alone?"

She said she was.

"Then can I go with you? I'm near Ju-an station right now."

He said it was urgent. He promised not to get in the way of her work. He begged her, saying that they could talk in the car. He said it was about Jiyoo. If only she had said no. But she couldn't. She knew that Joon-young didn't make requests often. And unlike Min-young, he wasn't someone who threw tantrums. In fact, he was a pushover who let other people take advantage of him, not the other way around. Jane figured there had to be a good reason for this. Even though she thought it strange that he wanted to talk to *her* about Jiyoo, she agreed to meet him.

Twenty minutes later, she picked up Joon-young at Ju-an station. She didn't recognize the man who got in the car. A head of matted, graying hair, lifeless pupils, shadowy eye bags, hollow cheeks, a shabby beard, and clothes that looked like they'd just been picked up off the floor. His appearance was enough to earn him a few dollars standing on the street with a sign. This used to be the brightest star at school.

Instead of a normal greeting, Joon-young offered an apology:

"Sorry for bothering you."

"What are you doing in Incheon this early in the morning?" Jane asked as she started driving.

"I just got off work and was in the area . . ."

Joon-young's words trailed off. He didn't say anything more until they left Incheon. He would stare at her as if he had something to say only to clamp up when they made eye contact. When he finally did speak up, it was to tell her he was going to take a nap.

"I feel a bit out of it. I haven't slept in days."

Jane glanced at him out of the corner of her eye. His dejected expression, the thread-thin red veins in his eyes, his dry cracked lips, his hoarse voice—he looked and sounded like an exhausted, broken man. Jane nodded. He could tell her what he wanted to say on their way back.

"Wake me up in an hour."

Joon-young reclined his seat and rested his head against the chair. He fell asleep as soon as he closed his eyes. His face, which was buried in the car seat, didn't look alive. Jane felt like she was looking at a hologram that had been beamed into her car from thousands of light years away.

They arrived at the Chungju Literature Museum around 11 a.m. She parked the car at the far end of the parking lot. Cold beams of late-autumn sunlight were illuminating his pale face. Jane could see his pupils moving slowly beneath his thin eyelids, as though he were dreaming of chasing birds.

Jane thought about waking him, but decided against it. She realized there was no reason to wake him right now. Even if she did, she'd immediately have to end the conversation and go inside. She was going to interview the director of the museum, after which she had lunch plans. And after that, she had to walk through the museum and take notes on the exhibits. In total, it would take about four to five hours. Jane adjusted the temperature and left the car running as she got out. As she walked toward the museum, she sent Joon-young a text message.

—I'm going to work. I've left the key in the ignition. You're on your own

for lunch.

When she returned to the car, Joon-young was gone. The door was unlocked. The key was still in the ignition, just how she left it. She wondered if he had gone to the bathroom, but she soon realized that couldn't be it. He would have taken the keys with him and locked the door. Only when she got in the driver's seat did she remember her cellphone. As soon as she took her phone off airplane mode, which she had turned on during the interview, she got a message.

—Something urgent came up. Sorry.

It was from Joon-young. The message was posted at 11:04 a.m., which meant he left just after she went into the museum.

All the way home, Jane was beating herself up for not swatting away the hand that had reached out from her past. Why had she agreed to meet him? No, more importantly, why had *he* wanted to meet her? Surely, he didn't ask for a ride just to sleep in her car, right?

But Joon-young didn't contact her again after that. So, where did he go after leaving her car?

Jane doubted he got into a car accident or something. If that was the case, the police would have contacted Min-young. Nor did it seem likely that he had been abducted. He wasn't famous enough to be worth kidnapping. Nor would he be easy to kidnap, as he was tall and well built. He didn't look well, but he was still in fundamentally good health. Jane also doubted that he would commit suicide. That just didn't fit his personality. He might have been introverted and sensitive, but he loved life. And from what she knew, he still had aspirations of becoming a respected playwright.

The only explanation that Jane could come up with was that he was lying low. He was probably fed up with people and the world. Or maybe he just needed a break. He'd resurface when the time came.

For the rest of that afternoon, Jane couldn't focus on her work because she kept seeing the phantom-like images of Joon-young's face from that day. She would try her best to think about other things, but before she knew it, she was thinking about him again.

But that all stopped when Jane got a text message from Yuna just before heading home.

—Please pick up Jiyoo today. Eun-ho's son has passed away suddenly. Everyone is devastated. I dropped her off at daycare in the morning. You can pick her up on your way home from work.

*

Yuna wasn't picking up her phone. Instead, an automated voice was telling Jane: "The number you are trying to call right now isn't available." It appeared that Yuna had blocked Jane as soon as she sent the message. This meant that one day of looking after Jiyoo would turn into two days, then three days, and so on until their mother returned from Russia.

Jane had wholly expected this. In fact, this was one of Yuna's best moves—getting her foot in the door. She would start with a small request, and then end up asking for extra favors. People would fall victim to this even if they knew about it. The person would just agree to hold her handbag for a second, and then before they knew it, they were holding all her luggage and following her around like a bag boy.

Jane had no choice in the matter. Whether she ignored Yuna's demands or accepted them, the result was always the same. If she didn't pick up Jiyoo, her teacher would call Yuna, and when Yuna didn't pick up, the teacher would call the emergency contact, their mom, who would frantically call Jane and beg her to pick up poor Jiyoo.

Their mom's trip to Moscow was done to reestablish relations with their aunt. Their aunt suggested the trip, and Mom had agreed. Her plans were to stay for a whole month. Yuna had planned on sending Jiyoo to Russia with her grandma. According to Yuna, it was a good opportunity to show Jiyoo other parts of the world.

But as always, Yuna's fickleness was as sudden as it was inexplicable. Last Tuesday, just five days before their mom's departure, Yuna picked up Jiyoo from daycare and left a text message on their mom's phone.

—I'm taking Jiyoo for a few days. I'll drop her off the day before you two leave for Russia.

Yuna didn't keep her promise. She didn't call or pick up her phone before their mom left the country. For Yuna, making promises was as easy as spitting out saliva, but keeping them was as difficult as licking it off the ground.

Jane's mom left Jane with Yuna's address, home phone number, and her husband Eun-ho's cellphone number. All the way to airport security, she pleaded with Jane to go to Yuna's place to make sure everything was all right, but Jane refused. Just before disappearing through security, Jane's mom made one final plea:

"I'm asking because of a horrible dream I had a few days ago."

Jane drove from the airport straight to Cheongyeon. She wanted to slap Yuna as soon as she saw her, but that wasn't why she was going to her house. Nor was it because of Mother's "horrible dream." She was going to tell Yuna that she wouldn't look after Jiyoo until their mom came back from Russia. She hadn't expected that Eun-ho would be home and not Yuna.

According to Jane's mom, Eun-ho was a good guy. And when Jane saw him herself, she knew that Yuna had a type. Just like Joon-young, he had an introvert's face and his eyes had the look of a sensitive child. But sensitivity was just another name for *weak*. And just like a weak person, he gave Jane the impression of being anxious and uncomfortable.

Yuna started her car. She continued to think about Yuna's text message all the way to Jiyoo's daycare. Was she telling the truth? Had her stepson really died?

It was possible that she was lying. Actually, the probability she was lying was very high. Yuna was so imaginative that she could lie about a genocide if she needed to. Everyone knew it, even and especially their mom. Jane decided she would pick up Jiyoo and take her to Yuna's house in Cheongyeon. She needed to confirm the truth for herself if she wanted to avoid being taken for a chump like she often had in the past.

Jane parked outside the daycare and went inside. The first thing she saw was a teacher stacking legos with a young boy. A moment later, she discovered Jiyoo sitting in the corner of the classroom reading a book. Jiyoo looked up as soon as Jane walked through the door, as though she had been focusing all her attention on the sounds around her.

"Auntie."

Jiyoo put down the book and jumped to her feet. She bolted toward Jane and hugged her waist. With her body glued to Jane's stomach, she looked up at Jane.

"Auntie."

She called Jane like this a third time.

"Auntie."

Jiyoo squeezed even harder and buried her face in Jane's ribs.

"I thought you weren't coming."

Jiyoo had never acted like this before. She never even acted like this to her own grandma. Jane could feel her heart sink. Yuna must be telling the truth. Jane hoped Jiyoo hadn't seen too much. But there was little that could explain Jiyoo's unusual behavior. Jane hugged Jiyoo and patted her on the back.

"I would never leave you."

Jiyoo's calling Jane "Auntie" three times had completely changed Jane's plans. She couldn't take Jiyoo back to that house, not when her stepbrother had died there. She had to take Jiyoo home with her. She could take her anger out on Yuna later.

"Jiyoo looks really happy to see you," the teacher said as she approached them. Jane asked when Yuna had dropped Jiyoo off.

"Around lunchtime."

According to the teacher, Jiyoo had sat in the corner of the classroom and hadn't said a word all day. She didn't touch her lunch or her afternoon snack.

"Make sure she eats something when you get home. She's probably starving."

Jane sat Jiyoo in the front passenger seat, something she wouldn't normally do. But today, she didn't want to leave Jiyoo, who looked anxious, by herself in the backseat.

"Should we pick something yummy up on our way home?" Jane asked as she started the car. She rattled off anything and everything that she could think of that a kid might like. Tonkatsu, pasta, jjajangmyeon. Jiyoo just sniffed once and shook her head.

"Or how about I pick up a Happy Meal from McDonald's?"

Jiyoo didn't answer. Her lips were clamped tight, and the tip of her nose was becoming red. She looked like she would burst out in tears if Jane suggested one more thing.

Jane was lost for ideas. Jiyoo wasn't the type of kid who often expressed her dissatisfaction. Most of the time, she would say yes to something that she didn't want to do to avoid upsetting people. For her to refuse food like this must have meant she was in a lot of pain.

"Then should we just go home?"

Jiyoo answered yes so quickly that it surprised Jane. There was even a look of urgency on her face. Jiyoo didn't say anything the entire ride home, nor did she look at Jane. She just hugged her school bag and looked down. She had withdrawn so much that Jane wondered if the warm welcome she showed Jane earlier had been her imagination.

Not much changed once they arrived home. Jiyoo went straight to her room, still hugging her backpack as though it were her favorite stuffed animal. Usually, Jiyoo would run to the bathroom to wash her hands first. She would then go into her room and come back out with a fresh pair of clothes on. But today, she didn't come back out of her room. In fact, she was still in her room by the time Jane changed out of her work clothes and knocked on the door.

"Jiyoo, are you asleep?"

No answer. Jane put her ear up to the door and asked again.

"Can Auntie come in?"

She could hear Jiyoo reply "Yes." A person shouting from a deserted island in the middle of the Indian ocean would have sounded louder. Jane opened the door and went in.

"What's wrong?"

Jiyoo was still in her kindergarten uniform and perched on the edge of her bed. She hadn't even taken off her coat.

"Nothing."

Jiyoo's complexion looked pale, and her face empty, as though she had just woken up from a nap.

"I'm going to make some instant ramen. Do you want to eat with me?"

This wasn't something Jane would normally offer Jiyoo, but now wasn't the time to be picky about nutrition. Her priority was getting food into Jiyoo's mouth, whatever it was. But Jiyoo answered no.

"Then should I make you some hot chocolate?"

"Okay . . ." Jiyoo said reluctantly.

Jane prepared a large cup of hot chocolate. Jiyoo barely touched it. Her eyes were beginning to droop.

"Do you want to wash up and go to bed?"

Jiyoo nodded her head.

"Then take off your uniform and come to the bathroom. I'll draw you a bath."

Jiyoo came into the bathroom when the tub was about half full. Jane sat Jiyoo in the water and started undoing her braids. It was obvious that the person who braided her hair that morning had been distracted. Not only was the back of her hair flat, but her hair was tangled like a bird's nest.

Jiyoo stared down at her feet as Jane fought with the tangles. When her hair was tangle free, Jiyoo leaned back into the water and surrendered her body to Jane as she stared up vacantly at the ceiling. Her large, deep eyes, which everyone ogled at whenever they saw her, were hazy and unfocused. By the time Jane dressed Jiyoo in pajamas and laid her in bed, Jiyoo's eyes were half closed.

"Are you not feeling well?"

Jiyoo shook her head. Jane placed her hand against Jiyoo's forehead. It was a bit warm from the bath, but it didn't feel like she had a fever.

"Are you sleepy?"

Jiyoo merely mouthed the word "Yes." Even after laying Jiyoo down, Jane continued to stand by her bed, reluctant to leave her side. Jane was bothered by Jiyoo's behavior and the fact that she hadn't eaten anything all day.

Jane bent over and whispered into Jiyoo's ear: "Do you want Auntie to sleep here with you tonight?"

"No."

Jiyoo's answer was as decisive as when she had rejected Jane's Happy Meal. Jane adjusted Jiyoo's blanket.

"Want me to turn off the lights?"

"After I fall asleep."

Jiyoo closed her eyes. Jane started hanging Jiyoo's clothes in the closet. She paused as she picked up the T-shirt that Jiyoo had been wearing underneath her dress. The collar and sleeves were black with dirt. And Jiyoo's leggings smelled musty. The soles of her knee-high socks were also shiny black and crusty. All her clothes looked and smelled like she'd worn them for over a week. Jane suddenly remembered what Eun-ho had said to her.

She's not home. You should know that.

Had Eun-ho been telling the truth? Was Yuna really not home? There were six days between when Yuna took Jiyoo and when she sent Jane that text message. What if she hadn't been in Cheongyeon that whole time? Where could she have gone?

Looking at Jiyoo's filthy clothes, Jane realized they were the same clothes Jiyoo had been wearing when Jane dropped her off at kindergarten last Tuesday—as though Yuna had taken Jiyoo on a sudden, unplanned trip and forgotten to bring extra clothes. This would explain Eun-ho's response. He didn't know where Yuna was. He really thought she was here.

Jane perched herself on the edge of the desk. Last Tuesday Joon-young came looking for her; last Tuesday Joon-young disappeared; last Tuesday Yuna took Jiyoo on a sudden, unplanned trip. A thought in her head bounced around for a while before she lost control of it and dropped it, letting it fall to the floor. Jane thought she would be able to pick the thought back up if she concentrated, but she just left it. She didn't want to. She was already exhausted. What she needed now wasn't concentration but rest.

Jane left Jiyoo's room. She threw Jiyoo's clothes in the clothes hamper and headed to the bathroom. But as she showered, the same word ran circles inside her head like a rabid cockroach. *Tuesday, Tuesday, Tuesday . . .*

By the time she came out of the bathroom, it was just past ten. Without drying her hair, she went straight to Jiyoo's room and opened the door. Jiyoo was lying face down with her cheek resting on a peach-shaped stuffed animal named Apeach and her arm dangling over the side of the bed. Jane doubted Jiyoo would answer if she called out to her.

Jane stepped into the room. She turned Jiyoo around to lay her on her back. It was then that Jane felt something under her foot. She picked it up and discovered it was a doll. It was a finger puppet, to be exact, with the word "Dad" written on its chest. It looked familiar. *Where have I seen this before?* At that moment, a memory emerged from the dark recesses of Jane's mind, sucking the air out of her lungs.

Jane ran from the memory by running out of the room. She went over to the couch and sat down, only to realize she hadn't escaped. The puppet, which she meant to leave behind, was still being squeezed to death in her hand. Jane could feel light emitting from the puppet and passing through the blood vessels in her hand. In the end, she couldn't run from the memory. She was dragged by the scruff of her neck back to the summer when she was seven, when the silk tree in the front yard was blossoming with inflorescences of deep magenta.

That spring, Jane's mom was diagnosed with end stage renal disease. It struck their family without warning, like a bolt of lightning. Later, Jane learned that the underlying cause of the disease was a tumor that had appeared on her mom's adrenal gland. Her condition worsened before their eyes, and their only option was a kidney transplant.

It was fortunate that Mom had an identical twin who was willing to give up one of her kidneys. The preparations before the surgery were long and complicated. Jane's aunt, who was to donate one of her kidneys, made sure she stayed in good health, and Mom received daily dialysis treatments.

Their dad had just gotten out of the military and was starting his own business. Jane was in first grade at the time, and Yuna was in kindergarten. There couldn't be worse timing. With two young daughters, a new business, and their mom's illness, the fate of the family was resting on a knife-edge.

Between work, caring for their mom, looking after two girls, and house chores, Jane's dad was the busiest man in the world, not a moment of free time. They were too poor to afford a helper, and there was no one they could ask for help. Jane's grandmother on her mother's side was dead, and her grandmother on her father's side had just moved to a village in Woohyeri, Gapyeong. They were returning to the home village of their grandfather, who had just suffered a stroke and was having trouble walking. To make things worse, their dad was an only son, meaning there were no aunts or uncles to help.

Perhaps that was why Jane's grandmother on her father's side eventually offered to look after one of the girls. The catch was that the daughter they chose would have to live with the grandparents in Woohyeri. Their father picked Yuna, and their mother agreed. They didn't have any choice; Woohyeri was a small town, and there wasn't any elementary school for Jane to attend within walking distance.

In their dad's opinion, however, Jane, who was the oldest, would have been easier to handle. She was seven already, and could look after herself. Their grandma would only have to worry about washing her, feeding her, and helping with homework. Not to mention the fact that Jane was old enough to help with chores.

But it didn't matter because Jane's schooling came first. So, it had to be Yuna. Yuna didn't understand why she had to go, nor did she go quietly. On the day she left, she clung onto their mom and begged not to be sent away. "Why are you sending *me*?" "Send Jane." "Why does Dad hate me?" "Grandma's house is full of bugs." "I'd rather die than live in the country!"

Jane thought for sure that they would bring Yuna back by winter. All she had to do was wait, and winter would solve everything. But winter solved nothing. In fact, that winter only taught Jane two painful truths: tomorrow never comes in the way you expect it to, and just because you wish desperately for something doesn't mean it will happen. Yuna didn't come back that winter, nor did she come back the following spring.

During Yuna's absence, the house existed in a dark, quiet shadow. Jane's mom took longer than expected to recover from the surgery. She suffered from dermatitis and had to take immunosuppressants to help her immune system accept the new kidney. Her mom also fell into a deep depression after their aunt, who had already made a full recovery, left for Russia. She talked less, lost weight, and avoided contact with other people. Sometimes, she would spend hours in Yuna's empty bedroom, not saying a word. She would just stare into Yuna's picture and cry silently to herself, streams of tears rolling down her cheeks.

She became terrifyingly cold-hearted to Jane. She didn't welcome her when she came home from school. And she was irritated by everything Jane did. When Jane watched TV, she would tell her to turn if off without reason; when Jane asked her a question, she would tell her to shut up; when Jane tried to help her around the house, she would swat Jane's hand away; when Jane asked how she was feeling, she would tell her to mind her own business and focus on her chores.

During those long days, Jane learned a lot. She learned how to move without being noticed by Mom, how to behave herself, how to hold her tongue, how not to cry when she felt humiliated, how to read the look on her mom's face, and she learned that she had to be a good girl to survive in their house.

Jane avoided any situation that would result in her and Mom being alone together. After school, she stayed at the playground or a friend's house until it was time for dinner. When she had nowhere to go or play, she would crouch beneath the silk tree in the front yard and wait for her dad to come home. Going inside the house without her dad was like stepping into a dark, scary tunnel. Jane would rather die than face her mother alone. And the hardest thing in the world was pretending not to hate something that you loathed.

Jane's dad went to her grandma's house in Woohyeri every weekend. And he would always take Jane instead of their mom. When Jane asked why Mom didn't come, he said it was because it would ruin her. This had two meanings. Literally, she was too weak to get into Dad's company truck and travel all the way to Grandma's house. The other meaning was that she couldn't emotionally handle seeing Yuna.

Yuna was always waiting for them, everything packed and ready to go. Some days, she would be standing in front of the gate dressed in her kindergarten uniform and a school bag over her shoulder. When Dad got out of the truck, Yuna would throw a tantrum, blocking the gate and telling him not to go inside. She wanted him to put her in the car and take her straight home to Incheon.

She always made a scene, even though she knew she wouldn't be going home. She would throw Dad's presents on the ground, whine about why he came if he wasn't going to take her home, and kick and scream as she rolled about on the floor. When it was time to go, she would change her behavior suddenly and cling to Dad's legs.

"Daddy, take me with you. I don't want to go back to the storage room."

When Dad asked what she meant by this, Grandma would pry Yuna off him and answer for her.

"Go. Don't mind her. She'll be back to normal in no time."

After they got home, Dad called Grandma to ask how Yuna was doing, but Grandma always told him the same thing.

"Don't worry. Your father and I will take her to the Half Moon Marsh to play."

Mom had no idea what unfolded whenever they visited Grandma's. Dad did a good job of hiding it. He probably didn't want to worry her. And, of course, Jane couldn't say anything. Especially not about what happened that one day.

It was a day in February, several months into Yuna's stay at Grandma's. It was Spring vacation for Jane, and Father was finally going to bring Yuna home. Jane didn't remember the exact date, but she knew it wasn't a weekend, as Yuna wasn't waiting in front of the gate for them when they arrived.

Yuna and Grandpa had gone out to the Half Moon Marsh. According to Grandma, Yuna was unaware that Father was coming to take her home that day. Grandma hadn't told her, in case plans suddenly changed.

"They'll be back before lunch. She can pack her things after we eat."

The three of them went their separate ways: Grandma to the kitchen, Dad to the bathroom, and Jane upstairs. Jane had been to Grandma's house countless times before, but she had never been inside Yuna's room—Yuna had never offered to show her. But today was Yuna's last day, so Jane figured it would be okay to look. She wanted to know if she could see the Half Moon Marsh from Yuna's large bedroom window, something she had always wondered about when looking up at the window from the front yard.

There were three rooms on the second floor. Opening the door to the right, Jane found what looked like a storage room. The room in the middle was Yuna's room. As Jane opened the door and went inside, she forgot all about the Half Moon Marsh. Jane couldn't believe her eyes. It looked just like she was back in Incheon. Aside from the large window, everything was identical to Yuna's room back home. Butterfly-decorated lace curtains, white bed sheets on a white bedframe, a pale pink canopy, lights in the shape of cosmos flowers, a vanity desk with a round mirror, large dolls lining the shelves, a wardrobe with a blue roof.

Jane knew immediately who had decorated the room for her. It wasn't Grandma because she had no idea what Yuna's room in Incheon looked like. There was only one person who could decorate the room like this, and that was their dad. He had either had the furniture delivered here or brought it here himself.

Jane walked over to the window. Strange little things were placed on the windowsill, which was as wide as a bench. Five tiny tables and five chairs that had long poles for back rests. On each pole was a finger puppet that could move its mouth. Each had a name tag on its chest. Dad, Mom, Yuna, Baby.

The last puppet wasn't a person nor was it free to move. It was a duck bound to the chair with rubber bands. One eye was missing, and there were dozens of holes puncturing its stomach. Even the duck's webbed feet were tattered as though someone had brought a razor to them. Just like the other family members, this duck had a name tag.

Jane.

Jane remembered the wave of darkness and nausea that was pulled over her eyes. She remembered screaming and falling over. Jane had never been, and would never again, be so afraid of her own name.

With trembling hands, she untied the duck and removed it from the chair. As she did this, the foot of the puppet got caught on the pole, causing the chair to fall to the ground and break into several pieces. Jane quickly started picking these up. She was so flustered that she didn't notice the bedroom door opening. Nor did she sense when someone came in. And then a hand reached out and snatched the puppet from her hand.

Jane turned around to see who it was. Immediately, her vision was blocked by the duck as it hit her in the face. Tears welled up in Jane's eyes, blurring her vision. Through the tears, she could hear Yuna's voice.

"Stealing bitch."

Yuna's voice felt like a large nail being driven through Jane's ear. Jane grabbed her head and took a step back. With her shoulders hunched over, she blinked and tried to hold back her tears.

"What did you just say?" Jane asked as she tried to hide the fact that her voice was shaking.

"Stealing bitch."

Yuna stuck her face up to Jane's neck.

"Stealing bitch."

A strange light, bright enough to fill her irises, was flickering in Yuna's pupils. She whispered again through her lips, which were slightly cracked as though she were grinning:

"Stealing bitch."

Jane couldn't respond to this. All she could do was try to keep her shaking legs from buckling. She didn't know at the time why she was tearing up and trembling in front of her younger sister like that. But now, she knew it was because she had sensed a hatred so deep and intense that it could destroy everything.

"You want this?"

Yuna went over to the desk drawer and pulled out a pair of scissors. She took the scissors and snipped off one of the duck's legs. She then cut off the other leg and the duck's remaining eye. In seconds, the duck became a lump of yellow fuzz scattered about Yuna's feet.

"Then pick it up."

Yuna took the duck's head, which was the only body part left in her hand, and tossed it to the side.

"What's wrong with you?" Jane asked.

"You stole everything from me," Yuna said as she held the scissors like she was holding a knife. "Mom, Dad, our home."

This wasn't Jane's fault. It was their parents' decision. The only thing that she had taken from Yuna was Mom's resentment. Jane wanted to argue with Yuna, but she couldn't get the words out. It wasn't easy defending herself in front of such intense hatred. She needed to be more courageous than Yuna was hateful, but she didn't have such courage. She didn't even have the guts to stand here and take this.

Jane retreated through the bedroom door, taking one step at a time backwards, all the while receiving Yuna's hateful glare. Once Jane reached the doorframe and turned her body, Yuna shouted out a warning to the back of her head.

"Just try to tell Dad about it. You'll end up just like that duck."

Jane didn't tell her dad. But it wasn't because she was afraid of what Yuna might do, but rather because she didn't want her dad to think she and Yuna were the same. Jane had to be the kind, mature, wise daughter. At least in the eyes of her father.

Because of this, the terror of that day was Jane's to deal with, and Jane's alone. She tried to forget about it. She would repeat to herself, "It didn't happen. It didn't happen." But the memory never fully went away, sometimes appearing in her mind like a tsunami on the horizon.

But if Jane was the duck, then who was the baby?

Jane looked down at the puppet in her hand. Was this the same puppet she saw that day? According to the name tag on its chest, it was. Jane didn't remember Yuna's handwriting, but she knew Jiyoo's. And the word "Dad" which was written in felt pen was not Jiyoo's handwriting. The puppet had to have come from Yuna. She had probably held onto the thing for twenty-nine years before giving it to her daughter.

Jane tried to think about where Yuna had stored these puppets. She searched her memory and realized she had never seen the family of puppets again after that day. Nor did she see the tables or chairs. It seemed like Yuna hadn't taken them with her from Grandma's. Indeed, Yuna left all her stuff at Grandma's that day. The only thing she took with her was her school bag, the same one she wore every weekend as she waited for Dad outside the front gate. Yuna was stubborn about not taking anything else. When Grandma asked her why, she said, "Grandma, don't touch my room. I'll come back to see you."

Jane had no way of knowing if Grandma did as Yuna asked her. Despite visiting Woohyeri several times before Grandma died, Jane never stepped foot upstairs again. She was too afraid because it felt like the phantom of the previous inhabitant was still lingering inside its walls. And Jane was afraid that malignant spirit would attach itself to her chest—like a name tag.

Even after Grandpa died, Grandma continued to live in Woohyeri. After she passed away, Yuna inherited the house and the wetlands. That was what Grandma wanted for some reason.

Jane heard from her mom that Yuna was disappointed by their grandma's inheritance. This was understandable from a financial perspective. The house was old, and the wetlands, although worth a lot of money, were locked in a green belt. The soil was soft and there were several places where sinkholes had formed, making the land unfit even for a family cemetery. Not to mentioned the fact that Yuna must have hated the memories that house conjured for her. It was only human nature to cut off painful memories.

Yuna never went back to Woohyeri, not even after grandma died. Nor did she go on the holidays to perform ancestral rites for their grandfather. She always chose to stay at home alone. It was as though she had completely forgotten about her promise to return.

Jane had thought that Yuna had no plans of ever going back to that cabin in Woohyeri. But it seemed like she had thought wrong. Was she using the cabin as a weekend vacation home? If that was true, it was possible that Yuna had taken Jiyoo there last Tuesday. That would explain why Jiyoo had this hand puppet.

Yuna put the puppet down on the sofa. *But so what?* It wasn't a crime taking your own daughter to the house you inherited. Nor was it a crime to give her your old finger puppet.

It wasn't a crime, but it bothered Jane. She wanted to know why. But why did she want to know why? After Jane turned nineteen, she and Yuna became strangers. Jane made great efforts never to see or think about Yuna.

Jane paused. She could hear something. Something quieter than the whir of the refrigerator. It didn't take long for Jane to realize the sound was coming from Jiyoo's room. Jane shifted her weight to her two feet and leaned in toward the sound.

"Dad!"

The sound had grown into a faint scream. Jane ran into Jiyoo's room. Her eyes were closed, and she was screaming in a hoarse voice as she squeezed her blanket.

"Dad!"

Jane ran in without turning on the lights, leaving the door open so the light from the hallway would guide her. She gently shook Jiyoo's shoulders.

"Jiyoo—"

Jiyoo opened her eyes halfway. She extended her arms as if asking Jane to hold her. As soon as Jane took her hand, Jiyoo pulled Jane toward her. She was strong enough to cause Jane to fall on top of her.

"Dad—" Jiyoo whispered.

It sounded like sleep-talking.

"Dad—He's calling me."

Jiyoo's eyes were still half shut, and she was whimpering through her dry lips. She looked like she was having a nightmare about her father. Jane lifted herself up and brought Jiyoo close to her.

"It's okay, little one." Jane patted Jiyoo on the back. "Don't worry. It's just a dream."

But this did nothing. The more Jane tried to calm her down, the deeper Jiyoo was being pulled into her nightmare. Before long, her whimpering turned into sobbing.

"Wake up, little one. Wake up."

Jane wasn't used to dealing with upset children. And this was the first time she had ever seen Jiyoo upset. Jane didn't know what she could do for her outside of hugging her and offering her words of comfort.

"Jiyoo, it's me, your Auntie. Auntie is here."

There was a trembling sound coming from the back of Jiyoo's throat. Her sobs were halting, and between the sobs, she would gasp for breath or mutter incoherent words.

"Beneath the attic . . . a loon is howling . . . Dad . . . the Half Moon Marsh . . . he's calling me."

Two things surprised Jane. The first was the name Half Moon Marsh. And the second was Jiyoo's body, which was burning up. Her cheeks were glowing like red-hot coils, her lips were as dry as dead leaves, and her breath was stale.

Jane realized Jiyoo must be suffering from a high fever. That was why she sounded so delirious. Jane pried Jiyoo from her and laid her down on the bed.

"I'll get the thermometer."

Jane's mind went blank when she arrived in the living room. She couldn't believe she didn't know where the medicine was kept. She searched all over the house—in the living room, in the hallway china cabinet, in the bathroom cupboard—but she couldn't find the medicine. Jane started cursing at her own stupidity when she remembered that her mom liked to throw things away. Jane started slamming cupboards in anger when she stumbled upon the medicine drawer in the kitchen.

Jiyoo's condition had gotten worse in the time it took Jane to find the medicine. Her hands were shaking, her head was turning side to side, and she was squirming. Jane held Jiyoo as she put the thermometer up to her ear. 38.9°C. Jane didn't know if this was a high enough temperature to make a six-year-old act like this. Was it enough to warrant a trip to the emergency room or would some Tylenol do the trick?

What did Mom usually do when Jiyoo had a fever? Jane ran to the kitchen and started rummaging through the medicine drawer again. She grabbed a bottle of white syrup and read the instructions, which were written in felt pen on the front of the bottle.

Ibuprofen. 10 ml, 4x per day.

There was about 20 ml left, which must have meant this had been opened and prepared before. But how long ago had that been? Was it still good? Jane didn't know if this was safe to give Jiyoo, but she took the bottle to the room anyway. She opened Jiyoo's mouth and poured half the bottle's contents into her mouth. She then pulled back the blanket, took off Jiyoo's pajamas, and placed a wet towel on her forehead.

But after that, there was nothing else for her to do except watch Jiyoo until her eyes hurt. Thirty minutes passed, but it felt like three hours. The change was slow, but the signs were clear. Her fever subsided leaving cool beads of sweat on her forehead. Her breathing returned to normal, and her facial expression looked peaceful. Before long, she was fast asleep.

Jane waited for another thirty minutes. She didn't move from Jiyoo's side. She was afraid that the moment she left the room, Jiyoo's temperature would blaze up again, afraid that the medicine had lulled her into a false sense of security, that Jiyoo really needed to go to the emergency room.

Jane finally understood why her mom always stayed up whenever Jiyoo was sick. But every time this happened, Jane's mom would burst into Jane's room in the middle of the night like a bolt of lightning. "Your child is dying. How can you sleep at a time like this?" These words were really meant for Yuna, not Jane.

Jane couldn't sleep, not tonight, not when she was the only person around to look after Jiyoo. Jane lay sideways next to her. She watched her eyelashes, which were trembling ever so slightly. Even though they'd lived together for the last three years, this was the first time Jane had ever looked after Jiyoo this closely before. It was also the first time she had felt so frustrated while watching Jiyoo.

Jane had intentionally kept her distance from Jiyoo for the last three years. She made special efforts not to become attached to Jiyoo and show her indifference. Sometimes, Jane's mom would ask her, "Do you hate Yuna's daughter or something?" She didn't hate her. Nor did she keep her distance just because it was Yuna's daughter. Actually, Jane didn't know exactly why she was so cold to Jiyoo. Perhaps it was because she was Joon-young's daughter. Indeed, she was just like him, in both appearance and personality. She even had the same dislike for ice cream.

Dad.

Jiyoo's voice hovered around Jane's ears. Had Jiyoo ever talked about her biological father before? Not that Jane could remember. In fact, she wondered if Jiyoo even had memories of him. If what Min-young told her earlier that day was true, the last time she would have seen him was when she was three.

Jane took Jiyoo's sleep-talk and translated it into full sentences.

Beneath the attic a loon is howling. From the Half Moon Marsh, Dad is calling.

Jane had no idea what this meant. Even if she changed the order of the sentences, it still didn't make sense. Was there even an attic at their grandma's cabin? Did loons trust humans enough to come that close to the cabin? Were loons active during the day or night? Jane had no answers. But as she searched her mind, she did stumble upon a memory related to the loons.

Jane didn't remember the exact day, but it had to be one of the many times she went with her father to Woohyeri. What she did remember clearly was that it was a summer evening when the red sun was setting behind an overcast sky of ashen gray. Everyone was sitting at the kitchen table eating dinner. And then, across the road from the wetlands there came a sound so eerie that it made the hairs on Jane's neck stand up. It sounded at once like the howl of a wolf and cry of a widow. Jane was so startled that she dropped the black bean between her chopsticks.

"Are there wolves in the marsh?" Jane asked.

Yuna started laughing hysterically. From the back of her rice-filled mouth came the sound of nails on glass. Watching this, Jane worried Yuna might choke. Sure enough, the rice went down the wrong pipe, and Grandma had to answer as she patted Yuna on the back.

"It's the call of loons from the Half Moon Marsh."

Jane turned over and lay flat on Jiyoo's bed. Her laptop was downstairs, so she used the ceiling to mentally type out her notes:

Tuesday afternoon, Yuna picks up Jiyoo from preschool.

2 p.m., Joon-young talks with Min-young on the phone.

Says he's in Kyochon. Hasn't been seen since.

One week later, Yuna drops Jiyoo off at daycare in grubby clothes.

I find Jiyoo with Yuna's finger puppet.

Jiyoo sleep-talks about looking for Dad.

"Beneath the attic a loon is howling. From the Half Moon Marsh, Dad is calling."

Based on this, Jane created a plausible explanation: Last Tuesday, Jiyoo went with Yuna to their grandma's old cabin in the country. There, she met her father.

Based on this hypothesis, she imagined Joon-young's movements: At around 11 a.m. on Tuesday morning, Joon-young received a call from Yuna. She told him he could see Jiyoo, and he ran to her without hesitation. If they had planned it in advance, he wouldn't have gone with Jane to Chungju. Joon-young has never been to Woohyeri because Yuna inherited the house after their divorce. That meant that they had to have met up in the middle somewhere and gone together. There was a good chance that "somewhere" was Kyochon. The three of them would have stayed in the cabin together. Jiyoo and Joon-young must have gone to the Half Moon Marsh together, where they saw loons. Jiyoo and Yuna must have come back to Cheongyeon after Jane and Eun-ho met on Saturday morning.

Joon-young hadn't returned.

So, where was Joon-young?

*

Early the next morning, Jiyoo turned into a fireball again. This time, her fever came with coughing and vomiting. Jane lifted Jiyoo onto her back. There was a large children's hospital just five minutes away, and taking Jiyoo to the ER herself would be faster than calling an ambulance.

The doctor said Jiyoo had the flu and pneumonia. She was immediately hospitalized and put in a single-patient quarantine room. Her fever began to go down once they gave her an antipyretic IV. And by the time the doctors made their morning rounds, Jiyoo was peacefully asleep.

While Jiyoo slept, Jane informed the kindergarten that Jiyoo would be absent for the next several days and called her manager to get some time off and reschedule her visit to the Han Yong-un Museum in Baekdamsa Temple for the following week. She then went home to get the things she would need to stay several nights at the hospital: toiletries, blanket, clothes, notebook, and the critical biography of Han Yong-un.

Jane couldn't tell Yuna of the situation. She had no means of getting ahold of her. Jane's number was still blocked. She tried calling Yuna through a public payphone, but Yuna still wouldn't answer. She gave up on trying to get in contact with her. She was able to reign in her anger when she convinced herself to imagine that Yuna simply didn't exist.

Jiyoo awoke around lunchtime. At first, Jane hadn't noticed that she was awake. As she organized the items she brought from home, she turned around to find Jiyoo staring at her in silence.

"Jiyoo, you're awake."

"Yes."

Jane walked over to her.

Jiyoo looked Jane in the eye and asked, "Auntie, am I in the hospital?"

"I brought you to the ER earlier this morning. You don't remember?"

"A little. You called out to me, right?"

"You heard me?"

Jane extended her arm and brushed back Jiyoo's disheveled bangs.

"I heard your voice in my dream," Jiyoo said. "I tried to call back, but I couldn't make a sound."

"What was your dream about?"

Jiyoo's eyes bounced around Jane's face. She looked like she was thinking hard about something.

"I don't remember."

Of course she didn't. With a fever like that, it was amazing that she remembered anything at all.

"Jiyoo, when did you start feeling sick?"

"My head hurt the day I went to Stepfather's house."

Jane was just about to ask what day that was when she heard a knock. The door opened and a nurse entered the room. The nurse put Jiyoo's noontime medicine down on the table and left. After her, the lady who served meals came in and handed them a tray of food. Rice porridge, watery soybean paste soup, tofu, unseasoned steamed white fish, and a side of lightly cooked zucchini. This was the kind of meal that Jane would only eat if she were dying of starvation. Without even batting an eyelash, Jane lied about the food:

"Wow, looks delicious."

Jane set up the bedside table and put the tray on top of it. She narrated her actions as she sat Jiyoo up for lunch.

"All right, Jiyoo. It's time for lunch."

Jiyoo looked down at the tray and sighed with her shoulders. Apparently, she didn't agree with Jane's lie that this looked delicious.

"If you spoon some rice porridge, I'll put side dishes on top. Deal?"

Jiyoo reluctantly picked up her utensils. Jane used her chopsticks to pull fish meat off the bones. Thankfully, Jiyoo seemed to like the side dishes. Although, not enough to swallow, apparently.

"You have to swallow, silly. Once you eat all your food, then you can take your medicine. And once you take your medicine, then your fever will go down."

Jiyoo winced as she swallowed the food in her mouth. She looked like she was being fed poison. Jane picked up some of the zucchini with her chopsticks. Utilizing all manner of persuasion and coercion, she eventually managed to get Jiyoo to finish a whole bowl of rice porridge. After making Jiyoo take her medicine, Jane fed her two strawberries as a palate cleanser. But when Jane offered her a third strawberry, Jiyoo gave an exaggerated sigh with her shoulders. It was her way of telling Jane not to push her luck. Jane took the hint.

"Jiyoo, can I wash your face before laying you down?"

Jiyoo nodded.

Jane prepared a wet towel and wiped down Jiyoo's face and hands. As she did this, Jiyoo's eyelids started to droop.

"Thank you, Auntie," Jiyoo muttered in a sleepy voice as Jane laid her down and pulled the blanket over her.

Jane stopped what she was doing and looked Jiyoo in the eye. There was guilt in Jiyoo's voice. Yuna had probably drilled into Jiyoo that she always needed to be grateful whenever someone did something for her.

"If you have another bad dream, just call for me." Jane then leaned over to whisper into Jiyoo's ear. "Auntie's not going anywhere."

Jiyoo fell asleep shortly after this. Jane put her laptop on the edge of

Jiyoo's bed and used the guest bed as a chair. She opened the document file for Chungju Literature Museum and opened the recording file. She felt like she was going to collapse from exhaustion, but she couldn't do that just yet. Even though she had taken a few days off from work, she was still responsible for getting this article out on time.

It was dark out by the time Jane checked her work email. There were dozens of emails accusing her of being a trash journalist. Most of them were lambasting her for last week's article about the Chae Man-sik Literature Museum. "I guess pro-Japanese collaborators enjoy luxury even in death." "Should murderers be forgiven just because they apologized?"

One email subject among these caught Jane's eye.

Jane, it's Min-young. Please read this.

Yesterday's events at the café flashed through Jane's mind. She closed her eyes to suppress the emotions that followed. Her intuition was telling her to press the delete button. It warned her that she would get tangled up in Min-young and Joon-young's problems if she opened the email. Jane clicked delete. After quickly organizing the rest of her inbox, Jane closed the window. And then, just before she turned off her computer, she remembered what Jiyoo said last night.

From the Half Moon Marsh, Dad is calling.

Jane also remembered what Min-young had said.

I haven't heard from him since Tuesday afternoon.

Jane could hear a voice inside her head telling her this wasn't a coincidence.

Jane searched through the trash bin and found Min-young's email. The email started with the words, "Jane, I'm sorry." The next paragraph caught Jane off guard.

I know you must be angry. I'm sorry for embarrassing you like that. There must have been a lot of your coworkers around. Please forgive me. That's not why I asked to meet you. I lost my cool . . .

Jane didn't quite believe this apology. It seemed insincere. Jane skipped over these pointless apologies until she got to the body of the email, which started on paragraph three.

Jane, I'm in Wonju now. I live in a small one-bedroom apartment. I moved here when I got my job. My company is nearby. For the last few years, I haven't been able to see my big brother often. He was just too busy after the divorce.

Last Tuesday, I was in Seoul for work. I hadn't seen him in a long time and decided to give him a call. But I couldn't get through. His phone was turned off, as

I told you yesterday.

Nothing seems right. My big brother has never turned off his phone on purpose. He's never gone off the grid. I can't take time off work to go looking for him. We just started an audit. I thought he might have gone back to Geoje Island to see our parents, but when I called, they said they hadn't heard from him.

I wasn't able to return to Seoul until Saturday. The first place I went was his apartment. But he wasn't there. I couldn't tell when the last time he had been home was. The place hardly looked like someone lived there. There wasn't a speck of dust on the floor. I tried calling his friends and coworkers, but no one had seen him recently. And the delivery company he worked for said he quit the week before. I was the last person to talk to him.

I've already gone to the police. I tried to make a missing person's report. But the police wouldn't take me seriously. When I told them everything, they just told me to wait a few more days. They seem to think a grown man can't be in danger.

I had no idea what to do. Then I realized I needed to meet Yuna, somehow someway. That's why I came to you. I thought you could help me arrange a meeting.

You probably want to know why I want to meet her so badly. After all, they got divorced so long ago. I shouldn't have any business with Yuna. I thought for sure you would understand. I thought you were playing dumb. That's why I got so angry. I'm not sure why it never occurred to me that you wouldn't understand.

I only remember what my big brother did to you on my way back to Wonju. You and he dated until you were nineteen, and then he dumped you and married your sister. If it were me, I would have killed them both. That must be why you decided to cut ties with them. But that's why I'm sending you this email . . .

Jane looked up from her laptop. The letters in the email were jutting out of her screen like two tightly clenched fists. Her nose felt like someone had punched it. Her breath was unsteady, and her head was beginning to spin. She was filled with deep regret. She shouldn't have run out of the café like that yesterday. She should have broken Min-young's fingers. That way she wouldn't have been able to send Jane such an infuriating email.

Jane got to her feet suddenly and walked over to the windowsill. She brought her face close to the glass and looked out into the darkness as it consumed her field of view. She could hear Joon-young's voice from all those years ago.

"Jane, I'm getting married."

Joon-young was always busy in college. If he wasn't working at one of his many part-time jobs at a café or barbeque restaurant near school, he was studying, tutoring, or at drama practice. But whenever he had a few minutes of free time, he would come to Jane's studio apartment, which was located just off campus. He would ask her to let him sleep there for just an hour or two. He didn't have enough time to go all the way back home.

True to his word, he came to her apartment only to nap. He was even respectful enough to sleep on her sofa and use the cushion as a pillow. But while he slept, Jane couldn't focus. The slightest flicker of his eyelashes was enough to ignite all the nerves in her body. The light radiating from her nerve endings was so intense that she felt like she might explode if as much as a strand of hair fell from his head.

The light in Jane's body went out as soon as he left. Despondent, her shoulders would drop. She felt like she was a human motel.

Jane never expressed her feelings to him, but desperately wanted to believe that he felt the same way about her as she felt about him. She held onto this belief like a morning prayer, the kind one makes daily despite never receiving a sign.

The club members all thought she was his girlfriend. Strangely, he didn't deny it. Their friends all called him the "perfect boyfriend." And in terms of personality and smarts, she agreed. But no one knew that he had one fatal flaw that prevented him from being the perfect boyfriend.

He didn't look at Jane like a woman. He looked at her as if she were something else. The closest thing Jane could think of would be a vegetable. Not sweet, but something you needed by your side, something you didn't love but which was safe, the kind of thing that was beneficial, not necessarily enjoyable. Indeed, Jane was the kind of person he could visit late at night without hesitation, the kind of person he could casually ask to put him up for the night, the kind of person who would be considerate enough not to wake him up while he was napping.

And Jane never crossed the boundaries he set between them. At the very least, she didn't grab him by the collar and demand he sleep with her. But she regretted this every time he left her apartment. She should have grabbed him by the shirt and demanded he sleep with her if he was serious about their relationship. And if there was no convincing him, she would have kicked him into orbit.

A long time passed as Jane idled her time away and did nothing about her relationship with Joon-young. There was no change in their intimacy, not after graduation, not after she started working, not even after he debuted as a playwright. Whenever he was burnt out from writing, or whenever he took a break from his part-time job, he would come to Jane, like some neighborhood cat that appears at a restaurant for a dish of milk once in a while. He would even leave behind two tickets to a play whenever he left, like a stray leaving behind a dead mouse for their human friend.

The reason this relationship continued for so long was clear: Jane was always available. The reason their relationship ended was just as clear: he had become *unavailable*.

Yuna had just got back from Russia. She showed up at Jane's work just before it was time to go home for the day. She said she was in Gwanghwa-mun and was "just stopping by." She asked Jane to buy her dinner. That night just so happened to be the first time one of Joon-young's plays was being shown on a live stage. Jane was planning on going to the showing in Daehak-ro with a bouquet of flowers and a fancy ballpoint pen with his name engraved on it. Yuna invited herself to go with Jane, saying something like she liked plays, too.

The play was good. And so was the audience's reaction. The only thing that wasn't good was Jane's mood. Yuna offered Joon-young the bouquet of flowers as though *she* had bought it for him. Jane didn't even need to introduce Yuna; she did that on her own.

"Are you Jane's boyfriend?" Yuna asked as she smiled teasingly.

Joon-young just laughed slightly without answering. Jane never found out what happened after that. She thought it strange when he didn't show up at her place for several months, but she didn't give it much more thought than that. Little did she know, her cat had found another dish of milk to drink from every night.

He only showed up again later that year in the autumn. He didn't come to nap. He was there to tell Jane he was getting married. He told this to her as she made an omelet. It had been four months since that night in Daehak-ro. She was more shocked by the short time frame than she was about the fact that he and Yuna were getting married.

"You're getting married to whom?" Jane couldn't believe her ears.

Joon-young replied by saying he was sorry.

"Sorry for what?"

"I know all about it. Your relationship with your sister."

In other words, Joon-young was apologizing for something else, not the fact that he was leaving her for her sister. She was so enraged by the shameless look on his face that she almost took the hot frying pan and hit him across the face with it, omelet and all. If only she had screamed out in anger and told him to fuck off, she might have felt less resentment toward him in the future.

Yuna asked Jane to catch the bouquet at the wedding. Well, not directly. She asked through their mom, something she intentionally did to put even more pressure on Jane.

"I think Yuna doesn't have any friends who can catch it. They all got married while she was off in Russia."

Jane was surprised all over again. Yuna was even less human than she had imagined. She was nothing but an animal wearing the skin of a human. Jane had once read in college that the most useful personality attribute was audacity. Jane doubted Yuna was marrying Joon-young because she really believed she loved him.

Jane refused outright.

"It's not like she's asking you to buy the flowers! What's so hard about catching a bouquet at your own sister's wedding?"

Min-young was right. Jane *had* cut off ties with the two of them. She had no interest in getting involved in their problems. And to this end, she needed to block Min-young and permanently delete this email, not just send it to the trash. Jane sat down in front of her computer again, but she immediately lost sight of her goal. The moment her eyes met the screen, she was caught in Min-young's trap again.

I want to tell you everything I know. I'll assume you know nothing about why my big brother decided to get a divorce, about the divorce proceedings, about what happened after the divorce, about why Yuna is a fraud and a con-artist.

I actually don't know all the details of Joon-young's marriage. I had assumed they were getting along well. But I learned that wasn't true when he showed up at my place in Wonju one day.

I didn't have to go to work, so it must have been a Sunday. He showed up at my place in the early morning with a backpack over his shoulder and a blue bruise on his chin. His lip was busted, too. He looked like he had gotten in a fight. But I never would have imagined it was with Yuna. He told me she hadn't hit him with her fist. She had thrown an iPad at him.

At the time, I couldn't ask him for any further details. He looked so exhausted. He asked me to let him use my bed to get some shut eye.

I was thinking about going to the grocery store to buy him food so I could make him something to eat when he woke up. Something that would cheer him up. After all, it was the weekend, and I had a lot of time.

Anyway, when I went back into the room to organize his clothes, he was already asleep. I picked up his clothes and hung them in the closet. That's when I saw it. There was a long cut through the front of his shirt. It wasn't torn like it would be if someone had ripped it with their hands. The cut had been made with a knife. Of course, I'm no forensics expert, but I'm positive it was a knife.

I lifted the blanket to see his body. I regretted it immediately. I couldn't believe that Yuna had made such marks. There were bite wounds on his forearms. And beneath his neck were three claw marks, the kind that someone could only make if they had the intent of drawing blood. Between the thumb and index finger on his right hand were three or four stitches. His shins were also covered in bruises as though someone had kicked at them.

I felt dizzy. I tried my hardest to convince myself that those wounds weren't proof that Yuna had attacked my big brother. I wanted to believe that they could be injuries from him trying to stop her from hurting herself.

Joon-young woke up later that evening. I asked him about the marks as we ate. He just told me that he left the house after asking for a divorce. He was probably too embarrassed to tell me about how she had attacked him. Or maybe he was worried that I would find Yuna and confront her. As you know, I've got a bit of a temper—especially when it comes to things involving my big brother.

I asked him why he wanted to get a divorce. His answer was simple. He thought he would die if he kept living with her. He said he thought about getting a divorce a long time ago. I would guess that he started thinking about it as soon as they got married. I also think he tried his hardest to save the marriage after Jiyoo was born.

Do you know how much Joon-young loves Jiyoo? This is also just my guess, but I think he endured it because he was afraid Jiyoo would get hurt. But then he reached his limit. In the end, he did it for Jiyoo. He couldn't allow her to grow up under a mother like Yuna. He didn't want Jiyoo to become like her mother. He didn't want Jiyoo to become Yuna's scapegoat.

Yuna refused his demands for a divorce. She said divorce didn't exist in her life. She had done everything in her power to protect their family, and she would continue to protect them. My big brother hadn't made much money during the four years of their marriage. None of his plays made it to the stage, and he rarely got commissioned. Yuna put food on the table by working at your father's company. And when they bought their house, it was thanks to Yuna that they qualified for a loan. Or so she said.

That day, Yuna told Joon-young they had been living off stolen money from your father's company. She did it because she didn't want the three of them living in poverty. The loan she said she took out was also just company money. As the lies piled up, your father eventually found out.

Your father told her to leave the company. He told her he wouldn't sue her if she returned everything she stole. Yuna signed a document saying that she would repay the money in installments after a ten-year grace period. That was the same day Joon-young asked for a divorce.

Joon-young wasn't able to get in contact with Yuna after he asked for a divorce and left the house. He returned to the apartment to find it empty and the padlock changed. He didn't know that your father had died. No one told him. It seems your mother was already aware that Yuna and Joon-young were getting a divorce.

He learned about your father after the funeral. He had gone to your father's company, where he heard the news. I guess he went to your parent's house after that but was chased away by your mother. He said she pushed him out the door like he was some beggar. In the past, she used to dote upon him.

The divorce wasn't easy. Actually, it was downright nasty. As soon as he filed for divorce, she matched him with her own divorce suit. My brother offered to pay back the money Yuna stole from her own parents. He even offered to give up his share of the apartment as a form of alimony. All he wanted was to maintain custody of Jiyoo.

But Yuna didn't just want custody; she wanted to strip Joon-young of his parental rights. And to accomplish that, she claimed he had repeatedly molested Jiyoo. Can you believe it?

In the end, Yuna won. Everything—alimony, child support, custody—went to her. Apparently, she hired a bigshot lawyer who specialized in divorce lawsuits. The only thing my brother got in return was visitation rights. I guess he offered to pay for everything as long as he had the right to see his own daughter once a month.

The problem was that Yuna didn't allow even this. She changed her number, moved her residence, and cut all contact with him. She even moved your mother, I heard. That made it impossible for my brother to find Yuna or Jiyoo, even though he faithfully paid all the child and spousal support. That was why he had several jobs. Sorry if I'm repeating what I told you yesterday.

Anyway, my brother must have made a request to enforce his visitation rights. But Yuna never showed up at court, even though the court summoned her several times. I've never met someone with such guts.

I met with Joon-young earlier this month. He talked about you that day. He said he was thinking about going to see you. I think he wanted to ask you for help. I doubt that was an easy thing for him to do. He knew what he did to you. He might act like an idiot sometimes, but he's not completely devoid of shame.

I think this should explain things, why I came to you, why I asked you if you'd seen him, why I think your sister is a con-artist. And now, I'll explain to you why I need to meet your sister.

Joon-young used to frequently send me pictures of Jiyoo. Because Jiyoo was just a baby back then, the pictures were usually of Yuna holding her. I showed one of those pictures to my boss. People like to brag about their nephews, and Jiyoo was so cute. I'm sure you won't like to hear this, but Jiyoo looked just like Joon-young. Even my parents think so. She looked just like him when he was a baby.

But my boss was more interested in Yuna than he was the baby. He looked at the picture for a long time and then asked if she graduated from Dong-a University. He knew her by name. He had never taken a class with her, but he could still recognize her just from her picture.

I didn't have a chance to ask him about Yuna after that. He was transferred to Jeonju. But then earlier this year in the spring, he returned to Wonju, and at the welcome party he took me aside to ask me if my brother was doing all right.

It was so unexpected. Why would he ask about my brother? I thought it was Yuna whom he was interested in. He then told me that at his college reunion, he had heard that Yuna had gotten remarried. In fact, one of his old classmates who was there that day was the friend of her new husband. The friend and Yuna's new husband were teachers at the same high school. He wouldn't tell me the name of the friend though. He just referred to him as "K."

Anyway, according to my boss, Yuna was notorious for jumping around from guy to guy. He told me she was the type of woman that attracted men like a magnet, despite not being particularly beautiful. Women like that have a talent for always being the center of attention.

He said there were two incidents in particular that caused an uproar on campus. The first was a suicide, and the second was a car accident.

Regarding the suicide, he told me that the body of her boyfriend at the time was discovered in a pond on campus. The police determined it was a suicide. Despite the fact the autopsy confirmed he had sleeping pills and alcohol in his system, they didn't find enough evidence to think there was foul play.

There were rumors, however. Apparently, at midnight of the day he committed suicide, there were two people who said they saw him commit suicide. The rumors were that they were drinking on a bench nearby when it happened. The problem is that these were just rumors. The two people never came forward as witnesses. And there were no CCTVs in the area to confirm their story.

The second incident happened two years later, when Yuna was a senior. I guess she was living with her boyfriend who also went to the same school. The night before he died, their neighbors said they heard shouting. But no one knew if it was because they were having a fight or just having really noisy sex. Rumor has it that they were planning on going to Moscow after graduation to study abroad together. Coincidentally, "K", Yuna's current husband's work colleague and friend, was a friend of her boyfriend at the time.

But then the boyfriend died in a car accident. They said it was because he fell asleep at the wheel.

My boss heard that the boyfriend had a change in heart and tried breaking up with Yuna. He asked his friend K to go with him to their apartment to collect his things. The accident occurred on their way back from the apartment. K was next to the boyfriend in the car when he fell asleep at the wheel and crashed the car. He had fallen asleep, too.

I wonder, could it really be a coincidence that both fell asleep in the car? People at school were all asking why Yuna Shin's boyfriends kept dying. After a while, coincidences stop being coincidences. If they drank something that made them fall asleep at the same time, that wouldn't be a coincidence. And I doubt they would drink soju just before hopping in a car.

K survived the crash. Only he knows the truth. But my boss says K's lips are sealed.

Jane took her hands from the touchpad. She was at the bottom of the screen, but there was still another page of email. Jane looked over at Jiyoo. The details of Min-young's story were being organized on Jiyoo's forehead.

Living together.

Break up.

Fatal car accident.

Falling asleep at the wheel.

This sounded familiar. She had heard a similar version of the same basic story before. The only difference was that the first time it happened, it had been in Russia, and the man had taken a week to die of his injuries. But now that Jane thought about it, the story Min-young told her must have preceded the incident Jane knew about. What if . . . ?

Jane shook her head and tried to rid her mind of hypotheticals. Jane didn't need to think twice about whether she was going to continue reading Min-young's email. Her trembling hand scrolled down the page on its own.

No one knew what happened to Yuna after graduation. But there were rumors that she went to study abroad in Moscow as she originally planned. One time, my boss brought up Yuna at his college reunion. He knew everyone would be interested to hear that he happened to work with the sister of Yuna's husband.

But when he told them this, K, who was at the reunion laughed out loud because it had been years since Yuna got divorced and remarried. It's such a small world. Everyone is either an old college classmate or related in some way.

After my big brother disappeared, I started to question Yuna's past. But I couldn't just go off rumors. I needed facts about what had really happened. I asked my boss if he knew how to get in contact with Yuna. He said he didn't. So, I asked him to give me the name of his friend K, but he refused. He wouldn't even tell me what school he worked at. I kept pestering him about it until he lashed out at me. I guess he was annoyed. He was probably worried about me damaging his name.

I was so lost. If only I knew where K works, I would be able to narrow my search. My boss's major in college was biology. And he said they were in the same department. There are only so many male high school biology teachers living in Seoul. I'm sure I'll be able to find him eventually.

But there is an easier way. Jane, you could give me Yuna's number. Or perhaps the workplace of her new husband. I know you broke off relations, but you should at least know what school your brother-in-law works at, right?

Of course, what I really want from you is to set up a meeting with her. Even if I did get her number, I doubt she would stay on the phone once she learned it was me.

And don't tell me to try her workplace. I've already tried. They told me she won't be coming into work for a while because of family troubles. And they wouldn't give me her phone number or address. Of course, I'm planning on calling the company every day until I get through, but perhaps you could spare me the trouble.

Why do I want to meet Yuna? I know Yuna received a court order to allow Joon-young to exercise his visitation rights. She has a history of ignoring court orders and has been fined before. If she doesn't follow through by the end of this month, she could be found in contempt of court and even face jail time. She's backed into a corner. Either she lets Joon-young see the child, or she goes to jail. Seeing as today is the 23rd, she has a week left.

I need to find Joon-young before then. He had a car, although it was a piece of junk. I need to stop this before he mysteriously dies in a car crash. Jane, I believe that you will help me. I'm sure of it.

PS: Do you know when your father found out about Yuna's stealing from the company? I'd guess that his death happened dangerously close to this discovery. By any chance, did he die because he fell asleep at the wheel?

Jane could feel her eyelids becoming stiff. There was sour saliva pooling up beneath her tongue. She could hear the ticking of a clock deep inside her ear as she was shot back in time to that fateful day.

It was the anniversary of their grandpa's death. Jane went early with her mother and Jiyoo to their grandma's house. Their father was planning on getting there around seven after he left work. But he never made it.

They said his car had rolled down a hill around Namyangju after ramming into the central barrier. The car was split into several pieces, and her dad died at the scene.

Jane didn't remember how she got to Namyangju that evening. She even forgot who was sitting next to her in the car. All she remembered was gripping the steering wheel and grinding her teeth as she put all her weight on the accelerator. The way she drove was as if her dad would come back to life if she made it there quickly enough.

But he didn't make it. What was waiting for Jane when she arrived was nothing but a collection of body parts as fragmented as the pieces of car they found him in. The police said it looked like he had fallen asleep at the wheel. Jane just stood there without saying anything. She couldn't open her mouth. She couldn't make a sound. She didn't even cry. The body in the emergency room didn't look like her dad. She couldn't accept the fact that he could die. To her, he was an eternal being. He was never going to die.

Jane was unable to get a hold of Yuna. Jiyoo stayed in Woohyeri while Jane and her mom held Dad's funeral. For all four days of the funeral, Jane was trapped in a memory from the past.

It was the first day of spring, about a year into Yuna's stay in Woohyeri. The house was a perpetually dark and quiet cemetery, and Jane's mom, who was still in a deep depression, was in the hospital because her flu had turned to pneumonia. With no one to watch Jane, Dad decided to take Jane to work.

Even though she was perhaps old enough to know better, Jane still thought her dad was the kind of business owner who worked in a fancy office and whose only job all day was to sign contracts with an expensive fountain pen. She never imagined that his company would be a musty smelling warehouse with boxes stacked to the ceiling. Even his office, if you could call it that, was nothing but two desks stuffed in the corner of the floor space—the other desk belonged to his partner, Mr. Choi.

Mr. Choi had been Dad's subordinate in the military. After they got out of the military, they decided to make a partnership when my dad started his company. They split the work without any overlap. Mr. Choi took care of administrative work and Dad took care of the sales.

"Stay here with Mr. Choi," my dad said. "I've got to go make sales. Read a book or something and order jjajangmyeon if you're hungry."

Jane said she wanted to go with him. She didn't know Mr. Choi, and she was curious about how Dad actually made sales. He hesitated for a moment before sitting her in the pickup truck.

That day, Jane learned what it meant to be an owner of a new company. It meant driving around the city and knocking on the door to any business that used grease: tractor repair shops, car shops, gas stations at the harbor; it meant going inside and handing strangers his business card; it meant asking people to consider using his engine oil; it meant getting rejected by almost everyone he talked to. But every time this happened, Jane's dad would just let out a hardy laugh before leaving them with a sample.

When her dad laughed like this, Jane would be reminded of the good times, when he would pick up Jane and Yuna one after the other to hug them in the morning before heading to the military base.

As they headed toward the next business, Jane's dad would sing a song.

Maria, Maria, you are my love, Maria…

After I sent you far away, I planted a flower

I planted a flower in my weeping heart…

He never sang any other song, as if there was an infinite repeat sign at the end of this one song. Tapping to the beat with his fingernails on the steering wheel, he would hum the song to himself.

Spring has returned and the flower has bloomed

The flower has bloomed like my longing for you

Jane wanted to know. For whom did he plant a flower in his heart? Was it for Mom? Would spring return to their home? Would Mom ever smile again like a blossoming flower?

When it was time for lunch, Dad parked the pickup truck at a rest stop. He asked if Jane wanted anything to eat.

"You can have whatever you want."

Jane shook her head. She didn't want to eat. Or rather, she *couldn't* eat. She couldn't eat anything that had been bought with Dad's money while he was out here planting flowers in his heart and running around begging people to buy his engine oil.

"Then do you want to share my lunchbox with me?"

"Yes."

Dad took out a thermos and a lunchbox from behind the driver's seat. Jane immediately recognized the leftover rice and side dishes from earlier that morning. Father poured some hot water into the thermos cap and put it in Jane's hand.

"The rice is cold, so mix it with some hot water."

Jane followed her dad around all spring break. The lunches she ate with him in his pickup truck blossomed like flowers inside her memory. Although, at the time she didn't know it. She only learned those memories were beautiful flowers when the snow thawed and spring returned. Those flowers protected her from everything: despair, madness, even death.

Another year passed, and the following February, Yuna returned from Woohyeri. But when she returned, she bore a knife in her heart. A knife that was aimed not at Dad nor Mom, but Jane. Yuna believed that Jane should be sent away, just like *she* was sent away. She made no efforts to hide her feelings. In fact, she deliberately worked to make her desires a reality.

First, Yuna didn't call Jane *unnie* like she was supposed to. In some ways, it was thanks to Yuna that Jane learned so many alternatives for the phrase "big sister." Her favorites, were *Hey*, *You*, *Idiot*, *That Thing*, *It,* and *Bitch.*

Yuna had to have the best things: clothes, school supplies, even her hairpins had to be better than Jane's. And she also had to receive all her meals and snacks before Jane. If Jane got as much as a single slice of apple before Yuna did, Yuna would turn the house upside down. On days their dad wasn't home, she would throw plates and cups. On days he was home, she would roll at his feet and cry bitterly.

Yuna also liked giving quizzes to their mom. The subject of the quiz was always her and Jane.

"Mom, who do you like more? Jane or me?"

At first, Mom would answer these questions like any responsible parent.

"What are you talking about? You're both my daughters."

"Who said we weren't? I asked who you *liked* better."

Even up to this point, Mom tried to work her way around the question.

"Well, you are the youngest. So I guess that would make you cuter."

"I'm not asking about cuteness. Who do you like better."

There were flames flickering in Yuna's eyes—flames that threatened to burst into an inferno. To put out this fire before it spread and consumed everything, Mom gave Yuna the answer she wanted.

"I like you better."

But this wasn't enough for Yuna. She always had to take it one step further.

"Mom, you hated sending me to Grandma's, didn't you? You wouldn't have sent me if it weren't for Jane, right?"

After a while, Mom stopped resisting and merely glanced at Jane with an expression that asked for forgiveness. She hoped that Jane would understand she was doing it to maintain the peace.

Yuna's game of quizzes became a daily occurrence, and Mom stopped looking to Jane for forgiveness. There was no hesitation in her answers. "Of course," she would say. "You're my favorite, Yuna."

Every time Jane heard answers like this, she felt conflicting emotions. She was disappointed in her mom for not taking issue with the flawed questions, angry at Yuna for treating Jane like a thief who stole everything from her, and felt guilty that it was because of her that Yuna had to stay in Woohyeri for two years with Grandma. Among these, it was always guilt that won. And it was precisely because of the guilt that she endured the humiliation and never fought back.

Yuna fought over control of Dad as well. She used their guilt over abandoning her for two years to put both parents under her thumb. Mom's humoring Yuna was the easiest and most direct way of reducing her guilt. And Yuna knew this all too well. Because she had complete control of Mom, she used Mom to manipulate Dad.

One time, Father took Jane to the movie theater. They were showing *Mrs. Doubtfire*. Father couldn't take Yuna because she wasn't old enough. He probably chose this movie on purpose because he wanted to make things up to Jane without the threat of Yuna trying to take it away from her.

That day, Jane laughed for the first time in ages. Jane wanted to cherish the happiness she felt that day forever. But then she made the stupid mistake of coming home with a half-eaten bag of popcorn.

Jane could see Yuna's eyes rolling to the back of her skull. Everything that happened next happened exactly as Jane expected, in exactly the same order and manner. Yuna's final magic trick was banging her head against the wall as she cried about how she wanted to die.

That was the first time Dad ever used physical discipline on Yuna.

"If you want to cry like that, I'll give you something to really cry about."

Mom tried to stop him, and the struggle that ensued led to her falling and needing to be taken to the ER. After that, Dad never laid a finger on Yuna again. Which was just what Yuna wanted. There was no one to check her power anymore. She took everything that belonged to Jane. With no one to protect her, Jane used whatever excuse she could find to stay out of the house. At first it was her friends' houses and the playground, but once she got older, it was study rooms or cram school.

Jane had no intention of standing up to Yuna. Confronting Yuna meant confronting her mom. Her only choice was to bide her time. She dreamed of the day she would graduate from high school and could leave for college in Seoul. Her dad swore he would pay for an apartment for her near campus so she could live by herself. All she had to do was endure Yuna a bit longer.

Two years after Jane graduated, Yuna also succeeded in getting into a college in the capital. It would have been economical to make them room together, but Dad shelled out the money to get Yuna a small apartment of her own near campus. He said it was because their schools were too far apart. But Jane knew it was because he was afraid of what Yuna might do to her when no one was around. Thankfully, his business was doing well, so he had the wherewithal to make this work.

Thanks to this, Jane and Yuna stayed out of each other's hair. And because Yuna didn't attend family gatherings in Woohyeri, they almost never crossed paths. Jane only heard news about Yuna through Mom. She was a bit shocked to hear Yuna had abruptly ended her studies in Russia, but her concern stopped there.

After Dad passed away, Mom's depression relapsed even worse than before. She had depended on their dad her entire life, so she needed to lean on Jane for support. She tormented Jane with nightly phone calls that lasted forever and were invariably filled with sobbing. She blamed Dad for leaving her, complained about how the house was haunted, and lamented the fact that no one would know if she suddenly had a heart attack and died. And she did all this while crying her eyes out.

And then one day, she made a sudden apology to Jane.

"I'm sorry, Jane."

Jane figured she must have run out of things to cry about.

"For what?"

"I'm sorry for being so cold to you when you were young. I just felt so guilty about Yuna. There was nothing else I could do. I cry sometimes when I think about what I did to you."

But to Jane, this was a confession she could neither understand nor accept. She was still making excuses, and the apology didn't seem particularly sincere. Jane felt like there had to be an ulterior motive behind this sudden confession.

"Can't you come home to live with me?" Mom finally asked after crying her eyes out. "We can go shopping together, eat together, watch movies together."

"Really, Mom?"

Jane's mom spent her entire life solving problems by crying and feeling sorry for herself. Jane didn't need any time to think about her mom's request.

"No."

A month later, Jane moved in with her mom. She hadn't been convinced by her overtures of shopping and eating together. But she just couldn't stand to lose any more sleep by her mom's nightly pity pleas.

Jane didn't involve herself in what happened between her mom and Yuna. On the days that Yuna came over, Mom gave Jane a heads-up. This was the agreement they made when Jane agreed to move in with her. Because of this, Jane knew almost nothing about Yuna's private life.

But even so, there was one thing she knew with certainty. When Dad died in that car accident, Yuna was not in the country. Jane heard from Mom that Yuna had gotten on a plane for Vladivostok that day. That's also why she couldn't attend his funeral. Nor could they get ahold of her. Yuna claimed she was in a remote area where she didn't have service or Wi-Fi.

Yuna had a solid alibi. But even without that, Jane refused to accept Min-young's theory. It had to be just a coincidence. It would be unwise for Jane to consider any other possibility.

But there was a nagging voice of doubt whispering into Jane's ear. She tried to change the channel in her brain. But the voice eventually broke through.

What time was Yuna's plane on the day of the accident?

Yuna knew Dad's schedule. She knew he would be leaving work early that day, and that he was headed for Grandma's house in Woohyeri. And it was only about an hour to the airport. Even if she met Dad in the late afternoon, she could probably still catch a flight in the evening. But did an evening flight to Vladivostok even exist?

Jane hesitated for a moment before looking up plane tickets. There were more direct flights than she expected. And Aeroflot even had flights that left as late as 10 p.m. Most of these had layovers; Yuna would have had to arrive late the next afternoon if she bought one of these. Catching an evening flight would be inconvenient, but not impossible.

Once Jane realized it was possible for Yuna to meet Dad and catch a flight the same day, she remembered something. Mr. Choi. She had saved his number to her phone at her dad's funeral. Mr. Choi had known her dad for nearly half his life, and he was the last person to see him alive. He also stayed at the funeral home for all four days of the service until Dad's ashes were enshrined, something only closest family members were required to do. Jane hadn't seen or contacted him since. All she knew was that he had submitted his letter of resignation after Yuna inherited the company.

Before pressing call, Jane thought once more about what exactly she wanted to know. And what would she do if she heard something she didn't want to hear? No answers came to her mind. She was just afraid.

Once you know something, you can never return to ignorance. And sometimes, to know something is to cope with it. Jane's instincts as a thirteen-year journalist were telling her she would have to cope with what Mr. Choi told her.

Jane looked at the clock. 10:40 p.m. It was too late to call him. But she pressed call anyway. She knew that if she didn't do it now, she would never do it. By tomorrow, she would convince herself that this was all "a mere coincidence" and never think about it again. After a few rings, Mr. Choi picked up.

"Hello?"

"Mr. Choi, this is Jane."

Mr. Choi was both surprised and pleased to hear from Jane. He asked how her mom was doing, how Jane was doing, and if there was something she needed help with. Before Jane told him why she was calling him, she thought one last time about what she was about to do. She would ask him several questions, and he would give her several answers. And depending on his answers, she might become swept up in Yuna's problems again. But she needed to know.

"I'm calling about my dad. Before he died, did he fire Yuna?"

Mr. Choi didn't answer. That meant yes.

"When did he fire her?"

"About a week before he passed away."

Jane felt all the veins in her neck wriggle to the surface.

"Was it because of money?"

He sighed. "Yes. I discovered she'd been stealing money from the company and told your dad."

"Why didn't anyone tell us?"

"Your father wanted to sweep it under the rug."

Jane still had her most important question. She focused all her energy on calming her heavy breathing.

"On the day of the accident, did Yuna come to the office?"

"Yes. I think she came around four in the afternoon. It was just before your dad left for Woohyeri."

"Did she bring anything with her?"

He said she brought coffee. They talked in my dad's office for half an hour, and when they came back out, it looked like they had made up. Yuna was beaming as she said goodbye to him. Dad patted Yuna on the shoulder and wished her safe travels.

"I was so relieved. No one wants to fire their own daughter. I was afraid money had ruined another family. I thought your dad should have just taken her word that she wouldn't do it again and let her stay at the company. She wasn't just another employee. She was his daughter, after all. There were other options besides firing her. Anyway, it looked like they had made amends, so I felt relieved."

"She left the office around 4:30?"

He said yes and that she left before my dad did. Two hours later, he died in a car accident. Despite knowing it was a shot in the dark, Jane asked one more question.

"The coffee Yuna brought . . . by any chance was it iced coffee?"

"Hmm . . . That I'm not sure about."

It didn't matter. Dad liked his coffee black and on ice. He would always chug the coffee before the ice even had a chance to melt. Yuna, who worked as a bookkeeper and secretary for him for several years, had to know how he liked his coffee.

"But Mr. Choi, why did you quit? I thought you would have wanted to help Yuna run the business."

Silence followed. Jane felt sorry and embarrassed for not knowing the reason. After all, Mr. Choi was the person who got Yuna fired. And Yuna valued loyalty above all else.

Jane hung up the phone. She leaned against the wall and closed her eyes. She was thinking of something, but even she wasn't quite sure what that was. She was confused to the point of being nauseous—and scared. She felt like she had just stepped into a swamp of unknown depth. Her ego was being split into two voices. One voice was stubbornly trying to persuade her this was all just a coincidence, telling her not to overanalyze things. And the other voice was asking her a question.

What did Yuna do to Dad?

PART 2: WHO IS SHE?

CHAPTER 4

Jiyoo lay on the bed at the cabin. The night sky was tinted red. Down the street, dogs barked. A loon was nearby. This wasn't the loon call Jiyoo was used to. It sometimes sounded like weeping, or groaning, or screaming. The cries weren't coming from the wetlands, but from beyond the wall.

The attic.

Jiyoo sat up and looked around, as though under some powerful spell. She didn't see any loons. She saw nothing that could make a sound on its own, not even a cricket. The loon called again. This time it sounded like gurgling. The source of the sound had moved downstairs.

Before Jiyoo knew it, she was walking down the stairs. She took one step after another, but the steps seemed to go on forever. Was she under yet another spell? No matter how far she went, she couldn't reach the bottom of the stairs. She started counting steps but would lose count and have to start over again. And then the loon went silent.

A voice came from outside the front gate.

Jiyoo, let's go.

Jiyoo stopped on the stairs. She had heard this voice a long time ago. She remembered the words clearly. This is what Father used to say to her. He would say it before taking her to the playground. But they weren't going to the playground. It sounded like he wanted to take her to the Half Moon Marsh.

Jiyoo, let's go.

The voice was getting quieter. Father seemed to really want to go to the Half Moon Marsh. No, he was already there, heading to the gorge. Jiyoo unconsciously reached out into the empty air.

No, Father. Don't go beyond the Half Moon Marsh.

Her voice didn't form into words. It merely echoed inside her head. Jiyoo started running down the stairs. By the time she realized she had misstepped, her body was already tumbling through the air. But even as she fell, she called out to Father.

Don't go! There's a cliff!

Jiyoo's long tumble only ended once her body fell to the floor of the kitchen. Jiyoo tried to lift herself up, but her body wasn't listening. She couldn't move a single finger. Lying face down on the cold wood floor, she could hear Mother's voice in the darkness.

Jiyoo, what are you doing there?

Jiyoo couldn't see Mother. All she could sense was a fishy smell. Jiyoo answered:

A loon is calling from beneath the attic.

Mother spoke in a cold whisper.

All the loons are in the Half Moon Marsh.

Jiyoo still couldn't see her. Jiyoo shouted in frustration.

No! Father is at the Half Moon Marsh.

It's okay. It's just a dream. It'll go away when you wake up in the morning.

Jiyoo shook her head.

No. Father is calling me from the Half Moon Marsh.

"It's okay, child. It's just a dream."

This time, a different voice was calling out to Jiyoo. It sounded distant, as though it were coming from another world. It was Auntie's voice. Jiyoo wanted to hear what Auntie said again.

Right? This isn't real. It's just a dream.

Jiyoo couldn't open her mouth. Nor could she open her eyes. She couldn't escape the dream. A powerful force was keeping her in the dream. Auntie's voice cut out like a dying radio.

Jiyoo was back in the cabin. She was holding Dad Puppet as she sat on the windowsill and looked out at the wetlands. Under the moonlight, the marsh sparkled like a pond of dark blue. This new dream looked like her second night in Woohyeri. She knew because there was a light moving through the wetlands.

The light approached the house. It gradually got larger and brighter. But Jiyoo couldn't see behind the light. All she could see was a dark shadow-like figure glimmering in its halo. The light exited the wetlands and disappeared outside the front gate. Suddenly, the surroundings went dark as the moon disappeared behind the clouds. The only light that remained was the halo of white from the lamp hanging on the maple tree in the front yard.

Jiyoo could hear something just beyond the lamp's halo. The sound of the gate opening, the sound of a wheel rolling through the dirt, the sound of the gate closing. Something entered the halo of light. A wheelbarrow, the one they used to bring the ducks their food.

Something cast a time spell on Jiyoo. Her vision became fragmented, like the panels of a comic book. One still frame appeared at a time in front of her eyes, each illuminated by the light from the maple tree. The wheelbarrow handles. Two hands pushing the wheelbarrow. A shadowy figure.

The figure glimmering beneath the lamp belonged to a person. They wore what looked like a black raincoat and a black rain cap which covered their face. Jiyoo could clearly see a pair of blue boots beneath the hem of the raincoat.

Mother.

These words echoed inside Jiyoo's head. The shadow suddenly turned to look up at Jiyoo's window, as though it had heard her. Jiyoo let out a shriek.

There was nothing beneath the rain cap—only more shadow. And yet, Jiyoo could sense someone looking at her through the darkness, a pair of formless eyes looking straight up at her. Jiyoo couldn't escape their pull; she was glued to the window. She couldn't look away.

Then suddenly, a pair of eyeballs appeared out of the darkness and started to move toward her. They flew through the air, like a pair of black butterfly wings. When they reached the glass, their black pupils encompassed the entire frame. The large, ravenous pupils glared at her.

Jiyoo could hear Mother's voice.

Jiyoo, what did you see from there?

*

"I didn't see anything!"

Jiyoo was shaking her head as she opened her eyes. She couldn't see in front of her. The black pupils were covering her view and wandering around like a school of tadpoles. Inside her head, a voice was repeating excuses and trying to hold back tears.

"I didn't see anything. I swear."

Warm tears started to flow down her cheeks and behind her ears, melting away the spell of the dream. Slowly, Jiyoo's senses started to return to her. Warm, dry air. The faint smell of disinfectant. The gentle pressure of a blanket wrapped around her body. The peacefully rhythmic beeping of machines.

Jiyoo slowly was freed from the grip of the dream. Her sobbing subsided and the muscles in her legs relaxed. The eyes disappeared completely, and she began to take in her surroundings. A bluish ceiling and a large, dark window, the languid drip of an IV, a guest bed next to hers, a laptop, a pair of earbuds lying on the bed. The bluish light filling the room was coming from the laptop screen.

Jiyoo remembered she was in the hospital with Auntie. She had woken up several times before. She remembered eating a meal here. But where was Auntie now? Fear seized her again. Perhaps she was still dreaming. Perhaps she was being taken back to the cabin. She had to yell out for Auntie before that happened.

The sound of running water was coming from the bathroom. The door opened. She could hear Auntie's footsteps as she walked over to the bed. Jiyoo felt relieved. This wasn't a dream. She was really in the hospital with Auntie.

Jiyoo closed her eyes. She decided to pretend to be asleep. She wanted to stay awake with her eyes closed until morning. She could still sense the presence of the dream from earlier hovering in the room. She was afraid that if she called out for Auntie, the dream would realize she was trying to escape and drag her by the nape of her neck back into the darkness.

Auntie stopped at the head of the bed. A moment later, Jiyoo felt a wet towel on her forehead. Her nose breathed in dry air with the smell of soap. Her throat tickled, as though she were about to sneeze.

Jiyoo tightened her throat and held her breath. Her fever must be gone. Her head didn't hurt anymore. It seemed like she was all better. But she wanted Auntie to remove her hand from her forehead.

Auntie eventually took her hand away and pulled the sheets up to Jiyoo's chest. Then she whispered to Jiyoo as if she knew she were awake.

"Go back to sleep. I'm not going anywhere."

Jiyoo almost replied to this. Her face blushed and her eyelashes twitched.

But she stubbornly kept her eyes shut. She was too embarrassed to open her eyes now that she had been caught. Auntie didn't say anything more and retreated.

The room became quiet, so quiet that when Jiyoo swallowed the spit in her mouth it sounded like thunder. She carefully cracked open one eyelid. Auntie was sitting against the wall with her earbuds in and looking down at her laptop. Jiyoo let out a sigh. Thank goodness. Auntie really hadn't gone anywhere.

Feeling safe, she shut her eyes again.

Inside her head, Mischievous Mouse was whispering to her.

Why did Mother go to the Half Moon Marsh?

Jiyoo answered this.

To feed the ducks, of course. Why else would she take the wheelbarrow?

Mischievous Mouse asked another question, this time sarcastically.

At night? By herself? Couldn't she wait until morning?

Jiyoo didn't have an answer. Now that she thought about it, Mother had prepared the duck feed on her own. She told Jiyoo not to come down from upstairs. This had never happened before. She *always* let Jiyoo watch her make the feed. She called Jiyoo her little assistant and gave her all sorts of chores and tasks. And if Jiyoo had a question, Mother would answer her kindly. When she was in a good mood, that was.

Mischievous Mouse asked another question.

Did Mother see you sitting on the windowsill?

She must have. At first, she thought Mother hadn't seen her. But then Mother shined a light on Jiyoo's window, and there was no doubt that she had seen Jiyoo. As soon as their eyes met, Jiyoo let out a yelp. She bent her body backwards as though she had been stabbed by something sharp. This caused her to fall to the ground. The back of her head hit the floor with a loud thud. As she lay there, she could hear the front door opening.

Frightened, Jiyoo jumped into bed. She didn't even have the time to feel the pain in the back of her head. She hid Dad Puppet under her pillow, pulled the sheets up to her armpits, and closed her eyes. She listened carefully to the sounds coming from downstairs. The sound of Mother going into the bathroom, the sound of the shower running, the sound of her coming out of the bathroom and going into the bedroom.

Mother didn't come back out of her room after that. She didn't eat, either. Morning came and went. There was a rainstorm that afternoon. And then evening came. But Mother stayed in her room sleeping. Jiyoo spent all day sitting at the windowsill and playing with Dad Puppet. She didn't even go downstairs.

Actually, she did go to the kitchen just once when she was hungry. But the fridge was completely empty. There wasn't a single apple or egg. Jiyoo climbed onto the kitchen sink and opened the cupboards. Nothing. There were only two things for her to eat. The yellowing rice in the rice cooker and the hardened goulash that had been left out.

Where did all the juice, cheese, and bread go? Did Mother throw them away? Or did she eat all of them herself?

Jiyoo felt her stomach burn with hunger. She had no choice but to dish some rice onto a plate. She poured a ladleful of gelatinous goulash onto the rice and tiptoed back upstairs. Perched on the windowsill, she ate all her food. She placed the empty bowl on the windowsill. She did this because she didn't want to go downstairs and risk running into Mother. If she saw Mother right now, she wouldn't be able to look her in the eye.

Mother's hibernation continued into the next day. Jiyoo decided to leave her room. It was forbidden for her to go to the wetlands on her own, but what Mother didn't know wouldn't hurt her. Of course, there was the possibility she might wake up while Jiyoo was gone, but Jiyoo's desire to visit the Half Moon Marsh was too great.

The sky as Jiyoo looked out the window was tall and blue. Sunlight was breaking through spotty clouds. A flock of birds flew over the wetlands, and loons howled from the marsh. Their calls weren't like the screaming Jiyoo had heard two nights ago. They had returned to sounding like lone wolves at dusk. Jiyoo felt relieved. Mother was right. What happened that night was just a dream.

Jiyoo took her coat from the wardrobe and threw it on. With furtive footsteps, she walked down the stairs and snuck out the front door. She crossed the front yard to where the window to Mother's bedroom was. Even though the window was blocked by a thick curtain, Jiyoo had no problem peering into the room because the curtains were slightly parted in the middle. She didn't even need to stand on her toes or crouch. The gap was just at the level of her eyes.

At first, she didn't see anything. The interior of the room was too dark. Only when she brought her eye right up to the glass and stared into the darkness for several seconds did she see what she had been hoping for. Mother was sleeping on the bed with her belly to the mattress and her head turned to the window. Judging from the fact that her eyes were closed, Jiyoo figured she must be asleep.

Standing with her body pressed against the glass, Jiyoo counted to five hundred. The entire time it took for her to do this, Mother didn't budge once. This meant she was in the clear. Jiyoo went back to the front yard, passed under the maple tree, and arrived at the shed.

She opened the shed door and walked past the wheelbarrow. There were chunks of mud plastered to the wheels and the frame. A black raincoat that was just as dirty hung from one of the handles. A pair of muddy blue rain boots had been tossed into the wheelbarrow. Jiyoo thought of what she saw last night and the moment she and Mother made eye contact.

Jiyoo shook her head and rid her mind of that thought. She entered the shed through the gap between the wheelbarrow and the wall. Her and Father's rain boots were placed side by side next to the ladder. It was just after putting on her rain boots that Jiyoo noticed the cardboard box behind the ladder. It was the same kind of box they sold at the post office. The lid was closed, but it wasn't sealed with tape.

Was this box always here?

Jiyoo's memory was telling her no. She knew everything that belonged in the shed. She came to the shed often, and sometimes she played all day inside the shed by herself. Jiyoo searched her memory several times, but she couldn't remember ever seeing this box before. The only thing Mother took from the trunk of the car when they got here was a shopping bag with groceries.

Jiyoo thought about opening the box before shaking her head. She rid herself of curiosity and hurried out of the shed. She was already worried enough that Mother would find out she had opened the finger puppet box. If she had one more thing to worry about, her chest would explode. The last thing she needed was to get caught twice for opening boxes that weren't hers.

It was cold outside. Much colder than Jiyoo had expected. The sunlight was like shattered glass: dazzling, yet cold and dangerous. The wind blowing in from the Half Moon Marsh smelled of winter. The wind was fierce enough to give Jiyoo's shoulder a hard shove. She buried her chin in her neck and ran along the trail.

The marsh looked as though it had been through a tornado. Reeds were drooping with mud, and the side path was black with sludge. The soil was so soggy that every step forward was a triumph. And every time she picked up her foot, the sole of her boot croaked like a frog. The trail felt twice as long as normal. When Jiyoo finally arrived in front of the feeding rock, her legs felt like she had climbed a mountain.

There was a lone loon napping atop the feeding rock. Jiyoo thought she recognized this one. It seemed like the same rascal that had attacked Father and her from the water that day. It was about the right size and color.

Should we get back at it for scaring us?

Jiyoo could almost hear her father's voice. Jiyoo jumped up onto the rock and slammed her feet down next to the loon. Just like before, Jiyoo swiped her thumb across her nose as she said, "Go away, you bully!"

But this wasn't as fun as last time.

Jiyoo went to the same places she and Father had visited on their walk, but her mood didn't improve. In fact, she only became sadder. Why did Father leave? He promised he would take her back here in the morning.

Jiyoo crouched down by the water. This was the same place from which she and Father viewed the loon nest. But now there was nothing. No nest, no eggs. The grass was flat and submerged in water. It looked like last night's storm had forced the loons to relocate. Or perhaps they were at the bottom of the marsh.

Jiyoo circled the Half Moon Marsh about ten times. She tried counting the numbers of ducks hanging around the swamp. She even stood at the end of the footpath and stared down the gorge. She was doing everything Mother told her not to do. And not just once, but ten times.

The gorge wasn't as scary as she thought it would be. But that's not to say it was fun. Before long, the red sun was setting over the mountain peak on the other side of the gorge. The wind rising from the bottom of the valley scratched at Jiyoo's cheeks, as though the wind itself had nails. Dark clouds were gathering on the distant horizon. It looked like it was going to rain again.

Is Mother awake?

Jiyoo looked back at the house. There had been more than enough time for her to wake up. If she was awake, she would probably be looking for Jiyoo. She might have even found Dad Puppet, which Jiyoo had hidden under her pillow.

Feeling anxious, Jiyoo quickly left the marsh. The sun had set by the time she arrived home. The first thing she did was check Mother's bedroom window. Mother seemed like she was still sleeping, although Jiyoo couldn't be sure because Mother was facing the other direction now.

Jiyoo went to the faucet in the front yard. She used the hose to wash the mud off her boots and went into the shed. She was planning on taking off her boots and changing into her normal shoes. But this changed when she saw the carboard box from earlier.

Just have a look.

It was Mischievous Mouse.

Just don't touch what's inside. Mother will never know if you just look.

Jiyoo was really planning on only looking. And she would have, too, had she not discovered something familiar inside it. Father's bag, the one with the bumblebee keychain. Jiyoo felt something in her stomach drop. Her pulse was buzzing inside her ear like a bee.

Things would have been all right had she stopped there. She would have been able to think that Father simply forgot his bag. But Jiyoo didn't stop. Her hands removed the bag on their own. Under it was a neatly folded jacket, a shirt, and jeans. These were the clothes Father had been wearing. And the brown sneakers at the bottom of the box were also Father's. Inside one of the shoes was Father's cellphone.

Questions rushed into her head. What did Father wear when he left? How did he leave without clothes or shoes? Why did he leave his bag behind? Won't he come back looking for his cellphone? Why did Mother store these in the shed?

But Jiyoo had more important things to worry about. If she stayed much longer, Mother would catch her. Jiyoo put the items back in the box in the order she had taken them out. Shoes, jeans, shirt . . .

But once she put the bag on top, the box wouldn't close. It was so full it looked like it was about to burst. Jiyoo took everything out and tried placing them in the box again. But the result was the same. She tried a third time, but nothing changed. She didn't try a fourth time. She just decided to edit her memory. The box was always this full. Its lid never closed in the first place.

Jiyoo left the shed without looking back. She went right up to her bedroom and closed the door. The view from her window had already turned pitch-black.

An hour or two passed, but Mother didn't wake up. Jiyoo pulled the covers over her head and tried her hardest to fall asleep. Perhaps because she was hungry, the harder she tried, the more awake she became. Her thoughts were unable to escape the box in the shed. She had no clue what the things inside that box meant. She turned toward the puppet still hidden under her pillow and spoke to it.

"Why did Father leave all his things behind?"

A loon howled in the distance as if to answer Jiyoo. She pulled the sheets over her head again and covered her ears. But the calls didn't disappear. They were slowly getting louder and wilder. But they weren't coming from the marsh. Nor was it coming from the attic. The cries were coming from inside her. And there was nothing she could do to stop them.

Jiyoo threw off the blanket and sat up in bed. As she did this, she realized there was a light shining in through her window. It also smelled like something was burning. Drawn to the smell, Jiyoo stepped down from her bed. She walked over to the window, and hiding her body behind the curtains, looked down at the front yard.

The lamp beneath the maple tree was lit, and a fire was burning inside the fire pit beneath the tree.

The ashen smoke rising from the pit was being carried far into the distance by the wind. Mother was sitting at the faucet near the firepit. Perched on a rock, she hugged both knees as she stared into the fire.

Shadows of flames were dancing atop her white cheeks. Placed by her feet was a cardboard box. Jiyoo realized immediately what was burning in the fire. Jiyoo was so close to banging on the glass and yelling at Mother to stop.

Mother! Don't do that. Don't burn Father's things.

Afraid that she might really yell out to Mother, Jiyoo covered her mouth with her hand. She went back to her bed, took out Dad Puppet, and lay down as she hugged him. She closed her eyes and waited to fall asleep. By some miracle, she managed to do this. She didn't remember falling asleep, but it was clear she had fallen asleep because the next moment, she was being awoken by a sound.

It was the sound of a car. As Jiyoo thought this to herself, she sat up in bed suddenly. A car? Is Father back?

Jiyoo jumped out of bed and ran to the sun-lit window. It wasn't Father, but Mother's white sedan leaving the front gate. A few seconds later, it turned the corner and disappeared.

Jiyoo's jaw dropped. She sometimes had nightmares about Mother leaving her. Each time this happened, she would wake up crying. And when she ran out of her room, she would always find Mother either cooking in the kitchen, sleeping in her bedroom, or taking a shower in the bathroom. This happened both at Stepfather's house and the countryside cabin. But Mother had never *actually* left her. It was always just a bad dream.

Jiyoo thought this time had to be a dream, too. No, she needed it to be a dream. Jiyoo ran out of the room. She bounded down the dark stairs two steps at a time. The kitchen had its lights off and was as dark as the stairs. Jiyoo sensed no one was in the kitchen. That might mean Mother was still sleeping.

Instead of calling out for Mother, Jiyoo cautiously opened the door to the living room. Darkness was waiting for her. When she flipped the light switch, an empty living room appeared before her. She crossed the living room and opened the door to the master bedroom. It was dark, and Mother was nowhere inside. Jiyoo opened the backdoor and went out into the backyard. Mother sometimes liked to take walks in the pine forest beyond the retaining wall.

But she wasn't there either. She wasn't anywhere, not in the front yard, not the shed, not beyond the front gate. Jiyoo felt herself getting nauseous. The strength was being sapped from her legs, eventually causing her to slump down beneath the maple tree. When she looked at the pile of ash inside the fire pit, all she wanted to do was cry. This wasn't a dream. Mother really had left her.

That day felt like an eternity. Jiyoo spent the hours sitting on the windowsill as she held Dad Puppet. She didn't wash herself. She didn't even go into the shed or the attic to snoop around. The whole house was completely still.

A harsh voice took control of her ears. It blamed Jiyoo for Mother's abandoning her, and pointed out everything she did wrong.

Mother left because you went downstairs in your dream when Mother told you not to, because you went into the attic and stole Dad Puppet, because you saw her come back from the marsh, because you went to the wetlands without permission, because you opened that cardboard box.

Jiyoo began to cry. She begged for Mother to come back. She promised that she wouldn't disobey Mother again. She swore to stop listening to Mischievous Mouse.

Because of this, Jiyoo hadn't heard the car come up the road. Nor did she hear the front gate open. She did, however, hear Mother calling her name, "Jiyoo—" but she didn't believe her ears. She wasn't sure if it was really Mother calling her, or if she was just so desperate for Mother to return that she was hearing things.

"Jiyoo Cha—"

The voice was calling from the bottom of the stairs. She wasn't hearing things. Mother had returned. She wanted to call back to Mother, but the words wouldn't form. She just whimpered like a puppy as she got down from the windowsill. As she did this, Dad Puppet fell to her feet. The sound of Mother's footsteps coming up the stairs was echoing through the room.

"Jiyoo—"

Mother's voice was close. Jiyoo could sense her on the landing. She sucked her whimpering back into her stomach. She suddenly became lucid. Mischievous Mouse appeared inside Jiyoo's ear.

Quick! Quick! Mother will be here any moment.

It was already too late to hide Dad Puppet. Mother would come into the room before she had time to even reach the bed. Jiyoo kicked Dad Puppet under the desk. She rubbed the tears and snot with the hem of her T-shirt. The door opened as she did this, and Mother entered.

"Jiyoo, why didn't you answer me?" Mother asked as she walked toward Jiyoo.

The look on her face was neither angry nor annoyed. She looked exhausted, like someone who was ill. Her right hand was wrapped in bandages and tucked away in a sling hanging from her shoulder. The fingers poking out of the bandages were bloated and red like sausages.

"I didn't hear you," Jiyoo said as she took a step forward.

Jiyoo had already given up on the idea of running toward Mother and hugging her. Even if she ran toward her, Mother didn't have another hand to receive her. In her left hand was a bag of salad.

"Why is your face like that?" Mother asked as she stopped in front of the desk.

Jiyoo dropped her gaze and looked at Mother's feet. She was inches from Dad Puppet. All she had to do was bend over, and she would see him. Jiyoo's mouth opened on its own and began lying effortlessly.

"I fell asleep while waiting for you and had a scary dream."

Mother turned her head slightly to look at the bed. The sheets were messy as though Jiyoo had just gotten up. But of course they were messy. Jiyoo hadn't made her bed in the morning. This was the first time Jiyoo had ever not made her bed, and it was fortunate that she hadn't.

"What kind of dream?"

"You . . . left me behind."

Mother's head tilted to the side slightly in a tender way. There was a barely perceptible smile on her lips.

"Is that why your eyes are all puffy?"

"I thought it was real."

Jiyoo's eyes were glued to Mother. She wasn't even blinking. She was afraid that if she looked beneath the desk again, Mother's eyes would follow.

"Were you waiting at the windowsill for Mommy?"

Jiyoo nodded.

"My child . . ."

Mother put the salad on the desk. The bag was filled with peas and lettuce. It looked like feed for goats.

"Come here."

Mother extended her left arm toward Jiyoo. When Jiyoo took a step toward her, Mother hugged Jiyoo's shoulder and patted her on the back.

"Mommy would never leave you. My hand was hurting, so I went to the hospital. I'm sorry I was so late. I had to get it disinfected and stitched up. They also wanted to give me an IV."

Jiyoo twisted her body slightly and escaped Mother's embrace.

"Are you all better now?"

"I'll feel better once I go downstairs and get some rest. I'm sorry, Jiyoo. I feel bad that you cried while waiting for me."

Mother smiled.

"Should I rest up here with you? We can share the salad."

Jiyoo frantically shook her head. She could already feel the peas becoming stuck in her throat. Because of this, her voice when she spoke sounded like a goat's yodel.

"No."

"Really? Are you mad at me?"

Jiyoo shook her head with a smile.

"I might hurt your hand if you sleep here. I kick in my sleep, remember?"

Mother stared into Jiyoo's eyes as if to ask if she was sure. She just stood there without saying anything, like she was giving Jiyoo the chance to change her mind. Jiyoo tensed her shaking legs and endured Mother's intense gaze. Just a few minutes ago, Jiyoo had been desperately wishing for Mother to come home. Now, all she wanted was for Mother to leave.

"Okay, then I'll sleep downstairs."

Finally, Mother left the room. The pea salad she left on the desk looked like a spy.

It was Sunday morning when they left the countryside house. Mother said they were going to Cheongyeon. Mother didn't say anything as she drove. Jiyoo sat in the backseat as usual. As soon as she got in the car, she took out *Frozen II* from her bag and started reading it. All her attention was drawn to her school bag because hidden at the bottom of the bag was Dad Puppet. She had many opportunities to put him back in the attic, but eventually she ended up taking him with her.

At first, Dad Puppet was just an object that gave her comfort. But now it had become something that protected her. He protected her from long hours alone in her room, he protected her rekindled longing for Father, and he protected her from the incessant cries of the loons, the recurring nightmare, and from the guilt of doubting what Mother said.

"Jiyoo, I have something to ask you," Mother finally said as they got on the highway. "You have to answer honestly."

Jiyoo glanced upwards without lifting her head. Immediately, she made eye contact with Mother in the rearview mirror.

"Did you open the box in the shed?"

Jiyoo heard a rattling inside her body, as though she had the hiccups. Jiyoo had almost forgotten about the box in the shed. Mother hadn't mentioned it their entire stay in Woohyeri, so Jiyoo thought she didn't know, even though she knew there was no way Mother wouldn't know.

"Yes."

Jiyoo's face turned bright red as soon as she answered. She was embarrassed for trying so hard to hide it. Mother's voice, which sounded like she didn't mind Jiyoo's peeping, terrified Jiyoo.

"Why?" she said.

"Well—"

Jiyoo reluctantly lifted her head. Mother's eyes were smiling inside the rear-view mirror. It was faint, but her smile was giving Jiyoo hope. Perhaps Mother would forgive her if she told the truth, even though that had never happened before.

"I went into the shed to put on my boots. I wanted to play in the Half Moon Marsh. But then I saw the box—"

"And opened it."

Mother said, cutting off Jiyoo and finishing her sentence for her.

"I shouldn't have."

"It's okay. Those things weren't mine. Father left them behind."

Mother told Jiyoo that a long time ago, Father had left a suit and dress shoes at the house. Mother brought these to give to Father. But it just so happened that Father received a phone call that his friend had died in a car accident that night. The funeral was being held the next day, so Father left in the suit and shoes Mother had brought for him.

"He told me to throw away the clothes he brought because they were old work clothes. But I didn't have anywhere to throw them away. The dump truck doesn't come to the cabin."

Jiyoo nodded her head despite not knowing if this last sentence was true.

"I burned them. After all, we couldn't take them back to Cheongyeon with us."

Mother glanced at Jiyoo again through the rearview mirror. Once Jiyoo nodded her head, Mother focused her eyes back on the road.

"Your stepfather can't know that we were with your real father. Do you understand what I'm saying?"

"Yes."

And she did. Jiyoo knew what Mother meant immediately. There was just one thing she didn't understand.

"Good. You're such a clever girl."

Mother's eyes returned to the rearview mirror. Jiyoo liked these eyes. Eyes that were like warm water that could melt away Jiyoo's worries. Eyes that said she forgave Jiyoo's disobedience. Jiyoo didn't ask Mother if she forgave her. She just believed it to be the case.

"And it's a secret that we went to the cabin. We've been at Grandma's the whole time. Got it?"

"Yes."

"If someone asks you where we've been, that's what you say."

"Yes."

Jiyoo didn't ask why because that was the first rule of secrets. She wasn't allowed to ask questions about things she didn't understand—because if she did, the warm water in Mother's eyes would freeze. Jiyoo pushed the words forming in her mouth back down her throat.

But then why didn't Father take his cellphone?

*

It was morning when Jiyoo opened her eyes. The curtains were open, but Jiyoo couldn't see outside. The window was filled with harsh reflections and was white with condensation. The hospital room door was shut, but Jiyoo could hear loud noises from the hallway: the rumbling of people's voices, footsteps going up and down the hallway, wheels rolling along the floor.

There was a knock on the door. A group of doctors and nurses entered the room and stood in front of the bed.

"Hi, Doctor."

Auntie appeared and greeted the man who looked like he might be the chief physician. He bowed back to Auntie. Jiyoo could feel her toes tensing up. She was nervous that the doctor was going to suggest they do something painful to her.

"Did we sleep well?" the doctor asked as he looked down at Jiyoo.

Jiyoo looked up at Auntie, who made eye contact with Jiyoo and nodded, as if telling Jiyoo to say hi to the doctor.

"Hello, Doctor."

This made him laugh. The other doctors and even Auntie laughed, too. Jiyoo was confused why they were laughing.

"I guess that means yes?"

The doctor raised his eyebrows seeking confirmation. Jiyoo thought for a moment about whether she should lie and say she slept well.

"In some ways yes, in some ways no."

The doctor pursed his lips and looked at Jiyoo. But judging from the crow's feet lingering round his eyes, Jiyoo could tell he was still smiling.

"That's fine. In some ways you slept well, in some ways you didn't. I'm going to ask you a few more questions. All you need to do is answer thoughtfully, just like you did with the first question."

He asked Jiyoo a series of questions: if her head hurt, if she had any problems breathing, if she was coughing, how she was feeling. Jiyoo answered each question truthfully. Her head didn't hurt, she had no problems breathing, she hadn't coughed since waking up, and that she wasn't in a bad mood.

"By not in a bad mood, do you mean you feel okay?"

Now he was putting words in her mouth. Jiyoo thought he had asked her to answer truthfully.

"I guess."

"Do you get dizzy or feel any pain when you move?"

"I haven't tried moving yet."

The doctor glanced over at Auntie and said, "Then should we try moving her a bit?"

Auntie hurried over to Jiyoo, who put her arm over Auntie's shoulder and sat up. She didn't get dizzy or feel any pain.

After placing his stethoscope against Jiyoo's chest, he asked, "So you're not in any discomfort?"

"I don't think so."

The doctor nodded. Before leaving the room, he said something that scared Jiyoo.

"I'll see you again later today."

The other doctors followed him out of the room. Auntie followed them out into the hallway, then came back with a tray full of food.

"Okay, Jiyoo. Shall we have a bite to eat?"

Auntie had bought a bowl of instant ramen for herself and sat across from Jiyoo. Jiyoo asked something that was on her mind.

"Auntie, was I really that sick?"

"Do you not remember anything?"

Jiyoo thought hard about Auntie's question. The first thing she remembered was someone hugging her and patting her back with their hand and the damp feeling of a towel. She also remembered Auntie's voice. *Wake up, little one. It's okay.*

Jiyoo had thought she was dreaming. The only people who called her little one were her biological father and Grandma. But now she knew for certain that the person who had been calling her while she was unconscious was her real Auntie, not some fake Auntie from her dream. It was really Auntie who had said, "If you have another bad dream, just call for me." And it was really her who had fed Jiyoo rice porridge, who had taken her to the bathroom, who had changed her clothes, who had given her a sponge bath.

But Jiyoo had a hard time believing it. The Auntie Jane that Jiyoo knew wasn't as kind as this woman. She was like Stepfather, always watching from afar. Sometimes Auntie would come to pick her up at daycare or teach her cool words, but never had she called Jiyoo "little one" and hugged her.

"No. I remember everything," Jiyoo said as she spooned herself some rice porridge. "I was awake for a minute last night and saw you on your laptop. Were you watching a movie?"

"*Bzzzt*! Wrong."

Auntie smiled.

"That was a dream, too?" Jiyoo asked in shock.

"No, it happened. But you got the date wrong, young lady."

This was the fourth day Jiyoo had been in the hospital, and the night Auntie watched a movie was two nights ago, not last night. All the while, Jiyoo's fever had been coming and going. She only stabilized last night.

"Once you started to look better, I was finally able to get some rest. The doctor says we have nothing to worry about now."

Jiyoo pushed some more rice porridge into her mouth. She could smell the scent of soggy grass.

"I talked on the phone with Grandma a bit ago. She was happy to hear your fever had gone down. She told me to tell you she loves you."

Jiyoo could feel her throat constricting. The back of her tongue retreated into her throat as if she was about to throw up.

Auntie never mentioned where Mother was. And Jiyoo didn't ask. She didn't want to hear Mother hadn't come to visit her in the hospital. She tried to make herself understand. If Mother hadn't come, there was a good reason for it. Mother already told her beforehand that Jiyoo would be spending a few days with Auntie. She said she would be too busy to look after Jiyoo because of what happened to Noah.

Jiyoo didn't know why Noah had died. But she remembered what happened that night. Jiyoo had woken herself up from a bad dream. It was that same nightmare she always had about the endless flight of stairs. Jiyoo hadn't had the dream for two days because she slept with Dad Puppet under her pillow. But once Stepfather came with Noah and Noah's grandma, Jiyoo had to sleep with Mother in the master bedroom and wasn't able to take Dad Puppet with her.

When Jiyoo opened her eyes, she realized Mother wasn't beside her. The door to the master bedroom was slightly ajar. A faint light was shining through the crack in the door. Jiyoo walked over to the door and peered out.

Someone was going upstairs. They were using their cellphone flashlight to illuminate their feet as they tiptoed up the stairs. Because the light was in front of the person, Jiyoo couldn't see who it was. All she could see was the vague outline of the person's back.

At the top of the stairs, the person paused. They shined the flashlight on Jiyoo's bedroom door and then on Noah's door, which was on the opposite side of the upstairs living room. As the light moved, it momentarily illuminated the person's face. Jiyoo could only see the side of their face, but she knew immediately it was Mother.

Mother went into Noah's room. Jiyoo felt relieved. It wasn't a thief. Mother probably had gone to sleep with Stepfather. They always slept together.

Jiyoo went back to bed and closed her eyes. She wasn't sure if she fell asleep after that or remained awake. All she remembered was the moment Mother came back to bed. Jiyoo could smell the sour scent of sweat and heard Mother ask her in a whisper: "Jiyoo, are you asleep?"

Jiyoo couldn't answer her. Her voice wouldn't leave her throat. When she woke up, Jiyoo heard Stepfather's screams coming from upstairs. His screaming was so loud and sudden that it sounded like someone had attacked him in his sleep.

Mother jumped out of bed and ran out of the room. By the time Jiyoo made it to the bedroom door, Mother was already running up the stairs. A few moments later, Noah's grandma and Stepfather began screaming in unison.

Jiyoo didn't know what to do. Something horrible was happening, and she didn't have the courage to go up and see for herself. Nor could she just go back to bed. Even though she didn't know what was happening, there was one word that she could make out through the screaming and the crying.

"Noah!!!"

Jiyoo waited. She waited despite not knowing what she was waiting for. Dozens of times, she had gone to the foot of the stairs only to turn around and run back to the bedroom. The screams and the crying were getting louder. A siren was blaring in the distance. When the sirens sounded like they were right outside, Jiyoo ran over to the glass door to the balcony.

An ambulance was parked outside. The door opened and two people jumped out of the vehicle. One was a tall man, and the other was a woman wearing glasses. Jiyoo ran to the front door without thinking and opened the door.

"They're upstairs!"

The paramedics ran up to Noah's room, and the house went quiet. Jiyoo waited anxiously at the bottom of the stairs. She still didn't know what she was expecting to come out of Noah's room. But she knew for certain it wasn't Noah on a stretcher.

The skin around his eyes was black, and his lips were purple. His mouth was clamped shut, as though his jaw were made of stone. His body, which was covered in a blanket, wasn't moving.

Jiyoo took several uncertain steps backwards. Her legs were trembling. Her head was spinning with questions. Why was Noah's face like that? Why wasn't he moving? Had he had another asthma attack?

Stepfather followed behind Noah. He looked like a completely different person. His hair was soaked with sweat, his shirt was completely unbuttoned, and his hollow eyes were red as though someone had brought a hot iron to them. He staggered with every step down the stairs. He lost his footing several times and almost fell. He was descending the stairs like a blind man.

Stepfather got into the back of the ambulance with Noah. The ambulance turned on its siren and left their driveway. A while later, Noah's grandma came down the stairs with the help of Mother. She looked like she didn't even have the strength to straighten her legs. She slumped down on the stairs several times as she called out for Noah. Finally, Mother succeeded in sitting her on the sofa.

"Grandma, are you okay? Do you think you can make it to the hospital?"

Mother's voice trembled like a whimper as she asked this. The tip of her nose was red, and tears were flowing out of her bloodshot eyes.

"My little baby!"

Noah's grandma prostrated herself on the sofa and buried her face in the cushions. Mother went into the master bedroom and came out holding her coat and bag. Jiyoo was still standing at the foot of the stairs.

"Jiyoo, can you be alone for a few hours?" Mother asked.

"Where are you going?"

"To the hospital. I'll call you later. Make sure you pick up."

Mother helped Noah's grandma up and walked out the front door. A minute or so later, her car left the garage. Jiyoo sat on the sofa, which was bathed in sunlight, as she waited for Mother's phone call. She didn't want to go anywhere, especially not upstairs.

Mother called sooner than Jiyoo expected. She said she was on her way home.

"I'll arrive soon. Get your school bag and meet me outside."

Mother really meant it when she said she would arrive soon.

"Mother, what happened to Noah?" Jiyoo asked as soon as she was in the car.

Mother's eyes looked at Jiyoo through the rearview mirror. She had been crying earlier, but now there were no traces of tears anywhere. Her eyes were so clear and white that Jiyoo wondered if she had been dreaming when she saw Mother crying earlier.

"He's dead."

Mother's voice shocked Jiyoo. It was the same voice Mother used when she told Jiyoo that Father had left the countryside cabin. Jiyoo worked up her courage to ask another question.

"Mother, are you sad?"

Mother's eyes disappeared from the rearview mirror. They were passing through an intersection, and she seemed like she was focused on the road.

"Mother doesn't have time to be sad," she said only after getting onto the freeway. "Noah's grandma collapsed and is being treated in the ER. I need to go to the police station. Your father can't do it. He's too out of it. Mother is going to be busy for a while."

"But Noah is your son, too."

Jiyoo didn't know where this courage was coming from. She wanted an answer, even if it meant asking more than once. Perhaps Jiyoo just wanted to know if Mother's tears were for real.

"Noah isn't my son. The only son I know is one I give birth to."

After this, Mother didn't say anything. She didn't even glance at Jiyoo through the mirror. She focused only on her driving until they arrived at Jiyoo's kindergarten. When she left, she only said one thing.

"Your Auntie Jane will come to pick you up later."

Jiyoo thought of the dark skin around Noah's eyes. Jiyoo had another question that she wanted to ask Mother but couldn't.

Why did you go upstairs last night?

"Auntie has a question for you, Jiyoo."

Auntie Jane's voice pulled Jiyoo out of her memories. Jiyoo nodded as she spooned some more rice porridge into her mouth.

"Last week, you were at the cabin in Woohyeri with your father and mother, weren't you? Not your stepfather, but your real father."

Jiyoo almost bit her tongue in surprise. The porridge that she had just swallowed became stuck in the middle of her throat.

"When did your father leave?"

How did she know? Did Mother tell her? Jiyoo winced as she tried to force the porridge down her throat. Auntie's eyes were carefully studying Jiyoo's face. Her gaze was just like Mother's. It told Jiyoo not to lie. But if Jiyoo couldn't lie, she wouldn't be able to say anything. It was a secret—that's what Mother said.

CHAPTER 5

Wife parked the car in the driveway, and Eun-ho stepped out holding Noah's altar picture.

"Eat something," Mother said from the back seat. "If you keep starving yourself like this, you'll be dead, too."

"I'll drive her home and be right back," Wife said.

Eun-ho and the family had just gotten back from Yong-in Cemetery. It had been more than six days since Noah died. Because the police needed to perform an autopsy, they hadn't gotten permission to bury his body until this morning.

Eun-ho needed to prove it was an accident, that he hadn't murdered his son on purpose. No one said it out loud, but everyone doubted his innocence. In Korea, there were many stories of children from previous marriages dying under suspicious circumstances.

Eun-ho didn't know when the results of the autopsy were going to be ready. And there was no guarantee that his situation would change once they did. Nor did he have the strength to do anything about it right now. Whether it was an accident or intentional, it wouldn't change the basic fact: he had killed his own son. Eun-ho would never be able to forgive himself, even if the legal system did.

Eun-ho's father, who got on a flight as soon as he heard the news, never said a word during the funeral—not to Eun-ho, not to Mother, not to Wife. All he did was man his post at the funeral home and take care of what needed to be taken care of. After they buried Noah, Father bid Eun-ho farewell at the entrance to the cemetery and said he was headed back to Jeju Island. As he hugged Eun-ho, he whispered something into Eun-ho's ear:

"Trust no one."

Eun-ho entered the house and just stood there. The house had an overwhelming sense of calm. It felt less like he had come home, and more like he had traveled into the past. A clean kitchen, the spotless marble living room floor, carefully arranged sofa cushions, tied curtains with evenly spaced creases in the fabric. The green leaves of the Bengal rubber tree were vibrant from being watered recently. They even had a sheen to them, as though someone had wiped them down with a wet towel. The soccer cones and soccer ball, which had been lying between the flowerpot and sofa when they left the house, were gone now.

The upstairs playroom was organized and cleaned, too—not a single piece of Lego remained on the carpet. The window curtains were drawn back to let light in; two large bean bags had been placed up against the wall; the blue-roofed dollhouse basked in the red evening sunlight; and Noah's toy chest was closed.

Eun-ho walked over to Noah's closed bedroom door and stood there for several minutes. He wanted to put Noah's picture in his room but didn't have the courage to open the door. He was afraid that if he opened the door, the screams from that morning would come rushing out again, like terror escaping an unsealed jar. In the end, he turned around without going inside.

Eun-ho hurried downstairs like someone being chased. He ran inside his study and closed the door behind him. When he saw his study, his mind went blank again. The blinds were wide open; his bag had been stored neatly on the bookshelf; his laptop was in the middle of the desk with a squared off stack of books to the right of it; someone had remembered to turn off the power strip; the chair was pushed into the desk; and the shiny glass on the desk looked like it had been touched by the same hands that had tended to the Bengal tree's leaves.

Someone had pressed the reset button. The entire house had returned to the past, when times were simpler. The air was flawlessly placid, like the surface of a glass lake. This was the holy kingdom of a family that had achieved happiness of mythical proportions. It was as if nothing had happened. At least, that's what the house was trying to claim.

When did Wife have the time to cast such an elaborate spell over this house?

Which one of the past days while Eun-ho was too overcome with grief to see, hear, or say anything had she come home from the funeral home to organize and clean? Was it when he rambled like an idiot at the police station? Was it when he waited for Noah's body to be returned after the autopsy?

The tidiness of the house was, incompatible with the chaotic emotions in Eun-ho's head. In fact, the peacefulness of the house put pressure on him. It was almost perfect. There was just one more thing that needed to be reset for the transformation to be complete: him.

Eun-ho went over to the desk. He placed Noah's picture next to the laptop. His shoulders and back crumpled as he collapsed into the chair. His chest was tight. He felt like he was sinking into a ravine in the ocean, his hands tied behind his back. He was desperate for air.

Eun-ho thought about what he could do to clear his mind. The thought of cleaning out the refrigerator, doing laundry, washing his face, all crossed his mind. But then he realized what was the most urgent matter.

He needed to open his laptop and search his email for the name Yoon-hee Lee. But this simple task seemed like looking for an eyelash that had fallen in the sand. The incessant voice in his head started teasing and mocking him for this.

You really think she still uses the same email address? It's been five years. And even if she still has that email, what are you going say? 'Our son died in his sleep?' 'I don't remember what happened because I was sleeping on top of him?' 'I accidentally smothered our son to death in my sleep?'

Eun-ho was confident she hadn't deleted her email. Yoon-hee had sent him an email just before she went to study abroad in America. She told him that she would keep this email address just to communicate with him. She often used it to ask for updates or pictures of Noah. But Eun-ho never once replied. He never sent her pictures or news of Noah. Yoon-hee abandoned her own son to start a new life in America; she didn't deserve to know how Noah was doing. There was only one reason why Eun-ho kept her emails. One day, Noah would start asking about his biological mother, and he wanted to be able to give him a way of contacting her.

Dear Yoon-hee...

Eun-ho didn't know how to start. In his mind, Noah's face was blinking like the cursor in the middle of the blank white page. Perhaps having a drink might help? But Eun-ho quickly shook his head. Getting drunk might deprive him of the little willpower he had left.

Yoon-hee was Noah's biological mother. The person he should have contacted first about Noah's death. At the very least, he should have told her about the funeral. Had he been himself, he would have done it, too. But Eun-ho wasn't himself. The reality of what had happened was just too much to bear without numbing his consciousness. Every time Eun-ho had a moment of clarity, he was immediately confronted with a reality that stabbed at his heart.

The reality of Noah's death lingered in the living room of Eun-ho's mind like a stuffed bird. Two voices were waging a never-ending war inside his head. One was denying he could have killed Noah, and the other was asking sarcastically, *Then who did it? Ghosts?* Seared into his consciousness like a hot iron was despair over the finality of what he'd done.

The only one who was functioning was Wife. He heard from others that it was Wife who did everything: she called the ambulance, she contacted Eun-ho's father, she drove Eun-ho's mom to the hospital. All he could do was hold Noah's lifeless hand on the way to the hospital as he cried and begged God not to take his son, clinging to the naïve hope that when they got to the hospital, the doctors would be able to save Noah.

But there was nothing the doctors could do. They said the window had passed a long time ago. From that moment on, Eun-ho was lost. All the blood drained from his heart. Sounds grew distant as he hunched over and fell to his knees.

The next thing he remembered was sitting alone in the funeral home. Wife, Mother, and Father were nowhere to be seen. Eun-ho turned to find Noah's picture sitting on the altar. In the picture, Noah was holding a soccer ball in his arms and running toward the camera with a large smile on his face.

Who prepared this? The answer came immediately to Eun-ho's foggy mind. Who else? Eun-ho wanted to know how Wife had opened his phone without him. After all, it was she who had suggested they never share passwords.

Eun-ho stood up and walked toward Noah's picture. He raised his hand and touched the glass. Rosy cheeks, a snaggle tooth, round nostrils. When the tips of Eun-ho's fingers met Noah's face, a memory from last summer appeared in his mind.

It was the day before summer break. Eun-ho was in the middle of teaching a class and was unable to take Wife's phone call. When he called her after class, she didn't pick up. Because he had more classes and a faculty meeting after that, he couldn't try her again. He received a long message from her just before heading home from work.

—I can never seem to get ahold of you when I need you the most. I went to the hospital because I had a sudden bloody discharge from my vagina. They said I had a miscarriage. I didn't even know I was pregnant. I couldn't contact you, so I ended up going into surgery alone. It felt like shit. I wanted to assure them that I had a husband, that I wasn't pregnant with a bastard child. I have a lot of things I want to say, but I'll leave it at this. I'm planning on spending some time with Jiyoo to take my mind off things.

Eun-ho re-read the message several times. He felt like he had been struck twice by lightning while crossing the street. He couldn't believe it. A pregnancy *and* a miscarriage?

Eun-ho and Wife's first fight as a married couple was over children. It happened on the first night of their honeymoon in a hotel in Seogwipo, Jeju Island. Eun-ho took out a condom, but Wife stopped him. She wanted a child. She wanted one before she got any older.

Eun-ho didn't. They already had two children that they couldn't raise themselves. Not to mention the fact that one of them was sick. Having another child wasn't just irresponsible, it was borderline criminal. Eun-ho was sure he had this clear while dating. That night, Wife responded to this by saying, "I understand." They even promised that they would discuss it more later and that he would get a vasectomy when the time was right.

Eun-ho reminded Wife about their agreement. But then they started fighting about semantics. According to Wife, "I understand" wasn't the same as "I agree." What she meant was "I understand your position. But I don't feel the same." And what she had agreed to wasn't a vasectomy but discussing it more later.

They stayed up all night arguing but still couldn't reach an agreement. There was just too much ground to cover between the extremes of getting pregnant and having a vasectomy. Wife shut down the conversation by saying, "You're such an ass." The next morning, she left the hotel and got on a plane for Seoul. But she was going to her mother's, not their new home.

Ownership of the pants in any relationship isn't decided during the first fight. It is decided during the make-up, when one forces the other into submission. After that, the hierarchy becomes fixed.

Eun-ho abandoned his stance in just one day. He called Wife and "persuaded" her to come back. He agreed to have another child and asked her to wait until they took Jiyoo and Noah in with them.

While Eun-ho wanted to think it was persuasion, in reality, it was closer to begging. He regretted flipping his stance later. If he'd stood his ground, he might have been able to prevent his Wife from reusing this tactic of disappearing to her parents' whenever they had a fight.

Wife accepted his proposition. This was why Eun-ho was so shocked by the news of the miscarriage. Hadn't they agreed to wait until they brought the kids to live with them?

Eun-ho called Wife. When she picked up, she sounded a lot less angry than Eun-ho had expected. She quickly accepted his apology. And when he asked her if she was feeling all right, she said she was. But when he said he would come to pick her up, she told him no. She would return with Jiyoo after a few days.

Eun-ho accepted everything without arguing, like an idiot. Because he had nothing better to do, he decided to go ahead with their summer plans on his own. He and Wife had made plans to spend the summer vacation with the kids. While Wife was at work, he would babysit. So, Eun-ho went to pick up Noah from Grandma's. On his way there, he stopped at the toy store and bought both kids a present. For Jiyoo he bought a book titled *Frozen II – A New Destiny*, and for Noah, he bought soccer cones and a soccer ball.

As soon as he returned to Cheongyeon, he set up the cones in a zigzag pattern on the living room floor. Noah looked down at the dribbling course with gaping eyes. Eun-ho put the soccer ball in Noah's arms.

"You can kick the ball as much as you want."

"What about as hard as I want?" Noah asked with a doubtful look on his face. His cheeks were as red as apples as he looked up at Eun-ho.

Eun-ho nodded his head.

"And can I scream?"

Eun-ho took his phone out of his pocket.

"Before that, let me take a picture."

Noah wrapped his arms around the ball. "Cheese!" Noah said as he showed Eun-ho a toothy smile.

Noah engrossed himself with his new toys as Eun-ho posted the picture to his KakaoTalk profile. Two hours later, he got a message from Wife.

—I'm glad you're having a happy time with your son while I'm in the hospital getting a dead baby removed from my womb. Does a child cease to be yours once it's dead?

Eun-ho's mind went blank. His joyful mood disappeared in a flash. Thinking about how thoughtless he had been, Eun-ho wanted to bite his own tongue.

He swore he hadn't meant to anger Wife. It wasn't like he wasn't worried. He'd just forgotten about it for a moment. Another thing he'd forgotten was the fact that Wife was a pro at taking the smallest of gestures or comments and making them into an indictment of guilt. By uploading that picture, he had given Wife a flamethrower and permission to blast him into oblivion.

Eun-ho quickly deleted Noah's picture from his profile. He called Wife even though he knew she wouldn't pick up. When it sent him to voicemail, he sent her an apologetic text message. All he could do now was wait for his punishment. Taking Noah with him to his mother-in-law's place to apologize in person wasn't an option.

And yet Wife had chosen this picture as the picture to be placed at Noah's altar, this picture that Eun-ho posted on the day of her miscarriage. But Eun-ho didn't have the time to ponder the significance of Wife's choice because as soon as Wife appeared, the detectives showed up and demanded he come with them. As he left the funeral home, Wife whispered something into his ear.

"Only tell them the facts. And keep your answers short."

The detectives repeated the same questions over and over again. They asked him why he wasn't raising Noah himself, whether he drank the night before, why he didn't notice anything strange while he slept, what position he found Noah in when he woke up. They also grilled him about his relationship with Wife and how they met.

Eun-ho searched his blurry memory as he answered a series of yes-or-no questions. It was only after giving a contradictory testimony, which was the result of a million misleading questions, that Eun-ho realized he was being interrogated to determine whether Noah's death was intentional.

The detectives asked Eun-ho what the chances were that a five-year-old boy, not a newborn by any stretch of the imagination, could be accidentally smothered to death by his father in the bed. Surely Noah would have screamed or struggled. What were the chances that he wouldn't have noticed Noah's struggling desperately for air?

He had been so shocked by Noah's death that he had never bothered to ask himself such an obvious question. Indeed, how did this make any sense? In the end, Eun-ho answered the detectives.

"Not likely."

Wife was called into the police station yesterday afternoon. She said they asked her about Eun-ho's sleeping habits. Wife told them that once Eun-ho falls asleep, nothing will wake him up, not even an earthquake. She said he thrashes in his sleep, and that one time, he almost strangled her to death in his sleep. She said when he woke up, he didn't remember it. She said she'd been wondering if he had a sleeping disorder since they first got married.

But this was hard for Eun-ho to believe. If he had any sleeping disorder, it was that he was a light sleeper, not the other way around. In fact, he was such a light sleeper that Wife woke him up whenever she changed positions in bed. And he had never strangled Wife in his sleep, at least, not as far as he remembered.

"You don't remember? I sent you a message about it before."

Eun-ho leaned his back against the wall and closed his eyes. He was tired of this. He didn't remember, and even if he did, what did it matter?

"Look at this," Wife said as she shook his shoulder.

Eun-ho slowly opened his eyes and looked at the phone she was holding in front of his face. It was an old text message between the two of them.

—You almost crushed me to death last night. Do you remember? Your sleep disorder is getting worse. And you sleep-talk a lot. Is something going on at work?

Now Eun-ho remembered. Wife sent him this message a few months ago. He also remembered being completely befuddled because he didn't know what she was talking about, and she had never talked to him about his supposed sleep disorder. But he had a class to teach, so he couldn't reply to her. By the time work ended, he had forgotten about the message completely.

"I showed the detectives this message," Wife said.

Eun-ho closed his eyes again. He knew she had good intentions, but he doubted this would help. The detectives had already asked him about his sleep patterns. And when he told them the truth, they looked at him in disbelief:

"Then why didn't you wake up that night?"

Eun-ho wanted to know just as badly as they did. Why hadn't he woken up? He wished someone would tell him what happened to him that night. There was only one reason that Eun-ho could think of.

"I hadn't slept in over five days."

Noah's death was changing direction, from accident to homicide. The detectives didn't say this out loud, but they didn't need to. Eun-ho was out of it, but he wasn't stupid.

The police said they would call him back to the station when they got the autopsy results. That, or they would come to him with a pair of handcuffs and read him the Miranda warning. It appeared that Eun-ho would have to deal with the shock of Noah's death and these murder charges at the same time.

But would he be able to? He was skeptical. When people want to believe someone, they'll accept almost anything as evidence. But when they don't want to believe someone, they demand the world—proof, alibis, testimony. And even if Eun-ho did satisfy all their demands, there was no guarantee they would believe him. First impressions are important, and no one likes to admit they're wrong. Eun-ho would remain a murderer in everyone's eyes, no matter what evidence he produced.

Not only did the cops not want to believe Eun-ho, but Eun-ho also didn't have the willpower to seek exoneration. What he needed was sleep, not innocence. And not just sleep, he wanted dreamless oblivion. Reality was hard enough to deal with, but the things that came to him while he was asleep were terrifying.

Indeed, Eun-ho was suffering from a recurring dream, the same dream he had the night Noah died. Explosions of light. A white hand appearing from the darkness. An endless abyss. Trapped at the bottom of a frozen lake.

Dear Yoon-hee,

I'm writing to you because I have something to tell you. Six days ago in the early morning . . .

Eun-ho wanted to write only about the facts, like he was giving a testimony. He tried his best to be detached. He had to control his emotions; that was the only way he could avoid rambling, that was the only way he could avoid pathetic excuses. As a result, the letter turned out more concise than he had even intended. Eun-ho read it again to check if he had missed anything or if there was anything that needed more context.

But when Eun-ho read it back to himself, he was disgusted by his own account of what happened. His throat felt tight, and he could hear the whirring of the blood rushing through his heart. Eun-ho hated his own tone in the email. Was this all he could manage after agonizing over it for several hours? The letter read like a notification. It could be boiled down to two sentences: *I killed our son. I thought you should know.*

Eun-ho thought about how he would feel if he were his wife and had received such a letter. He didn't need to think long. He'd buy a gun and get on the next plane to Korea. But Eun-ho didn't dare try writing it again. His mouse hovered over the send button until someone knocked on his door, pulling him back to reality.

The door to the study opened without making a sound. Wife stuck her head in the room. She stepped inside as soon as she made eye contact with him.

"There you are, honey."

Eun-ho glanced down at his computer screen. Despite knowing he was summoning the firing squad, he pressed send anyway. Eun-ho had no reason to hide his email to Yoon-hee from Wife. But she didn't need to know if she didn't have to. And knowing Wife, he doubted she would praise him for it. He could already imagine her response. First, Wife would demand him to explain why he was sending her an email, even though it should be obvious. And she would ask to see the contents of the email. And then she would start meddling and pretending that he needed to censor graphic details when she was really just fearful of the email becoming public. At this moment, this was the last thing Eun-ho wanted to do: having his own work censored by Wife.

"I've been looking all over for you."

Wife came over to the front of the desk. She looked like she was growing ten inches taller with every step she took toward him. A notification that the email was sent successfully appeared on Eun-ho's screen. It also displayed the name and email address of the recipient. Eun-ho moved his finger once more and pressed the confirmation button. Wife stood next to him with her body pressed against his shoulder.

"Sending emails?"

She placed her hand on his shoulder. Her eyes were looking down at his screen. The message had disappeared, but his email inbox was still open for all to see. He closed his email and logged out of the computer.

"Who were you emailing?"

Eun-ho turned his head and looked at Wife. She was wearing the sleeveless dress that she often wore at home. Eun-ho's nose was filled with a clean scent, as though Wife had just gotten out of the shower. Her long hair was down, and she was giving off the familiar smell of body oil.

When did she come home? Why didn't I hear her? Eun-ho was so confused. He had two ears; what were they doing while he was writing the email? Why hadn't they heard her taking a shower, drying her hair, and putting on clothes? Or maybe she was coming back from the local public bath house.

Eun-ho looked at Wife's feet which were visible beneath the hem of her dress. She had gotten a pedicure and her toenails had a fresh coat of red nail polish. It was then that Eun-ho realized she was barefoot. He remembered that Wife moved like a cat when she was barefoot.

"I was sending a message to the principal that I'm starting work again tomorrow."

Wife's clear eyes looked at him silently before replying, "Are you sure you'll be okay?"

Instead of answering, Eun-ho dropped his gaze. Noah's picture, which was next to his laptop, caught his eye.

"It hasn't even been three days since the funeral."

Wife perched herself on the edge of the desk. Her body naturally turned into him. It felt like Noah and Wife were both staring at him, Noah from the left, and Wife from the right.

"Don't overdo it."

Wife's hand moved from his shoulder to his face. With her thumb, she gently caressed the middle of his rapidly pulsating forehead. With each stoke her delicate fingers made across his skin, Eun-ho felt a chill spread deeper into his spine.

"I'm okay with it if you quit your job."

Wife started brushing his messy bangs.

"Quit and go on vacation with me. We can go away for a long time, until the pain goes away."

Eun-ho knew that this was her way of trying to comfort him. He also knew that she expected him to accept immediately. But there were times when he didn't want to accept anything. No jokes, no criticism, no consideration, no comfort—times when he wanted nothing.

And right now was one of those times. There was just one thing he wanted from Wife. And that was for her to get her hands off him. Even better would be if she left him alone.

"I'll think about it."

Eun-ho's downcast gaze met Wife's hand, which was propping her up on the desk. Her bandages were gone now, and he could see red lines, both long and short, on her fingers. There was one on her thumb, two on her first finger and pinky, and four on the edge of her palm. There were dark scabs where they had pulled out the stitches. What did she say happened again? She cut her hand while cooking?

Eun-ho felt a sudden rush of nausea. The white hand from his dream had appeared in front of his eyes. But he didn't understand why he was seeing this image now. Eun-ho turned his head to the side and fled from the hand. He pushed the chair back and put distance between himself and Wife. He used his arms to lift himself up. His inner thighs were shaking as he tried not to fall.

"I'm going to look at Noah's room for a moment."

The smile on Wife's face disappeared as though someone had pulled the plug. The whites of her eyes became icy cold, like chilled porcelain. She always gave off this cold aura whenever someone rejected her kindness. Eun-ho picked up Noah's picture and left the study. As he started up the stairs, he could hear Wife calling out from behind.

"Come back soon. I'll prepare dinner."

Eun-ho continued up the stairs. He could feel the daggers shooting out of Wife's eyes and stabbing him in the back of his skull. This time, he didn't hesitate and went straight into Noah's room. Inside, he was met with darkness.

In the city, it never got completely dark. Rooms were always invaded by light from streetlamps, apartments, neon signs, and cars. One of the reasons Eun-ho liked this house was because it was located in a forest. When night fell, it became shrouded in proper darkness, as though they were living out in the mountains. It was a luxury to have such darkness in the middle of Seoul.

But right now, Eun-ho didn't feel that way. This darkness was a specter, threatening to pull him back into the nightmare from that night. It wanted to drown him at the bottom of a frozen lake. Eun-ho frantically groped around until he found the light switch.

This time, a second wave of nausea rushed over him. His eyes were met with a sight he hadn't been prepared for. Neatly closed curtains, an empty desk and bookshelf, and a bed with new sheets. Eun-ho put the picture on Noah's desk and looked around the room again. Pengsoo was gone, and so were Noah's school bag, soccer cones, and soccer ball.

Eun-ho opened the closet. Noah's padded jacket and all his clothes were gone. The drawers and hangers were empty, too. There was no sign of Noah anywhere, as though he had never existed.

Eun-ho felt steam rising from the top of his head. He straightened his back as though a large amount of electricity was flowing through his body. Something heavy and hot was working its way up his throat.

Eun-ho ran out of the room. He bounded down the stairs two steps at a time and then marched toward the kitchen. Wife was washing something in the sink when she turned around to look at him.

"What's the meaning of this?"

*

A telephone was ringing in the empty faculty room. It appeared that Eun-ho was the first one in today. Eun-ho put down his bag and picked up the receiver.

"Hello?"

"Oh—is that you, Mr. Cha?"

Eun-ho immediately knew it was the student who helped as an administrative assistant in the principal's office.

"The principal wants to see you—"

Eun-ho was planning on seeing the principal, anyway. He hadn't been in for a week; it was protocol to drop by and check in. Eun-ho figured the principal wanted to know what was going on. Eun-ho didn't want to reveal more than he needed to, but he still needed to tell the principal that he would be making frequent visits to the police station for a while.

"Have the autopsy results come back?" the principal asked as soon as Eun-ho sat down. This wasn't exactly the warm welcome Eun-ho had been expecting.

"No, not yet." Eun-ho hesitated for a moment before adding: "I wanted to let you know that I'll need to go to the police station a few more times. I'll try to schedule my visits so that they don't interfere with—"

"That won't be necessary. I want you to take some time off to take care of the situation and look after your health."

Eun-ho took a moment to think about what the principal meant by this. Was he telling Eun-ho to take a break because he thought Eun-ho couldn't teach? Or was he simply *informing* Eun-ho that he couldn't teach?

"You'll be contacted later about your position."

So, it was the latter. It seemed like the principal had taken the speculation surrounding Noah's death as fact. Or perhaps the police had contacted the school about the investigation. Even if that was the case, Eun-ho thought this was an overreaction—and completely one-sided, at that. Shouldn't he be given the chance to defend himself?

"Can I at least—"

Eun-ho opened his mouth only to immediately close it again. Even if the principal was willing to listen to Eun-ho's defense, there was nothing Eun-ho could say except for an emotional appeal.

"We called an emergency meeting last Friday and came to this decision. We didn't want to have to go there, but we had no other choice. The school homepage crashed. My office was flooded by angry parents from the PTA. The department of education is even receiving signed petitions demanding your removal. They say it's unethical to allow you around children."

The principal stood up from his chair.

"Personally, I think this is a real shame."

And yet, he didn't look the least bit sorry. The look on his face was telling Eun-ho that he had nothing more to say, and to get out of his office. Eun-ho turned and left. His mind was completely blank. His body was shaking as though he had been dunked in the Arctic Ocean. It was finally starting to dawn on Eun-ho that he was a pariah.

His realization was confirmed again only a few moments later. Most of the other teachers had clocked in by the time he returned to the faculty room. As soon as he entered the room and walked over to his desk, everyone went silent. No one made eye contact with him. No one even gave him a perfunctory greeting. Everyone just sat at their desks and busied themselves with their work.

Eun-ho didn't see Jinu. It was then that he realized that aside from Jinu, none of his coworkers had come to the funeral. To them, Eun-ho already wasn't a coworker. He wasn't even an unfortunate father who lost his son. He was a child-killer. And worse yet, he was shameless enough to come into work as though nothing had happened.

I'm okay with it if you quit your job.

Wife's words flashed through Eun-ho's mind. Wife already knew this would happen. Eun-ho had had no idea. The thought hadn't even crossed his mind. Of course he had been out of it for the last several days, but how could he be this stupid?

Eun-ho got his bag and left the office. He didn't even want to look if there was anything in his desk drawer that he should take with him. His skin felt hot, and his teeth dry. He felt like he was walking not on the office floor but through the air. It was as though he were sinking one meter for every step he took forward. No one was looking at him, but it still felt like they were shooting nasty looks his way.

Eun-ho could finally breathe once he arrived in the parking lot.

"Eun-ho! Eun-ho Cha!"

Eun-ho turned around to find Jinu running after him.

"I was just getting in when I saw you leaving," Jinu said as he stopped in front of Eun-ho. He was bent over trying to catch his breath. "I heard you talked with the principal."

Eun-ho nodded.

"Just think of it like a vacation. The truth will come out, sooner or later."

This was a welcome yet pointless attempt at consoling Eun-ho. Not even

Eun-ho knew what the truth was. The best outcome was that the police concluded there was no intent to harm Noah, that he hadn't purposely crushed Noah's tiny throat. The weathervane of Eun-ho's intuition was pointing in an ominous direction. Indeed, there was a greater chance that Eun-ho's situation would only get worse. And Eun-ho wasn't ready for that. Nor did he have the willpower to brace himself.

"I'm going."

Eun-ho had to wring his throat just to utter these three syllables. And it took every ounce of strength Eun-ho had just to remain upright as he walked to his car. He didn't want to collapse, not in front of Jinu. Right now, that was the most important thing in the world.

Jinu came to the funeral home every day even while Noah's body was still at the coroner's office. He stayed there with Eun-ho late into the night. He was the only friend of Eun-ho's who agreed to be a pallbearer, and he was the only coworker who offered him words of consolation. Eun-ho didn't want to collapse in front of him. He was afraid that he might start crying at Jinu's feet. He was terrified that he would fall and never be able to stand back up.

As Eun-ho got in the car, Jinu grabbed the door. "I'm just saying this in case you don't know. You can call me anytime if you have something you want to ask."

The school bell started ringing. Jinu closed the car door and took a step back. Eun-ho started the car and left the parking lot. He mulled over what Eun-ho said to him as he drove. What on Earth was he talking about? Was there a question that Eun-ho needed to ask Jinu about? And was that question something that Jinu already knew? All Eun-ho knew was that Jinu didn't sound like he was joking. His face, his tone, this situation—none of these things were telling Eun-ho that Jinu was joking.

Eun-ho decided to bury his curiosity. He already had enough to think about. Even if he wanted to satisfy his curiosity, Jinu had classes to teach. Eun-ho would be better off first asking a question that he could get an answer to. Indeed, what exactly were students' parents saying about him?

But just because he could get an answer didn't mean it would be easy. He realized this anew once he got home and sat down at his desk. He never knew that opening his laptop, connecting to the internet, and going to the school's homepage could feel so difficult and terrifying. When he went to the open forum, he felt like he had voluntarily lain down at the guillotine. There were several pages of postings regarding him.

He got divorced only a year into his first marriage. And three years after that, he got remarried to a wealthy businesswoman. He was so crazy for her that he left his own son to be raised by his grandma. How could a five-year-old boy be smothered to death by his father unless it was intentional? His new wife must have hated the boy. He and she might have colluded. The police are investigating it as a potential homicide. Why else would they order an autopsy?

Eun-ho could feel sour saliva pooling up beneath his tongue. His throat constricted just like it did right before vomiting. His intestines twisted into a knot. It felt like a large hand was squeezing his bowels—and not just once, but multiple times and at regular intervals. Was this what contractions felt like?

Eun-ho lay with his forehead on the desk. He wrapped his arms around his stomach and curled up. He was desperately trying to steady his breathing. It wasn't working. Every time he breathed out, a whimpering groan escaped his lips. Some liquid was trickling down Eun-ho's chin, but he didn't know if it was tears, sweat, or saliva. Eun-ho felt like he was an animal.

It took a long time for the spasms to stop. When he lifted his head again, his whole body was covered in sweat. His brain felt like a battlefield that had just been bombed to oblivion. It was all he could do to stop himself from getting on the floor and curling up into a ball.

He wasn't on the ground because he was exhausted from pain. Nor was he bothered by the baseless attacks of a bunch of kids and parents. Although there were some exaggerations, these were just side branches. As with all things, when you took away emotions and the backstory, you were left with just the essence of what happened—things that were clearer to others than they were himself, things that he knew but didn't want to admit. These online comments opened Eun-ho's eyes to the truth, breaking him into a million pieces.

This was how Eun-ho had lived up to this point—like a dog that ignored its own tail. The past was like a tail. Even if you cut it off, it wouldn't disappear completely because there was always at least one person who would remember it used to be there.

Eun-ho closed the school homepage. He didn't open the email he got from the department of education. He didn't even open his search engine, afraid that he might see himself on the news. But there was one thing that he couldn't avoid checking. Eun-ho went into his personal email inbox. There was a reply from Yoon-hee. It had arrived faster than he expected. The subject was simply his name with a period.

Eun-ho Cha.

Eun-ho opened the email.

I never knew I would hear from you again, especially not under circumstances like this. If you're hoping for forgiveness, don't. And if you think you can run from this, don't. We can never run from the truth. I can't run from the fact that I abandoned my son, and you can't run from the fact that you killed him.

PS: Think about it carefully. Be honest with yourself for once and ask yourself, Could you really have done that in your sleep? We were together for seven years. The Eun-ho I knew would have woken up. You're the Princess and the Pea. Perhaps you were drunk or took a handful of sleeping pills before bed.

Eun-ho didn't drink that night, nor had he taken any sleeping pills. He'd already told the police this several times. Eun-ho knew this was unfavorable for him to admit, but it was the truth. The only thing he had that night was quince tea. The one Wife made him…

Without warning, the primary-colored teacups flashed across his eyes. Red for him, blue for Mother, and yellow for Wife. No. Yellow for Mother, blue for Wife . . .

Eun-ho shook his head and tried to rid himself of these images. He also threw dirt onto the thoughts, which were flickering like dying embers. He knew he could remember whose cup was whose if he focused, but he didn't want to. Asking questions about that would only lead him to preposterous conclusions. He had no choice but to forget about it.

Eun-ho brought another matter into his mind. The question of which wife was correct: his current wife, or his ex-wife? Just regarding his sleeping habits, the two women had vastly different opinions. He needed the opinion of a credible third party.

What about Mom? Jinu? No, neither would do. Opinions based on memory were meaningless right now. The person needed to be someone who would give him an objective record of what he did while asleep.

Eun-ho searched up the words "psychiatric clinic" and "sleep disorders." He got several articles about sleep disorders and depression. When he moved on to the second page of results, he started to see links to clinics that specialized in sleep disorders. He clicked on one of these.

It was an article explaining polysomnography: a test that analyzes brain waves, electrocardiograms, breathing patterns, and muscle movements of patients while they sleep to diagnose sleep disorders. The National Health Insurance covered conditions such as sleep apnea, narcolepsy, or hypersomnia. It seemed like Eun-ho couldn't count on insurance to help with the cost for the exam, but that didn't matter. The bigger problem was that the clinic was across town.

Eun-ho narrowed his search results to clinics in Cheongyeon. There was a clinic close to his house. According to their website, they had next-day results. Eun-ho organized his thoughts for a moment. Why did he have to take this exam? What was he trying to prove? And what would come of this?

Eun-ho couldn't accept that he had killed Noah. Even though there was undeniable physical evidence, he couldn't accept it. If what Yoon-hee said was right, things would get worse for Eun-ho by taking this sleep study. If the study results agreed with Yoon-hee, and if he gave the police his study results, he might be charged with murder. Should he still do it?

Yes. He could think later about what the police might do with the information. He needed any kind of evidence that said he didn't kill Noah. That was the only way he could go on living. Whether it was manslaughter or not, he couldn't live knowing he had killed his own son.

Eun-ho called the clinic and made an appointment. He was able to get a same-day appointment. He could get everything done at the same clinic. He would have a consultation at 5:40 and start the test at 8:30. He would be able to check his results the next day.

Eun-ho turned off his laptop and went up to Noah's room. He didn't have a reason for going there, but his legs had a mind of their own.

There was a box lying on Noah's desk. It was one of the large blue boxes they had used during the move. He had brought it here from storage last night. Inside were all of Noah's belongings: his clothes, school bag, soccer ball, and Pengsoo.

Wife, who had packed the box, couldn't understand why Eun-ho was upset about it. She said she did it for him, that she was afraid seeing Pengsoo would remind him of that day. She was afraid that the soccer ball would fill him with guilt. She was planning on burning the clothes and school bag after the three-day mourning period passed.

"I just did it because you were incapable of doing it yourself."

The look on her face was asking what the big deal was.

"You always do this. Why do *you* always decide what it is that *I* want?"

"When have I ever?"

Wife's face was bright red now. Her half-moon eyes were filled with bulbous tears.

"How much longer are you going to be like this, Eun-ho? I am tired of your constant irritability."

There were faint vibrations of a whimper in Wife's voice.

"If I knew this was going to happen, I wouldn't have made an issue about Jiyoo getting hit by that soccer ball. I should have just bitten my tongue. If only I hadn't said anything..."

Finally, the tears welling up in Wife's eyes started to flow down her cheeks. Her voice also started to tremble in earnest.

"I'm human, too. I get angry, too, sometimes . . ."

Wife had the extraordinary ability to evoke pity from someone who was angry at her.

"I didn't know you would discipline him so harshly. All I wanted you to do was have a word with him. It's all my fault that he had an asthma attack."

Wife also had a talent for stabbing people in just the right place.

"I think that's what started it all. He probably had another episode that night, while you were fast asleep."

The sound of the doorbell pulled Eun-ho out of his daydream. Eun-ho went downstairs. Through the intercom video, he could see two unfamiliar men standing outside.

"Who is it?"

"Police."

Eun-ho felt all his strength leave his body. They've finally come for me. The autopsy results had finally come back. There was only one reason they would come to his door instead of giving him a call. They had come to put handcuffs on him. Eun-ho stepped outside.

"Is this the residence of Yuna Shin?" one of the police officers in a blue windbreaker asked as he held up his badge.

Eun-ho blinked in confusion. "It is."

"Is she home?"

"No. May I ask what this is about?"

The two men glanced at each other before turning back to Eun-ho.

"Do you know where she went?"

"She should be at work."

"Aha." The police officer in the blue windbreaker nodded. "We came here because we heard she had gone home early from work."

Eun-ho didn't know what to make of this. These police officers seemed only interested in Yuna.

"She hasn't come back yet. May I ask what this is abo—"

"It's nothing. We just had a few questions for her." Blue Windbreaker handed Eun-ho his business card. "When you see her, tell her to give us a call."

Eun-ho looked down at the card. This man was a detective from the Seodaemun Police Department. This wasn't right. Seodaemun was about as related to Wife as Antarctica was related to crocodiles.

"If you tell me what this was about, I'll be able to relay it to my wife," Eun-ho said.

The detective thought for a moment before accepting this proposition.

"Yuna Shin's ex-husband Joon-young Seo is missing. He was last seen twelve days ago on Tuesday. We're looking for any leads, and we thought your wife might be able to help us."

This date lingered in Eun-ho's ears. The Tuesday before last was the day Yuna left the house. Eun-ho also managed to dig up the distant memory that he had been suspicious that Yuna had been with her ex-husband. It seemed like ages ago that he last thought about her strange absence. In fact, he had never had the chance to ask Yuna about where she had been from Tuesday to Saturday.

"Does anything come to mind?"

Blue Windbreaker studied Eun-ho's face. The stare was so intense that it felt like he had pulled out his gun and pointed it at Eun-ho's forehead.

"No. I'm a bit confused because this is concerning her ex-husband." Eun-ho put the business card in his pocket. "I'll deliver your message to my wife."

Eun-ho turned to look at their car, which was parked across the street, and signaled that it was time for them to go. Blue Windbreaker craned his neck to peer into the house through the glass window before going back to their car. Standing at the front door, Eun-ho observed the two men retreat. Only when they disappeared from view did Eun-ho go back into the house.

He took out the business card and looked at it with a grave expression on his face. He had to decide before Wife came home. He either had to just forget about it and simply hand her the business card, or he had to ask her about where she was for those five days.

Eun-ho decided on the former. His head was already saturated with his own problems. He would need undivided attention and immense luck just to make headway on the mystery of Noah's death. His problems with Wife could be dealt with later, if ever.

Eun-ho went into the master bedroom to change outfits. He put on a workout shirt and pants and a padded jacket. He packed his bag with his wallet, phone, and laptop. Just as he was walking out of the study with his car keys, he saw Wife enter the living room.

"You're home early," she said.

She looked a bit surprised. She was holding a large basket in one hand. It looked like she had just gotten back from the grocery store.

"Are you going somewhere?" she asked as she placed the basket on the dining room table.

"I'm going to the hospital."

"What?" Wife asked with a concerned look on her face. "Are you not feeling well?

"No. I'm just going to the sleep clinic."

Aha . . . Wife nodded.

"I understand. That's a good idea. You haven't slept in a week." As she pulled items out of the bag, she added, "Hurry home. I'm cooking something delicious."

"I won't be coming back tonight. I need to stay overnight for the test."

Wife's hand became frozen inside the bag. Her eyes turned to him.

"What kind of test requires you to stay the night?"

"It's a test that records my activity while I'm asleep. I'll see you tomorrow."

Eun-ho moved his bag to his other shoulder and headed for the front door.

"Why are you taking such a test?" Wife asked as she walked after him. "Did the police order it?"

Eun-ho said yes.

"Did the autopsy results come back yet?"

"Not yet."

"Then why are they asking you to take this test?"

Instead of answering, Eun-ho took out the business card from his pocket and handed it to her. Her eyes scanned the card before returning to his face. She was waiting for him to explain.

"Two detectives came by the house earlier looking for you. They want you to give them a call."

"For me?"

A strange look flashed across Wife's eyes. It disappeared so suddenly that Eun-ho couldn't be sure, but it looked like trepidation.

"They said Joon-young's gone missing. Since last Tuesday."

Eun-ho opened the shoe closet, and as he looked for his sneakers he glanced back at Wife. She was staring down at the business card with an unsettled look on her face. While he was curious what it meant, he was just thankful that the business card was acting like a get-out-of-jail-free card. Eun-ho closed the front door, being careful not to make a sound. He started his car and headed for the hospital.

The first stage of the study was easy. They measured his height and weight, calculated his BMI, asked about underlying conditions and drugs he was currently taking, then explained the study procedure. They also gave him a sleeping pill in case he needed it. By the time this was all done, he had two hours left before the start of the study.

Eun-ho killed time in the first-floor café. He ate a piece of cheesecake as he looked up articles on sleep disorders. The cake was the consistency of Vaseline, but he was able to wash it down with a soda. Eun-ho wasn't hungry, but he would need to feed his brain if he wanted to continue thinking clearly.

8:30. Eun-ho went into the exam room in the annex. The nurse led him to the sleep room. It felt like a business hotel. Small, clean, dark, and quiet.

"I'll be back in thirty minutes."

The nurse left the room. They didn't say it explicitly, but it seemed like they were giving him time to shower, change into the gown, and use the bathroom. Eun-ho meticulously prepared himself. He removed everything that would interrupt his sleeping. He turned off his phone, took off his watch, and even removed his ring.

Once he lay on the bed, the nurse came back to start attaching the electrodes. The nurse attached wired patches to his head, forehead, and temples. She also stuck what looked like tubes of oxygen into his nose, strapped two belts around his chest, and attached sensors to his fingers. Finally, she put a bottle of water on the table next to the bed.

"Here's some water for you."

Once the nurse turned off the light and left, Eun-ho closed his eyes. He thought about the "How to fall asleep in two minutes" video he watched on YouTube earlier. Relax your body. And repeat the following as you take deep breaths: Don't think. Don't think. Don't . . . think . . .

Eun-ho's thoughts burst like fireworks in the night sky. Every time Eun-ho said the words "Don't think" to himself, another firework would go off, brighter and more brilliant than the last. The sensor on his finger felt like it was crushing his fingernail. And the belts on his chest were constricting his breathing. Eventually, Eun-ho took the sleeping pill. He tried to suppress his heavy breathing as he waited desperately for sleep to come.

Eun-ho was finding it hard to breathe. A puttering sound was coming from deep inside his lungs as though he were a machine that desperately needed oil. And then he saw Noah.

Noah was thrashing as Eun-ho crushed him. Noah was trying to push Eun-ho off him. Noah's purple lips were searching for air.

Eun-ho trembled. He felt like he was about to have a seizure. He wanted to pull off all the sensors and run out of the room. He clenched his teeth and glared at the infrared camera.

Eun-ho had thought they could live happily ever after. If only he had endured for a little while longer, the four of them would be living a normal life under one roof. That's all he wanted. Nothing more, nothing less. Was that really too much to wish for?

Eun-ho closed his eyes. A white hand appeared and disappeared inside his mind. And something occurred to him.

That night, did I turn off the light before falling asleep?

*

"There's nothing that sticks out to me," the doctor said.

Eun-ho looked at the monitor on the doctor's desk. On it was a graph that Eun-ho couldn't read.

"You never stopped breathing, nor did you have any unusual movements. Although, I wouldn't say that your quality of sleep was particularly good."

He explained that Eun-ho had frequent interruptions to his sleep; he either woke up or had muscle movements. And his dreams lasted for a long time.

"Is there anything else you want to know?"

Eun-ho asked first what he was most curious about.

"You said I move a lot while I sleep. What kind of movements are we talking about exactly?"

"You toss and turn. Specifically, you like turning to your right to lie face down.

Eun-ho's tongue felt dry. Noah had been on his left. Eun-ho was afraid of the answer, but he asked his next question anyway.

"Do I ever turn left?"

"No."

The definitive nature of this answer caught Eun-ho off guard.

"You only turn to your right. It's a bit unusual."

"I didn't turn left once?"

A suspicious look appeared on the doctor's face. It looked like he wanted to know why Eun-ho was so hung up on not turning left. Eun-ho gave the doctor a plausible reason for his curiosity.

"I sleep with my baby, and I'm always nervous that I might smother him. Do you think I should put him on my left when I sleep?

Aha . . . The doctor nodded.

"If he's a newborn, yes, I would suggest putting him on your left. And leave a bit of room between yourself and him. Although, there are no guarantees in life. Have you thought about a crib?"

"He's not a newborn, he's five. But he's frail."

This made the doctor laugh. It was obvious that he thought Eun-ho was being ridiculous.

"Five? Then you have nothing to worry about. A better solution might be getting him his own bed."

Eun-ho thought of the first time he slept with Wife. It was about a month after returning from Russia. The morning after, Wife was furious. She asked why he slept with his back turned to her. She said she felt like he had cut her off, like she had been abandoned. She said she even felt insulted. After that, Eun-ho tried to hold her while they slept. But it didn't help. Every morning when he woke up, he was always sleeping with his back to her.

Now he knew why. He had a preferential direction when turning in his sleep. If Wife had ever slept on his right, they would have woken up facing each other or in each other's arms. Somewhat absurdly, they had never tried switching sides. It seemed they hadn't given it much thought.

Eun-ho's thoughts trailed off as he began thinking about the message Wife had shown the police. There was a good chance the message was a lie. Eun-ho trusted science more than he trusted people.

But why? Why would she send him that text message? It was as though she knew she would need it in a few months. Seeing the way his thoughts were getting out of control, Eun-ho suppressed his curiosity. Right now, he had more pressing questions. Questions he had paid money to get answered.

"I took the sleeping pill you gave me last night. Is it possible to be lucid after taking a sleeping pill? I felt like someone came into the exam room late last night. It felt like they were touching my fingers. I thought it might just be a dream, but I wasn't sure."

"Ah, yes. It was probably the nurse. The nurse usually goes into the room early in the morning to check on the patient. What we gave you was

Zolpidem, which doesn't have the sedation effects of benzodiazepines. You might be lucid without being completely awake or aware of what's happening. Sometimes people will interpret things as dreams."

Eun-ho could feel his pulse quickening. He had to make sure he heard the doctor correctly.

"You mean I might mistake things that really happened to me as elements of a dream?"

"Yes."

"And, if I took more than one pill, could I still react to external stimuli? Like a light or something?"

"Well, it would depend on the exact drug and how much you took. Even if you take one or two more pills of the drug we gave you yesterday, you would probably still be able to sense an external light or something. Of course, your senses as a whole would be somewhat dull. Everything would be hazy and dreamlike."

"And if I took the same test on a different day, without sleeping aids, could the test results be completely different?"

The doctor shook his head without hesitation.

"They would be more or less the same."

Eun-ho returned home. He took out his cellphone, which he had stashed away in his bag. He had ten missed phone calls and eight unread messages. They were all from Wife. She had sent them throughout the night and into the morning. Eun-ho read her last message.

—Why aren't you picking up? It's so frustrating. Where are you? Are you still at the hospital?

Eun-ho was getting a strong sense of déjà vu. These messages were exactly like the ones Eun-ho sent when Wife disappeared. Eun-ho now knew the emotional superiority that Wife must feel all the time. He felt like she was a keyboard that he could play on to his heart's content, a dog on a leash that he could screw with.

He didn't send a reply; if he did, she would call him immediately and demand explanations for everything. Eun-ho wasn't in the mood for such a phone call. He needed time to himself with no distractions. He needed to think about what the results of his sleep study meant, why his wife sent him that untruthful text message, and how he was going to interpret that lie about his sleeping habits.

Eun-ho switched his phone to silent and went into the study. He sat at the desk and laid out the test results in front of him. He caught all the thoughts that were scattered about his mind like fallen leaves and wrote them down on a notepad.

Sleep study—Zolpidem, 10 mg

Only turn right while sleeping—Wife's contradictory text message.

Noah slept on the left.

Lucid while asleep—Confuse reality for dream. Bright light. White hand.

Wife's right hand—Bandages on her hand. Stitches on her fingers and palm.

Quince tea—Red, blue, and yellow cups.

Mom—

That night—fell asleep with the lights on.

Wife's miscarriage and Noah's picture—

Tuesday the 16th—Wife leaves home, ex-husband disappears.

Jinu—Tells me I can call him if I have "something I want to ask him." What does that mean?

Eun-ho called his mom. She answered the phone in a voice that was stronger and brighter than he was expecting. She asked him questions until she was out of breath. How are you feeling? Have you eaten? What did the school say? When she ran out of questions, Eun-ho was finally able to ask his own.

"Mom, the night it happened, did you come into Noah's room to turn off the lights?"

"You mean the night Noah . . . ?"

"Yes."

"No. I was so tired that I fell asleep right after washing up. Why do you ask?"

So, she hadn't turned off the lights. And Eun-ho doubted Noah did it. And definitely not Jiyoo.

"Then you slept straight through the night?"

"Yes. Completely unaware what was becoming of my baby—"

The strength drained from her voice. Eun-ho knew if he didn't stop her, she would start weeping again. He asked another question to quiet her.

"Mom, do you always sleep through the night like that?"

"You still don't know your own mother's sleeping habits? Your father used to always grumble about how you were just like me, always waking up in the middle of the night and going to the bathroom. But strangely enough, I slept like a corpse that night. I haven't felt that way since that time they took out my appendix and gave me anesthesia." Noticing something odd about this line of questioning, she paused before asking, "Why?"

"I was just curious."

Eun-ho hung up and looked down at the notepad again.

Mom—Slept like she was on anesthesia.

Eun-ho tore off the paper and hid it with the test results under his rubber floor mat. He put his cellphone in his pocket and left the study. He went into the master bedroom and started opening the drawers to the vanity. After that, he rummaged through the jewelry box and the bags in the walk-in closet. He was thorough in his search, even turning out coat pockets, like he were a forensic scientist.

At first, he didn't know what he was looking for. Only when he stopped his search of the master bedroom and came out into the living room did he realize what it was: sleeping pills.

He stood at the bottom of the stairs and looked down at the thousand won bill he had in his hands. This was all he had found after snooping around for an hour. All at once, he was overwhelmed with relief that he hadn't found anything, guilt over suspecting his wife, and embarrassment for tearing apart their master bedroom in search of evidence. He would have stopped there had there not been a wriggling doubt at the bottom of his subconscious.

If it were me, I wouldn't hide it in the master bedroom either.

Eun-ho's watch was pointing to five. He went up the stairs. Wife would be leaving work soon. Even if she left right now, she wouldn't arrive until seven. That meant he had about two hours to play with.

Eun-ho went into Jiyoo's room and turned on the light. This was the only place in the house he never ventured. The room was oozing with Wife's taste in interior design. A pink bed canopy, white sheets and white pillows, lace curtains with butterflies on them, a cabin-shaped wardrobe, and an old-fashioned roll top desk. In the desk drawer were new stationary items that hadn't even been taken out of their packaging yet. Pencils, colored pencils, felt pens, markers, sketch books and notebooks.

There wasn't anything unusual in the wardrobe either. Just two sleeveless summer dresses. But there was something between the wardrobe and the wall. It was obscured by the curtains, but Eun-ho could tell that it was large and thick. He stuck his hand behind the wardrobe and fished the object out.

It was a thin brown cardboard box, about the dimensions of a laptop. Inside, there were yellow files sealed with strings. Eun-ho checked his watch. 6:15. He had a bit of time before Wife returned.

Eun-ho untied the string and flipped over the cover. There were clear plastic document folders in a binder. They were organized and labeled by year and month, from newest to oldest. The first file was from last month, and the last was from eight years ago. Eun-ho opened the stack to the middle where he found a document from two years ago in January.

Inside the plastic folder was a divorce petition. It had been filed not by Wife but by her ex-husband, on January 11. Eun-ho searched his memory. He didn't need to search long, though. He had met Wife at Lake Baikal on January 18.

I'm divorced. As of last week.

Eun-ho could almost hear her voice, as well as her enchanting laughter.

The next file contained a copy of the countersuit filed by Wife. It was dated January 25. Eun-ho, Jinu, and Wife returned to Irkutsk on the 21st in the afternoon. That was where they said goodbye. That night, he and Jinu had to get back on the train. And two days later, Wife needed to return to Korea in the morning.

Eun-ho bought another SIM card and put it in Wife's cellphone. He was determined to continue texting her after he got on the train. The first thing she got when she had service again was the news of her father's death. The message had been sent a week prior, the same day she lost her SIM card at Vladivostok International Airport.

Eun-ho remembered how heavy his footsteps were as he walked to the train station and how swollen her eyes were. If he could have his way, he would have stayed with her in Irkutsk. He wanted to stay with her until her flight to Korea. The reason he couldn't was because of a voice in his head. *Don't ruin Jinu's vacation just because of some woman you met four days ago!*

Two days later at a random train station, he received a message from Yuna. She said she was getting on the plane. If he remembered the days correctly, that would mean that four days later, she would have filed the countersuit.

Eun-ho's mind was foggy with confusion. He couldn't quite grasp what these dates meant, except for the fact that she had been married, not divorced, when they first met.

Why had she lied? Surely, she didn't think that "I'm divorced" and "My husband asked for a divorce" could really be equivalent expressions? He also couldn't understand how someone could file a divorce countersuit just four days after hearing the news of their father's death. She had looked so despondent when she got the news. She even buried her face in the table and cried. Could someone get over their grief that quickly?

Suddenly, Eun-ho was overcome with a sense of fear. What other lies were waiting for him in this box? Should he start making a list to keep track of everything? Were there lies he'd rather not know? Lies too great to bear?

Perhaps it would be better just to close the box.

Eun-ho looked down at the papers with a distraught look on his face. Two emotions were waging war inside his head. One was the desire to unmask every secret. The other was dread that these secrets might destroy the bits of normalcy that remained in his life—that was assuming there were any remaining at all.

He flipped over to the next page, and the next page, and the next page... All of them implied a long divorce trial and an intense struggle over parental rights. It was a year later when the divorce was finalized. It appeared that for that year, he had been Yuna's mistress.

But even after the divorce, Yuna continued to receive things from the court. They were all documents related to her ex-husband's visitation rights. It appeared that on this account, he had won. Wife had paid a fine of three million won for ignoring the court's orders, but it looked like she was still receiving court orders. The period that she had to execute the most recent court order ended today, November 30.

Had Wife allowed her ex-husband to exercise his visitation rights? And if she didn't this time, what would her punishment be? It would probably be worse than just a fine.

As far as Eun-ho knew, Jiyoo was at her grandma's house. That's what Wife told him. She said she would stay there until things settled down. Did that mean her ex-husband had met Jiyoo there? Or perhaps before that? Suddenly, Eun-ho remembered the detectives that had showed up at their door. Didn't they say he was missing? Since last Tuesday . . .

He had to stop his thoughts from multiplying and blinding him. When he turned the page, he found a white envelope. Inside were two Polaroid pictures. The colors were faded, but Eun-ho had no difficulty in making out the subjects.

The first picture was of a Caucasian man sitting at a kitchen table with his hands wrapped around a teacup. What interested Eun-ho wasn't the man but the object in the alcove behind him. He recognized it immediately. It was a music box in the shape of St. Basil's Cathedral. It would probably play Moscow Nights if you wound the spring. Eun-ho had bought the exact same music box at Izmailovsky Market in Moscow—four of them, in fact. Three as presents, and one to keep in his study.

The picture had been taken eight years ago on January 20. As far as he knew, that was the year Wife had returned from Russia after studying abroad there. Eun-ho searched his memory. What month did she say she had come back? March? April? It definitely wasn't January because she said she came back right before school started in March. If he remembered correctly, that would mean this picture had been taken in Russia.

There were two men in the second picture. The format was similar to the first picture in that they were sitting at a dinner table and with teacups in front of them. One of the men was someone he knew. The picture was thirteen years old, and his face was blurry, but Eun-ho could be sure it was Jinu.

Eun-ho recalled a memory. He could almost hear Jinu's voice from that day at the Shaman Rock.

"You made me coffee one time. At your apartment, when Jiwoon moved out."

Eun-ho put the picture on the floor. He pulled out his phone and opened his camera. He didn't know what this picture meant, but he had a feeling he might need this later.

Eun-ho looked at the clock to see it was past 7—time for Wife to come home. He put the documents and envelope back in the box and put the box back where he found it. He turned off the light and came out of Jiyoo's room. As he closed the door, he realized the whole house was shrouded in darkness. Of course it was. He hadn't turned on the lights when he came upstairs because it was still light out, but that was almost two hours ago.

Eun-ho suddenly felt lost. What should he do now? He didn't have the confidence to act like someone who knew nothing. If he ran into Wife right now, he would end up asking her questions: who she was with when she disappeared, what was she lying about and why, what was the meaning of the box in Jiyoo's room.

And even if he didn't ask, Wife would know something was up. She was a pro at reading his face. Most likely, she would ask him if he had something he wanted to tell her.

But neither could he avoid seeing her. Unlike him, Wife couldn't stand not knowing things. Even if he tried locking himself in his study, she would come in and pester him about what was wrong. Why didn't you pick up the phone? What were the test results? What did you do all day? Why didn't you answer my text messages after you read them?

Eun-ho went over to the window and parted the curtains to look outside. Headlights were moving toward the house. He waited for a while until a white sedan pulled up under the streetlamp out front. It was Wife.

He'd lost his chance to go downstairs. Wife would have already seen that the lights were off. Eun-ho went into Noah's room. He reached out and found Noah's desk. He took Pengsoo out of the box and crawled into bed with it. He then took off his socks and threw them onto the ground, as though he had tossed them while half asleep. He then focused all his attention on his ears.

He heard the car door opening. He also thought he heard the faint sound of the front door opening. After that, silence. At least until Wife knocked on the bedroom door.

Eun-ho sucked in his breath. He had almost said "Come in." Then the voice in his head whispered to him. *What are you doing, man? Pretending to be asleep, in your own home, because you're afraid of your wife?*

Eun-ho could sense the door opening and a light shining into the room. It wasn't the ceiling light. It was too faint. It must be coming from the playroom.

"Eun-ho. What are you doing here?"

She spoke as if she knew he wasn't asleep. The loud voice inside his head directed him. *Pretend to open your eyes. Naturally. And don't embarrass yourself by getting caught with bad acting!*

Eun-ho wanted to know. He wanted to know who his wife was, this woman whom he had once been head over heels for, whom, aside from a few exhausting personality flaws, he *still* loved. Did he really know her? What exactly was she doing behind his back? And how were those things related to what was going on right now? To answer these questions, he needed to put to sleep the voice in his head.

He started singing a silent lullaby to the voice in himself.

Hush, hush, little baby. Cuckoo, cuckoo, quiet chicken. Don't you wake up the baby.

Eun-ho sensed Wife coming closer. It sounded like she was barefoot again. Even Eun-ho's own heartbeat was louder than her footsteps. It took an unbearable amount of time for her to reach him. He didn't know a human could move this slowly. As the suspense drew on, Eun-ho felt like his spine was going to start spasming. The tingling sensation travelled all the way down to his toes. This caused his toes to move on their own.

"Eun-ho? Are you asleep?"

Her voice was right above his face. He continued to focus on singing the lullaby that his grandma used to sing to him.

Don't you bark, little doggy. You will wake up the baby.

"What are you doing sleeping here? It's so cold."

Wife's cold hand touched his cheek. Immediately, his breathing started to quicken. He might have even flinched slightly. He continued to sing the lullaby as though he was casting a spell.

Don't you bark, red doggy.

Don't you bark, blue doggy.

Don't you bark, yellow doggy.

Wife's whispering tickled his ears. "Sleep. I'll turn on the heat for you."

Eun-ho could feel Wife getting farther away, unbearably slowly, just like when she had approached him. It felt like a century passed before he heard the door closing. Once the dark silence returned to the room, he was able to let out the breath he'd been holding in. At the same time, he unleashed in his mind the loud voice he'd been suppressing.

Well, what are you going to do now?

Thankfully, he had all the time in the world to think about this now.

3 a.m. He got up from the bed. He walked out of the room barefoot, just like Wife. Without turning on the light, he felt his way along the wall and moved toward the edge of the stairs. The house from the top of the stairs looked like a large pit of darkness. Unable to see the light from the street, Eun-ho figured all the curtains in the house had been closed, from the balcony and the back door all the way to the kitchen windows.

Eun-ho pulled out his cellphone. He turned on the flashlight and descended the stairs in silence. He crossed the living room, being careful not to bump into anything. When he arrived in front of the master bedroom, he lowered the intensity of his flashlight to the lowest setting. In the instance that Wife was still awake, he would pretend like he was coming back to bed.

When he arrived at the head of the bed, he paused. Wife was lying on her side and facing the wall. Eun-ho couldn't tell if she was awake or asleep because he couldn't see her face. On the bed next to the nape of her neck was her phone. Just from the position of the phone and her hand, it seemed like she had fallen asleep while looking at her phone.

Eun-ho picked up her cellphone. He pressed the home button and was met with the lock screen. Eun-ho knew it would be locked. But he had to check anyway. The palm of Wife's right hand was face down on the bed just beneath her chin. He would need her right thumb if he wanted to unlock the phone.

If Wife had been lying on her back or if her side of the bed wasn't right up against the wall, this would have been easy. But because Wife was facing away from Eun-ho, and because there was no way for Eun-ho to walk to her side of the bed, getting at her right thumb was going to be difficult. He would either have to bend her arm and bring her hand to the phone, or he would have to bend over and bring the phone to her hand.

He picked the latter. If Wife woke up, he could fall on her and pretend that he was trying to cuddle with her. Eun-ho first put his own phone down on the floor and shined the light toward the ceiling. Next, he raised one knee up onto the bed and shifted his weight onto the mattress. The mattress shook slightly, but Wife didn't show any reaction. He brought his torso over her body and placed one hand on the bed for support. He looked down and studied her face.

Although it was still fairly dark in the room, thanks to the light from his cellphone which was illuminating the ceiling, he could see the outline of her pupils beneath her eyelids. He leaned his ear toward her and was able to hear her slow and steady breathing. Her lips were slightly parted. According to what he read yesterday, she was probably in REM sleep, which meant he would need to do a lot to wake her up.

Eun-ho slid Wife's phone under her thumb and lined up her fingerprint with the phone button. He then pressed down lightly on her finger until he heard a click.

The screen turned on, and the phone was successfully unlocked. At the same time, Eun-ho thought he saw his Wife's eyelids move slightly. Her pupils moved slowly toward the corner of her eyes, as though she were watching what he was doing through the skin of her eyelids. Eun-ho held his breath. He stopped moving and prepared himself to pretend to throw himself onto her.

Wife's breathing steadied itself. Her pupils returned to the middle of the eyelids. Eun-ho quickly retreated before the screen turned off. He lifted his torso and brought his legs down from the bed; after that, he picked up his cellphone and left the room. He went into his study and sat down at the desk. He cautiously let out a long sigh.

It looked like Wife had been watching YouTube before she fell asleep. The last video she had watched was a video about immigration to Russia. Eun-ho scrolled through the recent watch history: Investor Immigration, How I Made It in Vladivostok as a Small-time Investor, Living in Moscow as a Married Couple with Children, Why I Came to Russia, The Cheapest Way to Gain Russian Citizenship . . .

Eun-ho surveyed his memory. Had Wife ever mentioned anything about immigrating to Russia? Never. The only thing she had ever mentioned were her experiences studying abroad there.

This time, Eun-ho clicked on the search field in YouTube. To his surprise, her previous search terms had nothing to do with Russia or immigration: deboning, removing bones from meat, how to make pork bone soup, how to mincemeat . . .

Eun-ho searched his memory again. Had Wife ever made him pork bone soup? Never. Although, she did like eating it.

Eun-ho looked up at the battery indicator. She had 8% left. He quickly closed YouTube and went through her call history. Among a list of unfamiliar contacts was one he recognized. Jinu Kim. Yesterday 2:37 p.m. Eun-ho guessed that she had called Jinu after failing to get through to Eun-ho. If that was true, then she would know about his situation at school.

Eun-ho scrolled down the list. The name Joon-young Seo caught his eye. November 16, 11:01 p.m. Fifty-one seconds.

Had Wife really met up with her ex? Perhaps that would explain the detectives who had come to their house yesterday. Eun-ho could feel his temper flaring. Perhaps Joon-young wasn't missing, after all. Maybe he was just in hiding, waiting to run away with her to Russia.

Eun-ho took a picture of the call history with his own cellphone. He continued scrolling down but found nothing of interest. Wife had only called Joon-young this one time. Why would she only talk to him once? Eun-ho couldn't understand what this meant. All he had was the hunch that the two of them didn't meet regularly. This gave Eun-ho a sense of relief. Perhaps it had just been a one-night fling.

Eun-ho then looked at her text messages. He couldn't find any from Joon-young. But there was a notification informing her about a package.

—Great news, Yuna! Your mountain climbing rope has been delivered to your front door.

The date was November 15. There was no other information about this purchase. Eun-ho thought for a moment. Had Wife ever gone mountain climbing? As far as he knew, the tallest mountain Wife had ever summited was the small hill behind their house.

Eun-ho continued down through her text messages but couldn't find anything else of interest. There was also nothing of interest in her KakaoTalk app. The only name he knew was his own. He also failed to find anything in her calendar or notes.

Her photo album was more barren than he expected. There weren't many photos, and most were either selfies or family photos. And they were almost all taken on vacation, at kid cafés, or on date nights. If there was anything that struck him as odd, it was that each picture had the same composition. Wife was always in the middle, and everyone else was standing around her in the background, like extras in a movie. Every picture looked like a selfie, regardless of how many people were in the frame.

Eun-ho closed the photo album and thought to himself. What else could he look at? He only had 2% battery left.

He decided on opening her internet browser. There were quick access buttons to a search engine, shopping websites, and her email. Eun-ho clicked on her email and was immediately taken to her inbox. He was relieved to find it was an email address he knew. She had three hundred archived emails—too many to skim through with just 2% battery left. Eun-ho moved to the "sent" folder.

At the very bottom of the first page were emails to which only photos had been attached. The first email contained a photo of an elderly man. He was wearing a necktie and a black suit. A disposable coffee cup was placed on the table in front of him. It looked like Yuna's father. He had never met him in person, but he had seen his photo when they performed ancestral rights at his mother-in-law's house, and the man in this photo looked the same. Eun-ho took a picture of this with his phone.

The second email was a picture of Jiyoo and a man. They were sitting next to one another, cheek to cheek, and Jiyoo was smiling like the happiest girl in the world. She was wearing her preschool uniform, and the man was wearing a checkered shirt. It was obvious they were father and daughter. Every feature of their faces, even their forward-cupped ears, was a carbon copy of each other's. On the kitchen table were candles, a blue vase with three roses, two glasses of champagne, a glass of juice, and dinner plates. Eun-ho squinted to get a closer look at the dinner plates. It looked like they ate goulash for dinner.

When had this picture been taken? The file was uploaded on November 20. That was the day before she returned with Jiyoo. Unlike her other photos, this wasn't a selfie. It had clearly been taken by someone outside the frame. There was no question in Eun-ho's mind that Wife took this picture. As Eun-ho feared, Wife had met with her ex-husband. Eun-ho took a picture of this photo as well.

The last email had been sent on November 22 at 3:42 a.m. Eun-ho had an ominous feeling. He couldn't explain it logically, but the feeling was clear.

Eun-ho clicked on the email, ignoring the voice in his head telling him not to.

His intuition had been dead on. As soon as he opened the email, his breath was severed from his throat. In the picture, he and Noah were lying face down on Noah's bed. Noah was hugging Pengsoo on the left side of the bed, and Eun-ho was curled up on the right like a kidney bean.

The dream from that night appeared again in Eun-ho's head. He remembered a sudden burst of light in his dream. Eun-ho had been suspicious of this element of the dream. But now he was convinced. The light had been real. It had come from outside his dream. The explosion of light he saw must have been the flash of a camera.

But why did Wife take this picture? Why in the middle of the night, while everyone was asleep? Eun-ho's arms were shaking. Something was pulling his skin two notches tighter. He felt like he had just opened a door, behind which was an unfamiliar woman who had stolen the face of his wife.

It took all of Eun-ho's focus to hold up his camera and take a photo of this image. His hands were shaking so much that his thumb could hardly find the shutter button. He also dropped his phone several times. Once he finally got his picture, he closed Wife's email. But just as he did this, the phone screen went black.

Eun-ho looked down at the phone in a daze. Which happened first? His closing her email, or the phone shutting off? He wished he had video review to check. If the phone had shut off first, then Wife would know he'd been snooping. As soon as she went into her email, she would see the last email he had been looking at.

This made Eun-ho uneasy, but there was nothing he could do. Eun-ho changed the passcode on his own cellphone. He put Wife's phone in his pocket with the intent of going upstairs to put it back where he found it. But at that very moment, he sensed someone opening the door. Eun-ho looked up and almost screamed in shock. Wife's head was sticking through the crack in the door.

"What are you doing in here?"

Wife came in and walked up next to him.

"It's so dark in here."

Wife looked down at Eun-ho's phone, which was lying on the desk.

"Watching YouTube," Eun-ho said as he pulled his hand out of his pants pocket. "I couldn't sleep." To Eun-ho, his own voice sounded like a distant echo. His vision was also trembling slightly. His whole body might even have been shaking, but he had no way of knowing. Wife reached out and grabbed his elbow, as if to prop him up.

"You were sleeping when I got home. Are you hungry? I can cook you some instant ramen."

Eun-ho shook his head.

"It's too late to eat. We should go back to bed."

Wife followed Eun-ho as he moved toward the door. Her hand was still holding his elbow. And when they entered the bedroom, her hand sat him down on the bed. He felt like he was being detained by the police; the only difference was that he had Wife's hands instead of a pair of handcuffs. Wife got into bed once he lay down.

"Don't try to do this all on your own."

Wife lifted her hand and touched Eun-ho's cheek, then forcefully turned his chin to look at her. With his back flat on the mattress, his head was turned ninety degrees toward her.

"I'm here, too. You can lean on me."

She looked up at him, her eyes within just one finger width from his chin. With her hand still on his cheek, she stroked the skin next to his eye with her thumb. She did this so slowly and delicately that Eun-ho could sense the grain of her fingertips and the warmth radiating up from her capillaries.

Finally, Eun-ho turned the rest of his body to face her. He wrapped one leg around her butt and pulled her toward him. Using this motion as a distraction, he pulled out her phone and placed it under her pillow. After completing its mission, his right hand transitioned smoothly to the back of her head. Eun-ho cupped the back of her head, which was small and oblong like a melon, and brought her face to his chest. He didn't feel like he would be able to act well while looking her in the eye.

"Let's get some sleep," Eun-ho said as he brought his lips to her forehead. Wife wrapped her arms around his waist and brought the rest of her body in contact with his. Tucking her hand under his shirt and stroking the vertebrae of his spine, she whispered to him:

"No. What we need is comfort, not sleep."

CHAPTER 6

Jane left work as soon as her meeting finished to come home to Jiyoo.

Jiyoo wasn't allowed back at school even after being discharged from the hospital. The school asked that she stay at home for another week before coming back. They didn't seem to understand when Jane told them that it wasn't contagious. Because of this, Jane had to find someone to look after Jiyoo while she was at work.

Jane still couldn't get in contact with Yuna. No one was picking up the home phone. And when she called Yuna's company, they said she was on her "annual leave." Of course, if she really needed to get in contact with Yuna, she could take Jiyoo to Cheongyeon and bust through the door. But Jane didn't consider this a valid option.

Jiyoo was precocious. She was sensitive, self-aware, and didn't express her emotions often. In Jane's opinion, this was an extremely dangerous combination. Jiyoo might conclude that neither her mother nor her aunt wanted her. She might think that she wasn't welcome anywhere, and this might lead her to question her own worth, just like Jane had as a young girl.

Jane needed to look for a nanny. The woman she found was far from satisfactory. She boasted three decades of experience as a professional nanny, but Jane doubted this. Everything about the woman, from her patronizing tone to her preference for wiping her hands on her pants instead of washing them with soap and water, was unbecoming of a "professional" nanny. In fact, the only thing she seemed to be an expert at was calculating overtime pay and refusing work that wasn't in the contract. But Jane didn't have a choice. Unprofessional nanny was the only person who contacted her back.

It was raining outside and the roads were jammed. Once Jane entered downtown Incheon, she got stuck in stop-and-go traffic. It probably would have been faster had she walked. Jane turned off the main road several times looking for a faster route, but always ended up in yet another line of cars.

Her phone started ringing. It was coming from her home phone. It was most likely the nanny calling to complain about Jane being late. The ringtone sounded like it was nagging at her: "Hurry up so I can go home!" Jane reluctantly answered the phone call.

"Miss Shin, you didn't tell me someone was coming today."

The nanny's shrill voice came out of the earpiece and pierced Jane's eardrum.

"What are you talking about?"

"If she steals something, don't ask me. I'm not responsible. If you keep doing this, I won't be able to work in this house much longer. You're always late. And today some strange woman barges in and starts tearing the place apart—"

Jane had no idea what she was talking about. But the nanny was talking too fast for Jane to interrupt her. She just listened patiently. Combining the bits and pieces she gleamed from the nanny's nagging, Jane figured that a woman claiming to be Jiyoo's mother had showed up at the apartment. She said she was here to take Jiyoo home. When the nanny told her to wait for Jane to get off work, the woman told the nanny to go into the kitchen and wait there. She said she was going to pack Jiyoo's bags, but what she was really doing was tearing the house apart. The nanny wanted to stop her, but the woman was acting like she owned the place; there was no stopping her. The woman didn't answer when the nanny asked questions. She seemed more like a debt collector than someone coming to pick up her daughter. The nanny asked Jiyoo, who confirmed the woman's identity.

"Nanny, hold on a second," Jane said, finally managing to cut her off. "Does Jiyoo's mother know that you're on the phone with me right now?"

"She's in the master bedroom and I'm in the kitchen. I doubt she can hear us. Does this happen often? You don't sound at all surprised."

Jane had no reason to be surprised. Cutting into someone's lane suddenly without signaling was a perfectly "Yuna" thing to do. Nor did Jane have any desire to stop Yuna. Even if she tried, it was impossible. Jane would only end up hurting herself.

"Nanny, don't tell Jiyoo's mother that you talked with me on the phone."

"You mean you're not coming?" Nanny asked in an irritated tone. It seemed like she had misinterpreted Jane's simple request.

"I'm on my way. It's just that there's a lot of traffic. I'll be there in under thirty minutes."

"You want me to wait here like this for another thirty minutes? Do you know what time it is?"

Jane looked at the clock. 7:35.

"Fine, you can go home."

Nanny hung up without replying to this. Jane could feel her grip on the wheel beginning to tense up.

Yuna's world consisted of three types of people. Winners, losers, and strangers. She treated you differently based on which type she thought you were. Winners she treated like her tongue; losers she bit with her canines; and strangers she avoided like bad breath. To Yuna, Jane was a loser. And it was a rule of Yuna's not to explain things to losers.

In other words, Yuna wouldn't explain to Jane where she had been or why she was picking up Jiyoo without any warning. Jane just had to accept it, just like she had to accept it when Yuna first texted her to pick up Jiyoo from preschool. But even so, Jane wanted to say bye to Jiyoo and get some information, although she wasn't sure if either of these would be possible.

The roads finally started to clear up. At the very least, Jane wasn't stuck in stop-and-go traffic anymore. She whipped in and out of her lane like a delivery moped, using her high beams to warn other drivers. The last time she had driven like this was the night her father died. Jane arrived in the underground apartment garage in just under ten minutes.

Her timing was perfect; Yuna was just walking out of the elevators, a travel suitcase in one hand and her cellphone in the other.

Jane got out of the car holding her coat and bag. Jiyoo, who was following closely behind Yuna and with a small suitcase of her own, saw Jane first. Startled, Jiyoo stopped walking. Instead of calling out to Jane, Jiyoo turned to look at the back of her mother's head. Yuna was distracted by her cellphone. Based on how fast her thumb was moving, Jane figured Yuna was sending someone a text message.

Jane closed her car door. The sound caused Yuna to look up from her phone. Her eyes locked onto Jane like a prison searchlight. She put her cellphone in her pocket and stopped walking. Jane stared right back at her.

Father Time had favored Yuna. It had been years since they last saw each other, but Yuna hadn't aged a day. Long black hair, porcelain-white skin, peach-colored cheeks, and long, straight calves that looked like they belonged to a ballerina.

Yuna pulled her suitcase along as she marched toward Jane, chin tucked in, back straight, and hair flowing. The sound of her high heels hitting the concrete stabbed Jane's ears like pistol gunshots. *Pop, pop, pop.*

Jiyoo hurried along behind Yuna with her head down. She looked like a court dwarf to a medieval queen. The sight of this disgusted Jane, but she couldn't look away. Jane put on her coat and hung the strap of her bag over her shoulder. She approached Jane the way the heavyweight champion of the world enters the ring to stare down his challenger. The parking lot wasn't particularly cold, but Jane's spine was shivering.

Soon, Yuna arrived in front of the BMW parked next to Jane's car. It just so happened that Jane had parked right next to Yuna's car.

Yuna gathered the hair that had fallen across her cheek and tucked it behind her ear. She then turned her body to face Jane. Simultaneously, she took her keys out of her coat pocket and unlocked the car doors. With her eyes fixed on Jane and moving only her lips, Yuna spoke to Jiyoo:

"Jiyoo Cha, get in the car."

Cha? Since when had she changed Jiyoo's last name? Had Joon-young consented to that?

"Should I sit in the front?" Jiyoo asked as she poked her head out from behind Yuna, like a shadow at dusk.

"No. In the back."

Jiyoo stepped out from behind Yuna. She bowed her head and pulled her eyelids back to look up at Jane. Her eyes then arched sideways to glance at Yuna. With hurried steps, Jiyoo disappeared around the car. A few seconds later, there was the sound of the car door opening. Yuna and Jane waited to hear the door close, but it never did.

"Jiyoo, close the door."

"Yes."

And with that, the door closed.

"Did you just get back from a run?" Yuna asked. "You look out of breath."

Yuna's eyes became slightly longer. The light flickering in her pupils resembled a grin. Jane had seen this look many times before when they were young. And every time she saw it, she wanted to smack it with a heavy book.

"Were you worried? Afraid I'd touch your things?"

Yuna was taunting her, but Jane could tell she was caught off guard by Jane's appearance. When Yuna was embarrassed or flustered, her defense mechanism was to mock people. Jane's suspicion that Yuna wanted to take Jiyoo while Jane was gone was right. But it wasn't because Yuna felt uncomfortable around Jane like the way Jane felt uncomfortable around Yuna. It was just that Yuna resented having to acknowledge Jane's existence with a hello.

"Are you taking Jiyoo for good?" Jane asked.

Yuna tilted her chin to the side as she made a slight sneer. Jane stared silently into Yuna's brown eyes, which were twinkling in the lights of the apartment garage. Jane had always been amazed at Yuna's mastery over conveying emotion with just her eyes. One moment, her eyes could be as cold and menacing as an ice pick, and the next they could be as dazzling as a starry night, or as brilliant as a beam of spring sunlight. Right now, Yuna's eyes were that of a cat that just found a defenseless bird.

"You did a good job looking after Jiyoo," Yuna said.

Jane took a silent breath. Yuna's tone was the kind someone might use to tell a housemaid to go home. Jane couldn't let this bother her. She knew that Yuna would use her reaction against her: *Why are you so sensitive? I was just trying to thank you.*

Jane erected a wall made of mirrors inside her mind so that she could deflect whatever Yuna said.

"Did Joon-young agree to changing Jiyoo's last name?"

Yuna answered this question with one of her own.

"What, you think you're her mom now just because you looked after her for a few days?"

Jane did Yuna one better.

"Does Jinu Kim know?"

Yuna didn't react to this. She just blinked twice in silence. Jane decided to push Yuna a bit further.

"I heard he graduated from the same school as you. Were you two close?"

"How do you know Jinu Kim?"

This meant she knew him. Jane nodded.

"I met him by chance while doing research for an article I'm writing. He said he's a friend of your husband, and of yours."

"What's your point?"

Jane was convinced now. "K," the friend Min-young was talking about, had to be Jinu Kim. Jane had done research and found that there were two biology teachers at Cheongyeon High School. Coincidentally they were both males and both about the same age as Eun-ho. The reason she picked Jinu Kim, and not the other man, was because of his last name. There was a higher probability that someone nicknamed "K" would have the last name Kim and not Park.

"No point. I just thought I'd mention it."

Jane decided this was her time to retreat. She couldn't make Yuna feel like she was on to her. At least, not yet.

"Should I tell Mom? That she can relax and stay until New Year's because you've taken Jiyoo back?"

"Do whatever you want."

Jane turned her head and examined the inside of Yuna's car. Jiyoo was sticking her head out through the space between the two front seats. As soon as Jane and her made eye contact, she withdrew in shock. Jane looked back at Yuna.

"Can I at least say goodbye to Jiyoo?" Jane asked. "I did look after her for the last ten days, you know."

"Like I said, do whatever you want."

Jane walked past Yuna toward Jiyoo. She opened the back door and stuck her head in as she pulled out her business card from her bag.

"Auntie," Jiyoo called out in quiet voice.

Jane suppressed the urge to hug Jiyoo. She didn't want to make things harder for Jiyoo than they needed to be. She knew it would make Yuna jealous and start interrogating Jiyoo about her loyalty: *Since when were you so close to your Aunt?*

"Bye, Jiyoo."

After this, Jane withdrew her body from the car. Not surprisingly, Yuna was staring blatantly in her direction. Taking the full brunt of Yuna's gaze, Jane returned to her previous spot. Afraid Yuna might feel left out, Jane gave her a farewell, too.

"Let's not cross paths again if we can help it."

Yuna squinted her eyes at Jane. Her lips moved slightly as though she were about to say something. Jane ignored this and started walking. When she arrived at the elevators, she glanced back to find Yuna opening the driver's side door.

Just like the nanny had said, the house looked like a debt-collector had come through. But as Jane expected, it was way worse than that. Old sneakers, summer sandals, slippers—all Jiyoo's shoes were scattered across the floor. Her room was also a mess. The closet and drawers had been turned inside out and stripped of all Jiyoo's winter apparel: coats, padded jackets, sweaters, scarves, hats, gloves, earmuffs. On the bed were all the other articles of clothing that Yuna decided not to take.

The desk drawers were either open or had been completely removed from the desk. Yuna had gone through everything, it looked like. Crayons, pencils, colored pencils, sketch books—everything was in one big pile. Jiyoo's school bag was under the desk, and the art set that Jane had bought Jiyoo was lying wide open on the ground.

Jane went into the living room to find a similar scene. The doors to the cabinets were all open. Even Mom's room hadn't been spared Yuna's wrath. The album she kept in the closet had been dragged all the way out to the middle of the floor. This didn't look like the work of someone who was simply trying to pack their things. It was clear that Yuna had torn the house apart looking for something.

But what?

Jane's cleaning started in Jiyoo's room. She reorganized all the items in the drawers and hung the clothes piled on the bed back into the closet. She returned Apeach to its proper place. It was then that Jane noticed Dad Puppet. He was lodged between the top of mattress and the bedframe.

Last Thursday, after being in the hospital for three days, Jiyoo asked Jane to bring her Dad Puppet.

"And where is Dad Puppet?" Jane asked, pretending not to know what Jiyoo was talking about.

"In my school bag."

Jane brought her the puppet. Jiyoo didn't let go of the puppet once after that. Nor did she really play with it. She just hugged it tight or put it on her finger and stared into its eyes. To Jane, it looked like Jiyoo was in constant conversations with the puppet—both when she was awake and when she was asleep. Strangely enough, Jiyoo stopped having nightmares after that.

"Jiyoo, are you not having any more bad dreams?"

"Yes. Dad Puppet is protecting me."

Jiyoo wouldn't leave Dad Puppet behind if she didn't have to. It was clear that Jiyoo had hidden the puppet from its original owner. Another way of saying this was that Jiyoo had stolen the puppet from Yuna.

Yuna didn't share, not even if it was just borrowing. She hated people touching her things. Jane thought it might be different if it was with her own daughter. But she had been wrong. People don't change that easily. Jane placed the puppet back where she found it so that Jiyoo could find it later.

Jane went into the master bedroom. The picture album, which was in the center of the mess, grabbed Jane's attention again. It was open to a page with two pictures of Jiyoo. Earlier, Jane had passed this by without much thought. But now she realized what it meant. It was telling her that Yuna had been looking for Jiyoo's passport.

On her way out of the country, their mom had brought Jiyoo's passport with her to the airport, hopeful that Yuna and Jiyoo might show up before she left for Russia alone. She only handed it to Jane at the last possible moment, requesting that she hide it inside the family picture album. The album was open right to the place where Jane had hidden the passport.

Jane was amazed by Yuna's tenacity. How had she found it? How could she even have guessed it would be there? But Jane's astonishment quickly turned to confusion. What could Yuna want Jiyoo's passport for? Surely, she wasn't planning on taking Jiyoo to Russia to see their mother.

Jane decided to call her mom while this was still on her mind. As soon as she picked up the phone, she started quizzing Jane.

"Jane, where do you think I am right now?"

It sounded like she was talking with a mouth full of food. Jane wasn't in the mood for a quiz, but she humored her anyway.

"A restaurant?"

"Wrong!"

She was on a high-speed train headed for St. Petersburg. She bragged about how Russian trains were like airlines, complete with attendants, meals, and free coffee. Jane didn't ask, but her mom told her all about the itinerary for their four-day trip.

"The first thing we're going to do when we arrive in St. Petersburg is visit Henri Matisse's paintings. Then we'll have dinner at a fancy restaurant, after which we're planning on going to see Swan Lake at the Mariinsky Theatre. I'm crossing off two items from my bucket list in one day. Isn't that amazing?"

Jane didn't want to ruin her mood. But she didn't necessarily have the patience to listen to this boasting. Plus, international phone calls weren't exactly cheap.

"Mom, I have something to ask you. Can you go out into the hallway?"

Jane's mom did as she was told but seemed confused.

"Okay, you can talk now. I'm in the hallway. What's wrong?"

"On the day Dad died, you mentioned that Yuna had dropped by the house, right?"

She said this was true.

"Did Yuna mention the divorce that day?"

"Yuna said that Joon-young had left the house and filed for a divorce. But why do you ask? That was years ago."

"I'll tell you why later. Tell me first what happened that day when Yuna came by the house."

Yuna had showed up at the house that morning with Jiyoo. Noticing a bandage on Yuna's hand, Mom asked what happened. Yuna said she and Joon-young had a big fight because she found out that he had molested Jiyoo. He picked up a knife and was threatening to kill himself and Yuna. Yuna cut her hand while trying to stop him. He left the house after that and filed for a divorce. This was all according to Yuna.

"I couldn't believe it. Joon-young of all people. He should have gotten on his knees and begged for forgiveness. Then again, what he did was unforgiveable."

Mom said he had no right leaving the house and asking for a divorce. She had treated Joon-young like her own son and felt a deep sense of betrayal. Her heart almost exploded from sadness when she heard what he did to Jiyoo. If only she could get ahold of him, she would have cut off his hands.

But Yuna didn't show up at their parents' home to ask for revenge. She merely came to drop off Jiyoo. She explained that she was planning on going to Vladivostok for about a week and needed a safe place for Jiyoo to stay. Mom agreed to look after Jiyoo without a moment's hesitation. If Yuna wanted to go off the grid for a while to figure things out, she was all for it. What Mom didn't know was that Jiyoo would be staying with her for the next several years.

"Did you believe everything Yuna said?"

"Why wouldn't I? My own daughter showed up at my door with her hand slashed to pieces." The temperature of Mom's voice suddenly dropped several degrees. "Jane, do you still hate Yuna?"

It wasn't a matter of hating or liking her. Yuna was a bitch and everyone, even Jane's mom, knew it. As far as Jane knew, Yuna might even be clinically insane. Jane suppressed the desire to say this out loud.

"Did Yuna not tell you then that she quit the company?"

"What are you talking about? She was the company's head accountant!"

"But then how could she leave for an entire week? And without any prior notice? Did Dad give her permission to take time off?"

"Did he give her permission? He was the one who was most in favor of it! When she told him what Joon-young did to Jiyoo, he told her to leave Jiyoo with us and take as much time as she wanted. He said he would take care of everything in her absence. But then he got into that accident..."

Jane nodded. She felt like she was looking at a tower of cards. If one lie was out of place, it would all come crumbling down to the ground. But Jane found it hard to believe that Yuna could spin such an elaborate web of lies. The fact that she hadn't been caught in a contradiction, not once, must mean she possessed an incredible memory.

"But why are you asking me about these things now?" Mom's tone then turned to one of disgust. "And why are you making trouble again? What did you hear?"

Again? Jane had no memory of ever making trouble, especially not when it involved Yuna. She had lived her entire adult life without ever speaking the name Yuna Shin. Jane understood this question as a plea to stop digging. But Jane had other plans.

"You can go, Mom. Auntie will get suspicious if you're away for too long."

"Don't mess with Yuna. She's finally happy. Don't you even feel bad for her?"

Why was Yuna the only one Mom ever felt bad for? Jane felt a mix of anger and sadness.

"Bye, Mom."

After hanging up, Jane sent a text message to her aunt.

—Auntie, it's Jane. I have something I want to ask you. My mom can't know. I'll call you in twenty minutes. Go out into the hallway to take my call.

Twenty minutes later, Jane's aunt pretended to answer the phone in Russian. After that, Jane could hear her aunt telling Mom in Korean that she was going to take a phone call.

"Jane, what did you say to your mother? She came back all red in the face and has been talking to herself ever since."

The way Jane's aunt was whispering gave Jane the feeling that she was enjoying the drama. At least someone found this amusing. Jane could imagine what her mom was saying to herself: *Spiteful child, trying to ruin what little happiness her younger sister has.* Jane cut straight to the point.

"Auntie, you said that Yuna's Russian boyfriend died in an accident just before Yuna returned to Korea, right?"

"Hm?"

Just like Mom, she sounded confused by this question from the past.

"Did her boyfriend fall asleep at the wheel?"

"Did I tell you that?" Jane's aunt seemed shocked.

"Didn't you?"

"Well, that's what the black box suggested."

"He was your TA, right?"

"Yes. I acted as his guardian until his parents came to Moscow."

Jane summarized the story for her aunt to fact check.

"He was living with Yuna at her apartment, right? And they were planning on getting married. But then he changed his mind. He packed up his bags and then died in a car accident. Is that right?"

"Why do you need to ask me this behind your mother's back? Your mother knows the story, too."

"You know my mom."

"So you're not going to tell me why you're asking these questions?"

"I'll tell you later. And one more question. What was his name?"

"Istvan."

After hanging up, Jane sunk into the chair. Entering her field of view was the family picture hanging next to the China cabinet. Four people sitting on four blue metal chairs placed side by side in front of a white wall. Sitting in the center were Mom and Dad, dressed in matching blue shirts and white pants. Jane was sitting next to her mom, in a shirt and pants, but with the colors reversed.

Yuna's place was next to Dad. A dense head of lustrous hair covered her back. She was wearing a white dress that exposed her shoulders and was holding a single blue balloon. The photo had been taken for their dad's sixtieth birthday, but because of Yuna's white dress, it looked more like Yuna's wedding photoshoot.

Yuna was twenty-two at the time and a senior in college. If what Min-young told Jane was true, then Yuna would have been living with her boyfriend at the time, the one who was driving with Jinu when he died in a car crash. But Jane needed confirmation. If it was true…

Dark storm clouds formed inside Jane's mind. She felt like she was standing in front of a door to a foreign world. She was almost at the threshold, but she wanted to turn around. It felt like once she opened the door, there would be no going back. She might lose Jiyoo, her mom, and everything else she cared about. She might even lose the solid earth upon which she was standing.

Jane hunched over on the table with her face buried in the wood. She was trying to prevent her feelings toward Yuna from drawing her in. It didn't work. A song was playing in her ear. A beautiful baritone voice. Fingers tapping on the steering wheel.

Maria, Maria, you are my love, Maria...
After I sent you far away, I planted a flower
I planted a flower in my weeping heart...

*

Jane sat inside the interrogation room of the Seodaemun Police Station. She was waiting for Detective Gibeom Kim. He was already twenty minutes late.

Before Jane transferred to culture and arts, she worked for ten years in local news. Back then, she spent more time waiting at the police station than she did working at the office. Despite knowing why the police isolated people in the interrogation room for long periods of time, Jane couldn't help but feel anxious and angry.

Jane's senses were focused on what was going on outside of the interrogation room. She could hear every voice and every footstep in the hallway. As someone who used to frequent the police station, Jane thought she could handle being interrogated without batting an eyelash, but now that she was here, she realized she was mistaken. It was completely different coming to the police station as a witness, or even potential suspect.

Jane got the call to come to the police station earlier that morning. She was at the press center, and the press conference for the new book of a so-called "writer of the people" was just about to stop. The man on the line revealed himself as Detective Gibeom Kim from Violent Crimes at the Seodaemun Police Department. He asked if she knew Joon-young Seo.

"I do."

"We have a few questions for you," he said without any further preamble. "Can you come down to the police station this afternoon?"

"May I ask why?"

He told her that Joon-young had been missing since the 16th. Jane felt the chair she was sitting in begin to shake. Even though she had anticipated the detective's answer, it still managed to rattle her. Jane had been hoping desperately she wouldn't get this phone call. But now that she had, it was clear something had happened to Joon-young. It also meant that they knew she had met with Joon-young the morning he was last seen. If they didn't know, they wouldn't have any reason to call her. Adding to Jane's sense of unease was the fact that Detective Kim worked in Violent Crimes.

"And what am I being summoned to the police station as?"

"A witness," he said. "Can you come in right now?"

"I can't right now. I'll be there by six."

Jane knew that she could delay her visit to the police station by a few days if she wanted to, but she didn't. If she had to pull off a Band-Aid, might as well get it over with quickly. Plus, Jane had already prepared herself mentally for the pain.

Jane knew she could get a lawyer, but she didn't want to because, at least for now, she wasn't a suspect. Jane put her materials on the desk: a piece of paper waiving her right to counsel, a notepad, a pen, and her cellphone, which was switched to airplane mode and ready to record the conversation. And at the front of her brain, ready to be summoned at a moment's notice, were the answers that she had been rehearsing all last week in anticipation of this. Jane went over these answers one last time to calm her nerves and kill time.

But it didn't help. When the middle-aged detective came into the room followed by his young sidekick, Jane's heart started racing like a horse. She lifted her body out of the chair. Afraid that her voice might shake if she greeted them verbally, she just looked at them in silence.

The middle-aged detective came over and stood across from her on the other side of the table. Putting both hands in his pants pockets, he met her eyes head on, as if to push back her gaze. He looked like he wasn't interested in introducing himself. Instead, the young detective who followed him in gave her a naïve smile.

"Sorry to make you wait. Something came up. Please, sit."

Jane sat down, but the middle-aged detective didn't. Standing there, he turned his chin sideways and inspected the things she had placed on the table, as though he had never seen someone come to an interrogation so prepared. Jane felt the fire in her reignite. Not only was he twenty-five minutes late, but now he was wasting even more of her time by acting needlessly tough.

"Thank you for so willingly coming down to the station like this," the young detective said as he sat down.

According to him, the middle-aged detective was the one she talked on the phone with earlier: Detective Gibeom Kim. With his introduction out of the way, they went right into checking her personal information. They asked her for her identification number, her name, her occupation, etc. After that, they informed her that she had the right to a lawyer and could refuse to answer questions at any time. Then, in a perfunctory tone of voice, he asked her if she would be exercising these rights. As far as Jane knew, they didn't do this for just any witness. Their asking these questions meant that she was actually a suspect.

"I'll exercise my rights as necessary."

The young detective looked back and forth between Jane and Detective Kim.

"Oh, yes, of course—" he said with his mouth half-open like an idiot.

"Also, can I record this?"

Jane picked up her cellphone and showed it to them. This time, it was Detective Kim who responded.

"Like a true journalist, always recording everything."

Although he didn't give her permission, he also hadn't said no. Jane pressed the button to start recording. Detective Kim's eyes followed her finger as she did this. It felt like his gaze would burn a hole through her fingernail if it lingered for too long. But Jane didn't sense any hostility in his eyes. His demeanor was simply informing her that he wasn't her friend, that it was his job to prove people guilty.

Jane felt the gears in her head starting to move. And like magic her shaking stopped.

"Jane, do you know why you're here?" the young detective asked. His tone made him sound like a missionary for some pseudo religion: *Do you know the Dao?* Missionaries like that always came in twos. If he was the cute one meant to make you drop your guard, Detective Kim was the tough one who started pressing you to join.

"No."

The young detective summarized what they knew about Joon-young's disappearance. He was last seen leaving his house in the early morning on November 16; they found his car parked at a public parking lot near Ju-an station in Incheon; they confirmed that the car had been parked there around 8 a.m. on the morning he was last seen; and they were treating this like a criminal investigation. Jane waited for them to continue.

"We want to hear where you were and what you were doing the morning of his disappearance," Detective Kim said.

"I left the house at around 8 a.m. That morning I went to Chungju to do research for an article."

Jane continued explaining what happened that day. But despite having practiced this many times before, the testimony coming out of her mouth wasn't at all organized. As a precaution, she wrote down everything she said on her notepad. Her rate of speech was half its normal speed, and her sentences sounded more like written language than spoken speech.

"So let me see if I got everything. You left the house around 8 a.m. Twenty minutes later you met Joon-young at Ju-an station. You then drove him to Chungju, and while you were gone from the car for a minute, he disappeared without a word. So you called him, but he didn't answer. Is that right?"

After writing down Detective Kim's summary on her notepad, she checked the information before correcting him.

"No. I said I was gone for four hours. He left me a message saying something came up. After that, I didn't try contacting him. So, I don't know if he would have picked up or not."

Detective Kim pulled the corners of his mouth into a wide grin. Crooked lion's teeth poked out between the gap in his lips.

"Isn't that what I said?"

She didn't answer this.

"What's your relationship to each other. You must be close to go to Chungju with him and let him take a nap in your car."

"I told you he's a friend from college."

"I heard he's your ex-boyfriend and he married your sister." Detective Kim looked at the young detective. "Sounds like a soap opera, doesn't it?"

Jane didn't react to this. All she did was record this comment on her notepad. She was hoping he might hold his tongue, but he seemed to have no intention of pulling punches. Detective Kim grinned at her again before continuing.

"It seems to me like you've been seeing your ex-boyfriend all this time, the man your sister married. Is that right?"

"I can't answer that question."

Detective Kim propped his cheek on his hand and stared brazenly at Jane, who used all her energy not to avert his gaze. This stalemate continued for a while. *Tick-tock, tick-tock.*

Detective Kim started over from the beginning. Jane for her part would glance down at her notes and repeat her answers from before as if reading a script. Getting angry or making any unnecessary comments would only hurt her. The more energy she allowed her emotions to consume, the greater the chance she would slip up. This was also the only way to get out of here faster. She had to repeat the same answers until the lion got sick and tired of her.

"Can you show me the text message Joon-young sent you?"

Jane paused her recording and looked for the message. Detective Kim glanced momentarily at the cellphone she gave him before returning it to her.

"Would you mind sending me a screenshot of that? I want to take a closer look at it later."

He talked as if she had just sent him a ten-page report. After taking a screen shot of the text exchange, she sent it to the number he gave her.

"At what time did you read the text message?" Detective Kim asked as he fiddled with his phone.

"Around 3 p.m."

"You said you got out of the car at 11 a.m. And this text message arrived at 11:04. You mean to tell me you didn't check your phone for four hours?"

"I put my phone in airplane mode just before going into the museum. I can't concentrate if I get phone calls while working. I'm required to record interviews."

Jane held up her phone and showed it to them.

"Just like this."

Aha . . . Detective Kim mouthed before changing the subject.

"Do you know Min-young Seo?"

"I do."

"She told us she met you last Monday."

"That's true."

"She said you hid from her the fact that you met Joon-young. Why?"

"I never hid it from her. She never gave me a chance to speak. I guess she didn't tell you the scene she made when she showed up at my workplace."

Detective Kim tapped on the desk with the side of his thumb as he stared at her. His facial expression was saying, *You tell me.* Jane agreed to this, but she spoke as casually as she could, and only gave him the most basic details.

"I find it hard to believe you ran away just because of a little disagreement. Did you record that, too? I'd like to hear what was said."

Jane didn't answer this. But he continued to push her buttons.

"What? You don't have it? I thought you were a journalist!"

"If you're so curious about what happened, then you can ask the staff who were working at the café that day."

Detective Kim didn't look that interested after all. He skillfully moved on to the next question.

"Min-young sent you an email asking for help the next day. You could have told her then."

Jane focused in on his choice of words. He said "Min-young sent" not "Min-young said she sent." The former implied that he had seen the email himself, and the latter implied that he'd only heard about it. Jane had to check to see if she was correct.

"Did you read the email?"

Detective Kim didn't respond. Jane took this as meaning he had.

"It was a hard email to reply to."

"You didn't tell her because she hurt your feelings—that's what you're saying? Come on, Jane. This is someone's life we're talking about. Can't you put your feelings aside?"

There was contempt in his tone. Jane's brain was telling her to ignore this, but her emotions took a direct hit. Her face became flush, as though someone had lit her skin on fire. Not only was she pissed, but she could also feel her eyeballs bulging. Her fingers, which were holding the ballpoint pen, tensed up. Her handwriting as she wrote on the notepad suddenly became messy, as though the pen were slipping on ice.

There were three reasons why she didn't reply to Min-young's email. The first was shock. In fact, she was still shocked by what Min-young had told her.

The second was blood ties. No matter how much she despised Yuna, she was still her sister. So Jane's natural inclination was to be a defense lawyer for Yuna, not a prosecutor. From this point of view, everything Min-young told her was circumstance and conjecture. She had no physical proof that Yuna had done anything.

The third reason was an emotional one. Simply put, she didn't want to help Min-young. She knew Min-young didn't know how to say thank you. Worse yet, if she did tell Min-young that she had met Joon-young, she would never hear the end of it. Min-young would chase Jane around and demand to know why she didn't tell her the truth from the beginning. In fact, this was probably the reason why Jane was sitting in the police interrogation room right now.

In the end, Jane had decided to wait things out. She knew that the police would step in if Joon-young really was missing. And if the police found out she had met Joon-young the day he disappeared, she could tell the truth to them directly. She had hoped the police would be more sensible than Min-young. But she had hoped in vain.

"Are your feelings really that important?" Detective Kim wanted an answer to this question.

"I'm not going to answer that."

Detective Kim turned his head to look at the wall. Jane could almost hear him clicking his tongue.

"Look, Jane. You were the only person to see Joon-young that day. He disappeared after you two met. Do you know what that means?"

Hearing this, Jane realized they must not have any evidence on Yuna. If Yuna had been caught on camera, they wouldn't be questioning Jane like this. If indeed Yuna had taken Joon-young to the cabin in Woohyeri, then she did a fantastic job of avoiding the network of CCTV cameras.

"Miss Shin?"

"I think your timeline is off. There's one person who talked on the phone with him after he got out of my car."

"And who's that?" Detective Kim asked with an unphased look on his face.

"The person who made the missing person report. I guess she didn't tell you. From what she told me, she last talked with Joon-young at around 2 p.m. that day. I was in an interview at that time."

"What kind of interview takes that long?"

Jane reached into her bag and pulled out her business card wallet. Thankfully, the museum employee's business card was at the very front.

"You can ask the person I interviewed that day. They will corroborate my alibi."

Detective Kim took the card and looked at it for a moment before stashing it in his pocket.

"While we're on the topic, I would like you to tell us if what Min-young said in her email was true."

"There was only one thing Min-young said that was factual. My dad died in a car accident. The rest of what she said are her own assertions."

"But it's also true that he dated you and then married your sister Yuna. And because of that, she said you cut ties with your sister."

Jane thought for a moment. Why was he continuing to push this narrative that she and Joon-young dated? Did he not understand the meaning of the word friend? Were they trying to frame this as an act of revenge by some resentful past lover? That *would* be the easiest thing for them to do.

"And on top of that, you kept meeting Joon-young behind your sister's back? This sounds more and more like one of those morning soap operas."

Jane bit down on the inside of her lip. She had to maintain her composure, even if it meant drawing her own blood. If she didn't, she would be engulfed by the fireball raging inside her chest.

"I told you that was the first time I'd seen him in seven years."

Detective Kim nodded his head slightly as if to say, *Of course you did.*

"Okay, so you met your old boyfriend for the first time in seven years. But nothing happened between you two. He just slept in your car until you left for an interview and then disappeared? Tell me, would *you* believe this story?"

Jane steadied her breathing.

"Whether you believe it or not, it's the truth."

The sound of nails on dry hair filled the room as Detective Kim scratched his temple with this index finger.

"And how am I supposed to believe that Joon-young left your car like you said he did?"

"I showed you the text message."

"It's not hard to forge a text message."

"Where was the last place his cellphone had service? Was it Chungju? According to what Min-young told me, Joon-young was in Kyochon when she last talked with him on the phone. At that time, I was inside Chungju Literature Museum."

Detective Kim tilted his head to the side as he looked down.

"I'm not sure that proves you weren't the last person to be with him."

Jane desperately wanted to tell them that they were talking to the wrong person, that they should be questioning Yuna, not her. But she just bit her tongue. It wasn't time yet to talk about that. Jane wasn't planning on voicing her suspicions until she knew exactly how everything was connected.

For now, her lips weren't sealed because Yuna was family, but because most of the information she had was based off rumors. If she jumped to conclusions based on circumstantial evidence, there would be no telling what kind of damage the shockwaves would cause. If she wasn't careful, Jiyoo, Mom, and herself would all be sucked into this.

"I think that's a question you can answer by asking the taxi driver who drove him to Kyochon."

Detective Kim tilted his head in a confused manner.

"Why are you so sure he took a taxi to Kyochon?"

"I doubt he took the bus. If he left at 11 a.m., he wouldn't have enough time to get there by 2 p.m. if he took the bus."

Detective Kim studied Jane's eyes for a while. She didn't look away.

"Fine. We can talk about that again later."

Detective Kim finally broke eye contact and looked at his notes.

"Where did you go after leaving Chungju?"

"Home."

"You stayed there until morning?"

"Yes."

"Is there anyone who can corroborate that?"

"No."

"Why not?"

This time it was Jane who tilted her head to the side in confusion.

"Because I was alone."

Aha . . . Detective Kim nodded. He bared his lion's teeth again as he grinned. Jane had the feeling she had made a mistake. But she couldn't figure out what they knew that she didn't.

"What did you do at home alone?"

"I worked on an article until two in the morning. This is something you can confirm for yourself, you know."

"Oh, really? Please tell me." Detective Kim crossed his arms and leaned back against his chair.

"Check the apartment CCTV. You'll see me drive into the apartment parking garage. If I had left my house before morning, it would be on the tape."

Detective Kim hit his forehead sarcastically as if to say, *Really? Why didn't I think of that?*

Jane was seconds away from stabbing him in the forehead with her pen. Had her hands been above the table, she might have done it, too. Jane crossed her legs and switched sitting positions.

That night, she finally realized why anyone would confess to a crime they hadn't committed. Detective Kim repeated the same questions and made her give the same testimony over and over for hours. She must have told him ten times about what she did after leaving Chungju. By the time the interrogation finished it was late into the night, and Jane felt nauseous just hearing Detective Kim's voice.

"Would like to read over our report, ma'am?"

This was the first time in hours the young detective had opened his mouth. Jane said she would. A minute later, they gave her a printed copy. Even the first sentence had been twisted to reflect their own bias.

"The subject of this sentence is wrong," Jane said as she pointed to the error with her pen. "It was Joon-young who called me. Not the other way around."

It took another hour to compare notes. The whole time, Jane found it hard to concentrate because Detective Kim was talking to himself for everyone to hear.

"What patience to keep one's lips sealed this whole time . . . despite knowing Joon-young was thought missing . . . and only she opens her mouth when we call her in."

Jane didn't know what his point was. Even if she wanted to share what she knew, it wasn't as easy as just opening her mouth and declaring it to the world. She didn't know at which police station Min-young made her report. Jane couldn't just go to any old police station and say she had information about the Joon-young Seo case. And besides, Min-young said the police dismissed her when she first tried to make a report. Until Jane knew the police were actually investigating Joon-young's disappearance, there was no reason for her to go to the police. And even if she did go to the police, what could she say? *I'm the last person who saw the missing person Joon-young Seo?*

Jane signed the report and handed it back to Detective Kim.

"One more question, Miss Shin. Would you show us your car's black box?"

This caught Jane by surprise. Why hadn't she thought about that before? Although, she doubted her black box went that far back in time. In fact, she was positive the footage had been written over by now. But perhaps forensics could retrieve the data. With the two detectives following her, she walked them to her car in the parking lot. Detective Kim received the black box from her car and then took a step back.

"We'll have a look and get back to you. It might take a few days."

The two men watched her as she left the parking lot.

Jane felt nauseous as she entered the river of cars. Her vision was blurry, and every muscle in her body was pulsing with built-up tension. Both her body and mind felt tattered and frayed.

Jane wanted to go straight to Woohyeri. Perhaps she should have gone there first. The problem was, she didn't have time. She was just too busy. Her sudden absence from work had left her with a lot to get caught up on. And after work, she was completely tied up with taking care of Jiyoo.

Jiyoo's lips were tight. Yuna must have instructed her beforehand not to talk about what happened at the cabin. No matter what kind of question Jane asked—direct, indirect, leading—Jiyoo wouldn't say. And Jane couldn't press Jiyoo. In the end, Jane was unable to get a single clue about the whereabouts of Joon-young.

And yet, it was clear to Jane that, at the very least, Joon-young had been and stayed at that cabin. But to get proof, she would need to go to Woohyeri. If she didn't do this soon, Detective Kim with his lion's teeth would be reciting the Miranda warning to her.

*

It was Saturday morning. Jane's body felt as stiff and heavy as a century-old tree, but she jumped right out of bed as soon as she opened her eyes. She had a lot to do today. Places to be, people to meet.

Jane had a cup of coffee for breakfast as she got ready to leave. But unlike her usual routine of makeup and nice clothes, she got ready by finding and putting on comfortable clothes that she could move in—beanie, face mask, sweater, leggings, and padded jacket. She put her wallet, lanyard, and cellphone in her coat pocket. Then finally she took out her zip-up high-top canvas shoes. As she did this, she felt something buzzing in her pocket.

Jane pulled out her cellphone. The caller ID said "Yuna's House." But Jane knew it wasn't Yuna. She had no reason to call Jane. Even less likely was Eun-ho. Jane pressed the accept button.

"Hello?"

"Auntie—" It was Jiyoo. Her voice was quiet and cautious, as though she were calling while lying next to a sleeping lioness.

It was at this moment that Jane realized something. She missed Jiyoo. The warm sensation in her chest was telling her this.

Jane was so caught off guard by her own emotions that she didn't answer Jiyoo. She was embarrassed. Why was she getting so emotional? Jiyoo had only been gone a few days. These emotions were something Jane thought herself incapable of feeling anymore. Jane thought herself a pile of dead leaves, too dry to produce a single drop of moisture. She'd felt like this ever since Dad died.

"Auntie, it's me—Jiyoo."

This time, Jiyoo's voice was even quieter.

"Yes, I know."

Jane wanted to bite her tongue. Was that all she could say? *Yes, I know*? Couldn't she think of something more affectionate to say? Even something as simple as "Hi, Jiyoo" would have been better.

"Auntie, are you busy today?"

Not surprisingly, Jiyoo was being considerate of people who weren't even around. Jane needed to act more enthusiastic to let Jiyoo know she wasn't bothering her.

"Not at all! It's Saturday, after all. I don't have anything to do. I was so bored and sleepy that I've been just twiddling my thumbs all morning."

Jane could hear a quiet giggle over the receiver. This shy laughter immediately put a smile on Jane's face.

"Jiyoo, does this mean you kept Auntie's business card?"

"Actually, I tore it up into really tiny pieces and threw it away. I memorized your phone number."

"Really?" Jane asked in genuine surprise.

"Really! I can show you—"

Jiyoo carefully recited each digit of Jane's phone number. Jane's lips pursed as the smile on her face turned bittersweet. Jane knew Jiyoo had done this to hide the card from Yuna.

"Is that right?" Jiyoo asked after she said the last digit.

Jane's facial expression changed again as a chuckle escaped her lips. *If it was wrong, would you be talking on the phone with me right now?*

"I practiced five times before tearing it up. I wrote the number on a piece of paper without looking at the card. But don't worry. I wrote it down—somewhere only I can find it."

Jiyoo's characteristically careful explanation made Jane chuckle one more time.

"But Auntie . . . I'm really sorry."

Caught off guard by this apology, Jane stopped laughing.

"What for?"

"I didn't take the art set you bought for me. Mother wouldn't—"

Jiyoo stopped mid-sentence as though she had just remembered something. Jane didn't ask her what she was going to say. She knew that Yuna forbade Jiyoo from taking the art set because Jane had bought it for her.

"It's okay. You can always play with it the next time you come over."

"Auntie, I might never go back there."

The remaining smile on Jane's lips evaporated.

"Is that what your mother said?"

"Yes." She sounded sad.

"Jiyoo, you don't like being at that house, do you?"

"No? It's not that." Jiyoo's voice perked up again. "It's just that I'm scared at night. I have to sleep alone."

"But you're alone when you sleep here, too."

"That's because Grandma's house is an apartment. Grandma's room is right next to mine. And so is yours, Auntie. But here I sleep alone on the second floor. And the room across from me is Noah's. I see his room as soon as I open my door. That's why—"

Jiyoo stopped again mid-sentence. But this time, it didn't sound like she was afraid of saying something off-limits. It sounded like she was contemplating whether to tell Jane the truth. Jane decided to help Jiyoo:

"You've been having dreams, huh?"

"Yes. Noah comes out of his room and keeps knocking on my door. He screams at me, asking for his soccer ball."

Jane had already heard about the soccer ball incident from Jiyoo. Even though Jane told Jiyoo it wasn't her fault, Jiyoo continued to blame herself. She seemed to believe that if she had given him back his ball, he wouldn't have had that asthma attack. And if he hadn't had that asthma attack, he wouldn't have died. The nightmare about the soccer ball had to be a result of her guilt. Jane offered her a solution.

"How about asking your mother to change rooms with you?"

"No, that won't work."

Jane didn't ask why. She didn't need to. Yuna never allowed her decisions to be changed by another person's will. Or perhaps it would be more accurate to say that she despised the will of others. Jiyoo had probably picked up on this from years of experience. Jane offered an alternative solution.

"Then should I bring you Dad Puppet?"

"Yes."

Jiyoo's response came out of her mouth like a bullet.

"If you want to come," Jiyoo added suddenly, as though she felt embarrassed for revealing her true intentions so easily.

Jane needed to go to Cheongyeon for something else anyway. But now that she also needed to bring Jiyoo her puppet, she had no choice but to drop by the house. The only problem was that she needed to give Jiyoo the puppet without

Yuna's knowing.

"Jiyoo, is your mother home?"

"No."

"What about your stepfather?"

"No, he's not home either."

Jane looked at the clock. 10:50. She quickly calculated the time it would take to get there. Five minutes to the gas station, five minutes to fill up, and then an hour to Cheongyeon.

"I'll be there by noon."

"But Auntie, do you know where Dad Puppet is?"

"I do."

Jane arrived outside Yuna's house a few minutes past noon. She was five minutes late because she stopped at McDonald's. After parking across the street, Jane got out of the car with Dad Puppet and a Happy Meal.

The weather that day was unusually windy and cold. Even the sky was an ashen color. Dead leaves were tumbling across the house's blue roof. Perhaps it would snow later today.

Jane ran across the street. She even ran up the front steps. The front door was opening just as she approached it. Jiyoo ran outside. She jumped into Jane's arms and let out a small cheer.

"Auntie!"

Jane reflexively pressed Jiyoo into her chest.

"Auntie, Auntie, Auntie—"

Jiyoo wrapped her arms around Jane's waist and buried her cheek in Jane's ribs as she continued to call out to her. Just like last Monday when Jane came to pick her up from preschool, Jiyoo's calls sounded like a feeble whimper. Jane glanced up at the second-story window. Three windows lined the wall of the house.

Which belonged to Jiyoo's room? Whichever one it was, Jane was sure that Jiyoo had been staring out her window waiting for Jane. Five minutes would have felt like fifty to her. Jiyoo had run out in her bare feet and was dressed in a white dress that revealed her white ankles.

"I thought you were never coming."

Jiyoo removed her cheek from Jane's stomach and looked up at her.

"I told you I would."

"But still."

Jane put Dad Puppet in Jiyoo's hand.

"Think of a place your mother won't find it. The crack between your bed and the wall is too dangerous."

"I know. A secret place—"

Jiyoo paused. Judging from the way Jiyoo's eyes were getting wider, Jane could tell that she finally understood the meaning of her words.

"You knew?" Jiyoo asked.

"Don't worry. I'll keep it a secret."

Jane held out the Happy Meal. Jiyoo's eyes grew with excitement.

"You said no one was home, didn't you?"

Instead of saying thank you, Jiyoo just looked down at the bag of fast food.

"I told them not to include the toy. Remember to get rid of the wrappers when you're done. Do you remember what I taught you about folding the paper box?"

"Yes. Fold it until it's flat, then put it in the trash. My stepfather takes out the trash."

Jane took a step backwards.

"Well, young lady. Go inside and hide him in your secret place."

Despite nodding, Jiyoo didn't move.

"If you need anything, call me. I'll keep my phone on for you."

Jane took another step backwards and down the front steps.

"I'm leaving."

Jiyoo didn't move. One step, and then another. Jiyoo continued to watch until Jane turned around and crossed the street to her car.

Jane stopped in front of her car and looked back at Jiyoo. Long tangled hair, the hem of her white dress fluttering in the cold wind, slender calves and bare feet, holding Dad Puppet in one arm and a Happy Meal in the other, staring quietly out at Jane.

Jane could feel something cold spreading inside her chest. Everything surrounding Jiyoo looked melancholic. The large two-story house towering behind her, the dead leaves tumbling about on the roof, the ashen sky—even the cypress on the front porch positioned like Jiyoo's shadow looked depressing. Jane thought she could hear Jiyoo whisper something to her.

Auntie, don't touch Mother.

A question popped into Jane's head, one that she should have asked herself before. If what she feared turned out to be true, and Jiyoo lost her mother, how would Jiyoo handle it?

The answer was "not well." Jane knew that Yuna wasn't simply Jiyoo's mother. She was an absolute monarch who had dominion over her daughter's soul. There was no replacement for Yuna in Jiyoo's world. If Jiyoo lost her mother, she would lose everything. But if Jane continued digging, that's exactly what might happen.

Jane turned away from Jiyoo. She pulled out her car keys and unlocked the doors. Just as she did this, Jane heard a car in the distance. She turned her head to discover a white SUV driving toward her. Without moving her head, Jane glanced out of the corner of her eyes toward the front door. Thankfully, Jiyoo had already disappeared.

The white SUV pulled up next to Jane's car. The driver's side door opened, and Eun-ho stepped out of the car. Jane was astonished by what she saw. How could someone change so drastically in such a short amount of time? It had been only two weeks since she last saw him. The hair to the left of his left ear was graying. There were dark bags under even darker eyes, and his cheeks, which had been as rosy as a child's, were now thin and hollow. He looked like he had aged ten years.

The cold wind cut across the back of her neck as she was struck by a sense of déjà vu. Eun-ho looked just like Joon-young had looked when he got in her car. It seemed like all Yuna's men turned out like this. If they didn't die first, that is.

"What are you doing here?" Eun-ho asked as he stood to the side of the front of her car. He looked out of breath. Jane wasn't prepared with an answer. So naturally, what came out of her mouth was a jumble of words.

"I just wanted to see how Jiyoo was doing. I missed her."

Eun-ho turned his ear slightly toward her. He looked like he was genuinely trying to hear her. Because of this, Jane felt the strange obligation to explain more to him.

"I didn't steal anything," Jane said, trying to make a joke. "I just peeked inside."

Jane's poor attempt at humor didn't get a laugh from Eun-ho.

"Please keep it a secret from Yuna. Don't tell her you saw me here. I came here because I heard she wasn't home."

Eun-ho looked down at his sneakers and started nodding. Once, twice, five times, six times. He looked like he was prepared to keep nodding until tomorrow if she didn't stop him. He looked like he was trying to find something to say.

But he didn't need to say anything. And besides, she didn't have time for this. Perhaps Eun-ho didn't mind, since he was just a few steps away from his home, but Jane had someone to meet. And most importantly, she had to get out of here before Yuna came home.

"Well, I should get going," Jane said.

Finally, Eun-ho stopped nodding and lifted his head.

"Wait, I have something to ask you."

Jane waited for him to continue.

"From Tuesday of last week to Sunday morning, November 16 to the 21, was Yuna with you and your mother?"

Jane wanted to know why he was asking this question. If he didn't have memory problems, he would remember Jane came here on Saturday morning specifically looking for Yuna. But since he asked, she might as well answer him.

"No."

"What about before that?"

This question implied that Yuna regularly left the house. Did that mean she was making frequent trips to Woohyeri?

"If you're asking if she stayed the night at our house before, then my answer is the same."

"Not once?"

He seemed desperate for assurance.

"Never."

A look flashed across his eyes. It was so fast that Jane couldn't be sure, but it looked like a head nod. Either he was thinking to himself, *I knew it*, or he was thinking to himself, *So, it's true*. Eun-ho stuck his hands in his pockets and looked down at his shoes again, as if his lines had been written on the nose of his sneakers.

Jane turned slightly toward the house. Despite it being daytime, she could tell that one of the three second-floor windows was lit. Jane couldn't see through the thin curtains, but she could imagine Jiyoo crouching near the window ledge and peering down at them. She'd be nervous, wondering how her auntie was going to take care of this sticky situation.

"Then where was she?" Eun-ho finally asked. "As her sister, you must know."

Jane turned back to look at him. This question didn't make any sense to her.

"Eun-ho. Do you know what you're implying?"

Eun-ho raised his eyebrows in surprise. He looked like he wanted to ask, *Did I say something?*

"You're implying that I was lying, that I asked you where she was when I already knew where she was, that I'm scheming with her to fool you."

Eun-ho dropped his head and drew air into his lungs through his teeth. She listened to the whistle of the air with suspicion. She thought he might start cursing at her.

"That's not what I meant." Eun-ho looked up as if he were looking for an excuse. "I just asked because I thought you might know something. You are family after all."

They say couples develop similar personalities, and Eun-ho's explanation sounded a lot like the way Yuna might ask, *Why are you being so sensitive?*

"I'm not Yuna's family. You are."

Eun-ho used his canine to chew on his bottom lip. Jane decided not to take any more questions. Her watch was pointing to 12:30.

"I've got to go now."

Jane turned around and opened the car door.

"Do you know what Jiyoo likes to eat?" Eun-ho asked suddenly.

This was even more surprising than his other two questions. Jane didn't answer him. She also sheathed her criticism: *You still don't know what she likes?* But Jane could understand his ignorance. He was just her stepfather, and they hadn't lived together apart from the weekends. But she couldn't understand why he was asking her and not his own wife. It was best not to answer nonsensical questions.

Jane got into the driver's seat. Just as she started the engine, Eun-ho thrust his head into the car, right between her and the front windshield. He had suddenly invaded her personal space and was looking straight into her eyes from a distance of what must have been no more than ten centimeters.

"Every kid has at least one takeout food they're crazy about."

Jane had to answer him. She couldn't start driving with his head caught in her car door like this.

"She likes McDonald's Happy Meals. Bulgogi burger, French fries, and a coke."

Eun-ho nodded and withdrew from the car. He was even kind enough to close the door behind him. Jane didn't like this sudden gesture of goodwill. He looked like he had finally got what he wanted, but what that was, Jane didn't know, and that was why she didn't like it.

Jane took off. The entire drive, her head was furiously trying to figure out what Eun-ho's questions meant. She felt like she had an idea why he asked his first question. And once she remembered her first encounter with him a few weeks ago, that hunch became a conviction. The question was meant to find the truth about where Yuna had been those five days.

The last question struck Jane as odd and out of place. Why had Jiyoo's palate suddenly become a topic of serious discussion? Was he finally doing his part to become a good stepfather? Perhaps he wanted to buy Jiyoo lunch. And if that was true, Jane was overanalyzing this. But if it wasn't, then she might have no hope of understanding his motives. It just didn't make sense for him to be worrying about Jiyoo's picky eating while he was asking questions about his wife's disappearance. He had to have another goal than just feeding Jiyoo.

Another goal . . . That was it. Jiyoo was the only one who could give him answers; she was the only one who knew where Yuna had been those five days.

Had Jane realized this earlier, she could have saved Eun-ho the trouble. He had no chance of getting Jiyoo to talk. She was Yuna's most devout follower. And Jiyoo knew that the punishment for apostates was hell. She would never open her mouth, not even for a truckload of Happy Meals.

Jane arrived ten minutes late. The café was full of people, but Jane didn't need to glance around to find him. She recognized him instantly.

He looked just like his picture on Facebook. Jane had never seen someone with such a rectangular head and body. Jane went over to the man and stood before him.

"Jinu Kim?"

Not sure whether to stand or stay seated, the man stood up halfway and greeted her.

"You must be Jane Shin."

"Sorry for being late."

"Not at all."

"Please, sit down," the two of them said simultaneously.

And yet, both she and he stayed standing.

"Do you want to order something?"

Jane said the first thing that came to her mind.

"Café latte, hot—"

Jinu disappeared without hearing the rest of Jane's order. He looked like he wasn't going to come back until he had the coffee. After ordering, he went over to the pick-up counter. Jane's impression of him over the phone was obstinate and intense. But now that she had met him, he seemed quite polite.

When she first called the school, she couldn't reach him. The person answering the phone said he was in the middle of class. Jane left them with her name and phone number.

She got a call back thirty minutes later. Judging from the caller ID, he was calling from the school phone and not his cellphone. When Jane introduced herself as Yuna's older sister, Jinu said suspiciously that he didn't know Yuna had a sister. He said he would make a phone call and get back to her once he knew she was telling the truth. Afraid this meant he was going to call Yuna, Jane suggested an alternative.

"How about I send you my driver's license?"

In a reluctant tone of voice, Jinu gave her his cell number. After hanging up and sending him the picture, Jinu replied with a message asking her what she wanted.

—I have something I want to ask you about my sister. I'm hoping we can meet in person. This isn't something I can talk about over text or a phone call. I promise I won't take up a lot of your time.

A minute or so later, he replied agreeing to meet her. Jane added that she didn't want Yuna to know about their meeting. Jinu replied with a simple "Okay." He chose the time and place for them to meet.

"Did you have lunch?" Jinu asked as he placed the latte in front of her. "I bet you're starving."

Jane hadn't but lied anyway. She didn't want to impose on him. Silence fell between them for a moment as Jane organized her thoughts and he sipped his coffee.

"You were college classmates with Yuna, right?" Jane finally asked. She didn't want to beat around the bush. She was going to ask him questions up front and directly. She hoped he would be equally direct in his answers.

"Yes."

"You were friends with the man she was living with, right?"

"Yes."

"I heard you went to the apartment just before your friend died in a car accident."

Jinu made an audible gulp as he swallowed hard.

"I came here to ask you about that day."

PART 3: PERFECT HAPPINESS

CHAPTER 7

Eun-ho watched as Jane drove off. Even after her car disappeared, he continued to stare down the road for some time. Her answers, though not necessarily friendly, were clear as day. But whether they were transparent and honest was another issue. He was particularly unsure about the latter.

Jane was a master of deception according to Yuna. She had conspired against Yuna and turned her into a problem child using all manner of lies and tricks. It was because of her that Yuna had to spend her childhood in the country with her grandmother. Yuna's grandmother pitied Yuna for this; that was why she willed her a cabin and large plot of land. Where was that plot of land again?

Eun-ho looked up at Jiyoo's room. He could see the curtain move beyond the glass. Eun-ho had a hunch that Jiyoo had been staring at him until he looked up. She was probably curious about what Eun-ho and her aunt were saying.

Where was Wife? Earlier when Eun-ho left the house, she acted like she was going to be home all day. It almost seemed like Jane had come specifically to make Jiyoo lunch. Jane was right; it would be best if Wife didn't know about her coming here today. To that end, Eun-ho needed to ask Jiyoo to keep this a secret.

Eun-ho got back in his car. He needed to see Jinu. He had something to ask his old college friend. On the phone, Jinu suggested they meet later that afternoon, as he had plans before that. After hanging up, Eun-ho considered checking on Jiyoo, but couldn't bring himself to go back into the house. Yuna would be home soon—at least, that's what he wanted to believe.

A voice was circling Eun-ho's ears as he drove around and avoided going inside.

Yuna and Jane are working together.

The voice wasn't Eun-ho's; it belonged to someone who had called him that morning. He had just gotten out of the shower and was drying himself off when his phone started to ring. Yuna brought the phone to the bathroom for him. It was a number he didn't recognize. Leaning against the door frame with her shoulder, Yuna asked:

"Aren't you going to pick up?"

Eun-ho stared at Wife. Why wasn't she leaving?

He let the phone continue to ring until Yuna got the message and left.

"Eun-ho Cha, correct?" a woman's voice asked as soon as Eun-ho picked up.

It was an unfamiliar voice. She introduced herself as Min-young, the sister to Joon-young Seo, Yuna's ex-husband. She wanted to meet in person.

"Why?"

"I'll explain later. You're looking for answers about your son's death, aren't you?"

Eun-ho's hand, which had been drying his hair, stopped suddenly. He was already aware that Yuna's ex-husband had disappeared. Could his disappearance have something to do with Noah's death? In Eun-ho's mind two pictures—one of Jiyoo and her biological father, and one of Eun-ho and Noah—were overlapping.

But he felt uneasy. Min-young must want something in return for offering information about Noah's death. She would demand something of equal value. But what that was, he didn't know. Try as he might, he couldn't think of anything he had that she could want.

He hesitated for a moment before accepting. He was grasping at straws, but it didn't matter. The enemy of my enemy is my friend. And even if this woman wasn't his friend, she might be able to show him the way. If she really was the sister of Yuna's ex-husband, he doubted she would be colluding with Wife, especially if she knew about the divorce.

Min-young must have already decided she was going to meet Eun-ho, no matter what. She gave him the address of the café she was waiting at, which was nearby, and told him what she was wearing.

"I'm at a café called Mojo. You know it, right? My hair is tied, and I'm wearing a black dress. You'll know when you see me. I look just like Jiyoo."

The café was on the forested road behind the townhouse. Eun-ho often stopped there with Yuna on their walks after dinner. This made Eun-ho feel somewhat uneasy, but he decided not to ask if they could meet somewhere else. After all, it wasn't like they were having an affair. And what were the chances Wife would go there in the morning?

"You're going out?" Wife asked as Eun-ho got dressed. He nodded as he headed for the front door.

"Where?"

"To meet a lawyer." He hadn't prepared this lie; it came out automatically, as though he were becoming a compulsive liar.

"When did you get a lawyer? And why are you meeting in the morning on the weekend?" Wife was out of breath as she intercepted him just before the front door.

"We'll get the autopsy results any day now," Eun-ho said. "I need to prepare myself legally."

"Prepare yourself legally? How?" Yuna looked genuinely curious.

"That's what I need to figure out."

"Just wait a minute. I'll go with you," Yuna said as she placed her hand on his arm. "I'll get dressed immediately and be right out."

Eun-ho hadn't expected her to go this far. Hoping that his surprise wasn't showing on his face, he removed her hand from his arm.

"Maybe next time. I want to go alone today."

"You shouldn't go alone. You need someone else there. Someone who can give an objective account of what happened…"

"I know how to talk for myself. I have my own mouth," Eun-ho said with a serious look on his face as he cut her off. To prevent her from saying anything more, in a cold voice he added, "You just worry about Jiyoo."

Eun-ho didn't look to see Yuna's facial expression after saying this. He didn't even look back after putting on his shoes and walking out the door. As he walked toward his car, he could feel Wife staring out at him from the window.

After parking his car outside the café, Eun-ho took out his cellphone. He put it in airplane mode and turned on the recorder. When he entered the café, he immediately made eye contact with a woman seated near the window in the corner, dressed in a black dress. She watched him walk over to her. Her eyes were intelligent and cunning. But unlike what she had claimed, she looked nothing like Jiyoo. The only thing they shared was a last name.

"Are you Min-young Seo?"

Min-young got up from her seat with a faint smile on her face.

"I think I know Yuna's type now," she said.

Eun-ho didn't know what she meant by this, but he didn't think it appropriate for a first greeting. He lowered his eyes and looked at the table. On it was a single cup of coffee. Eun-ho went over to the counter and ordered himself a coffee. By the time he returned to their table, five minutes had passed. Eun-ho wanted to get this out of the way so they wouldn't have to pause in the middle of their conversation.

After he sat down, neither of them bothered with banal greetings. Min-young just stared at him, as though she were studying him. Her eyes were impatient.

"My condolences," she said. "About your son."

Eun-ho didn't react to this. Instead, he just took a sip of coffee. As he did this, he was hit by the absurdity of the situation. He was sitting across from the sister of his wife's ex-husband; she was the last person he thought he would ever meet for coffee. What could she possibly want from him?

"I would like you to tell me everything that happened that day."

Eun-ho had no desire to do this. He had already told the police the story a million times. He didn't want to have to recount it again. Especially to some woman he had just met.

"I think you owe me an explanation first."

Min-young brought her lips to a sharp point and looked at him. She either had no idea what he meant or was just pretending not to know.

"How did you get my phone number and address?"

Aha . . . She mouthed as she lifted her chin.

"Is that so important?" she asked with a look of innocence. "What's important is that we're here now."

Eun-ho could guess that Min-young and Yuna were not that close. And it wasn't simply that they weren't close; they probably had it out for each other. From what Eun-ho saw, Min-young Seo and Yuna Shin were of the same ilk: people who thought the world revolved around them. Of course, he would need to see more before he could tell who the superior narcissist was.

"You seem to have received the help of a professional. I doubt my wife gave you that information, neither is there anyone around me whom you would be close with."

She again answered this question with another question.

"Didn't you come here today because you were curious about what I had to say?"

"I didn't come here to hear your story. Neither did I come here to answer your questions. I came here to find out why you're snooping around."

"Aren't you even a little suspicious of your son's death?"

Her voice seemed agitated.

"Do you really think you killed him?"

Eun-ho cheeks were starting to burn up. They might even be visibly red. He could keenly sense the eyes of the people sitting around and behind him. Instead of answering her question, he lowered his eyes. He inhaled through his teeth, letting out a slight hiss. Even the neighborhood dog would understand this as a warning sign, but Min-young didn't seem to notice.

"Are you always such a heavy sleeper? Don't you think it strange that you slept through everything?"

"I could report you to the police right now. For invasion of—"

"That night, did you drink something before going to bed?"

Eun-ho could feel his chest starting to pound. How did she know?

"What do you mean?"

She didn't answer him. She just studied his face, a smile in her eyes. He tried his hardest not to look impatient.

"Your wife. She wasn't home on the sixteenth of November, was she?"

Eun-ho could feel himself becoming more and more frustrated. How long was she planning on only asking questions and not giving answers?

"Yuna isn't a stay-at-home mom. She's not home on weekdays."

"That's not what I'm asking. She didn't come home that evening, right? She was with my brother."

Eun-ho closed his mouth to prevent the gasp from leaving his mouth. It felt like a hook had suddenly been stuck in his side. What made her so certain?

"According to the police, the last place my brother used his credit card was at a McDonald's in Kyochon. They say he bought a Happy Meal. I doubt many grown men enjoy Happy Meals."

Eun-ho leaned against the back of his chair and sunk deep into the seat.

"He bought it for Jiyoo. He must have met Jiyoo. And there's no way Jiyoo came alone. Yuna brought her. The last time I talked to my brother on the phone was at 2 p.m. Although we didn't really talk for long. He hung up on me, and his phone has been off ever since."

She let out a dry cough twice and reached for a cup of water. She lapped at the water the way a cat would. A few moments later, she continued.

"This is what I think happened. My brother was already riding in Yuna's car when he received my phone call. She picked him up where there weren't any security cameras. The reason he hung up on me was because of her. I'm not sure if you know this, but my brother had fought a long time in court just to see Jiyoo. He probably didn't want to upset Yuna. It had been three years since he last saw his daughter. He probably wanted to make sure he could keep seeing her. They say my brother's cellphone signal cut off in that area. It wasn't just that he hung up on me. He turned off his phone. He's been missing ever since."

Eun-ho thought about that picture of Jiyoo and her father. Where had it been taken? It didn't look like a hotel. Was it a vacation home? Or perhaps . . .

"I heard the police are checking every street camera near Kyochon. They want to see if Yuna's car was in the area."

Eun-ho straightened his back. Min-young pulled her thin lips to the side and smiled.

"Odd, isn't it? That Yuna and her sister Jane are both connected to my brother."

But Eun-ho didn't know what she was talking about. What did Jane have to do with Yuna's ex-husband?

"The police probably wouldn't have started their investigation if they hadn't found my brother's car. Do you know where they found it?"

Eun-ho waited silently for Min-young to answer her own question.

"At a public parking lot near Ju-an station in Incheon. The police asked me if I knew how Jane and my brother knew each other. Apparently, my brother got into Jane's car after parking his car there. But I knew exactly what happened. Jane and my brother had dated a long time ago. And not just for a little while. For eleven years."

Eun-ho swallowed a wad of dry spit. Did this mean Joon-young had left Jane and for Yuna?

"Jane and Yuna are working together."

Min-young said this without further explanation. She just stared silently at Eun-ho, as if to ask, *You understand, don't you?* Eun-ho had to ask what she meant.

"It means the two of them kidnapped my brother, together. Jane picked up my brother and drove him to where Yuna was waiting. Yuna used Jiyoo as bait to lure my brother into her car. My brother would go to hell and back just to see Jiyoo again."

Something wasn't right. If Joon-young really wanted to see Jiyoo so badly, why use Jane? All Yuna needed to do was dangle a piece of Jiyoo's clothing in front of Joon-young's eyes and he'd come running.

"They probably did it to confuse the police. That's why the police are running in circles right now. They can't figure out which Shin to focus on. The way I see it, they're accomplices."

Eun-ho couldn't understand this either. Why would Jane collude with her estranged sister to kidnap her ex-boyfriend? Especially after so many years? Min-young was so convinced of her theory that she was ignoring the most obvious facts. She seemed incapable of differentiating between what was true and what was convenient.

"How do you think you would feel if your boyfriend of eleven years suddenly left you to marry your sister? If it were me, I'd kill him. Perhaps she was just waiting for the right opportunity."

Eun-ho was tired of this. Min-young was still withholding information. What was the connection between the disappearance of her brother and Noah's death?

"I'll ask you again about that day, the sixteenth of November. Yuna didn't come home that night, did she?"

Eun-ho felt he needed to answer the question this time. Only then could they move on.

"I heard she was at her mother's."

Min-young shook her head.

"Wrong. Yuna was not at her mother's. She took my brother somewhere. And that night, my brother was given something to drink."

Eun-ho thought again about that picture of Jiyoo and her father. There was a champagne glass in Joon-young's hand, and a glass of juice in Jiyoo's. Eun-ho took another sip of his coffee. His throat itched. He was feeling impatient. So impatient he wanted to pry open Min-young's mouth and pull out everything she wasn't telling him.

"Yuna," Min-young continued, "lived with a man in college. He died in a car accident. They said he fell asleep at the wheel. It was the same day he broke up with Yuna and moved out. But the person in the car with him that day managed to survive."

Min-young lifted her chin and looked Eun-ho in the eye.

"That man was none other than your friend, Jinu Kim."

Eun-ho could feel his diaphragm suddenly tighten. Hot coffee became stuck in the back of his throat. That picture of Jinu and another man sitting at a kitchen table with coffee flashed before Eun-ho's rapidly blurring vision. He could hear Jinu's voice in his head. *You can call me anytime if you have something you want to ask me.*

"And there was another who died in a similar car accident. Yuna's father. The accident happened after she was fired from her company. He, too, fell asleep at the wheel. They say Yuna inherited the company after his death."

Despite Eun-ho's disbelief, he was nodding his head. They had learned about Yuna's father's death when they were in Irkutsk together, a week after the incident. Eun-ho tried to remember where Yuna was a week before that, but his brain was scattered. All he could see in his head was a picture and the face of his father-in-law holding a cup of coffee with a broad smile on his face.

"I'm curious, have you asked your wife for a divorce recently?"

This question he could answer the most confidently. He hadn't.

"Or perhaps you've given her a reason to?"

Eun-ho wondered, was not getting on his knees and begging for her to come back reason for her to divorce him?

"As pay back, you drank something, the day before your son died."

Eun-ho had already suspected this. The problem was he didn't have any evidence to back it up.

"Your son died, while you were fast asleep."

Eun-ho thought of the picture of him and Noah. The muscles in his cheeks started twitching furiously. But why Noah and not him?

"It was a warning. A warning that you could be next."

Min-young stared at Eun-ho quietly. She looked like she wanted to see his reaction to her theory. Eun-ho stared straight back at her. She seemed crazed to him. People didn't just murder children to send warnings.

"I know you want to prove your innocence. And I want to find my brother. I believe he's still alive. To get what we both want, you need to tell me the truth before it's too late. Where was Yuna on November 16? At least tell me where she might have gone—"

"Min-young."

He couldn't accept what she was saying. She was forcing incompatible jigsaw pieces together to arrive at the conclusion she wanted. Her story seemed unlikely to him, if not impossible.

"You mean my wife and sister-in-law kidnapped your brother? And they also killed my son?"

"If you don't show Yuna the change in behavior she wants—" Min-young stopped and looked Eun-ho in the eyes. "Then you'll be next, I'm positive of it."

Eun-ho got up from his seat. He'd heard enough. The only thing left for him to do was leave this café. He didn't have the desire nor the ability to give Min-young what she wanted.

"Don't come back. And stop spreading dangerous lies. If you don't, I'll call the cops." Eun-ho removed his cellphone from his inner pocket. "I have it all recorded."

Min-young pursed her lips and glared at him. Before she could say anything, he turned around and left the café. He got in his car and took off before she could come chasing after him. But perhaps what he was really running away from was a truth he didn't want to believe.

Eun-ho was outside his home when he finally pulled himself out of his thoughts. He was shocked when he realized he had driven home on autopilot. But even more shocking was that it was his sister-in-law Jane, not Wife, who was waiting for him outside when he returned. But this was good. Now he had the opportunity to get answers.

She likes McDonald's Happy Meals. Bulgogi burger, French fries, and a coke.

Jane's last answer flashed through Eun-ho's mind. Min-young said Joon-young had bought Jiyoo a Happy Meal that day, too. Doing some math, Eun-ho could guess that Joon-young and Yuna had gotten divorced when Jiyoo was three. That was too young an age for hamburgers. How did Joon-young know what Jiyoo liked to eat? Had he asked Jane? Or perhaps Wife?

Later that afternoon, Eun-ho went to Jinu's apartment. He parked his car in the underground parking garage and went up to the sixth floor. Jinu was dressed in nothing but a pair of shorts. Eun-ho glanced at Jinu's arms, which were as wide as Eun-ho's thighs. His broad chest was glistening with perspiration.

"I thought you were meeting someone earlier. You looked like you just got back from the gym."

Jinu flexed his chest muscles as he laughed.

"I don't go to the gym these days. Don't you remember? I set up a home gym."

Jinu said he spent a fortune installing a squat rack. He bragged that his bench press, deadlift, and squat now combined to a total of 500 kilograms. It seemed he traded in his Nintendo Switch for dumbbells and plates.

"The people downstairs haven't complained?" Eun-ho asked in genuine concern.

"I renovated the apartment and soundproofed the floor. Wanna see?"

Eun-ho shook his head. He didn't want to listen to Jinu for the next two hours giving a lecture about sound insulation and home exercise equipment.

"Are you hungry?"

Jinu pointed to the kitchen table with his thumb.

"What are you in the mood for? I've got it all."

Laid out on the kitchen table was chicken breast prepared in every form known to man, from sausages to steaks.

"Got any beer?" Eun-ho finally asked.

"Beer? It's not even five."

Jinu stepped out onto the balcony and came back in with a sixpack of beer. For something to nibble on, Jinu prepared his own choice of tandoori chicken. The wind rattled the balcony window. The sky was a gloomy grey. It seemed like snow or sleet would start falling from the sky soon.

"Have you gotten the autopsy results back yet?" Jinu asked as he sat down next to Eun-ho.

"Not yet."

Eun-ho immediately emptied the entire can into his mouth. As the alcohol entered his gut, his body began to relax. Eun-ho hadn't realized how tense he had become on the ride over here. He also realized that this was the first time he'd touched a drink since two weeks ago, which was coincidentally the last time he saw Jinu. Eun-ho couldn't believe he had managed without the mind-numbing effects of alcohol.

"I thought of something I wanted to ask you."

Eun-ho took his phone from his pocket and placed it on the table between them.

"Have a listen, and then I'll explain."

Eun-ho emptied a second can of beer into his mouth as Jinu listened to the recording. Jinu didn't budge and only stared down at his feet. He didn't even react when his name was mentioned. Only when Eun-ho stopped the recording did Jinu look up. He let out a strange sound, something in between a grunt and "Hmmm."

"And I have something you need to see," Eun-ho said.

He opened his photo album and scrolled to the pictures stolen from Yuna's phone. He clicked on the picture of the Caucasian man and handed the phone to Jinu.

"Flip through the pictures."

Jinu did what he was told without saying a word. With each picture, he showed more emotion. The first picture brought about subtle surprise, the second confusion, and finally an emotion that Eun-ho could only describe as shock. Jinu had found the same pattern Eun-ho had.

"You know what I've come here to ask you, don't you? You must think I'm stupid for taking this long to figure things out."

Eun-ho opened his third can of beer. After guzzling half of it, he continued:

"You should have just told me."

Jinu's response came many seconds later.

"There were a lot of rumors . . . but even I wasn't convinced. Until earlier today, I still wasn't sure what I would do if you came asking questions. I didn't know if telling you what happened would be the right thing to do. And what would be the point of telling you?"

The words "until earlier today" rang inside Eun-ho's ears.

"What happened earlier today that changed your mind?"

"I met with someone for lunch who asked the same questions as you are right now."

Eun-ho paused in surprise as he brought the beer to his lips.

"Who?"

"Yuna's sister. Jane Shin."

Eun-ho was speechless. He had expected Jinu to say the police or perhaps Min-young. But Jane? How did Jane and Jinu know each other?

"Jane learned about Yuna's mysterious past through Min-young, just like you. It seems like Min-young went to Jane before she went to you. But I'm a bit surprised by the recording you just showed me. Jane and Yuna? Working together? And I can't believe Yuna married her sister's ex-boyfriend."

"So, what did you tell Jane?"

Jinu stared quietly out the window. A mountain pigeon was hooting in the distance.

"At first, I didn't want to tell her. It's not an easy thing to talk about. But then she told me about her father. She said she had to know the truth. When I asked her if this could all just be a coincidence, she told me that Yuna's boyfriend in Russia also died in a car accident. Apparently, he fell asleep at the wheel, too."

Eun-ho's eyes drifted down to his cellphone. Was the Caucasian man in the Polaroid the same boyfriend from Russia? Eun-ho's intuition was telling him yes.

"I'm still a bit lost for words. I'm not sure if such a conspiracy is even possible. What if she's innocent? And I'm worried my memory isn't reliable."

Eun-ho turned his head back toward Jinu.

"Tell me what happened," Eun-ho said.

It was as Eun-ho anticipated. The man in the second Polaroid was named Jiwoon, the same man Jinu mentioned at Lake Baikal several years ago. Jinu told Eun-ho a story eerily similar to the one Min-young told him.

Everyone at school knew Yuna, everyone but Jinu, who had just come back to school after finishing his two years of mandatory military service. The first time he met Yuna happened to be the day of the accident.

At the time, Jiwoon and Yuna were living in an apartment together off campus. They had plans to go to Russia together to study abroad after graduation. But the night before the accident, Jiwoon suddenly showed up at Jinu's front door. They went to a bar near Jinu's house to talk, and there Jiwoon told him that he had just broken up with Yuna. According to Jiwoon, it had been a week since he ran out of their apartment without taking his things. It wasn't just a verbal fight or a fight of passion between two lovers. Jiwoon was genuinely scared of Yuna.

Yuna was intense; the kind of woman whose emotions were always dialed up to ten. Because of this, she was always vacillating between extremes. One moment she was beckoning her man to come closer, and the next she was pushing him away. Depending on her mood, she was either an angel or a tyrant. She nitpicked about the smallest things, and if Jiwoon tried to get her to stop nitpicking, she would get angry, claiming he was trying to push her away. And when she got angry, she always took it to the extreme. Jiwoon and Yuna almost broke up several times before. And when this happened, Yuna would always ask, "How can you do this to me?"

Jiwoon said he was afraid of confronting Yuna alone. He had come to Jinu to ask if he would go to the apartment with him to get his things. Two days later, the two of them went to the apartment together.

"Because of what Jiwoon told me, I was expecting a flamboyant and violent woman with long nails."

But he was completely caught off guard by the woman who greeted them at the door.

"You know better than I. It's probably why you fell in love with her. Her smile looked like the great opening of the heavens after a heavy rain. Not an ounce of malice anywhere. She looked pure and innocent and was unusually mature for her age at the time. I started to doubt what Jiwoon had told me. I thought he was making up stories about a perfectly normal woman just to give himself an excuse to break up with her."

Yuna just stood in front of the kitchen and watched them as they packed Jiwoon's things. When they finished, she offered them some coffee before leaving. Jiwoon wanted to get out of there as soon as possible, but Jinu thought it would be rude. The coffee, which had been filled to the brim from the coffee machine, looked so pitiful; he couldn't just reject her offer and leave it there. Eventually Jiwoon sat down at the table with Jinu. It was then that Yuna pulled out her Polaroid camera.

"She said she wanted a picture, as a souvenir. Jiwoon was reluctant to give her permission."

She took three pictures, one for each of them. After the photoshoot, no one said a word. Yuna just said one thing as they left the apartment.

"Goodbye, Jiwoon."

Her voice was so quiet and calm that Jinu couldn't help but turn around and look at her. When he and Yuna made eye contact, she said again, "Goodbye, Jinu."

Jinu emptied the can of beer in his hand and looked down at the floor.

"How could I have known? Actually, what Min-young told you wasn't completely accurate. I guess she believed one of the many rumors that were going around at the time. I wasn't in Jiwoon's car at the time of the accident. He was on his way to his parents in Bundang. I had done my job and didn't need to go all the way with him. Plus, I had plans later that night. But then . . ."

When he got home, he became exhausted. Up to that point, he hadn't felt that anything was amiss. He just figured he was tired from helping a friend move and from the tense air in the room. He lay down in his bed, telling himself he was going to take a five-minute nap. He woke up two days later. As soon as he awoke, he heard the news of Jiwoon's accident. They said he fell asleep at the wheel and drove his car into Han River from Olympic Highway.

"Do you know what I thought the moment I heard the news?"

The coffee. They both drank that coffee; one of them was passed out for two days, and the other fell asleep at the wheel and died. Could that be a coincidence? Yuna didn't come to the funeral. You couldn't find her at school either.

All Jinu heard was that she went to Russia right after the accident. Jinu said that ever since then, he lived with a terrifying question mark in his heart. But then he met her again at Lake Baikal in Russia.

"Why didn't you tell me then?"

Eun-ho asked this question even though he already knew the answer. Jinu *couldn't* tell him, and if he did, Eun-ho would have thought Jinu as the world's worst saboteur. At the time, Eun-ho was already resentful for Jinu's mention that he was divorced. Finally, Eun-ho understood the meaning of Jinu's words those two weeks ago at the bar.

If you're not careful, you might go in your sleep.

But the person who died in their sleep wasn't him but Noah. Why Noah? It was he who angered Wife. The only person who could answer this question was Wife.

"That's what I thought as soon as Noah died. Even if you hated me for it, I should have stopped you from marrying her. I regretted saying hello to Yuna at Lake Baikal. If only I hadn't suggested we go out for drinks together, she would have been someone who just passed through your life.

"But why did you suggest we go out for drinks together?"

"I was curious. I wanted to know if she had really done it. It's funny now that I think about it."

Jinu let out a wry laugh.

"I don't know what I was expecting. If she had killed him, she wouldn't have told us. It's not like someone walks around with a guilty note posted to their forehead."

Jinu opened another can of beer. He took a large swig but didn't say anything after that. Eun-ho also didn't ask any more questions. He had thought that once he talked with Jinu, things would clear up, but things were only hazier now. He still didn't believe it, and he still didn't see a way forward. His head was just spinning with more questions.

Yuna, who are you?

*

It looked like sunset all afternoon. There was thick fog, and the cast iron sky was becoming darker by the second. It wasn't even 5 p.m. yet. Jane straightened her back and repositioned her hands on the steering wheel. She needed to keep her attention on the right side of the road so she wouldn't miss the sign.

Jane would miss the entrance to Woohyeri if she blinked. Not only was the road hidden by trees, but there was no sign except a bus stop sign that was barely the size of Jane's palm. Neither was the village visible from the highway.

Woohyeri
1001, Bukmyeon, Mt. Suri

Jane made a sharp right after the sign. After driving through a kilometer of terraced rice patties littered with bales that looked like dinosaur eggs, Jane finally began to see people. The village was comprised of two dozen houses that were scattered along the foot of the tiny mountain.

Once Jane turned the corner of the terraced farmlands, she came upon an abandoned house and the perfect place to hide her car. The house, which was up the street from her grandma's cabin, hadn't changed much since the last time Jane came to Woohyeri three years ago. The wall surrounding the house was all but missing, the front gate had fallen off its hinges, and the greenhouse in the front yard had a large cut through its plastic roof. Jane never thought she'd have a reason to enter the front yard of this abandoned house, but now she did. Jane drove her car inside the front yard and parked behind the greenhouse. It wouldn't be wise to park her car at her grandma's cabin.

Jane walked back out through the front gate of the abandoned house to see if she could see her car from the road. From there, she could just barely see it if she was looking.

Jane jogged more than five hundred meters up the hill toward her grandma's cabin. The cabin was at the end of the road, in the deepest pocket of the village, and surrounded on three sides by an overgrown pine forest. When Jane arrived, she was met with an unsightly front gate. Its blue paint was chipping, there were rust stains that looked like dried tear stains of red, and beneath the gate were winter weeds as large and gnarly as thick jungle vines.

Jane tried pushing the gate. Not surprisingly, it was locked. She pressed the bell on the gatepost. No response. As her final attempt, Jane called out at the top of her lungs:

"Is anyone home?"

No answer. Jane figured that if someone hadn't answered by now, she could be relatively certain no one was home. Jane turned toward the iron fence which was intertwined with rose vines. It looked like it could only endure four more seasons before becoming scrap metal, and yet the posts were firmly planted in the ground. Pushing and kicking had no effect. Even when Jane climbed onto the fence, it was sturdy enough to support her weight.

Jane made a soft landing just beneath the maple tree. When she looked up, though, she was met with something she hadn't been expecting. The cute, colorful two-story cabin that looked like it had come straight out of a fairy tale was gone. Jane felt like she was staring at a house that had been abandoned for decades.

The maple tree was nothing but barren branches, and the unpruned juniper in the planter had lost its shape. Vines had climbed the walls of the house and were blanketing the roof. The deck was rotting and piled high with dead leaves. And the windows were even dirtier than those at the abandoned house down the road.

Jane crossed the front yard and headed toward the front door. Locked. The window to Grandma's old room was also locked. And because thick curtains were blocking the window, she couldn't even see inside.

Jane went into the back to find an even more desolate sight than at the front of the house. The retaining wall was cracked and crumbling, the garden was overrun with pieces of plastic and weeds, and lying beneath the persimmon tree was a pole pruner. The soggy earth was green with moss, and fierce mountain winds were blowing in from the shadows of the forest.

Jane hopped across the soggy ground and arrived at the back door. Not surprisingly, this, too, was locked. Jane even checked the window to the first-floor bathroom, despite knowing that even if it was open, she would only be able to fit her head through it. She bent her neck backwards and looked up at the second floor. On the left was a window just big enough for her to squeeze through. Of course, she would have to get up there first to know if it was open.

Jane went over to the shed. When she opened the door, a small wheelbarrow was blocking her way. It was the one Grandma used for working in the vegetable garden. The wheels and hull of the thing were caked in dirt, as though someone had been gardening recently. Inside the wheelbarrow was a pair of dirty blue work boots.

When Jane switched on the lights, an eight-step folding ladder standing next to a stack of firewood met her eyes. This was what her grandparents had used when picking persimmons or fixing the roof. Beneath the ladder were two pairs of boots placed side by side. Based on their size, the pair of black boots looked like they were for men, the yellow boots for children. Both were as dirty as the one in the wheelbarrow.

Three dirty pairs of boots . . . Jane stored the boots in her memory and closed the door. Right now, she had to drag the large ladder out of the shed and set it up beneath the window.

As she dragged the ladder out of the shed and set it up against the roof, Jane thought about how much easier life would be if she were stronger. The window wasn't locked. That was fortunate because that meant she wouldn't need to break any windows. It was also large enough that she could comfortably fit through.

Jane pushed the window open and stepped inside. She was now in the bathroom. Next to the sink were rubber hair ties, a box of soap, and on the shelf were children's shampoo, an Apeach toothbrush, toothpaste, and a cup. The bathroom slippers placed at the entrance to the bathroom were also Apeach-themed. Apeach was one of Jiyoo's favorite characters. She collected everything from stickers and pencils to pillows and socks.

It looked like Yuna used the first floor and Jiyoo used the second floor. Jane took off her shoes and left the bathroom. Because the hallway was dark, she left the door to the bathroom open as she went to the next room. Inside, she was confronted with a sight from thirty years ago. The bed, desk, wardrobe, even the lights were all exactly the same as when Yuna had lived here. Jane was drawn to the windowsill as though under the influence of some magic spell.

A family of puppets with name tags were sitting at a table and drinking tea. Mom, Dad, Yuna, and Baby. Jane's puppet, who was missing its legs and had its belly slashed open, was lying at Jane's feet and staring up at her with its single back eye.

Run, before Yuna comes home!

Jane squeezed her eyelids shut.

This isn't real. It's a hallucination, a specter that's crawled out of my memory. Open your eyes and do what you came here to do.

When Jane opened her eyes, there was nothing on the windowsill. The only thing there were yellow butterflies dancing above white laced curtains. Jane retreated from the room. She pushed shut the door to the room and the door to her memories. As she walked toward the room at the end of the hallway, she used her pants to wipe her hands, which were wet and sticky like the back of a toad. There was a lock on this door.

Jane searched her memory. Had this room always been here? She couldn't remember. But she did remember how Jiyoo had sleep-talked almost every night at the hospital.

Beneath the attic a loon is howling.

Was this the attic? If it was, then based on her memory of the layout of this house, "beneath the attic" would technically be the kitchen on the first floor. But Jane needed to confirm her memory. Jane took out her cellphone from her jacket. She turned on the flashlight and started down the stairs toward the bathroom. She brought her shoes with her and placed them outside the back door.

The bathroom wasn't as dark as the hallway. There was light coming in from the small bathroom window. Jane picked up and inspected each of the items in the bathroom. Toothpaste, toothbrushes, shampoo and conditioner, white hand towels. The waste basket was completely empty. In the cabinet there was bleach and drain cleaner, and next to the toilet were two toilet brushes.

There was nothing that hinted at Joon-young ever being here. Jane even shined her cellphone flashlight toward the bathtub drain cover, but there wasn't a single hair caught in the grate. There were also no signs of any loons, although this didn't surprise Jane. She hurried out of the bathroom. The smell of bleach was tickling her throat and causing her to cough. She felt like her bronchial tubes were getting bleached every time she breathed in.

She walked through the hallway and entered the kitchen. Here, too, the first thing that greeted her was a smell. But this time, it wasn't the smell of bleach. This was closer to the fishy smell of meat that seeped into the air when you made bone broth.

Jane opened the refrigerator. There was no food in the refrigerator, let alone freshly made broth. In fact, the refrigerator wasn't even plugged in; its interior was room temperature and dark. Placed on the island in the middle of the kitchen was a scented candle and a blue flower vase. And on the shelves of the overhead cupboard were bowls and cups. In the cabinet next to the kitchen sink were silverware and miscellaneous culinary tools like a wine bottle opener. Most of the things were old and what you would expect to find in a typical kitchen.

What surprised Jane was what she found in the bottom cabinets. On the first shelf was a wooden cutting board and four knives on a rack. One knife was long and thin, one was short, one was a sashimi knife, and one looked like a small hand axe. Jane opened the next shelf to find a mincer. And on the next shelf were two stock pots that looked big enough for a small person to bathe in. The pots reeked of the fishy smell of meat that was permeating the kitchen.

Jane had come here and helped prepare food for their grandpa's ancestral rites many times, and she had never seen these kitchen tools before. This wasn't the kind of stuff you found in a typical family kitchen. These were the tools of someone who butchered cows, pigs, chickens, and ducks.

What had Yuna done with these tools? The purpose of the tools was too clear to imagine anything else. The knives were for dismemberment, the pots were for boiling, and the mixers were for grinding. The words dismember, boil, and grind all seemed to be pointing in the same direction.

A cold breeze cut across the nape of Jane's neck. An image appeared in her head like a light being turned on. Jane shook her head as she got to her feet and went into the living room.

Her cellphone flashlight illuminated a familiar scene. A ceiling fixture made of two long fluorescent tubes, a bookcase filled with Grandpa's books, and an old fabric sofa and round coffee table. The calendar on the wall was two years old and still open to September, the month Grandma passed away.

Grandma's old room, which was connected to the living room, was also untouched. Even the sheets on the bed were the same ones she had used when she was alive. The outside of the house looked like an abandoned house, but the inside looked frozen in time, like Grandma still lived here. Jane could almost see Grandma's ghost wherever she shined her flashlight. It looked like Yuna had no intention of living in this house. If she had even the slightest intention to come here on the weekends, there would be no reason to keep this place looking like a mausoleum.

Jane started going through the wardrobe. She then moved on to the drawers and the vanity. But there was nothing that looked like it belonged to Yuna. Nor was there anything that struck Jane as odd. After a while, Jane had nothing left to search, as she had gone through everything, even the sewing box. But just as she was heading out of the room, she paused. The voice inside her head was pulling at her hair.

What are you looking for? Are you looking for evidence that Joon-young was here? Or are you looking for evidence that he wasn't here? Get it straight. Don't just look at what's convenient. You've forgotten that you're not just some bystander or witness in this case. You're their top suspect!

Right. Jane had forgotten her predicament. She had forgotten why she was here. Because of this, she had closed her eyes even when she discovered something suspicious, dismissed it as meaningless. She was trying to deny her intuition. She didn't want to accept the unacceptable. Her subconscious was resisting.

She hurried out of the living room, like someone who had been spooked. Her legs gave out, causing her to slump over on one end of the couch. As she sat down, she heard the sound of cracking plastic beneath her.

Jane stood up. She pulled out the cushion of where she had just been sitting. A long, small object was stuck halfway between the folds of the sofa frame. She picked it up to realize it was a ballpoint pen. Her fingers started to tremble. Engraved on the clip of the cap were the initials JYS. This was the same ballpoint pen that Jane had given to Joon-young on the day his play was performed on stage, the day she introduced Yuna to him.

Speaking of Eun-ho, I overheard him talking with the police at Noah's funeral.

Suddenly, Jane remembered what Jinu had told her.

The night before, he drank quince tea that Yuna had made. He was in such a deep sleep that he didn't know his own child was dying.

If it was possible to sleep through someone else's death, was it possible to sleep through your own? Jane started recalling the things that she had seen in the kitchen. The professional-grade knives, the grinder, the pots.

There are moments in life when everything suddenly comes into focus, when it feels like you can see the entire universe. This was one of those moments. The curtain of unconsciousness that had been covering Jane's eyes had been torn down in one swift motion. The wall of resistance had been toppled in one blow. The imagination that had been locked away burst like a dam. Jane was terrified of her own imagination for being able to accept such a possibility.

Go see for yourself.

The voice in her head gave her another command.

See with your own two eyes what is locked inside the attic. Break down the door if you must. If Joon-young is inside, then you've let your imagination get the best of you. If he's not…

Jane put the pen in her pocket and went to the kitchen. She opened the bottom cabinet and pulled out the knife rack. She picked up the knife that looked like it had the best chance of breaking a lock. Something big and heavy, yet sharp. She picked up the cleaver and was standing up when she heard a click from behind her. As her senses turned outward, she could sense the front door opening.

A cold draft grazed the back of her neck. It looked like her luck had run out today. Jane slowly turned toward the front door. Yuna was standing in the yellow light from the front porch bulb. She didn't look surprised. Then again, it was Jane who should be surprised.

"Looks like I've got a guest."

Yuna took off her shoes and stepped onto the wooden floor. She was dressed in a black dress, scarf, and black coat. And in one hand she had a foldable cart and in the other, a handbag with a head-sized horseshoe key chain.

"I don't remember inviting guests."

Yuna set the cart up against the wall, walked over to the living room door, and turned on the lights. Her facial expression was bright and joyful, like an actress taking the curtain call. Jane watched quietly as Yuna walked over to the kitchen island and stood before her. She was trying her best to steady her trembling vision.

She felt like she was back in the past. Standing in front of Yuna with the murdered duck stuffed animal in her hand, trying in vain not to shake. And just like that, her legs were trembling, the back of her neck was burning, the skin on her stomach was becoming taut with uncontrollable spasms. And in her chest, her heart was galloping.

"What's wrong with your face?" Yuna said as she took off her scarf and placed it on the table. "You look like you swallowed a wasp."

Yuna's voice was tight, as though she was holding in a cackle. Jane couldn't think of how to respond. All she could do was bring an extinguisher to the chemical fire that had ignited in her body.

Stop shaking. You're bigger and stronger than Yuna. Smarter, too. And you're holding a cleaver. Act like it!

But it wasn't easy. Despite all these years, it looked like her body still hadn't produced antibodies to defend against Yuna.

"Why are you here?" Yuna asked. "You even hopped the fence like a thief. Once a stealing bitch, always a stealing bitch."

Yuna continued to grin. Jane turned off her cellphone flashlight and put the phone in her pocket. Then with her sweaty hands, she adjusted her grip on the cleaver.

"Where's Joon-young?"

"If you want to see Joon-young, I don't know why you would come looking for him here."

"You brought him here. About twenty days ago. Don't you remember?"

Yuna suddenly tilted her head sideways. Her oblique gaze was brazen, as if she had nothing to hide.

"The last time I saw that man was three years ago."

Yuna's ability to lie with such a straight face never ceased to astonish Jane. She could lie about anything with eyes like that. Jane pulled out the pen from her pocket.

"I gave this as a present to Joon-young seven years ago. I found it here under the sofa."

"So what?"

"That's why I asked where he is."

"And I'm asking, why are you looking for him?"

"I was contacted by the police yesterday. They wanted to know if you were really at Mom's from the 16th to the 20th. When I asked why, they told me Joon-young disappeared on the 16th."

Yuna raised one eyebrow, as if to say, *Keep going.*

"I thought something was strange, too. I couldn't get in contact with him for almost a week."

Jane hoped this lie would strike a nerve.

"That day when you called Joon-young, he was with me in Chungju."

Yuna straightened her head. The smile that had been dancing around her eyes vanished.

"I drove him to Kyochon. And I watched from afar as you drove off with him in your car."

"You've been meeting him behind my back?"

The tail end of Yuna's words quivered minutely. It was a sign that Jane had found the right button. Finally, Jane felt herself starting to relax. She now had the courage and leverage to push the issue.

"Where's Joon-young?"

Jane put the pen in her pocket again and walked around the table toward Yuna, who turned her body to keep Jane in front of her. Yuna was mumbling in Jane's direction like someone in a trance.

"You did it again, didn't you?"

Jane stopped walking about twenty centimeters from Yuna.

"You touched my things again, didn't you?"

Yuna continued to mumble to herself. She had the special ability of selectively only hearing what she wanted to hear and tuning everything else out. In hopes of shaking Yuna out of her trance, Jane refocused the conversation.

"Yuna, where is Joon-young?"

"Stealing bitch."

Not this time. Jane raised the cleaver and put it up to Yuna's neck.

"Think carefully before you say that again."

Jane could feel through the blade the muscles in Yuna's neck twitching.

"Well, well. Look at you."

Yuna's tone suddenly became calm.

"Is this any way to treat your younger sister?"

Yuna was a hypocrite, but that didn't make her wrong. Jane decided to give Yuna a quiz.

"Jiwoon, Istvan, Dad. What do these three people have in common?"

Yuna stared at Jane without answering.

"They all drank coffee that you made for them, and then a few hours later, they all fell asleep at the wheel and died in car accidents."

Jane tightened her grip on the cleaver. Yuna's jugular wriggled beneath the blade.

"And they all abandoned Yuna Shin. In fact, Dad did it twice."

Yuna made her eyes into slivers. Flames of a blazing inferno were escaping between the slits and burning Jane's skin.

"You were too young the first time it happened to do anything about it. But you weren't going to forgive him a second time."

Jane took one step forward.

"Of course, Joon-young did something even worse than Dad. Not only did he abandon you, but he was also a thorn in your side for several years, and threatened to put you in jail if you didn't let him visit Jiyoo. Knowing you, you wouldn't be satisfied with just sending him off in his sleep.

"You should have been the writer, not him."

Yuna's lips barely opened as she said this. Her pronunciation was half jumbled. Her words were hissing through her teeth.

"I want you to show me the room upstairs. The one with a lock on it. If I'm really just imagining all of this, then prove it to me."

Jane moved to the side and pointed to the stairs with her chin.

"You first," Jane said.

Yuna started moving. She walked toward the stairs with light footsteps. Jane followed behind her, leaving about two feet between herself and Yuna. As Yuna passed in front of Jane, the edge of the cleaver went from pointing at her throat to pointing at the back of her neck. Her arm was tingling, and her hand was shaking. And yet Yuna looked not the least bit nervous.

Jane was amazed by Yuna's temerity. From the moment they saw each other, Yuna hadn't shown much more than a flinch. Even right now as Jane had her at knife point, Yuna didn't seem very nervous. Jane couldn't judge if it was because Yuna didn't think she was a threat or because she simply didn't fear death. If she was just acting like she wasn't nervous, she was the best actor Jane had ever seen.

Jane stopped thinking. But by the time her eyes moved to the handbag hanging from Yuna's wrist, it was already too late. The handbag was slicing through the air and flying toward her head. Jane instinctively leaned back, but it wasn't enough to dodge the surprise attack. The heavy horseshoe key chain on the handbag smacked her in the right eye.

Pain shot through her head as though her eyeball had been shattered. At the same time, Jane felt an immense force shoving her shoulder. Jane had the wind knocked out of her as her body bent backwards and her heels lifted off the stairsteps. She went flying through the air and landed on the hardwood floor headfirst.

It happened so fast that she didn't even have time to scream. Even before she had the chance to open her mouth, darkness overtook her. The last thing Jane saw was Yuna picking up the cleaver off the ground. Just before Yuna brought the back of the blade down on her, Jane blacked out. From the darkness, she could hear Yuna's voice.

"Stealing bitch."

*

Mother came back later that night. Jiyoo was sitting on the living room sofa, mindlessly watching *Ballerina*. Felicie and Camille were in the middle of a dance battle when Jiyoo heard Mother's voice.

"Jiyoo Cha."

Jiyoo was suddenly brought back to reality. She turned her head to find Mother standing at the entrance to the living room. In one hand she had her coat, and in the other a large plastic bag. Jiyoo jumped to her feet.

"You're still up?"

Mother glanced once toward the wall clock. Jiyoo followed Mother's gaze. 11:00. Jiyoo had no idea it was so late.

"I was watching a movie and didn't know—"

Mother headed into the kitchen. After placing the plastic bag and her coat on the table, she sat down on one of the chairs with her legs crossed.

"Turn that off and come over here."

Jiyoo did as she was told. With her eyes, Mother motioned Jiyoo to the seat across from her. Again, Jiyoo did as she was told.

"Have you had dinner?"

"No."

"You must be hungry. I was going to save this for tomorrow—"

Mother took out a Happy Meal from the plastic bag and placed it in front of Jiyoo. Then, she took out a bag of French fries and put this in front of herself.

"Eat."

Jiyoo hated cheeseburgers. She never ate mozzarella sticks and didn't like milk. And yet, all three of these things were included in the Happy Meal. And Jiyoo already had three SpongeBob and Krusty Krab toys. It would be difficult to have such a perfectly horrible Happy Meal without trying. It almost seemed like this was Mother's cruel way of punishing Jiyoo. But for what?

Of course, Jiyoo couldn't express her discontent. That was the kind of thing that Mother never allowed, not even when she was in a good mood. And right now, because Mother had caught Jiyoo watching a movie when she should be sleeping, because Mother didn't look like she was in a good mood, it was even more important that Jiyoo eat the food with a happy look on her face. And yet despite knowing this, Jiyoo's mouth didn't do what she told it to do. Feeling like she was about to throw up, Jiyoo simply nibbled on the edge of the bun.

"Why are you eating like you're a rabbit?" Mother asked.

But as always, this wasn't really a question. It was a command to stop picking at her food and eat already. To show she understood, Jiyoo took a big bite out of the burger. She swallowed the whole thing without chewing to avoid tasting the cheese. The same way Father did that day in the car.

"What did you eat for lunch?" Mother asked as she picked up a single French fry. Jiyoo quickly swallowed the food that was stuck in the back of her throat. But it didn't go down easily because her throat was dry. She let out a sound as if she was being strangled.

"R—rice."

"What rice? The curry rice is still there."

Mother pointed to the three-minute curry rice that was placed next to the microwave. Jiyoo frantically opened the carton of milk. She guzzled the milk until she washed down the bite of cheeseburger lodged in her throat. As she did this, she searched her brain for an appropriate answer.

"Actually—I didn't eat."

Mother blinked once. Jiyoo lowered her head.

"I'm sorry for lying."

Mother tapped on the table with her long nails.

"Why didn't you eat?"

Jiyoo hated curry rice as much as she hated cheese.

"My tummy hurt." Jiyoo lied without thinking.

"Does it still hurt?"

Jiyoo was feeling more and more uneasy. Mother didn't seem like she was asking out of concern. Even though her tone was gentle, it sounded insincere.

"A little."

Mother nodded. And that was it. Jiyoo worked up the courage to ask another question.

"Can I stop eating?"

"Fine."

Mother stuck another fry into her mouth.

"Did your father come home earlier today?"

For a moment Jiyoo didn't know what Mother meant. Was she asking about her real father or stepfather? Once she remembered that this home was stepfather's home, her chest suddenly became tight. If she answered honestly, she would have to mention Auntie Jane. And if she lied, that might get her into trouble in the future. If Stepfather told Mother the truth, that would ruin everything.

Don't worry. Your stepfather will keep our secret.

This is what Auntie Jane said when she called Jiyoo after Stepfather drove off. But Jiyoo wasn't sure if she could believe this. She didn't know Stepfather very well—aside from the fact he didn't smile or talk much. Jiyoo decided to trust Auntie Jane. If she said he would keep their secret, then he would keep their secret.

"I don't know. I was napping all day because my stomach hurt."

"He didn't even call?"

Jiyoo thought for a while before finding the best answer.

"I didn't hear the phone ring."

Mother didn't say anything. She didn't even nod. All she did was chop a French fry into segments on the table with her long nails. Jiyoo hesitated for a moment before asking:

"Can I go to bed now?"

"Okay, go to bed."

Mother's eyes were fixed on Jiyoo's unfinished cheeseburger, as if she was telling Jiyoo to sleep inside the cheeseburger. Mother did this often. Looking at one thing, while talking about another thing. This was a sign that she was irritated by what Jiyoo was doing. Even after being told to go to bed, Jiyoo found it hard to get up from her seat.

"What are you waiting for?" Mother asked as she lifted her gaze from the cheeseburger. Only then did Jiyoo get out of her seat. As she walked out into the living room, she could sense Mother's gaze. She slowly went up the stairs, pretending like her stomach still hurt. She wanted to get to the top of the stairs in one giant leap, but she tried her best to resist this urge. Jiyoo wondered how nice it would be to have the power of transformation. Then she could turn into a small caterpillar and crawl up the stairs. That way she wouldn't attract Mother's attention.

But even when she got upstairs, she still wasn't at ease. She felt like Noah was standing in front of his bedroom door glaring at her. She could almost hear him say, "Give me back my soccer ball!" Jiyoo put her hands over her ears, dropped her head, and hurried past Noah's bedroom door toward the bathroom to wash her face and brush her teeth. She did the same thing when she came out of the bathroom. It was just a few steps from the bathroom to her room, but the whole time, two different urges were fighting each other. One was the urge to turn around and see if Noah was really there. And the other was the urge to run into her room.

Jiyoo did neither. She kept her eyes forward as she walked to her room. She wanted to lock the door, but she didn't do this. Mother hated it when she did that. She became furious when she came to say goodnight to Jiyoo and found the door locked. She said it was no different than telling her to "Go away."

Jiyoo turned off the light and crawled into bed. She turned on the nightlight sitting on the bedside table and lay flat on her back. Her eyes naturally drifted to the top of the wardrobe. That was where she hid Dad Puppet. Now, all she had to do was wait for her Stepfather to come home. When that happened Mother would go into the master bedroom, which would mean it was safe for Jiyoo to take Dad Puppet from his hiding spot and place him under her pillow.

Jiyoo started counting. *One, two, three . . . Nine hundred ninety-nine*. Still her stepfather hadn't come back home. She counted to one thousand again. She counted to one thousand five times, but still her stepfather hadn't come home. The house was quiet. There were no sounds of Mother moving. Jiyoo figured Mother must have gone to sleep. Did that mean it was safe? Mischievous Mouse said it did.

Jiyoo got down from the bed. She got up on her desk and took Dad Puppet down from the wardrobe. Then she got back into bed and placed the puppet under her pillow. Relief washed over her. Now she felt like she could finally relax and fall asleep. Jiyoo regretted not taking Dad Puppet with her when

Mother came to take her from Grandma's house. Had she taken him with her, she wouldn't have needed to call Auntie Jane.

Jiyoo had been eating dinner when Mother came to pick her up from Grandma's. She didn't like most of what the nanny cooked—things like egg bibimbap and marinated chicken. But that day, Nanny had cooked her beef bulgogi and mushrooms. The bulgogi was good, but she was only able to eat a couple bites before Mother suddenly appeared and started turning the house inside out. The nanny tried to stop Mother, but Mother ignored her. After hiding Dad Puppet, Jiyoo stood nervously next to her bed.

Mother told Jiyoo that she wouldn't be coming back to Grandma's. She also told Jiyoo to leave behind most of her things: clothes, books, and an art set that Auntie Jane bought for her, even her school bag. Jiyoo lost her chance to take Dad Puppet with her. Because of this, Jiyoo suffered from nightmares ever since coming back to stepfather's house. It didn't matter when she slept; night or day, she always had nightmares when she closed her eyes.

Now that Auntie had brought Dad Puppet for her, Jiyoo thought she would be able to sleep better now.

Father will look after me. He will protect me from the loons, the endless staircase, the voice calling me to the marsh.

But now with Dad Puppet under her pillow, Jiyoo realized something. Even though she wouldn't be having nightmares, the fear of Mother finding Dad Puppet would keep her up at night. But still, that fear was better than the nightmares. She could hide the puppet, but she couldn't hide from the nightmares. And it wasn't like Jiyoo could keep her eyes open forever. She would have to fall asleep eventually.

Jiyoo turned on her side and stuck her hand under the pillow. She felt her body relax as soon as her hand met Dad Puppet. Even the knot in her stomach was beginning to unravel. She was just about to fall asleep when a bright light caused her to open her eyes. A harsh white light was shining in her eyes. Jiyoo brought her hand up to her face to block the light.

"Jiyoo Cha."

It was Mother's voice. Jiyoo put down her hand, but she still couldn't see Mother clearly. A blurry white object was approaching the bed. Jiyoo saw double of the objects in the room. But by the time her eyes adjusted, it was already too late. Mother had pulled back the sheets and taken Dad Puppet from Jiyoo's hand.

"Get up," Mother said in a soft whisper. This was the scariest whisper in the world. Jiyoo sat straight up.

"What is this?"

Mother waved Dad Puppet in the air. Sitting in bed, Jiyoo was frozen in place. Her vision was going blurry again. If felt like the room was starting to spin. Dad Puppet was coming in and out of focus.

"Are you not going to answer me?"

Mother's voice got even quieter.

"I'm sorry."

This was what instinctively came out of Jiyoo's mouth.

Mother shook her head.

"I don't want an apology. I want an explanation."

Jiyoo dropped her head and stared at her knees. What should she say? She didn't have an answer.

"Jiyoo Cha," Mother said again. Her tranquil voice was warning Jiyoo that tonight wasn't going to be peaceful, whether she told Mother the truth or not.

"I'm sorry."

"For what?"

"For taking Dad Puppet, without your permission."

"Is that all?"

Jiyoo could feel saliva as sour as vinegar working its way up her throat. Her lower stomach was tightening, and she was overwhelmed with the urge to go to the bathroom.

"And keeping him without telling you."

"And?"

"And—"

Jiyoo swallowed the saliva welling up inside her mouth. Her mind was dark with hesitation and fear. And . . . and . . .

"Did your stomach really hurt today?"

Jiyoo realized Mother knew everything. And she realized that she had missed her last chance to tell the truth. Mother held up a phone receiver, which she had been hiding behind her back, and brought it up to Jiyoo's eyes.

"My little Jiyoo's so smart. I'm sure you know what this is."

Jiyoo held in her breath. Auntie Jane's name was shown twice in the call history.

"You left the puppet hidden at Grandma's house. Then you call Auntie Jane this morning to ask her to bring it to you. But Auntie Jane didn't just bring you the puppet. It was lunch time, after all. That's why you didn't eat Mother's

Happy Meal. Even though she bought you your favorite meal."

Jiyoo shook her head.

"No, Mother. My tummy really did hurt."

Mother took something out of her cardigan pocket. It was the Happy Meal bag that Jiyoo had folded neatly and put in the trash.

"You still want to lie to me?"

Jiyoo could feel the organs inside her torso suddenly contract. Her breath was short and halting.

"Mother gave you a chance to tell the truth."

Mother threw the puppet and receiver on the bed and the Happy Meal paper bag on the floor.

"You should have told me when I gave you the chance. If you had, I would have only punished you for stealing the puppet. But now, I must punish you for also lying to Mother." Mother took a step back from the bed. "Out of bed."

Jiyoo got down from the bed and stood before Mother.

"Take your suitcase out of the wardrobe."

Mother's voice was a cold and fierce blizzard. Jiyoo could feel all the hairs on the back of her neck stand up. Why was Mother asking her to take out her suitcase?

"You disobey me, steal from me, and lie to me. I would have forgiven you if I thought it was just a mistake."

A foreboding thought flashed across Jiyoo's mind like a conviction. Jiyoo was too terrified to even tremble. She shook her head furiously.

No. Mother wouldn't do that.

"But you knew. You knew what you were doing. You conspired with your Auntie and made a fool of me." Mother then lowered her voice even further. "Even if everyone in the world betrayed me, I thought I could trust that you would always be on my side."

Jiyoo desperately shook her head.

"No, Mother. I—"

"I can't live with a backstabbing little cunt."

Jiyoo heard a scream-like plea burst from her own mouth. "Mother! No. I didn't mean to—"

"Take out your suitcase."

Jiyoo's intuition was right.

Jiyoo took a step back. She brought her hands together as if praying to Mother.

"Mother, I was bad. I won't do it again—"

"I already told you. Twice. If you make me say it again, I'm going to run you out of the house in your pajamas. Take out your suitcase!"

Jiyoo took another step back. Her thigh was up against the bed. She could hardly see now, and warm tears were beginning to well up around her eyes. She couldn't believe what was happening. She wanted to believe that Mother wasn't really going to chase her out in the middle of the night like this. She wanted to think that Mother was just giving her a harsher scolding than usual.

"Mother, stop."

Jiyoo collapsed to her knees at Mother's feet. Her voice started to shake with sobs.

"Don't kick me out of the house."

Jiyoo started choking on her own tears. The back of her throat was contracting rapidly with convulsions. It felt like her head was going to explode with pain. Jiyoo was too distraught to realize she was making things worse.

Jiyoo had already made two mistakes. She wasn't allowed to cry when begging for forgiveness. Crying annoyed Mother and made her even angrier. The proper thing to do was to explain what she did wrong and why she did it. Jiyoo's second mistake was asking Mother to stop. Mother decided the punishment, not Jiyoo.

"Just take me to Grandma's house. I won't come home until you tell me to—"

And with that, Jiyoo had made a third mistake. An unforgivable mistake. Telling Mother what to do.

Jiyoo's left cheek turned suddenly to the right. Lightning struck the other cheek. Pushed back by the force of the slap, Jiyoo hit her head on the corner of the bed and fell to the ground. A scream erupted. The ceiling was spinning above Jiyoo's head. Everything became distant.

"Get up."

Mother's voice sounded distant. Jiyoo lifted her head. The taste of iron trickled down Jiyoo's throat. She felt nauseous and started to hiccup.

"Faster."

Jiyoo got up. She staggered. The floor beneath her feet felt unsteady. Something was dripping from her chin. Specks of bright red were dotting the floor and her pajama bottoms. Jiyoo desperately focused her vision and looked at Mother. She hoped that Mother would see that she had a nosebleed. But it was in vain. A cold hand grabbed Jiyoo's shoulder and pushed her.

"Go to the wardrobe."

Jiyoo staggered to the wardrobe. Mother followed and stood behind her.

"Open the door and take out your suitcase."

Jiyoo opened the door, but she didn't want to take out the suitcase. If she did that, she would really have to go outside.

"Please, Mother. I said I was sorry."

Jiyoo turned around and pulled Mother's waist toward her.

"Let go of me."

Mother tried to push Jiyoo away. Jiyoo buried her head in Mother's stomach and shook her head furiously.

"No. I don't want to go. Mother, please!"

Jiyoo didn't realize she was shouting. She also didn't realize how desperately she was holding on to Mother.

"Let go of me, you lying cunt!"

Mother's voice erupted like thunder. Jiyoo went flying toward the wall. She felt her head hit the wall. There was a loud thud, and then Mother's face grew distant. Her vision was going black. And then the world vanished.

"Jiyoo, wake up. Jiyoo."

It was Jiyoo's stepfather's voice. She opened her eyes. Stunned eyes were looking down at her.

"Can you see me?"

Jiyoo tried to say yes, but her mouth wouldn't open. Instead of answering, she just blinked at him.

"Are you okay?"

Jiyoo didn't know. But she knew that even if she could get up, it would be best not to. If she pretended to be unconscious, Mother might show mercy. Jiyoo closed her eyes again.

"Don't interfere."

Jiyoo could hear Mother's voice from her right. Jiyoo's stepfather lifted her up with both arms.

"Put her down!" Mother shouted.

Stepfather brought Jiyoo over to her bed. Jiyoo's heart was beating so fast she thought it might leap out of her body.

"Can't you hear what I'm saying?"

Stomping her heels on the ground, Mother walked over to Stepfather and shoved him out of the way.

"I said don't touch my daughter, you sick son of a bitch."

Jiyoo didn't want to believe it was Mother who was saying these things. She didn't want to believe Mother had called her that name. Stepfather fell on the bed while holding Jiyoo. Jiyoo opened her eyes out of shock. Stepfather stood back up and started shouting at Mother.

"What did you do?"

Mother reached out with both arms and shoved Stepfather in the chest again.

"I said don't touch my daughter!"

It seemed like Stepfather hadn't expected this second attack from Mother. He lost his balance and was forced backwards. The third attack started immediately. Mother rammed Stepfather into the wall. There was a loud thud and Jiyoo could feel the wall shake.

"I told you not to touch her."

Mother started thrashing and pounded her fists against Stepfather's chest.

"What has gotten into you?"

Stepfather grabbed Mother by the wrists. Mother writhed violently as she tried to free her hands from his grip.

"Let me go, you son of a bitch."

"Get ahold of yourself. Don't do this in front of Jiyoo."

Stepfather shook Mother a couple times before letting go of her with a gentle push. Mother then took several steps back before falling to the ground. Jiyoo held her breath as she watched them fight. She remembered that Mother and Father used to fight like that a long time ago. Mother would throw a fit like a child. She would shove Father and punch him. And then when Father couldn't take it anymore and pushed her back, she would run to the kitchen and come back with a knife.

"Did you just hit me?" Mother said as she got to her feet without breaking eye contact. The whites of her eyes were streaked with red, like a candy cane.

"If you want to keep going, let's do this downstairs," Stepfather said.

Mother pursed her lips and stood up straight.

"Go to the kitchen, drink some water, then meet me in the living room."

At this, Mother turned to look at Jiyoo, who closed her eyes as fast as she could. A moment later, Jiyoo heard a voice. It seemed like Mother had finally left the room.

"It's safe now."

Jiyoo opened her eyes. Stepfather was picking Dad Puppet off the bed and looking down at it quietly.

"Is this why she was mad at you?"

Jiyoo nodded.

"Because your father gave it to you?"

This time, Jiyoo shook her head.

"You mean this isn't yours?"

Jiyoo didn't answer. Stepfather stared motionlessly at her.

"Okay. You don't have to tell me if you don't want to."

Stepfather went out of the room and came back a while later with a wet towel. He perched himself on the edge of the bed and wiped Jiyoo's face.

"Does it hurt?"

"No, I'm fine." Jiyoo just barely was able to get these words out of her tight throat. But feeling like she should thank him, she opened her throat one more time.

"Thank you for helping me."

Stepfather had a strange look on his face as he stared at Jiyoo. She had never seen someone make this face before. All at once, he looked sad, angry, happy, and like he had something to say.

"Should I turn off the lights?" Stepfather asked as he pulled the blankets over her.

"Yes."

"Goodnight."

Stepfather picked up the receiver, turned off the lights, and left the room. Jiyoo pulled Dad Puppet close to her. She closed her eyes, but she couldn't fall asleep. Mother never let things go. And she never forgot. Stepfather had only delayed Jiyoo's punishment. This wasn't the end of it. She felt anxious and afraid. Mother had gone down to the kitchen. But what if she came back with a knife, just like before?

CHAPTER 8

Eun-ho waited for Wife inside his study. It had already been thirty minutes. When he came down the stairs, Wife was sitting on the sofa in the living room. He had no idea what she was doing. Not only was she sitting with her back to the stairs, but she had turned off all the lights, making everything pitch black. The only thing he could make out was the back of her head, which was dimly lit by the light shining in from the balcony window.

Even though she should have sensed Eun-ho coming down the stairs, she didn't turn around. He didn't call out to her or speak to her. He figured she would find her way to him eventually. But she did not. Nor did she march off to bed. Wife's personality was such that she had to resolve this before going to bed. But Eun-ho was nervous for a different reason. Tonight, he had something to tell her.

It was almost ten by the time Eun-ho left Jinu's apartment. He decided to leave his car at Jinu's and walk home. He did this for two reasons. Not only did he need to sober up after drinking for much of the day, but he also needed to organize his mind, which was scattered from shock and disbelief. Wife's voice was repeating itself inside his head the whole walk home.

Happiness is subtraction. It's getting rid of the possibility of unhappiness until life becomes perfect.

The possibility of unhappiness . . . He walked up from the riverside path onto the main road. As he stood waiting at the crosswalk, Wife's voice whispered to him again.

I've lived my whole life striving for that perfect happiness.

The light changed several times, but Eun-ho just stood there blinking. Wife's college boyfriend, Wife's Russian boyfriend, Wife's father, Wife's ex-husband—and then there was Noah. Wife believed that a flawless family was a happy family. There was a sudden rattling sound in Eun-ho's head. As though two broken gears had suddenly interlocked.

Synthesizing what Min-young and Jinu had told him, Eun-ho realized that the four men had all made Yuna unhappy for one reason or another. Breaking up with her, divorcing her, firing her. Noah was flawed in that he came from another womb. She must have believed that Noah was a threat to her happiness. Or perhaps she just couldn't accept his mere existence.

Bracing against fierce winds, Eun-ho started to shake. It wasn't the physical cold that made him shake, but the chilling nature of this realization. He could see something that he had been blind to. Those men were the focus of Wife's "efforts." And so were Jiyoo's adoption and Wife's insistence on having a child together. Everything was connected, like branches from the same tree.

From the beginning, the families that he and she imagined were incompatible. A flawless family to Wife would be her, Eun-ho, Jiyoo as Eun-ho's adopted daughter, and a child of their own. There was no room for Noah. These were the conditions of the perfect happiness that Wife dreamed of.

Even after arriving home, Eun-ho couldn't go inside. He just stood outside and stared up at the house in reluctance. The upstairs and downstairs windows were illuminated, but their light didn't reach him. What he was looking at didn't feel like a house but an abyss. Eun-ho was afraid to go inside. He was so afraid that he was trembling.

Eun-ho had to decide whether to go in. Turning around and leaving would be no different from running away. And such a decision would be consistent with the way he had lived his life until now, always ignoring the unbearable truth. Going in meant offering himself up as bait—something he'd never done before.

And going inside would ultimately lead to the same outcome. He would either die of old age in prison for murdering his wife, or he would be murdered in his sleep. Either way, walking through that door was suicide.

Eun-ho started toward the front door. With each step, Eun-ho could hear blood rushing through his ears. His body was pulsating, the back of his neck was prickly, and he was hearing bells inside his head. He wondered how he was going to confront Wife in such a pitiful state.

As soon as he opened the front door, he was met with the sound of Jiyoo crying. A few seconds later, he heard Wife's screams.

This had never happened before. He had never heard Jiyoo cry or seen Wife throw a tantrum because of Jiyoo. Eun-ho walked through the living room toward his study. He didn't want to get involved in their mother-daughter problems.

Eun-ho opened the door to his study but was unable to push himself inside. Jiyoo's cries had turned to screams. She was screaming like a child who was terrified. Eun-ho finally threw his bag down and ran upstairs.

When Eun-ho got to the door of Jiyoo's bedroom, he heard a loud thud. He opened the door to find Jiyoo on the ground with a heavy nosebleed. Wife grabbed Jiyoo as she started shouting.

"Open your eyes. Wake up. Before I kill you."

Someone had pushed Wife's self-destruct button.

Eun-ho was less surprised than he was disturbed. This wasn't the first time Eun-ho had seen wife lose it. But what did surprise Eun-ho was the way he responded. He pulled Wife off Jiyoo and picked the child up.

"Don't touch my daughter, you sick son of a bitch."

The blood started draining from Eun-ho's head as he heard these words. There was a sinister implication in what she said. She brought her fists down on him as she repeated this over and over again. The more appropriate thing to say would be something like "This doesn't concern you." At least, that's what most people would say. The only reason to say it this way was if he had touched Jiyoo inappropriately.

A chilling thought flashed through Eun-ho's mind. Was this how Wife cornered her ex-husband in the divorce suit? Was this how she stripped him of his parental rights?

Eun-ho's queries turned toward himself. What would happen if he asked for a divorce? As he searched for an answer, he pushed his imagination to the worst place.

He had no parental rights to be stripped of. And if Jiyoo was made to testify, she would agree with everything her mother said. Eun-ho wouldn't be just a child murderer; he would also become a child molester.

Telling Eun-ho not to touch her daughter wasn't just a slip of the tongue.

She was both threatening to ruin his life while simultaneously laying the groundwork to make it a reality. This was just how she fabricated the story about his sleep disorder with those fake text messages.

"Eun-ho."

He looked up from his desk. Wife was calling to him from outside the door to his study.

"Would you open the door for me? My hands are tied."

Eun-ho got up from his chair. When he opened the door, he was met with glossed-over hazel eyes. He could smell alcohol in her breath. He had told her to come to him after drinking some water, but it seemed she had drunk alcohol while sitting alone in the dark living room.

Could he really tell her when she was like this? Eun-ho nervously stepped aside to let her into the room. Wife took one step inside. In one hand she had two glasses of ice, and in the other, an opened bottle of vodka.

"Have a drink with me," Wife said as she lifted the bottle. She must have drunk a lot because she was slurring her speech. Eun-ho received the bottle and went back to his desk. He took out a folding chair, placed it next to the desk, then sat down in his office chair.

Wife didn't sit down in the chair he brought out for her. Instead, she perched half her butt on the edge of the desk and looked straight at him. She pushed the two glasses toward him. Eun-ho poured each of them a glass.

"First, a toast."

Wife held up her glass. Not knowing what else to do, Eun-ho held up his glass, too. Before he could ask what they were making a toast to, Wife clinked her glass against his.

"Today was the first time you've acted like Jiyoo's father."

Wife took a sip of her vodka before looking down at him. She stared at him with a stern look on her face, as if to ask, *Why aren't you drinking?* Eun-ho brought the glass to his lips but didn't drink. He had just sobered up, and the smell of vodka made him nauseous.

"I was really moved by what you did up there," Wife said.

Eun-ho didn't answer. Was that what Wife did when she was moved? Roll her eyes into the back of her skull and attack someone?

"Before, you never paid any attention to what I did to Jiyoo. But now you're willing to fight me to protect her." Wife rattled the ice in her glass. "What changed?"

Eun-ho focused his gaze on the ice cubes in her glass. He waited in silence because he wasn't sure what it was that Wife wanted to hear from him.

"I'll be honest with you. I was so mad today. Because of Jane and Jiyoo."

Wife let out a long sigh. She looked down at her feet and shook her head for a while. Just when Eun-ho was starting to think that she had forgotten what she was about to say, she continued.

"I didn't want to tell you this because it had to do with my family and because I was embarrassed, but Jane used to have feelings for my ex-husband. Although he never felt the same. She chased him all through college and even after they graduated."

Eun-ho looked down at the glass in his hand. He was biding his time, waiting for the moment his words would deliver the biggest emotional blow to her.

"Perhaps that's why Jane was so obsessed with Jiyoo. She's always acting as if she's Jiyoo's mom. She even came to the house today while I was out. I knew as soon as I saw the Happy Meal box in the recycling bin. She brought Jiyoo a creepy puppet, too. Jiyoo's young, so she likes those kinds of things. And because she's been buying Jiyoo gifts and treats, Jiyoo lied for Jane. I specifically asked her if Jane came by today, and she lied."

Wife drained the rest of the vodka into her mouth and held her glass out to Eun-ho, who filled it up for her.

"That's why I had to discipline her. But then you showed up and did something you've never done before, making *me* feel like the villain."

Eun-ho summarized in his head what Wife had said up till now. She got pissed because her sister brought Jiyoo lunch; she got angry because Jiyoo lied about it; and she was pushed over the edge because Eun-ho showed up at the worst time possible. She blamed the three of them for making her look like a crazy bitch. This was always how Wife defended herself.

"But after I thought about it, I was so moved by your heroic gesture that I thought we should celebrate over drinks. You understand how I feel, don't you?"

Instead of answering, Eun-ho just finished his drink. The alcohol warmed his throat as it trickled down toward his stomach.

"But it looks like you drank a bit today, too."

"A little." Eun-ho's voice dried up at the back of his throat.

"With whom?"

Eun-ho knew if he said Jinu, they would get into another fight. He could say he had drinks with a friend from work or college, but would she believe that?

Eun-ho suddenly felt disgusted by his own thought process. He was still walking on eggshells around her, despite knowing what Wife had done to achieve happiness, despite being convinced she had killed Noah, despite his only purpose for coming home was to know the truth.

"With whom did you drink, Eun-ho?"

"Jinu."

"Jinu? I thought you promised me you wouldn't talk to him anymore."

He had promised that. He had only promised that because at the time, he was desperately trying to prove his devotion to Wife. He didn't know the true reason she didn't like Jinu. Eun-ho turned to look at the ice remaining in his glass. He hoped the ice could extinguish the fire raging inside his belly.

"Jinu's my friend. And he was my only friend to stay by my side during Noah's funeral."

"Oh, right. I forgot. He's your friend."

Wife slowly nodded up and down. The ice jostled inside the glass to the beat of her nodding.

"So what did you talk about when you met your great friend Jinu? Did you talk about your controlling bitch of a wife?"

Eun-ho looked up and locked eyes with Wife, whose pupils were watching him like a hawk. The tipsy look in her eyes from when she first entered the room had vanished without a trace.

"I just wanted to vent a little."

"Is that all you did?" Wife asked as she brought her eyes up to Eun-ho's face, as if she could detect lies just by looking deep into his eyes. "Vent?"

Eun-ho averted his eyes as he changed the subject.

"Did you call those detectives back? The ones from Seodaemun Police Department?"

"What does that have to do with Jinu?"

Eun-ho figured he might as well push her a bit further while he was at it.

"Those detectives keep calling me and asking me all sorts of questions."

"What kind of questions?"

"Well, they really want to know if you were home on November 16."

Wife brought her head back to its original position and looked at Eun-ho out of the corner of her eye, as if to say, *Keep going, I dare you.*

"And actually, I've been wondering the same thing. Where were you those five days?"

"You weren't wondering, don't lie."

A grin formed on her lips.

"If you were so curious, Eun-ho, why didn't you call me once while I was gone those five days? What were *you* doing for those five days?"

This was a clever subversion. She had hit the ball right back at Eun-ho. If Eun-ho were his usual self, he would have gotten caught up in her trap and become emotional. But Eun-ho was becoming less and less receptive to these games.

"I thought you were at your mother's. But you weren't. Your sister came looking for you here."

The grin disappeared from Wife's lips. It seemed like the mere mention of Jane could put her in a sour mood.

"She said she came here to tell you that your Mom is out of the country and not to drop Jiyoo off at their house."

Wife's eyes momentarily looked left before returning to looking forward. Eun-ho knew what it meant when Wife's eyes moved like that. She made it when she was backed into a corner and was looking for a way out. Eun-ho continued:

"I told your sister that I thought you were at your mom's place. And she looked confused, like she didn't know what I was talking about."

"I never said I was going to my mom's place." It looked like she had found her way out.

"I went on a trip with Jiyoo. I needed time to think. Time to think about whether I wanted to continue living with a man who wouldn't accept my daughter as his own."

Eun-ho poured more vodka into his empty glass. It seemed like he wasn't going to get drunk no matter how much he drank.

"I came back because I decided to give you one more chance," Wife said. "Just one. But you haven't changed. I'm trying my best."

Trying her best meant killing Noah. Eun-ho dumped the entire glass of vodka into his mouth. His stomach lurched in pain.

"Didn't you promise when we got married that you would try too? Have you forgotten your promise?"

Wife moved so that she was all the way on the desk. She crossed her legs, one hand supporting her and the other holding her glass. With her right foot dangling in the air, her slipper slid off her foot, just getting caught on her toe before falling. Her smooth, white toes bobbed up and down ever so slightly. Eun-ho's nose was filled with the smell of her body.

"Are you finally ready to try?" Wife looked Eun-ho in the eye. This kind of seduction used to have an effect on him. But right now, her advances were only making it hard to breathe. He couldn't believe Wife still thought she could seduce him like this. It was clear she had a magic mirror inside her that told her she was a queen.

"So, you're not going to answer me?"

Wife brought her hand to Eun-ho's cheek. She stroked his bristles with her warm, soft fingers. As her fingers traced lines on his face, goosebumps appeared in their wake, like skid marks on a road.

"Yuna."

Eun-ho moved his head backward and distanced himself from her hand.

"I have something I need to tell you."

Wife glanced at her hand, which was left dangling in the air.

"No." She shook her head. "I have something to tell you first."

Eun-ho closed his mouth.

"I'm leaving the company. I relinquished my duties as CEO yesterday."

This was the last thing Eun-ho expected to come out of her mouth. Wife studied his reaction. Eun-ho used all his might not to let his eyes waver.

"I've thought about this for a while."

Wife explained that she wanted them to immigrate to Russia. She'd even gone to a Khabarovsk investment immigration info session. She'd made preparations to start a new business and had already found a house for them.

"I'm going to the real estate agency on Monday to put this house up for sale. It'll sell quickly if we ask for less than market value. After that, we'll be ready to start our new lives together, in Russia."

When had she had the time to do all this? She must have been planning this for months. Had she been working under the assumption that he would agree to this? That must have been what she believed. Either that, or she was planning on coercing him into agreeing. Eun-ho wondered if Noah had been one of the items she crossed off her to-do list.

"I know it's tough, but you've got to let Noah go. You need to move on with your life. You have a family. The ones who are still alive."

Wife scooted across the desk so that she was directly in front of him. The slipper that had been dangling on the tip of her toes fell to the ground. Wife used to straddle him like this when they were madly in love to get him to do things for her. She would get up on his desk, spread her legs, and put her feet on the armrests of his chair, trapping him in his seat. It wasn't long ago that he would sit helplessly in anticipation of her next move as he listened to the pounding of his heart. But now, he could hardly bear to look at her.

"The police investigation will end soon. You'll be charged with manslaughter and either be sent to prison or have to pay a fine. All we can do is wait. That's what my lawyer said. But don't worry. He has the highest win rate of any criminal defense attorney in Korea. When this is all over—"

Eun-ho could hear Wife's voice becoming distant. He was desperately fighting the urge to jump out of his seat and strangle her. Soon, he was going to be formally charged with the murder of his son. If he couldn't reveal the truth before then, and if he gave in to his current urges, this would turn into a double homicide.

"So don't do something as stupid as handing over those sleep study results."

Wife put her bare foot on Eun-ho's inner thigh. Her toes playfully crawled up his pants. Eun-ho's leg started to spasm.

At the same time, Eun-ho realized something. Wife knew something about Noah's death. She hadn't said anything that directly proved this, but she was talking with too much conviction.

"I'm trying my hardest to defend you, honey—"

Wife looked into his eyes and tried to cast a spell over him. The sour smell of her skin was seeping into every inch of his body.

"If you keep acting on your own, I won't be able to help you. Don't you think so?"

Eun-ho's intuition was right. She was threatening him, telling him that whatever it was that he knew, he should forget it. If he didn't, she would make sure he was convicted as a child murderer.

"Yuna."

Eun-ho looked Wife in the eye. He tried his hardest not to show any emotion on his face. He had to be calm and emotionless for his words to have an effect.

"I want a divorce."

Wife tilted her head to the side. She wrinkled the skin between her brow, as if she didn't think this was funny. He looked her straight in the eye and spoke clearly, so there would be no chance of her mishearing him:

"I'll leave the house. Tomorrow morning."

*

Dad Puppet had magical powers. When Jiyoo was asleep, he protected her from nightmares. And when she was awake, he gave her the strength to endure anything.

Jiyoo woke up several times throughout the night, and when she opened her eyes, she was immediately in pain. Lying in bed, she would confide in Dad Puppet. She told him about what she did wrong, the disappointment in herself for getting caught, her regret and sadness about losing Mother's trust, her suspicions about Mother and the guilt she felt for doubting her, and the fear about her impending punishment.

As she talked, the pain in her chest subsided and she was able to fall asleep again. When day broke, Jiyoo was well enough to stand up. She also had the courage to summon Mischievous Mouse. She was ready to figure out who could help her.

Not Stepfather. As far as Jiyoo saw it, Stepfather had no interest in her. He said hi to her like he would say hi to a random child on the street. He only helped her last night because he pitied her. Mother had knocked Jiyoo unconscious and given her a bloody nose. Anyone would have stepped in like he did. Anyone.

What about Auntie? Would she be any different? Would Auntie come running if she knew Jiyoo was in trouble? Would she look after Jiyoo until Mother decided to forgive her or Grandma came back from Russia? That's what she did last time Jiyoo was sick. She nursed Jiyoo back to health and stayed by her side at the hospital when Mother wasn't around. She even called Jiyoo affectionate names and hugged her when she was having bad dreams.

Jiyoo pulled her sheets over her head as she thought hard about how she could talk to Auntie without Mother knowing. But she couldn't think of anything. At least, not until Stepfather knocked on her bedroom door.

"Jiyoo, are you up?"

Even if Jiyoo hadn't heard his voice, she would have known it was him because Mother didn't knock before coming in. Mother always said that she had the right, not just to enter Jiyoo's room, but to have access to Jiyoo's thoughts. She could decide what Jiyoo thought and how she acted.

When Jiyoo asked why, Mother said, "Because you belong to me." As soon as Jiyoo protested with a "But—", Mother posed a question to Jiyoo: "When an artist paints, does the painting belong to the painter or the painting?" Finally, Jiyoo understood. She was a painting.

"Jiyoo, are you still asleep?"

Jiyoo stuck her head out from the sheets and answered, "No."

As usual, Stepfather didn't come into Jiyoo's room. He just stood outside the door and delivered his message.

"Come down for breakfast."

"Yes," Jiyoo said as she got up. She quickly made her bed and changed out of her pajamas. She did this twice as fast as she normally did. Mother would be downstairs, and Jiyoo didn't want to make her wait.

But Mother wasn't in the kitchen. Stepfather was sitting by himself at the kitchen table and drinking coffee.

"Good morning," Jiyoo said as she brought her hands together in front of her stomach and bowed to Stepfather.

"Did you sleep well?" he asked. The look on his face was unfamiliar. Even though he wasn't smiling, there was this kindness in his eyes. His tone was uncomfortable, but not cold or unfeeling.

"Yes." Jiyoo hesitated for a moment. "Where's Mother?"

"She had something to take care of. She'll be back around lunchtime."

Jiyoo nodded in excitement. It seemed her punishment had been delayed a few more hours. Suddenly, Jiyoo realized she might be able to call Auntie. But she immediately abandoned this idea. Mother would be checking the call history from now on. But perhaps she could ask Stepfather if she could borrow his cellphone.

"Well, don't just stand there. Sit."

Stepfather motioned to the seat across from him with his eyes. On the table was an omelet, cereal, yogurt, orange juice, bananas, toast, strawberry jam, and honey. It was enough to feed all the kids in the neighborhood. Surely he wasn't expecting Jiyoo to eat all this. Jiyoo stared at Stepfather in disbelief.

"I didn't know what you liked." He forced a toothy smile. "Just pick out what you want. I'll eat what you don't."

Stepfather didn't say anything more. He didn't even ask about last night's incident. He just took notes on a piece of paper as he finished two cups of coffee.

Jiyoo could feel herself relaxing. She was relaxing so quickly that she was surprised. Before long, she even felt comfortable, at ease. The cellphone placed next to the cup of coffee kept grabbing her attention. Courage was forming in the back of her mind—courage out of desperation.

"Excuse me—"

Stepfather looked up from the document. Jiyoo practiced a few times in her head before speaking.

"Can I ask you something?"

Stepfather put the papers down on the table and looked at Jiyoo eagerly.

"May I use your phone?"

For a moment, Stepfather looked like he was thinking.

"You mean my cellphone?"

"Yes."

Jiyoo could feel her voice retreating back into her throat. She wanted to take back what she had just said.

Stepfather opened his phone and handed it to Jiyoo. The phone was already unlocked.

"Can I go to the bathroom to make a phone call?"

"You can do it here." Stepfather got up from his chair. "I needed to go to the bathroom anyway."

Stepfather didn't ask whom she was calling or why. He picked up the papers he had been looking at and disappeared. Before the screen turned off, Jiyoo found Auntie Jane's number and pressed it. She could hear the ring tone. Once, twice, three times.

Auntie didn't pick up. Jiyoo got an automated message telling her Auntie's phone was turned off. Jiyoo hung up the phone and called again. She could feel her strength draining. No, that wasn't the right expression. Auntie Jane had taught her that for a situation like this, the correct word was "hope." She was losing hope. But why did Auntie turn off her phone? She said she would keep it on. Always.

Jiyoo tried ten more times. She put down the phone just as Stepfather came back.

"Done?"

"Yes."

Jiyoo wanted to thank him but couldn't. Her throat was tight and she wanted to cry. Jiyoo dropped her head and stuck a piece of toast in her mouth. She was afraid that she would really start crying if she made eye contact with Stepfather. But the toast got stuck in her throat, making her gag. Jiyoo reached for the juice and drank the whole glass.

"Are you all right?" Stepfather asked as she put down the glass.

"Yes, I'm all right."

And she really was. Her throat already felt better. The desire to cry that had been working its way up her throat disappeared with the toast.

"You don't have to eat if you don't want to," Stepfather said as he sat down. His brow was furrowed, but he didn't seem angry. He just looked concerned. Jiyoo shook her head.

"Are you going out?"

"No, I'm going to wait here until your mother comes home. Why?"

"Nothing. Can I go up to my room?"

Stepfather gave her permission to. But Jiyoo didn't get up from her seat. She needed to ask him another favor.

"Do you have something you want to say?"

Jiyoo was thankful that he asked. That gave her the courage she needed to speak.

"Can I ask something? Will you keep it a secret that you gave me your phone?"

"From your Mother, you mean?" Stepfather said, filling in the part that Jiyoo wanted to keep implicit. Jiyoo nodded.

"I have something to ask of you, too. May I?"

Auntie had told Jiyoo that nothing was free. If she received something, she had to pay it back. She told Jiyoo that if she didn't want to pay people back, she shouldn't ask for favors in the first place. As Jiyoo had already asked Stepfather for two favors, it was only right that she do him one. But Jiyoo was nervous that he would ask her a question that would be hard for her to answer.

"What is it?" she asked.

"The week before last, you were with Mother from Tuesday to Saturday."

Jiyoo's heart was beating faster and faster. She knew what he was about to ask.

"Where did you two go?"

This wasn't just hard for her to answer, this was impossible for her to answer. Her chest was becoming tight, just like earlier when she choked on the piece of toast. Jiyoo decided to use the white lie she had used before.

"Home."

But this time, Stepfather wasn't going to let it go. He demanded her to be more specific.

"Which home?"

Jiyoo needed to keep Mother's secret, but she didn't want to lie.

"Can't you ask Mother?"

Stepfather stared at Jiyoo in silence. Jiyoo averted his eyes by looking downward. It felt like minutes passed before he answered:

"Okay."

Jiyoo wanted to go back upstairs as soon as possible.

"Can I go now?"

Stepfather gave her the same answer from earlier. "Okay."

Jiyoo stood up from her chair. She bent at the waist and bowed to him.

"Thank you for the meal."

"Jiyoo—"

He called out to Jiyoo but didn't continue. He sat up straight in his chair and took a deep breath.

"Never mind. Forget it."

The entire walk up the stairs, Jiyoo could feel Stepfather's gaze. It was the kind of gaze that made her want to look back. She felt worried and confused. Why was Stepfather asking her and not Mother? What was he going to say to her before stopping? And had she given him the wrong answer?

The morning passed slowly. Jiyoo had nothing to do but stare out the window anxiously. But because this room didn't have a large window ledge like the cabin in the country, she had to sit on top of the desk to watch the occasional car pass by. And each time this happened, her heart would start racing with anticipation. But after a while, she wished that Mother wouldn't come home until later that night. Perhaps this would all be forgotten if she was asleep when Mother came home. If that happened, perhaps Mother would forget about punishing Jiyoo.

But Jiyoo knew that wasn't going to happen. Mother would never forget what Jiyoo did. Jiyoo was going to receive her punishment one way or another. In some ways, she just wanted to get it over with. If Mother took Jiyoo to the orphanage, Jiyoo could at least call Auntie Jane to come pick her up—assuming Auntie turned her phone on.

At some point, Jiyoo's vision started to go fuzzy. She could even feel her head nodding slightly in drowsiness. Jiyoo opened her eyes suddenly when she heard a sound coming from beneath her window. She quickly lifted her head and looked out the window. Mother's car was parked in front of the garage, and the door to the garage was opening. The moment had arrived.

Jiyoo quickly got down from the desk. But once she was down, she felt lost because she didn't know what to do, even though she had been thinking about this moment all day. Should she pretend to be taking a nap? Should she pretend to be reading a book? Should she go downstairs and welcome Mother home? And what should she do about Dad Puppet? Mother already knew about him, and she hadn't taken him away again. Even so, Jiyoo didn't have the courage to leave him in plain sight.

Dad Puppet eventually went under Jiyoo's pillow. She sat at her desk and took out *Frozen II* from the bookshelf. Although she knew Mother wouldn't pity Jiyoo just because she was reading, she thought it might make her less angry if she found Jiyoo reading. As Jiyoo did this, her ears were turned outward.

Jiyoo could hear Mother's movements as vividly as though she could see her. Mother got out of the car, entered the passcode on the padlock on the front door, crossed the living room, and entered a room. Jiyoo let out the breath that she had been holding in. Her shoulders, which had been up to her shoulders, dropped with a sigh. Now she needed to think. What would she say when she saw Mother? After all, it was only a matter of time until Mother came upstairs.

But Jiyoo's intuition had lied to her. It was Stepfather, not Mother, who came up to see her. Jiyoo got up from her chair.

"Your mother wants you to come down, dressed to go."

Jiyoo didn't ask why. She knew the answer. Mother was sending her to the orphanage.

"And she wants you to put your things in your suitcase. Only pack the things you need. Pajamas, underwear, socks."

This time, however, Jiyoo was confused. If she was going to the orphanage, wouldn't she need all her stuff?

"Do you need help?"

Jiyoo shook her head.

"I can do it." Then for some reason, Jiyoo added something she really didn't need to add: "I know how to do it. I've done it before."

"But still, you have to bring the suitcase downstairs."

Jiyoo shook her head. She wasn't going to the playground; she was going to the orphanage. If she was going to be chased out of the house, she'd rather do it *without* Stepfather's help.

"I'll be down in a minute."

Stepfather stared at Jiyoo with both hands inside his pockets. Jiyoo dropped her eyes and looked at her toes. It didn't matter; Stepfather wasn't going to be able to stop Mother. And if he couldn't stop Mother, he was of no use to Jiyoo. Plus, Jiyoo needed space to think about what to take and what to leave behind.

"I'll wait downstairs then."

Finally, Stepfather left. Jiyoo stood vacantly in the middle of her room. Now that she had her suitcase out, she couldn't decide. It both seemed like she needed to take everything, and that she needed to take nothing. Jiyoo looked down at her name tag, which was stuck to the top of the suitcase. She remembered what Auntie had told her about choices.

"When faced with a hard choice, just think about what's most precious to you."

Jiyoo chose Dad Puppet and *Frozen II*. At the very back of the book was the note with Auntie's phone number, which Jiyoo had prepared in case she ever forgot. Jiyoo filled the rest of the suitcase with the things Mother told her to: pajamas, underwear, socks.

Mother and Stepfather were sitting shoulder to shoulder on the sofa. They were both dressed in thick jackets. On the floor beneath the coffee table was a small travel bag. Jiyoo was confused. Was Stepfather going to the orphanage, too?

"Did you pack underwear?" Mother asked as she got up from the sofa.

"Yes."

"And your gloves and hat?"

Jiyoo showed Mother the gloves and hat that she had in her hand. Satisfied, Mother turned to Stepfather who grabbed the travel bag and stood up.

"Shall we?"

Outside, Mother got into the driver's seat as Stepfather put the bags in the trunk. He buckled Jiyoo in and then got in the back with her.

"How far is it?" Stepfather asked as they left downtown Cheongyeon.

"About two hours. I think you'll like it."

Jiyoo couldn't understand their whole conversation, but from what she could understand, it sounded like the place she was taking Jiyoo was two hours away. Stepfather seemed to also think it was a good idea to take Jiyoo to the orphanage. But was that really what he thought? Jiyoo glanced furtively at Stepfather, and he looked back at her. He smiled at Jiyoo with his eyes. But Jiyoo was confused because the rest of the muscles of his face didn't look like they were smiling.

"Let's eat lunch in the car," Mother said.

Mother parked the car in front of a building. There was a McDonald's on the first floor.

"Honey, would you go in and buy us something?"

Mother wanted a shrimp burger and a coffee. Stepfather looked at Jiyoo.

"Jiyoo, want to go in with me?"

"Yes."

Jiyoo was afraid of being alone with Mother in the car. Stepfather got out of the car first and gave Jiyoo his hand. In the past, Jiyoo would be afraid of what Mother would think, but not anymore. Stepfather was Jiyoo's last hope. If she begged him, he might be able to stop Mother from sending her to the orphanage.

"Jiyoo, you want a bulgogi burger with fries and a coke, right?" Stepfather asked when they got to the cashier.

"How did you know?"

Stepfather chuckled.

"Your aunt told me."

Stepfather's laugh immediately lightened the mood.

"You're taking me to the orphanage, aren't you?" Jiyoo asked cautiously.

Stepfather raised his eyebrows in surprise.

"Because last night I made Mother angry—" Jiyoo added when she saw Stepfather's reaction.

The smile of Stepfather's face was slowly disappearing.

"No. We're going on vacation. I think."

Their number appeared on the order screen.

"Let's talk about this later," Stepfather said as he got up.

When they were back inside the car with the food, Stepfather's cellphone started to ring inside his pocket. He took out his phone and checked the number. He looked like he was thinking about whether to answer. The phone continued to ring in a stubborn manner. Finally, Stepfather pressed accept.

"Hello?"

"Where are you?"

Jiyoo could hear a man's voice. Jiyoo immediately turned to look up at the rearview mirror. She immediately made eye contact with Mother. Stepfather simply looked out the window without answering.

"I wanted to make sure you were—"

"Aha, Mr. Park—" Stepfather said, cutting off the man. "I didn't recognize the number at first."

Mother reached over and turned off the radio. But the man on the line wasn't responding. Stepfather glanced up at the rearview mirror as he spoke:

"I don't think that'll work. I'm going somewhere with my wife and daughter right now."

The man on the phone said something, but his voice was too quiet for Jiyoo to understand.

"Yes. I'll call you back later."

Stepfather hung up the phone. They passed under a sign that read "Wirye-dong, Hanam City" and entered the highway.

"Mr. Park? You mean the lawyer?" Mother asked. "What did he say?"

"He wanted to meet me at his office early tomorrow morning."

"What about our promise?"

Stepfather's eyes turned to the rearview mirror again.

"Did you hear me? I told him I couldn't make it."

"No, I was asking about the fact that you said you'd call him back later." Before Stepfather could answer this, Mother continued. "Can't you put your phone down for just one day?" Mother held up her cellphone. "I've turned mine off. The only thing I want to focus on is us."

Stepfather took the hint faster than Father had. Mother didn't have to ask him twice about turning it off. Mother extended her hand toward the back seat.

"Give it to me."

Stepfather stared at Mother's hand with a flustered look on his face.

"Why? I've turned it off."

"Have you already forgotten? The promise we made this morning?" Mother paused before raising her voice slightly. "It's just one day. This will be the last time."

Stepfather eventually handed over his phone. Mother turned the radio back on. After that, no one said anything. Everyone simply ate their lunch in silence.

This situation wasn't unfamiliar to Jiyoo. Everything was the same as when they picked up Father. The only difference was that Jiyoo had no idea where they were going right now. There were signs on the highway, but all of them were places she had never heard of before.

It had been snowing since yesterday. At first it was just a light dusting of snow, but then at some point, it turned into a blizzard. They turned onto a two-lane road that barely had any cars. Mother then took a sharp right after a bus stop. Then like magic, a familiar sight appeared before them. Although everything was covered in snow, Jiyoo knew where they were. Mother wasn't taking Jiyoo to the orphanage. They were going to the cabin in the countryside.

Jiyoo thought about why she hadn't recognized anything up to this point. Perhaps it was because they had come from Cheongyeon. The day they picked up her father, they had come from Incheon. Whatever the reason, Jiyoo felt both relieved and excited. It seemed like Mother was going to forgive her.

The abandoned house that they always drove past on their way to the cabin appeared in the distance. The blizzard had blown away the plastic covering to the greenhouse, leaving nothing but its metal frame. Behind it was a parked car. As far as Jiyoo could remember, there had never been a car parked at the abandoned house. But because the car was buried in a foot of snow, Jiyoo could only make out the silhouette of the vehicle. It looked both like a small truck or a jeep, like the kind Auntie drove.

Once they rounded the corner, the roof of the cabin appeared. Mother parked the car outside the front gate.

"We're here."

"Where are we?" Stepfather asked as he unbuckled his seat belt.

"My grandmother's house. I've told you about it before. I inherited it after she passed away."

After getting out of the car, Mother opened the gate with a key from her bag. As she did this, Stepfather took out the things from the trunk. There was a shopping bag, the travel bag, and Jiyoo's suitcase. Jiyoo also got out of the car last.

It looked like it had been snowing all day. As soon as she stepped onto the road, she was up to her ankles in snow. The pine forest, the wetlands, the cabin roof, the vines on the wall, the front yard—everything was caked in white. Mother walked ahead toward the front door. Jiyoo dragged her suitcase through the snow as she chased after Mother. Stepfather came in last, carrying the shopping bag and travel bag. All the while, he was glancing around with a doubtful look on his face.

When Mother opened the door, a smell greeted them like an eager puppy. Jiyoo was used to this smell. It was the smell of duck feed.

"What's that smell?" he asked as he stood at the doorway and glanced around.

"It's the smell of an abandoned home."

Mother put her bag on the kitchen table and turned on the overhead fan. She also pulled out a lighter from the drawer and lit the scented candle lying on the table.

"It gets like this if the doors have been shut for too long. It will pass after a while. Don't worry."

Aha . . . Stepfather mouthed as he took off his shoes and stepped inside.

"Should I put the groceries in the fridge?"

"Just put them on the kitchen counter. I'll put them away myself."

Mother opened the door to the living room and lit the scented candle that was lying on the table next to the sofa. She then opened the door to the master bedroom and disappeared inside. Stepfather went into the kitchen and put the groceries down—not on the kitchen counter like Mother told him to, but on the kitchen table. As he did this, his eyes followed Mother into the master bedroom. He looked dazed, like someone under a spell.

"Mother, I'm going to put my bag upstairs." Jiyoo shouted out to Mother.

"Take off your coat and hang it up before you come downstairs," Mother replied from the master bedroom.

Dragging her suitcase along, Jiyoo started for the stairs. But just as she reached the foot of the stairs, she heard a loud thud from above. This was accompanied by what sounded to Jiyoo like the call of a loon. Jiyoo looked up at the ceiling before turning to look at Stepfather. He was also staring up at the ceiling. Before long, Mother was standing at the door to the living room.

"What's that sound?" Stepfather muttered to himself.

"The call of a loon—" Jiyoo replied as if muttering to herself.

"It's the roof," Mother said, correcting Jiyoo.

But just as she was finishing saying this, another thud came from above. And then another howling, even louder and longer than the first time. But this time, it didn't sound like a loon.

"That doesn't sound like a creaky roof to me. Should I go check it out?" Stepfather asked as he looked at Mother.

"There's nothing to check out. You don't know this house like I do. It always makes strange sounds when the wind blows. Old houses always do that."

Jiyoo thought this was strange. The roof had never creaked like that before. She had stayed here during windstorms. On those days, the only sound the house made was the rattling of windows. The howling at first sounded just like the loon from her dream, the one crying in the attic.

"Jiyoo—" It was Mother. "Do you want to show Father around? You can go to the Half Moon Marsh."

"Right now?" Jiyoo asked without thinking. Mother's suggestion surprised her almost as much as the sound coming from upstairs. Why would Mother want her to go to the wetlands when it was snowing so hard? And hadn't she told her just a second ago to go upstairs and put away her coat?

Mother pointed to the front door with her chin, as if to say, *Hurry up*. Jiyoo suddenly remembered that Mother had suggested the exact same thing when Father came to the cabin. Jiyoo couldn't help herself from asking the same question she had asked then.

"What about you, Mother?"

Mother gave her the same answer.

"Mother is going to prepare dinner. And clean. You spend some time with your father."

"What about my bag? Shouldn't I put it upstairs first?"

But it was the roof and not Mother who answered Jiyoo. There were two successive thuds, the second one quieter than the first.

"This house is falling apart," Stepfather muttered to himself.

Mother looked at Jiyoo. There was a menacing look in her eyes. She was scolding Jiyoo for not obeying her immediately.

"Just leave your bag. I'll take it up for you."

Jiyoo put her suitcase down and headed for the front door.

"Follow me," she said to Stepfather. But he didn't budge. He was clearly distracted by the sound coming from the attic.

"Eun-ho, don't keep Jiyoo waiting."

At this, Stepfather reluctantly left the kitchen.

"Make sure you're back before dark!"

Jiyoo went to the shed and changed into her boots. She hesitated for a moment before handing Stepfather the pair of men's boots. After receiving them from her, he stared down at them for a while. He looked upset. Jiyoo thought it best if she didn't mention they had belonged to Father.

The sky was becoming prematurely dark as black clouds were blocking out the sun. The usual sound of loon calls and birds rustling in the reeds was absent. The only thing they could hear was icy wind whipping through the wetlands.

"Follow behind me."

Jiyoo stepped onto the path. It looked like the wetlands had received much more snow than the cabin had. Falling snowflakes obscured Jiyoo's vision, making it hard to see the path. The heavy snow had also flattened all the reeds, removing the landmarks on which Jiyoo relied.

"I thought you said this was a marsh," Stepfather said as he looked at their surroundings. "All I see is snow." He seemed nervous.

"There are lots of reeds. But it's snowing. So, you can't see them."

Jiyoo used the difference in ground elevation to make out the path. She couldn't walk fast because of the thick snow, but at least the ground wasn't slippery. Every step filled the air with the sound of crunching snow.

"You must come here often. I can't see anything," Stepfather said.

Jiyoo decided to use an answer that she used before: "That's because this is Mother's home."

"Just because this is your mother's cabin doesn't automatically mean you can find your way like this so easily. You must have walked this path dozens of times before. Jiyoo, did you come here last time?"

Jiyoo knew immediately what Stepfather meant when he said *last time*. It was the same question he asked her this morning. Jiyoo couldn't answer this.

"I know you were here with your father."

Jiyoo stopped walking. Despite the cold wind, Jiyoo's face was burning. This happened every time she had to lie. Stepfather had known the answer when he asked her the same question this morning. But then why had he asked it? And why hadn't he scolded her for lying to him? Stepfather stopped walking, too, and looked down at Jiyoo.

"I'm not mad at you. I'm not trying to get you in trouble."

"I—"

"It's not your fault. I blame the person who made you lie."

Jiyoo instinctively came to Mother's defense.

"No. Mother didn't tell me to lie. It's just that I—"

Jiyoo stopped mid-sentence. She had the feeling she had just made a mistake. She made eye contact with Stepfather and shook her head. The look on his face confused her. All at once, he looked like he was mad, like he pitied her, and like he had something to say.

"I guess I'm putting you in a difficult position." He pursed his lips. "Let's just keep this between the two of us and never talk about it again. How about that?"

Jiyoo didn't answer. She was both anxious and suspicious. All she had said was that Mother hadn't told her to lie. Was that enough for him to know what he wanted? And how did Stepfather know that Jiyoo had been here with her father? And why did he keep asking the same question? Jiyoo studied Stepfather's face, but nothing was written on it.

"Shall we?"

Stepfather started walking again, but this time he was a bit distant from Jiyoo, with one foot on the path and the other on the snow-covered reeds. The silence continued for a while. Jiyoo started talking when she thought of something to say:

"You shouldn't step on the reeds. If you get stuck in the mud, you won't be able to pull your foot out."

Stepfather laughed once. "Don't worry. The ground is frozen solid."

"But still. You should let me go first. Just follow me."

Jiyoo felt at ease once she couldn't see Stepfather's face anymore. As the burning sensation on her cheeks subsided, she was finally able to concentrate on her walking again. The farther they walked, the harder it was to see the footpath. Just when Jiyoo thought they should have arrived at the Half Moon Marsh, she was met with an unfamiliar sight. Only when she discovered the feeding rock, which jutted out of the snow, was she convinced of their location.

"We're here."

Jiyoo climbed onto the snow-covered boulder. She did this slowly and carefully, testing each step so that she wouldn't slip and fall. Stepfather followed her onto the rock and stood next to her.

"Is this the Half Moon Marsh?"

"Yes." Although, it wasn't the Half Moon Marsh that she knew. The landscape was wholly unfamiliar. It had turned from a blue pond to a white sheet of ice, the way a swimming pool might transform into an ice rink. Jiyoo couldn't see any cordgrass or ducks. The only evidence Jiyoo had for this being the Half Moon Marsh was the feeding rock on which they were standing.

"The ducks are all gone."

"They must have migrated somewhere warmer. Do the ducks usually live here?"

"Yes. There are all sorts of ducks."

Jiyoo looked toward the mountain peak beyond the wetlands. But she couldn't see anything because of the snowstorm. Jiyoo perked up her ears and held her breath hoping for the sound of birds, but there was nothing. All she could hear was the howl of the wind as it blasted snow into the wetlands.

Jiyoo thought of the light she had seen that night moving along the path from the wetlands, and she thought of Mother in the front yard pushing the wheelbarrow. The questions that she had been suppressing in her mind surged forward like a bad dream. Why had Mother gone to the Half Moon Marsh alone?

"Should we go back now?" Stepfather asked.

*

Maria, Maria, you are my love, Maria...

Jane could hear her father's voice in the darkness. This must be a dream, she thought. She was seated next to her father in the front passenger seat of his truck. Sometimes his voice sounded like it was inside her head, and other times it sounded faint and distant. And then his voice would be carried away by the cries of the wind.

After I sent you far away, I planted a flower

I planted a flower in my weeping heart...

Cold and shivering, Jane awoke to find herself lying in the dark. She was in the fetal position with her legs bound and her arms tied behind her back. She wanted to open her eyes, but they were sealed shut. In fact, she couldn't move any part of her body, not her head, not even a single finger. Perhaps she was experiencing sleep paralysis.

Spring has returned and the flower has bloomed

The flower has bloomed like my longing for you

As Jane drifted in and out of consciousness, she realized something. She wasn't experiencing sleep paralysis. She was experiencing pain. It was pain that was keeping her down and preventing her from moving. Pain so intense it felt like her throat had been pierced by an arrow every time she tried to breathe. Pain that caused her nerves to throb in agony with every heartbeat. She hadn't been dreaming about her father's singing. No, his voice was ringing inside her ears like she were under some spell.

She tried to open her eyes again. But her eyelids stung and felt heavy, as though they had weights tied to them. She had a gag in her mouth, and her wrists and ankles were bound with rope. To make things worse, the rope connected to a noose tied around her neck. It had been tied so that the knot would tighten when she tried to straighten her body.

I cut the flower to cure my longing

I cut the flower as I wept for you, my love, Maria

Jane wanted to cry. She let out a silent scream. She wanted the voice inside her head to stop. She didn't need flowers. She hated flowers. What she needed was a knife. Something to cut this goddamn rope around her neck. Something with which to slit Yuna's throat!

Jane thought she could beat Yuna. Or more accurately, she thought she could overcome the guilt buried deep inside her and do what was necessary. But as she watched Yuna's handbag fly through the air toward her left eye, she realized she had been lying to herself.

Avoiding Yuna, cutting off relations, looking the other way when it was convenient—all those attempts to overcome Yuna were nothing but shadow boxing. Had she really won, she wouldn't have come all the way out here just to prove Yuna's innocence. She would have gone to the police, handed them this address, and let them take care of her. At the very least, she would have used the knife in her hand when Yuna appeared. That was what normal people did when faced with a threat.

But she hadn't done any of that. And for that, she let herself be overpowered and knocked unconscious. When Jane first woke up, she was lying face down at the bottom of the stairs with both hands tied behind her back. Yuna was standing to Jane's right, a cleaver in one hand and a rope in the other. In a matter of seconds, Yuna had gone from hunted to hunter.

"Time to get up. You've kept me waiting," Yuna said.

She lifted Jane to her feet. More than the knife, Jane was concerned about Yuna's foot, which she could see out of the corner of her eye. Jane's left eye, which was the one that had been struck by Yuna's bag, was already swollen shut. If Yuna decided to kick her right eye with her foot, she might lose her vision completely.

"Go up the stairs. I'll take you to the room you so badly want to see."

Yuna then brought the cleaver up to the back of Jane's neck and added, "Just so you know, I've handled more knives than you have."

She was probably right, but what did it matter? Knife or no knife, Yuna was in control now.

Jane walked up the stairs. But she tripped twice in just ten steps. The first time she only bumped her knee, but the second time, she hit the bridge of her nose on the edge of the steps and fell over. It was the fault of the blurry vision in her left eye and the poorly lit stairs.

She let out a groan as she lay face down. It felt like she had broken her nose in two places. She had just enough willpower to prevent her groan from turning into a whimper. Yuna, not surprisingly, didn't seem to be fazed by this trivial accident. She merely tapped the back of Jane's head with the cleaver:

"Would you hurry it up, *unni*. I've got to get home and feed Jiyoo."

This was the first time in thirty years that Yuna had referred to Jane as *unni*. It startled Jane so much that the hair on her neck stood up. Without saying anything, Jane got to her feet. A few seconds later she was standing in front of the door to the attic. Yuna took the key from the drawer in the dresser in the hallway and unlocked the door. When the door opened, a cold, damp breeze seeped into the hallway.

Yuna turned on the lights to the attic and showed her inside. Turning her head on a swivel, Jane surveyed the room with her right eye. A small, long room with no windows, a slanted roof, books, old fans, piles of junk against the wall, cardboard boxes, a large plastic tub and a plastic bucket.

This must be the attic from Jiyoo's dreams. Not surprisingly, Joon-young wasn't here. And there was no indication that he had even been here. If he were stuffed in a cardboard box or plastic tub, Jane would at least be able to smell him.

"Sit over there."

When they reached the end of the room, Yuna pointed to the wall with her cleaver. It was the side of the room where the ceiling was the highest. Judging from the layout of the house, it must be the wall connected to Jiyoo's room. Jane crouched as she pushed her butt into a space between the large and small boxes stacked against the wall.

"Good. I didn't even need to tell you where to sit."

Yuna was standing in front of her, her legs in a wide stance. She seemed to find this funny. She bared her teeth and smiled arrogantly.

"If you crouch like that, your legs are going to cramp. Sit with your legs extended."

"That's my problem, not yours," Jane said, causing Yuna to poke her with the back of the blade.

"You're even more stubborn than Jiyoo. If you don't put your legs out for me, how can I tie them?"

Yuna was someone who didn't understand the law of parsimony. You shouldn't use figures of speech when you can use straightforward expressions. Especially when having a conversation. Jane had mistaken Yuna's words as concern.

Jane extended her legs. With her back against the wall, she gazed down at Yuna's pale fingers as they tied the rope around her ankles. This didn't look like her first time binding someone. The knots were so well tied that Jane probably wasn't going to be able to escape without cutting off her own feet. When she was done, Yuna took her cleaver and brought it down on the leftover rope, cutting it.

Jane couldn't help flinching when this happened. The knife blade stuck into the wood floor, just centimeters from Jane's ankle bone.

"Did I startle you? You're more of a scaredy cat than I thought."

Yuna tossed the leftover pieces of rope to the side as she let out a laugh.

"Earlier when you came at me with that knife, what was it that you said with that ugly mouth of yours? 'Think carefully before you say that again?'"

She shot Yuna a glare. But because Yuna pulled the knife out of the ground and was now holding it, she stifled what she had wanted to say.

"Did *you* think carefully about this? Did you not think I might show up at my own property?"

Yuna brought the blade between Jane's eyes. She looked like she could barely contain her excitement.

Jane thought of the professional tools she had seen in the kitchen. The grinder, mixer, and pots. The things she thought couldn't be true were seeming more and more likely.

"Where is Joon-young?" Jane asked.

Yuna stopped smiling and stared at her. A serious question was lurking behind her eyes. *What's it to you?*

"Why did *you* go to Chungju?" Yuna asked.

Jane decided she should push Yuna's buttons. Yuna was the type of person to start spilling everything like rapid fire when you got her worked up. And Jane had nothing to lose. She was already tied up. She might as well make the most of her situation.

"I went to see the house," Jane answered.

A puzzled look flashed across Yuna's eyes. Soon that puzzlement came out as a question:

"What house?"

"Jun always said he wanted to live in a place that overlooked Lake Hoamji. He would be able to write, go on picnics with Jiyoo, and—"

"Ha! Picnics." Yuna said, cutting Jane off. "Who said I would let him spend time with Jiyoo?"

Jane wasn't finished with her lie.

"And he said it was a great house for newlyweds. That's why I went."

"A house for newlyweds? He was planning on getting married? To whom?"

Yuna was throwing out questions one after another. And with each additional question, her voice got two pitches higher. Blood vessels were starting to pop out of the middle of her forehead. If this continued, her forehead was going to become a barcode of veins. Jane realized she had found the right button.

"Me."

"In your dreams. This will end just like it did last time—with you kicking and screaming because he'll never love you."

Despite her words, Yuna seemed to have a creeping doubt. Every word she said was faster, higher, and fraught with anxiety. This was Jane's chance to deliver the final blow. She picked a cliché but tried-and-true option from her playbook.

"We wanted to get married before my stomach got too big. We found out three months ago."

Yuna's eyes snapped to Jane's stomach. Her gaze then zigzagged back to Jane's face. She would have been less shocked had an opossum been pregnant with a kitten. Jane added one final punch for good measure.

"Do you want to see the ultrasound of your nephew? It's in the car."

"Don't try to trick me."

With the cleaver dangling between her bent legs, she started to mumble like a crazy person.

"Shameless son of a bitch. If I knew he was fucking you while begging to see Jiyoo. I can't believe he threatened to call the police if I didn't let him see Jiyoo."

Jane was silently watching the veins that were exploding in Yuna's eyes like fireworks. It didn't take long for the fireworks to catch fire. Jane didn't need to fan the flames anymore. It would turn into an inferno without her help. But for the sake of time, Jane decided to pour a bit of gasoline on the flames.

"That's not an unreasonable demand. She's Joon-young's daughter, after all. Just like she'll be my daughter once we get married."

"What?"

Yuna tightened her grip on the cleaver that had been dangling.

"Your daughter? Did you just say she'll be *your* daughter?"

Jane fixed her gaze on Yuna's eyes so as not to flinch. Now that she had started, she planned on taking it a few steps further.

"Shall I tell you how I found this place? Jiyoo was in the hospital for a week after you dumped her off with me. She had a high fever for days and started talking deliriously. But there was something strange. Children usually want to find their mommy in times like that, but she didn't ask for you. Not once. All she did was cry and call for Daddy. She kept saying he was at the 'Half Moon Marsh.' And that Mother took him there in a wheelbarrow."

Yuna blinked as though she were wincing. Appearing for a moment beneath her fluttering eyelids was a look of shock. If Jane had to guess what that look of shock was about, it would be, without a doubt, a feeling of betrayal.

"Is there another Half Moon Marsh besides this one?" Jane asked.

Yuna responded with her own question.

"So, is that why you came here? To find out if what Jiyoo said was true?"

"Yes."

As soon as Jane said this, the cleaver came slicing through the air toward her neck. Jane instinctively ducked. The blade just barely grazed the crown of her head and stuck into the box next to her. Yuna pulled the knife out of the box and spoke:

"You want to know what I did to Joon-young?"

Yuna brought the knife down on the box. Again and again, until the box was reduced to slivers. Tumbling out of the box was a set of finger puppets and toy tables and chairs.

Jane looked down at the rolling bits of yellow fur that were among the things that had fallen out. According to her memory, this was what remained of the duck Yuna had stabbed to oblivion thirty years ago. Yuna used the edge of her blade to collect the tuffs of fur and bring them to Jane's feet, as though she were presenting Joon-young's corpse to her.

"Does that answer your question?" Yuna asked.

Jane was speechless. Even if she asked Yuna to clarify what she meant, she wasn't prepared for Yuna's answer. *Did you really do it, Yuna?*

"You seem surprised," Yuna said.

Jane clenched her jaw. She felt something working its way up her throat. Her needlessly wild imagination had already brought her to that place. It showed her the scene of Joon-young dying, drugged with sleeping pills and in a trance. Did it happen in the first-floor bathroom? Was the wail of the loons actually Joon-young screaming as he drowned in a pool of his own blood?

And about Eun-ho . . .

This time it was Jinu Kim's voice that Jane heard.

The night before it happened, he drank Yuna's quince tea. He fell into a deep sleep, unaware that his child was dying.

It appeared as though Yuna had done one for the ages. She had murdered a girl's father right next to her, and she had murdered a father's son right next to him.

"Open your mouth," Yuna said as she pointed the cleaver at Jane's lips.

Jane didn't need any time to think about this. Not only was someone holding her at knife point, but that someone had also lost their mind.

Yuna stuffed the head of the duck in Jane's mouth. She couldn't breathe and her jaw felt like it was going to break. The duck's head pressed against the back of her throat, making Jane gag.

Yuna went out of the room and came back with duct tape. She wrapped the tape around Jane's head, like tying a bandage, then lowered her hands. The uncut roll of tape was dangling by Jane's ear.

"What did you say you were going to do earlier?"

Yuna sawed off the dangling roll of tape with the cleaver.

"Didn't you say you were getting married to that son of a bitch? Didn't you say you were going to steal my daughter?"

Jane craned her neck like a lollipop and sat still. She was afraid. Yuna's hands were shaking with anger and looked like they might accidentally cut off Jane's head.

"You've grown a lot since we were kids, Jane. I bet that's why you thought you could take me."

Yuna put her hand in Jane's jacket pocket and, after a few moments, pulled out a ballpoint pen, a cellphone, and car keys. She turned the pen and inspected it from several angles, as though she had never seen one before.

"You're a real romantic."

A grin returned to Yuna's lips as she muttered to herself. A good idea seemed to have just come to her. Jane felt even more uneasy. What was a good idea for Yuna would be a very bad idea for her.

"Jane."

Yuna's voice was once again chirpy like a hummingbird. Jane felt like she was listening to a soprano jump back and forth between octaves. She had seen her sister's extreme shifts in mood countless times before. But, listening to her sister call her name with a grin on her face as she held the cleaver in her hand, she had never been as intimidated as she was now.

"If you want to marry that son of a bitch, be my guest," Yuna said as she put the pen back in Jane's pocket. "We'll have the wedding tomorrow. At the Half Moon Marsh."

Jane wasn't sure if she had heard Jane correctly. As she blinked one eye, she went over her sister's words, one syllable at a time. Tomorrow, at the Half Moon Marsh . . .

"I'll keep these with me."

Yuna showed Jane the cellphone and car keys.

"Sleep tight. And sweet dreams."

The lights in the room went out. Yuna closed the door and disappeared. Jane could hear the click of the door being locked and the sound of Yuna walking down the stairs. After that, she heard something clattering. This continued for a while until she heard Yuna drive off in her car.

Silence filled the house. Jane lay on her side in the cold darkness. She closed her eyes and tried to think. What should she do? What should she not do? What could she do to get out of this attic alive?

But her head was not in any condition to think. Despite knowing she needed to use her head to get out of this situation, she didn't want to think about anything. All she could do was listen mindlessly to the voice in her head blaming her for not preparing herself even though she knew she might run into Yuna here, for her poor handling of the situation after she did run into Yuna. Of course, Jane's anger was also directed at Yuna. But the emotion was so large that she didn't dare release it.

When she was young, Jane would often quell her anger by "praying for Yuna." Praying that Yuna would fall into a manhole, praying that the roof would collapse on Yuna while she slept, praying that Yuna would spontaneously combust and die. But now was the opposite. Nothing bad could happen to Yuna. It would be bad for Jane if the police suddenly wised up and arrested Yuna or chased her out of the country. If something happened to Yuna, there was a high probability that Jane would be discovered in this dark attic, dead from lack of water and food. And if she was really unlucky, they would never find her body, and this house would become a tomb for her mummified body. In other words, Yuna needed to evade the law a little bit longer so that she could come back to kill Jane. That was the only way Jane would get a chance to escape.

It was this that Jane decided to think about. How was she going to take advantage of the opportunity when Yuna came back?

One option was to pretend to be asleep and wait until Yuna got close enough for Jane to attack her. Of course, she would need to be willing to be cut or stabbed with Yuna's knife. There was no way Yuna would come empty-handed.

Another possibility was that Yuna would untie Jane's feet so that she could walk herself to the Half Moon Marsh. If that happened, Jane could make a run for it. If she could just make it to the village, she would be able to find someone who could help her. The problem was that this was unlikely. Yuna wouldn't be so careless. She would probably dump Jane into the wheelbarrow, ties and all, and cart her to the marsh to drown in the water.

Although Jane couldn't find an answer to the question of what she would do, it seemed like she did have an answer as to when Yuna would be coming back. Yuna would come back at night. That was the best time to drag Jane to the swamp to drown.

Jane's thoughts moved on to more basic questions. Why was Yuna doing this? Was she just crazy? Or was it because she preferred offense over defense? Perhaps she had never intended on killing anyone. Perhaps she only wanted to teach them a lesson, but accidentally killed them. Or perhaps there was some other explanation for all of this, something that could explain why she had to do what she did?

Trying to understand someone's actions means trying to explain the meaning of their actions on your own. This was impossible for Jane to do, no matter how hard she tried. She had always thought she understood her sister, but now she realized she was delusional. What she knew wasn't Yuna, but her own feelings about Yuna. As Jane lay there, she continued to ask a question that couldn't reach the only person who knew the answer: *Yuna, who are you?*

One moment, she was burning with rage thinking about Yuna, and the next, she was trembling thinking about what tomorrow would bring. It terrified her that she didn't know when Yuna was going to drug her with sleeping pills and drown her in the marsh. Jane was sure it would be tomorrow. But tomorrow could be ten hours away or ten minutes away. She had no way of telling.

But the pain she felt was more real to her than the fear. Her eyeballs were throbbing, her nose was swollen, the cotton in her mouth was causing her to gag, and she was unable to swallow her saliva. And her bladder was getting fuller by the second.

Jane's consciousness was starting to fade out. Her thoughts disappeared, her emotions became faint, and her senses became dull. Time continued to pass like this for Jane, neither awake nor asleep, but somewhere in between.

And then finally, Jane heard a car. But she was doubtful at first. Had she really heard a car, or was she just imagining things? She stopped breathing, perked up her ears, and waited for more sounds. She could hear the screeching of metal on metal. The image of the rusty front gate appeared and disappeared before her eyes like a mirage. The front door opened, and people were talking. First a man's voice, then a woman's, then a child's.

She couldn't hear what they were saying. The voices were a low hum and had to pass through layers of wood, making it impossible for Jane to distinguish syllables. The only thing Jane knew was that one of the voices belonged to Jiyoo.

Jane's entire body felt the pounding of her heart. Yuna was back. But Jane had no idea what kind of plan could include Eun-ho and Jiyoo. This was an opportunity for Jane. Eun-ho and Jiyoo definitely were not conspiring with Yuna; they would be unaware of the fact that Jane was tied up in the attic. Jane had to let them know, by whatever means necessary. Let them know that she was being held against her will up here.

Jane sat up straight. She stretched out her legs to see if there were any objects near her that she could reach. Her heel got caught on something. Judging from the material, she guessed it was the cardboard box that Yuna had slashed to shreds earlier. Next, Jane scooted sideways across the floor until her foot touched something large and flat. Based on the texture, this too felt like a carboard box. But it was heavy as though it was filled with books. It didn't budge even when she pushed it with her heel.

Jane put her bound hands on the floor, turned sideways, lifted her hips in the air, then kicked the box as hard as she could.

"Jiyoo! Jiyoo!" she screamed.

The box wobbled slightly, but it didn't fall over. Her heel was now throbbing, but that was about it. Not even the shouting seemed to escape her own mouth. And now she was coughing because small bits of the duck's head were tickling the back of her throat. As Jane coughed, the gag accidentally got stuck in her airway. She just barely managed to unblock her airway with the back of her tongue. But as she did this, she triggered her gag reflex several times, causing the muscles in her stomach and chest to painfully constrict.

Jane steadied her breathing as long streams of tears flowed down her face. To her disappointment, no one was coming upstairs. She didn't try screaming again. Instead, she scooted around the floor and kicked over everything she could find.

Between every object that fell, Jane would pause to listen. She still couldn't sense anyone coming upstairs. Even the low hum of people's voices had disappeared. And now, there was nothing left for Jane to kick over. Jane decided to explore further in the direction that she remembered there being a stack of cardboard boxes.

Her foot found another box. As she tried to identify the box, something came crashing down to the floor. Judging from the metallic sound, Jane figured they were her grandma's old stainless-steel dishes. This time, she was sure she had succeeded in alerting Jiyoo and Eun-ho. With a ruckus like this, she could summon every ghost in Woohyeri.

Jane sat up straight again. She steadied her breath and waited for whomever was going to come upstairs. A moment later, she heard someone's footsteps on the stairs. Then the sound of someone unlocking the door. They opened the door and turned on the lights. Jane reflexively closed her eyes.

"You're having fun up here."

It was Yuna. Jane opened her eyes. Yuna was standing at the threshold. Jane was confused. Why was Yuna alone? Where had Eun-ho and Jiyoo gone? Had Jane been wrong? Were they conspiring with Yuna? Or perhaps they had left already.

"You've got too much energy to spare, it seems." Yuna said as she stepped into the attic.

No sooner did Jane think Yuna was starting to approach her than Yuna slapped Jane across the cheek with all her might. Jane had no idea Yuna could move so quickly. Jane fell backwards, hitting the back of her head on the floor. Before she even had time to gasp in shock, Yuna took her heel and stomped on Jane's throat. Jane felt like a grenade had detonated inside her throat. Pain and heat immediately closed off her airway.

"With all that energy, you might try something."

Yuna then took her foot and kicked Jane in the side. But her foot felt more like a stake. Jane curled up and rolled on the floor in pain.

"Is that why you're making all this noise?"

Yuna grabbed Jane by the hair and forced her head backwards. She pulled on Jane's hair with such force that it left Jane's eyeballs trembling. As Jane gazed into Yuna's eyes, she found the answer to the question she'd been asking herself for the last thirty years.

Yuna was nothing but a small girl. Inside Yuna's eyes, Jane found the angry seven-year-old girl who had been sent to Woohyeri to live with her grandma. For all these years, it was this rage-driven girl who had been controlling Yuna.

"Keep it up. See if anyone comes to save you."

Yuna put all her weight into her fist as she cracked Jane across the left cheek. Jane's head snapped backwards. Yuna grabbed Jane's head with both hands and kneed her in the face. She continued to knee Jane, in the throat and on the back and side of the head. A loud eruption exploded in Jane's ears. Her surroundings went dark. And through the gaps in her consciousness, which blinked like a strobe light, Yuna's voice pierced her ears.

"Keep it up, you fucking cunt."

Jane let her body go limp. She could feel Yuna putting a noose around her neck as she drifted in and out of consciousness. Yuna rolled Jane over and tied the noose to the ropes on Jane's ankles. She then turned off the light and left the room.

When Jane finally came to, she realized something. Yuna was serious about killing her. The noose on her neck was giving her an option. She could either strangle herself here or last a little longer to die at Yuna's hands.

Jane didn't want to die. At least not here, not like this. But if she was going to live, she needed to do something. She couldn't just lie here and continue listening to her father's voice.

Jane started searching through her memory. When the lights were on, where had she been? Jane remembered vaguely being in the middle of the attic. Although Yuna had tossed Jane around, she hadn't moved far from where Yuna first discovered her.

Jane turned on the GPS inside her head. She used the place where she had first woken up as a reference. If she had gone straight while knocking over boxes, then all she had to do was go back in a straight line. If she ran into boxes while doing this, she had gone in the right direction; if she reached a pile of junk, then she had gone in the wrong direction. She might be able to move if she brought her legs up to her ribs and rolled her body along the floor.

But there was an unexpected variable she hadn't anticipated. The moment she moved her legs, her body began screaming out in pain from the beating she had just taken.

As soon as she brought her chin to her chest, it felt like her neck was going to break. And when she rolled on her side, her ribs felt like they were stabbing her lungs. Even her eyeballs felt like they were going to fall out of her skull when her forehead touched the floor. Jane rolled her body one more time, smashing her chin on the floor. A sharp, burning pain pierced her jaw. Jane couldn't take any more pain.

With every revolution, she let out a groan. Before long, her body was drenched in sweat. She was disappointed in herself. She couldn't believe she was in so much pain from just a few blows to the body and head. It wasn't even like it was a strong man who had hit her; it was just Yuna.

Finally, her forehead found the edge of a box. There was nothing touching her legs. She rolled one more time, hitting the wall with her knees. Jane let her body relax and lay down. Her cheek, which was slick with sweat, rested on the wood floor. She relaxed her tense shoulders and closed her eyes. She waited for the burning pain to subside.

In the meantime, she could hear a bell downstairs. A few moments later, she heard what sounded like a piece of classical music written for the violin, although she didn't recognize the piece. Through the sound of the music, Jane could make out the sound of a knife on a cutting board, as well as the clinking of bowls and plates.

Eventually, she heard people's voices, too.

Jane pressed her ear into the floor. As she tried to make out what was being said, she was able to hear Yuna say:

"Wash up. It's time for dinner."

CHAPTER 9

Honey, would you sit there?" Wife stood in front of the kitchen table and motioned with her eyes to the chair in front of the door to the living room. Without any reason to object, Eun-ho quietly took his seat.

"And Jiyoo, sit next to your father."

Jiyoo sat in the seat Mother told her to. Jiyoo's complexion was pale, and her eyes were fixed to the table. Eun-ho followed Jiyoo's gaze. A long blue flower vase, a scented candle, and wine glasses. Eun-ho could feel his jaw become rigid. These were the same objects he'd seen in the picture. Even the three roses in the flower vase were the same color.

"I'll sit here," Wife said as she brought the salad bowl over and placed it on the table. Her place, which was across from Eun-ho and closest to the kitchen, was already marked with a wine glass.

"It'll give me easy access to the kitchen."

Eun-ho furtively glanced at his watch. 6:00. It was a little early for dinner.

"Night falls early here," Wife said, reading his mind.

"Is there anything I can do to help?"

"No. Just sit. You can talk to Jiyoo if you want."

Wife made several trips to the kitchen counter. One by one, she filled the kitchen table—a bottle of champagne in a bucket of ice, orange juice, bread, jam, peanut butter, and three plates with goulash. As she did this, Eun-ho and Jiyoo sat in their seats without saying a word, like children in time-out.

Wife was more upbeat than she'd been the last several weeks. She was almost gliding across the kitchen floor. Her cheeks were rosy, and even the pitch in her voice was higher than usual. She had twice as much to say, too. "It's hard to bake the bread evenly with that old oven." "I can't believe they didn't have any fresher salad ingredients at the store." "We were low on ice, so the champagne might not be very cold."

When she finally sat down, she explained her choice in champagne—how the name Belle Époque meant "beautiful times," how the champagne made a perfect "aperitif" because it was light-bodied and had gentle but consistent bubbling and peach overtones. To Eun-ho, as someone who knew nothing about champagne, he had no idea what her explanation meant, nor did he care.

"As this is our first family vacation, we should celebrate." Wife smiled as she looked at Eun-ho. "Honey, would you pour the champagne?"

Her tone smelled sickly-sweet, like overripe peaches. Eun-ho uncorked the bottle of champagne and poured two glasses. Considering the fact this was a fresh bottle, maybe that meant it was safe to drink. As he did this, Wife poured Jiyoo a glass of orange juice.

"A toast?" Yuna said as she held up her glass. "To our beautiful, first trip together."

Both Eun-ho and Jiyoo lifted their own glasses.

"Actually," Wife said suddenly as she got up. "Don't move."

Jiyoo and Eun-ho meekly put down their glasses. Wife bent over and brought her phone out from under the kitchen table.

"We should take a commemorative picture."

Wife took several steps backward until she reached the kitchen sink.

"Honey, put your head against Jiyoo's like you mean it. Cheese."

Jiyoo glanced sideways at Eun-ho as he tilted his head toward her. It wasn't that hard to touch heads. The problem was saying cheese. Eun-ho's mouth spasmed, and a chill spread throughout his back. He realized that he, too, was now on the Yuna Shin Express bound for hell.

"Jiyoo, what are you doing? Look this way and say cheese."

Wife raised one hand in the air and curled her finger. Jiyoo turned to look forward. There was clear worry on her face. She tried harder to say cheese, but the corners of her lips merely contorted in pain. Her eyes looked like she was on the verge of crying. Wife counted slowly:

"One . . . two . . ."

The flash on her camera burst with a click. Wife walked back to the kitchen table as she checked the picture.

"It turned out great. Do you want to see?"

Eun-ho took the phone as Wife handed it to him. The moment he saw the screen, he was reminded of another picture that had been taken in this exact location. A man and child with their heads touching, two dark doors open behind them, roses and scented candles on the table, a bottle of champagne. The setting and structure of the two pictures matched perfectly. The only thing that had changed was the man sitting next to Jiyoo. Eun-ho returned the phone to Wife.

"Looks great. Send it to me. I'll save it to my phone."

"Later. Now is the time to enjoy our meal."

Wife turned off her phone and put it face down on the table. Lifting her glass, she proposed a toast.

"This time for real. To our happiness."

Eun-ho clinked glasses with Wife. He chugged the champagne in hopes that it would calm his nerves. As he waited and imagined what was coming next, Eun-ho wondered where the peach overtones she'd been raving about were.

"How were the wetlands?" Wife asked as she put down the glass.

"I'm not sure. There was nothing out there. Jiyoo says there are usually lots of ducks."

Jiyoo flinched and turned to look at Eun-ho. Her eyes were asking, *When did I say that?* It appeared Eun-ho had made a slip of the tongue.

"The ducks will come back in the spring," Wife mumbled to herself as she spooned some goulash into her mouth.

Eun-ho didn't touch his goulash. If Wife wanted to give him something special, it would be in the goulash. He had voluntarily walked up to the guillotine, but he had no intention of lying down and sticking his neck out, too. He picked up a piece of bread and spread peanut butter on it. He didn't particularly like peanut butter, but he had no other choice. Jiyoo had already taken the small amount of jam that was on the table.

Wife's gaze was fixed on his hand as it spread the peanut butter. Her elated mood from just a moment earlier had disappeared without a trace. Cast across her face was the shadow that always appeared when she was upset and feeling down.

"Has the Half Moon Marsh frozen over?" Wife asked out of nowhere.

Eun-ho nodded.

"Is it frozen *solid*?"

Eun-ho tilted his head in confusion. Why was she asking?

"Don't give me that look. What's so hard about just saying yes or no?"

Wife's voice was suddenly dripping with irritation.

Eun-ho waited a second before answering.

"The surface of the marsh was covered in snow. But I'm not sure if it's 'frozen solid.'"

Eun-ho put the bread in his mouth and started chewing. It was so dry that he would have been happier taking off his belt and chewing on that. He was incapable of tasting anything and felt like a prisoner on death row eating his last meal.

Wife didn't say anymore. The house was quiet. All he could hear was the clinking of dishware on the kitchen table. Suspicions were accumulating in his head like frequent flier miles. He wanted to know what the source of that sound earlier was. And why had Wife sent him and Jiyoo to the wetlands as soon as they heard the sound? Oddly enough, they hadn't heard that strange sound since.

Wife said it was the roof, but he didn't believe this. If that were true, wouldn't they still be hearing it? The wind hadn't stopped blasting the house. There was also something mysterious about the way Jiyoo called it a loon. It almost seemed like the loon was code for something or someone. That would make more sense. Could it possibly be referring to her father, Joon-young?

Eun-ho thought about the car at the abandoned house they had seen on their way here. That was an odd place to park a car. The village was barely populated, and no one lived in the old house, it seemed. Nor did it look like a junk car. Judging from its outline, it looked like a large SUV or jeep. The blue hue of its chassis had been just visible through the snow.

"Thank you for dinner." Jiyoo was the first to put down her utensils. The goulash on her plate had hardly been touched. The only thing she had eaten was two pieces of bread with jam and her glass of orange juice.

"Yes, thank you for dinner," Eun-ho said as he put down the butter knife in his hand. He, too, hadn't eaten much: only the champagne and two pieces of bread with peanut butter.

Wife showed no reaction. Her eyes were cast downward as she pushed the goulash around the plate. She looked even gloomier than before. Judging from the way her pursed lips were focused to a point, she seemed distracted by something.

"I'll do the dishes," Eun-ho added.

Wife looked up and made eye contact with him, looking like she had just been taken out of a dream.

"Would you? I'll take Jiyoo upstairs and tuck her in."

Jiyoo glanced over at Eun-ho. She looked flustered. As far as Eun-ho remembered, Wife had never tucked Jiyoo in. At least, not at their house in Cheongyeon. If anything, it was Jiyoo who had the honor of bidding Wife goodnight.

"Jiyoo, shall we go upstairs?"

Wife put down her utensils and stood up. Jiyoo hurried to her feet. A few moments later, the two disappeared upstairs.

Eun-ho started clearing the table. Even as he moved all the plates to the kitchen sink, his ears were sifting through the sounds upstairs. It seemed like they still hadn't entered Jiyoo's room. He could hear intermittent murmurs, but their voices were so quiet that he couldn't tell what they were saying.

As Eun-ho turned on the kitchen faucet, his brain became muddled from images popping in and out of his mind, as though he were about to fall asleep. His eyelids felt scratchy. He blinked several times, but it didn't help. It felt like his eyelids and cornea were stuck together. The room was starting to spin, and his sense of distance disappeared, as though he was looking at everything through a mirror.

Even his hands were moving strangely. This wasn't the first time he'd done the dishes, but his movements were clumsy like a baby's. Twice he dropped a plate. He even dropped a spoon on the ground while trying to bring it over to the drying rack. Following the loud sound, Wife called from upstairs.

"Honey, did you break something?"

Eun-ho didn't know what she was doing, but she seemed like she was still in the hallway.

"No."

Eun-ho's voice as he answered felt detached from his own body, as though he had plugs in both ears. The fishy smell that had been assaulting his nose this whole time suddenly disappeared. He couldn't tell if he had just gotten used to the smell or if his sense of smell was being shut off.

There was no way he had taken a sleeping pill. He hadn't touched the goulash, and the champagne was a new bottle. This had to be the effects of sleep deprivation. Eun-ho had been suffering from insomnia ever since the incident.

And last night, after asking for a divorce, he was too afraid to go to sleep.

Of course, the divorce wasn't his true goal. His true reason for asking for a divorce was to see what Wife would do if pushed over the edge. He didn't answer any of her questions; he merely told her he wasn't in love with her anymore.

This wasn't a lie, nor was it an exaggeration. After Noah died, he spent many nights sleeping in Noah's room. He also ended up sleeping there the night he stole Wife's phone. He tried his best to endure her advances, but in the end, he couldn't. He wanted to throw up as soon as her tongue slithered between his lips and into his mouth. He pushed Wife away and fled to Noah's room.

Using that night as an example, Eun-ho explained to Wife the extent of his disillusion. He didn't answer her when she asked what she had done wrong. Nor did he respond when she blamed him for making their marriage difficult.

There are two types of people when it comes to conversations. Those who listen to the person they're talking to, and those who don't. Talking with the latter is like playing an endless game of ping pong.

Wife belonged to the latter. Regardless of what he said, she would always ask him emotional questions or give him exhausting answers. This would continue until she started attacking him physically. And even if he kept his cool, things only got worse. Then she would lose it and start harming herself. This was the same tiresome pattern that Eun-ho had experienced since they got married. The only solution was avoiding her entirely.

He looked straight into Wife's eyes, which were shaking with rage. He tried his best to sound indifferent.

"I'm leaving tomorrow. I'm not taking anything with me."

"That's because none of this belongs to you." Wife's breath was damp and sour.

He could feel himself becoming nauseous again. He pushed away Wife's legs, which were still straddling his chair, and got up. He picked up his jacket, which had been thrown on the desk, and left the study.

"Eun-ho—" Wife called out to Eun-ho just before he closed the door behind him. "Come here." Her voice was a soft whisper.

This made Eun-ho flinch. Such a tone of voice always had power over him. Marriage with Wife was a train platform: on one side of the platform was the train for heaven, on the other side was the train for hell. "Come here" was the boarding call for the train to heaven. *Come here, I'll make you happy.*

Eun-ho didn't go to her and simply closed the door. He continued walking and went out the back door. He entered a trail with streetlamps, and walked until he reached a rest area in the forest. All the while, his phone was ringing tirelessly. The only times it wasn't ringing were the second-long intervals it took for the caller to hang up and dial again. He had no need to check who it was. There was only one person who could be calling him.

Eventually, he put his phone on silent. He sat down on a bench that was damp with evening dew. With his elbows on his knees and his hands clasped, he looked down at the lights beneath the hill. Fog was forming over the streets. Eun-ho felt like he could hear Noah's voice beyond the fog.

Dad, what are you doing there?

Good question. What am I doing here? How did my life turn out like this? Where had I gone wrong?

Eun-ho felt like he had stepped into a dark void. He felt like he had walked blindly into a place where there was no place to stand, where he couldn't see in front of himself. Ever since he had met Yuna, he had been completely bewitched, like a climber blinded by the beautiful peak of a tall mountain, who climbs the mountain even though he knows death awaits him. Eun-ho had paid the ultimate price for allowing himself to be so blinded by Yuna.

Something hot was burning inside his throat. His temples throbbed. Moisture filled the corners of his eyes. He held his face with his cold hands and started to cry. The sobs and groans slowly turned into an uncontrollable wave of grief. But this wasn't grief about losing Noah or resentment toward himself. His tears were from the sudden clarity of his own disillusionment.

After two hours he left the rest area. He wanted to hold out until daybreak, but he couldn't stand the cold anymore. When he pulled out his phone to use its flashlight, he saw Jinu was calling him.

"Where are you?" Jinu asked immediately.

Eun-ho was about to ask why Jinu was calling him at such a late hour, but stopped himself. He knew why. As Eun-ho expected, Wife had gone to Jinu and told him about their fight. He didn't need to ask why she went there. She had gone there because she was confident that Eun-ho would be there. Jinu was unable to stop Yuna from tearing the place apart.

"I told her you weren't there, but it was no use. I knew she was difficult, but I had no idea she was *this* crazy. She saw that your car was in the parking garage, and was convinced that you were hiding somewhere in the apartment."

Jinu let Eun-ho imagine the rest of what happened for himself. Eun-ho felt himself blushing. Now he knew what his students felt like when their parents came to school to demand better grades. It was fortunate that Jinu lived by himself. He didn't want to imagine what would have happened if Jinu had a girlfriend living with him.

Jinu asked Eun-ho again where he was. When Eun-ho said that he was on the trail behind their house, Jinu told him to come to his place to get his car and tell him what happened. But Eun-ho didn't want to go; he was too embarrassed to talk to Jinu, and he was afraid that Wife would be hiding in the bushes outside Jinu's apartment. But most of all, he didn't want to drag Jinu into this anymore than he already had.

"No, I should go home."

Eun-ho went to a nearby PC café. He needed to think about what Wife might do when he went home to pack his things. Would she offer him a cup of coffee before he left? Or would she take him somewhere?

It was unlikely that she would try to drug him now. She knew his car was still at Jinu's, so getting him drowsy on sleeping pills would do nothing.

Eun-ho thought about putting all his money on the former. Wife knew that Eun-ho knew. And because of that, she wouldn't be dumb enough to use her usual method. In fact, there was a good possibility that she would suggest they go somewhere so he would have time to reconsider. And that somewhere would be the same place she took her ex-husband.

That was what he wanted. But there was just one small problem. When the moment arrived, he would have no way of defending himself. He was using himself as a sacrifice. But even so, he needed to know the truth about Noah's death. He needed confirmation that he hadn't killed his own son. Not to prove it to the police or to the world, but to prove it to himself. This was the first time in Eun-ho's life that he realized the truth was more valuable than his own life.

Around 7 a.m. he returned home. Wife was sipping a cup of coffee and looking out the balcony window. She should have seen him come in. But she only appeared after he entered his study and started putting his things in his bag. She appeared in the room suddenly, without even knocking.

"Honey, please talk to me."

Their talk didn't go well. Wife was a poor negotiator. She was only good at giving speeches. She went on and on, pointing out how rash a decision he was making, sobbing about how much pain she was in, bragging about how much she had tried last night to fix this problem. But all Eun-ho could do was yawn.

"If you must leave, then go. All I ask is for one more day to change your mind."

Eun-ho could feel the drowsiness wearing off. His ears had finally heard what they'd been waiting for.

"The day after tomorrow is Jiyoo's birthday. Let's go on an overnight family trip to celebrate."

She asked him to make just twenty-four hours for Jiyoo, who never got to take a trip with her father. If by the end of it, he still hadn't changed his mind, she would accept the divorce.

After ten minutes of silence, Eun-ho answered, "Okay." Everything after that happened exactly as he expected. Before he could even blink, they were at the place where Wife had most likely taken her ex-husband. But there were two variables Eun-ho hadn't anticipated.

The first was that the Seodaemun Police Department had asked Yuna to come in early that morning. They wanted to question her as a potential witness. This was good because it allowed Eun-ho to talk with Jiyoo while she was out.

Just as Eun-ho figured, Wife had trained Jiyoo well. Her lips were sealed. But there was one exception. Eun-ho could sense a subtle but perceptible air of resistance and obedience within Jiyoo. It wasn't in her actions, but rather in her attitude. It was the resistance of a child who on the surface was obedient but was secretly talking back to their parents under their breath. Knowing how sensitive Wife was to subtle changes in behavior, there was no way she hadn't sensed this, too. It was likely that their fight the previous night was because of Jiyoo's newfound rebelliousness.

The other variable was that Wife had confiscated Eun-ho's phone. Not only had Jinu called him on their way here, but now he didn't have the ability to call for help. At the time, Eun-ho thought he would get his phone back eventually. His main goal was not to make Wife suspicious. Only now did he realize this was a lapse in judgement.

It was unconscious obedience. The same unconscious obedience that caused him to beg Wife to come home every time she left the house. Eun-ho wasn't that different from Jiyoo in that he, too, had been domesticated by Yuna.

Just before leaving the house, Eun-ho sent Min-young a text message:

—I'm going on a trip with my wife. I won't be back for a while.

He thought about giving Min-young more of a hint, but then decided against it. It would be problematic if Min-young showed up too soon. Eun-ho had drafted the text message when he was alone with Jiyoo and pressed the send button just before getting into the car. After it was delivered, he blocked Min-young's number so she couldn't call or text him.

He knew this would put Min-young into a frenzy and cause her to start looking for him. She would either get the help of the police or she would get the help of the private detective she had used to do background research on him. And once they realized he and Wife really weren't home, they would begin their pursuit. At least, this was the best-case scenario.

Indeed, Min-young was his only safety net. His phone was the guide that would lead his pursuers. But now that the guide was in Wife's hands, he was anxious that they would never find him. If he could only find the phone and turn it on.

It seemed like Wife was still doing something upstairs. With the water running, he started rummaging through the kitchen. Wife's phone was on the shelf beneath the kitchen table. He pressed the home button, but it was turned off. Thinking his phone might be in the storage closet, he opened every closet door, but he couldn't find it. Every shelf was empty.

"Eun-ho, are you looking for something?"

Eun-ho could hear Wife's voice coming from upstairs. He had tried to be quiet, but it seemed like Wife's ears had heard him opening the cabinets. He said the first thing that came to mind.

"Do you know where the paper towels are?"

To his own ears, his voice sounded slurred as though he were drunk. It felt distant and vague, as though the voice were coming from outside.

"They're under the kitchen table."

Eun-ho stood up. The room started spinning again. His vision lurched as though he were on a boat at sea.

"Did you find it?" Wife asked.

"Yes!"

As soon as he said this, he could hear a door closing. It seemed like Wife had finally gone into Jiyoo's room. Eun-ho leaned against the edge of the kitchen sink. His nausea was doubling with every moment. His feet looked impossibly far away, as though his legs were several meters long. This wasn't just a temporary phenomenon. And it wasn't sleep deprivation. Somehow, Wife had drugged him.

Eun-ho wasn't particularly receptive to sleeping pills. The only thing to go numb was his body; his mind was just fine. The sleep study he took had confirmed this. This was only the second time in his life that he had felt so drowsy—the other time being the night Noah died. Eun-ho figured Yuna had given him the same drug.

The dinner they ate slowly passed in front of Eun-ho's eyes. The goulash, the glass of champagne, the salad, the pieces of bread, and the saucer of peanut butter. Eun-ho paused on this last image. It had to be the peanut butter. He was the only one who touched the peanut butter.

Had Jiyoo known? Is that why she didn't touch the peanut butter? Had she betrayed him like she betrayed her own father? Puddles of sour saliva began to form around Eun-ho's gums. Eun-ho needed to throw up.

Eun-ho turned around and put his mouth over the faucet head. He held his breath as he drank until he felt full of water, then stuck his fingers down his throat and vomited into the sink. He repeated this five times until he was ready to collapse from exhaustion. His sweater was soaked, and there was a puddle of water on the kitchen floor.

He washed the vomit down the drain and turned off the faucet. He then took a handful of paper towels and mopped up the water on the ground. As he left the kitchen, he hoped this pitiful attempt at an exorcism had rid him of the drugs. His goal was Wife's bag which was in the living room. It should have only taken him five seconds to get there from the sink, but as things were, this short walk felt like he was crossing the solar system. Nothing felt normal or right.

Only the center of his vision was in focus; the peripheries were distorted like a Salvador Dali painting. Walls were bending, the ceiling was sagging, the front door moving back and forth like a yo-yo. Eun-ho's feet sunk into the floor with every step, as though the floor were trying to swallow him.

Wife's bag was on the coffee table in the living room. His travel bag was beneath the table, and Wife's jacket was hung over the sofa armrest. He opened the bag and looked inside. He couldn't see well. Not only was the opening to the bag small, but the inside of the bag was deep and filled with miscellaneous items. This was only exacerbated by the fact his eyes couldn't focus.

Eun-ho stuck his hand in the bag. The first thing he fished out was Wife's makeup pouch. As soon as he unzipped the pouch, one side of it sagged, spilling out all its contents.

Eun-ho held his breath as he watched. One thing rolled noisily under the sofa, another thing slid to the middle of the living room floor, and something heavy fell to his feet with a thud. He felt like he was watching a video in slow motion.

He sensed no movement upstairs. The surroundings went quiet again.

Eun-ho looked down at the fallen items. One of the items was his cellphone. He bent down at the knees and picked it up. With trembling fingers, he pressed the power button. The screen eventually lit up, showing him that he had several missed calls. Twelve in total. All from Jinu.

Eun-ho switched the phone to silent, turned on the recording app, then put the phone back into the pouch. He turned to the item that had slid across the floor. It was a bag of medicine. He crawled over to the bag and picked it up. Inside were five oblong-shaped pills. The name of the drug was printed on the bag:

Temazepam (10 mg)—Sleep sedative—Take one pill thirty minutes before bed.

The word temazepam looked to Eun-ho as if there were embossed lettering. So this was the drug that Wife had used. Eun-ho remembered his doctor explaining the difference between sleeping sedatives and sleeping aids. The side effects stored in his memory were exactly the same as the symptoms he was experiencing now.

The prescription had been written at a "Dr. G's Sleep Clinic," and the pharmacy was in Geomdan, not Cheongyeon. That was where Wife's company was located. It was likely the clinic she went to was also in that area. Not that it mattered anymore.

Just as he was putting the pills back in the pouch, something startled him. He had heard a voice coming from upstairs. When he perked up his ears, he could hear footsteps coming down the stairs. Crouching on the living room floor, he was frozen in place. There were still things left under the sofa to retrieve, but he didn't have time. His heart was beating out of his chest. A single droplet of sweat trickled out of his armpit. The voice inside his head was shouting at him in desperation. *Pull yourself together! Move! Quickly put everything back!*

"Eun-ho?" Wife called from the door to the living room.

This happened just as he was performing a feat of superhuman speed. He towed his body under the sofa like a broken truck, grabbed Wife's lipstick and hand mirror, put them in the pouch, put the pouch back in her bag, and then took off his soaked sweater and threw it on the coach.

"What are you doing over there?"

Eun-ho turned around to look at her. He wanted to say he was looking for a change of clothes because he had got his sweater wet, but his tongue was curled up toward the back of his throat. His words came out like a jumbled groan.

Eun-ho tilted his head to the side in confusion at the sound he had just made. As Wife approached him, the image of her split in two. The living room was being stretched like the rubber band of a slingshot. And then, as if someone had let it go, the entire living room smashed into his face. This time, he was unable to accomplish any feats of superhuman speed or agility. Eun-ho fell backwards, and everything went black.

When he opened his eyes, he was locked in a frozen lake—the same lake from his dream, the one in which he had been adrift the night Noah died. Just like then, his body was immersed in water trapped beneath the ice. A mysterious light was flickering above his eyes, and the wind was howling in the distance.

"Why did you do it, honey?"

Eun-ho could hear Wife's voice through the wind.

"Why didn't you keep your promise?"

She asked this question in an inflectionless murmur, as though she were talking to herself.

"I thought marrying you would make me happy."

The water swept across his forehead like a heavy breeze. The undercurrent was dragging his limp body through water.

"Do you know how much effort I spent trying—"

Wife's voice was momentarily swept away by the wind.

"—to make that dream a reality?"

Right. Effort. Wife's effort. That horrifying effort that had driven their family to ruin. Suddenly, a violent rush of water put Eun-ho on its back.

"Do you know how hard I tried to protect you?"

Eun-ho's body rose suddenly, hitting the ice, then sank deep into the lake. Wife's voice drifted in and out with the motion of his body. Rising, then dropping, surging, then falling.

"When Noah died and the police suspected you, I did everything to clear your name. I endured you and your irritability. I tried to forget the pain you caused me these last few weeks. I did it because this was our new beginning."

The wind swept away Wife's voice again. Eun-ho wondered how much time had passed since he lost consciousness. Two hours? Three? Five?

"But you kept pushing me away."

The wind returned with Wife's voice.

"You avoided me, hid things from me, betrayed me. You pretended to be asleep when I came home. You looked through my phone while I was asleep. You drank with Jinu behind my back and then came home and asked for a divorce. I forgave you time after time, and you still don't appreciate me. Do you know how much that hurts?"

Eun-ho tried wriggling his fingers. But he couldn't. He tried to open his eyes, but they were glued shut. The wind was blowing across the top of his forehead again. He could more vividly feel the shaking of his body. Wife continued to talk to herself.

"Even as we arrived here in the country, I was still hopeful. I wanted to believe that you would understand me once we talked about everything. I wanted to believe that you were always on my side, like I was always on yours. I wanted to believe that you weren't serious about getting a divorce, that you only said what you said because you were in a bad mood."

Eun-ho realized something. He wasn't adrift in a lake. He was being loaded onto something, being moved along a path above ground. The illusion had disappeared, but he wasn't completely awake. He was aware, but his body was still asleep, as if he were suffering from sleep paralysis. In other words, only his thoughts and senses were functioning.

"But if I was wrong to believe all these things, then why did you follow me here? Don't tell me you came here with the intent of finding evidence?"

Whatever Eun-ho was riding in was rolled over a dip in the ground. Eun-ho was tossed into the air. When he fell back down, his neck and back bent backwards as though they were about to snap. But Eun-ho barely felt any pain. Wife continued to talk to herself without taking a break.

"Even if that's why you're here, I need to know your true feelings. Many times, I've found that reality is exactly the opposite of my expectations. Actually, not just many. Every time. Always."

Eun-ho could guess that the thing he was riding in wasn't a car. He gradually started to feel more directly the sensation of the fierce wind. It had to be something with wheels that could carry a person. Something like a stroller.

"When I found out the truth, and if you passed my test, I was planning to give you one more chance. We could have started over, a new life in a new place. All you had to do was follow me. As you know, I'm always well prepared."

Suddenly, the wheelbarrow that had been in the shed flashed through Eunho's mind. It was one of those two-wheeled wheelbarrows that farmers used for transporting manure and tools. It would be too small to carry Jinu, but just big enough to carry Eun-ho's body. His legs were probably hanging over the side of the thing. Eun-ho didn't need to guess who was pushing the wheelbarrow. It had to be Wife.

"I was so sure of myself. The test was easy enough for a child to pass. You like goulash. And you don't like bread. And I've never seen you touch peanut butter. And yet, you didn't even touch the goulash. All you ate was bread and peanut butter. Why on earth did you eat that? Were you afraid I had put something in the goulash?"

Wife let out a snort. To Eun-ho, it sounded like a derisive laugh.

"And when I came back after putting Jiyoo to bed, you were going through my bag. Are you happy? You found the sleeping pills. You must have thought turning on your phone would save you. You must have thought turning on the voice recorder would give the police enough evidence to put me away. That's what you thought, right?"

Suddenly, the wheelbarrow flipped over, launching Eun-ho's body through the air. He fell to the ground, and rolled several times, eventually coming to a stop with his face in the snow.

Again, he barely felt any pain. But he did gain one more piece of information: his hands and feet were tied with something. But thankfully, his hands were tied in front of him and not behind his back. Had wife used the climbing rope she bought online? Or perhaps duct tape, which would have been easier to work with? Whatever it was, Eun-ho doubted he could free himself on his own.

He lay with his face buried in the snow. Listening to the sound of crunching snow, the sound of his wife's footsteps approaching him, the sound of death drawing near.

"Whose fault do you think Noah's death was?"

Wife's voice was right next to Eun-ho's ear. Following this question, a white light shined on the side of his face.

"You think it was my fault, don't you?"

Wife lifted his head by a fistful of hair and shined the light in front of his eyelids.

"It wasn't."

Wife brought her cold, moist lips to Eun-ho's earlobes. Eun-ho could feel his eyelids twitching.

"It was your fault."

Wife didn't sound angry. Nor did she sound like she was laughing at him.

In fact, Eun-ho felt no emotion in her voice. He had seen her lose it several times before, but he had never seen her snap like this. It was as if a critical part of her brain had experienced a fatal error—the part of her brain that made her human, that gave her a soul.

"My poor little Jiyoo. You should have adopted her as your own daughter when I asked you to. I told you I would take on the task of convincing Joon-young. I was still planning to do it, even when your bitch of a mother told us to take him back. You knew he couldn't live with us until we changed Jiyoo's last name. And yet you had the audacity to say you would bring Noah to live with us."

That was why she killed Noah? That was it? Eun-ho needed to ask her this, but his mouth wouldn't open. All he could feel was his wife's breath pounding at his ear.

"Why do you only care about your son?"

Wife pulled his head even further backward, as though it were the lid to a rice cooker. Eun-ho could hear his bones cracking.

"He's not the only child in this family, you son of a bitch."

Wife then slammed his head back into the snow. This time, he felt pain that was close to shock. It felt like his face had shattered. A low groan escaped his throat as his body started to shake. Finally, it seemed like he could sense pain.

"I have the worst luck."

Wife rolled Eun-ho onto his back. He could feel his bound hands being lifted above his head. At the same time, he was able to crack open his eyes just slightly. A black shadow glimmered through the haze in his narrow vision.

"No matter how much I do for people, they always betray me. Even my own father."

Wife grabbed Eun-ho by his bonds and stood up. Dragging him behind her, she started walking somewhere.

"For some reason, I thought you'd be different."

Eun-ho was being dragged through the snow with his hands above his head like a sled. He could see the bright light extending into the darkness and stopping on the wheelbarrow.

"I guess I believed you were more honest than those other men."

The wheelbarrow was standing upright, with its hull facing forward. It looked like its wheel had snagged on a rock or gotten stuck in a puddle.

"But now I know—you're the worst of them all."

Wife pushed him with her heel as she stuffed him into the wheelbarrow. A sharp pain pierced his stomach. As his head bent out of the wheelbarrow, he let out a sharp groan.

"Oh, you're finally awake."

This was the first time he was able to get a good look at her. Black boots, a black raincoat and hat, and a headlamp. Behind the light of her headlamp, Eun-ho could see two black, emotionless eyes.

"I know it hurts, but just wait a little longer. We're almost there."

Wife walked to the back of the wheelbarrow. She grabbed the handles and jumped up to let her weight lift the wheelbarrow with Eun-ho inside it. Once the wheelbarrow was upright again, they continued their journey. Eun-ho's head bobbed with the jostling of the wheelbarrow.

"Earlier, I borrowed a play from your book. You know, using someone's thumb while they're sleeping to unlock their phone. But I shouldn't have. Had I not looked at your phone, I might not have snapped like this.

Eun-ho's narrow eyes widened in shock. All the things that could have made her snap flashed before his eyes. The pictures he stole from her phone, the recording of his and Min-young's conversation, the email thread with his ex-wife.

"Didn't you say that the phone call earlier this morning was from your lawyer? Didn't you say you were going to meet him? I tried calling the number back. A very familiar voice answered. I didn't know Jinu went to law school. I was so shocked I didn't know what to say. But he was desperately calling out your name. Eun-ho Cha! Say something! Eun-ho Cha! It's Jinu!"

Wife started cackling. It was that same cackle he heard at Lake Baikal, the same laugh that made all the hair on his body stand up. But right now, his hair stood up for a different reason. It stood up because he realized Wife had finally lost it.

"But you know what, honey?"

Wife's laughing stopped as suddenly as it had begun.

"Why did you call Jane earlier this morning? She didn't pick up, but you called her ten times in a row."

What did she mean? Eun-ho was confused for a moment, but then he remembered what happened that morning. Jiyoo had borrowed his cellphone to make a call. She must have called Yuna's sister, Jane. But why hadn't Jane answered her phone?

"What could be so important that you would call my sister ten times in a row? And since when were you and Jane so close? Are you fucking my sister?

Don't tell me there's another secret I don't know!"

With every question, Wife's voice was getting higher and higher. Eun-ho looked around with blurry vision. The only thing that Wife's headlamp was illuminating was the snow on the ground. In desperation, he focused all his attention on his ears. But he heard no police sirens over the sound of the snow and wind. The earth seemed completely devoid of people and animals. It was just him, and this hysterical woman.

"So that got me thinking. I want to compose a masterpiece, something that will really knock the socks off the police. A story of star-crossed lovers, an adulterous man and his whore of a sister-in-law, who tragically commit suicide by drowning themselves. What do you think?"

The abandoned car down the street appeared in Eun-ho's mind. The blue SUV covered in snow.

Then finally, Eun-ho realized that the loon in the attic wasn't Joon-young; it was Jane.

And then he found the last piece to the puzzle. Yuna was taking him to the Half Moon Marsh to die.

*

A loon was crying just like before. But unlike that night, something scratched the wall between each call. The sound wasn't very loud. It was secretive, like someone was trying to whisper in her ear, coaxing her to come closer.

Jiyoo pulled the blanket over her head. She covered her ears so she wouldn't hear the sounds. But it was no use. The sound was too close. It was just beyond the wall next to her bed.

Every time the loon cried, Jiyoo's legs twitched. And every time it scratched at the wall, her tummy felt funny, just like when she felt nervous. Jiyoo thought about what happened when she came upstairs with Mother a few hours ago. Mother had stopped in front of Jiyoo's door and given her a command.

"Jiyoo, go to the bathroom."

Jiyoo looked toward the bathroom, then back at Mother. She didn't understand what she meant.

"Brush your teeth, wash your face and feet, and go potty."

"Yes," Jiyoo said, even though she still didn't understand. Jiyoo could wash up after Mother went back downstairs. Why did Mother have to wait for her?

"You won't be able to use the bathroom again until tomorrow."

This explanation confused Jiyoo even more, but she did as she was told and went into the bathroom. Mother stood at the door to Jiyoo's bedroom until she came back out. She looked lost in thought. Even as Jiyoo walked up to her, Mother seemed unaware. Only when Jiyoo called out to her did she finally regain her emotionless composure.

"Mother—"

"Done?"

"Yes."

Mother opened the bedroom door. Jiyoo went in first.

"Why do you think I followed you up here?" Mother asked Jiyoo as she closed the door behind her.

"Because I haven't—"

Jiyoo stopped mid-sentence and looked down at her feet. She knew the answer, but she was afraid to say it.

"What?" Mother wanted a complete answer.

"Because I haven't been punished."

"Then you know what must happen now, don't you?"

Jiyoo closed her eyes for a moment, then opened them again. She suppressed the urge to ask for forgiveness and said the words Mother wanted to hear, even though it killed her to say them.

"I must be punished."

Silence filled the room for a moment. But that moment was cold and unbearable, as though she were standing in the middle of a snowstorm.

"Everyone makes mistakes—" Mother finally said, breaking the silence. "I want to believe that this was a mistake, your first mistake."

Jiyoo stared up at Mother as she took one step toward Jiyoo. Jiyoo was confused. Was she going to forgive Jiyoo without punishing her? Or was she going to forgive her *by* punishing her?

"Jiyoo, did you bring Dad Puppet here with you?"

Jiyoo glanced furtively at the suitcase placed next to the desk. She couldn't lie. Even if it meant that Mother would take him away. After all, Mother would have looked in her bag when she brought it upstairs.

"Yes."

"Give it to me."

Jiyoo turned her body and crouched next to the suitcase. She laid it on the ground and took out Dad Puppet, which was hidden underneath one of her sweaters. She looked it once in the eyes to say goodbye. *Thank you.*

"What are you doing?" Mother asked. She pressed Jiyoo to hand it over. Jiyoo stood up and handed Mother the puppet.

"Where did you find him?" Mother asked as she took him.

"I . . . couldn't sleep . . . so I . . ."

Jiyoo could feel her cheeks starting to glow bright red. She was embarrassed to admit what she did because she knew it was embarrassing. It wasn't easy talking about something embarrassing without being embarrassed.

"I'm not mad at you. I just want you to tell me the truth."

"I waited for you to fall asleep then I left my room."

Jiyoo took a deep breath. She said the rest of it as though she were spitting out toothpaste:

"And then I took the key out of the dresser in the hallway and went into the attic."

"I see. So, if you hadn't left your room, none of this would have happened. Right?"

Probably. Yes, if she hadn't left her room, she wouldn't have stolen Dad Puppet.

"Then can you try tonight not to leave your room?"

Jiyoo looked up at Mother without answering. She didn't understand what she meant.

"It's my test to you. If you can stay in your room until tomorrow morning, I'll forgive you."

A test. Forgiveness. Jiyoo swallowed the saliva that was collecting beneath her tongue.

"And as a present, I will give you this puppet."

"Really? He'll be all mine?"

Jiyoo doubted she heard Mother correctly.

"Yes," Mother answered. "And if you don't pass my test, do you know what will happen?"

"I won't be forgiven. And I won't get a present."

As soon as Jiyoo answered, she realized why Mother had told her to go to the bathroom before going into her room.

"And what does it mean if you won't be forgiven?"

Jiyoo didn't want to say the word orphanage. Words were powerful, and sometimes all one needed to do was say them for it to become a reality.

"You don't know?" Mother asked.

"I—"

Jiyoo searched her mind for what would come next. She wanted to find words that would convey the meaning of orphanage without using the word orphanage.

"I won't be able to live with you. And I won't be able to live with Grandma either."

"Right. So, I'll ask you again. Can you stay in your room tonight?"

Jiyoo found nothing hard about this. In fact, to her, it seemed like a piece of cake. How many times had she spent all day in her room?

"Yes."

"And if I call you, what will you do?"

This was a very hard question. Jiyoo thought what the correct answer was. Jiyoo brought her hands together and prayed that she had the right answer.

"I won't leave my room. Not until tomorrow morning. No matter what."

"Good." Mother pointed to the bed with her eyes. "Well, you should get ready for bed then."

Jiyoo changed into her pajamas and got into bed. Mother turned off the light and left the room. Soon, Jiyoo heard footsteps going down the stairs. It was then that the loon started calling her from beyond the wall. It was almost as if the loon had been waiting for Mother to leave.

Jiyoo turned to lie on her side. The longer she lay in bed, the less sleepy she felt. After a while, she could pick out each sound individually. The wind, the snow pelting the window, the maple tree's branches whacking against each other, Mother's footsteps as she walked around downstairs, Mother's shouting, something heavy—like a steal ball—rolling across the wood floor, the front door opening and closing. And then eventually, she heard the front gate opening.

Jiyoo pulled back the sheets and sat up in bed. Mischievous Mouse, which had been quiet for some time now, poked its head out. And with a voice as sweet as honey, it started whispering in her ear.

Think carefully about what Mother said. She said not to leave the room, but she never said you couldn't leave your bed. Right?

Once Jiyoo thought about it, she realized Mischievous Mouse was right. She could walk around the room all she liked. And even though the lights were turned off, the room wasn't very dark. The white snow and the light in the front yard provided more than enough light to move around.

Jiyoo got out of bed and went over to the window. Using her palm, she wiped one corner of the frosted window and made a small window within a window. She peered out the hole and looked down at the front gate. Someone was leaving the front yard with the wheelbarrow. Someone dressed in a black raincoat and rain hat, someone with whom Jiyoo had made eye contact that one night, someone whom Jiyoo didn't want to believe was Mother.

Jiyoo jumped back from the window, but she was already a moment too late. She had seen something she shouldn't have. She wanted to convince herself that she had seen nothing, but she couldn't fool herself. She had immediately recognized the two long objects hanging over the side of the wheelbarrow. They were the legs of a person wearing white sneakers.

Jiyoo heard the front gate close. She went back to the window and peered out again. They were all gone—the black raincoat, the wheelbarrow, the white sneakers. All she could see was a white light floating down the footpath. The light soon entered the wetlands, which were engulfed in a flurry of snow.

The loon in the attic stopped whispering. Now that it knew Mother was gone, it was wailing. The loon also went from scratching the wall to pounding on it. *Thud, thud, thud . . .*

Jiyoo could feel the strength in her legs draining. Her knees gave out as she collapsed in front of the windowsill. Something was crawling out of the dream she had almost forgotten. She could see two legs with white sneakers on their feet ticking like the hands of a clock.

The call of the loon turned into Father's voice. She stuck her head between her knees and covered her ears with both hands, but Father's voice assaulted her ears like a powerful cannon.

Finally, the dream hiding in the thicket jumped out of the bushes.

Jiyoo didn't remember when she had fallen asleep that night. Actually, she couldn't even be certain that she ever fell asleep. All she remembered was that at some point, she started to hear the call of a loon.

At first, she thought it was coming from the Half Moon Marsh. It didn't bother her or hurt her ears. After all, she had come to the cabin before and was used to the loons. But as the call got louder and closer, she realized something was off. She realized the call wasn't coming from the wetlands. It sounded like it was coming from the attic.

Jiyoo sat with her feet hanging over the bed. It didn't occur to her that she should call Mother. Nor did it occur to her that she should wake up Father. At that moment, she wasn't thinking anything. She simply opened the bedroom door and went out into the hallway, as though she were possessed by something.

When she flipped the switch, electricity entered the candle bulb on the wall. The light was just bright enough for her to find the dresser in the hallway. Jiyoo found the key and unlocked the door to the attic. It didn't occur to her that she should be afraid. If anything, she thought she might be dreaming.

There was nothing in the attic. From her bedroom, it sounded like the loon was in the attic, but now that she was here, it sounded like the loon was downstairs. Jiyoo went back into the hallway and locked the door behind her. She returned the key to where she had found it. And again, with barely any hesitation, she started down the stairs. The loon's call was getting stranger and stranger. One moment it sounded like someone screaming, the next it sounded like someone crying, and sometimes it sounded like angry shouting.

Once she turned at the landing, everything became dark. The stairs bent at the landing, cutting her off from the light upstairs. All the lights downstairs were off. Only then did Jiyoo feel afraid. She thought something might jump out from the darkness and grab her ankles. And she was afraid that if she called out to Mother in the darkness, she would trip and fall.

But even so, Jiyoo didn't turn back. She continued downstairs, like a child bewitched by a magical flute. She would feel each step with her toes before moving forward. When she finally arrived in the kitchen, a shriek exploded from the darkness. The sound was so loud and sudden that Jiyoo almost shrieked herself. The sound had come from Mother, from the bathroom.

Jiyoo had no time to think, no time to turn on the lights. Something was happening to Mother. Something terrible, something that Jiyoo needed to stop. That was why Jiyoo ran to the bathroom and opened the door without knocking.

At first, Jiyoo didn't know what she was looking at. She felt like she was looking at a strange picture book.

Blood on the bathtub and wall. Mother standing next to the tub and looking back at Jiyoo. The cleaver in her hand. The blood splattered on her face. Two legs dangling over the side of the tub. A single twitching toe.

The moment each of these objects combined into one picture, something inside Jiyoo's mind broke. Darkness immediately enveloped her eyes. She had no memories of what happened after that. Except for the scream she let out before everything went black.

When Jiyoo opened her eyes, she was lying in bed. A dim light was on, and Mother was standing next to the bed. There was concern on her face.

"Jiyoo, are you okay?"

Jiyoo glanced around. She was in her room.

"I came upstairs because I heard you scream. Was there a monster in your dream?"

Mother was wearing a blue bathrobe. Her hair was drying in a blue towel. Nowhere was there anything that looked like bloodstains. A smile twinkled in her eyes, two locks of hair were plastered to her wet forehead, and her cheeks looked moist and clear. She looked like she had just come running out of the bathtub. Jiyoo let out a whimper-like sigh. It was just a dream.

"Are you feeling okay?" Mother asked.

The images of the bathroom appeared in Jiyoo's mind again.

"No," Jiyoo said as she shook her head and rid her mind of the images. "It's nothing. I just—"

"Good," Mother said with a nod. "It's okay. It was just a dream. It'll all disappear when you wake up in the morning."

"Shall I stay here until you fall asleep?" Mother asked in a concerned tone.

"No."

Jiyoo had never fallen asleep while being watched by Mother. At least, not as far as she remembered. She thought it would actually be harder to fall asleep if Mother was watching over her.

"Good. Then I'll go back to finish my bath."

Mother turned off the lights and went out of the room. She left behind a damp, fishy smell.

Mother was right. Jiyoo thought she was dreaming that same dream, but she wasn't. The dream always ended at the bottom of the stairs. And that was because Mother's voice always stopped her before she got to the bathroom. Because of this, she had forgotten all about the bare foot dangling over the side of the bathtub. At least until she saw the legs with white sneakers dangling from the wheelbarrow.

Jiyoo wondered if the white sneakers were also a dream. If they were, then the loon in the attic had to be a dream, too.

Yes. It was a dream. The kind of dream that Dad Puppet protected her from, the kind of dream that disappeared as soon as she woke up. Jiyoo lifted herself off the floor. Immediately she looked out the window again. The light was motionless in the middle of the footpath. Although the snow was obscuring the light, she could see it clearly enough.

But isn't that strange? Mischievous Mouse asked. *I don't remember you falling asleep tonight. But don't you have to fall asleep to dream?*

Jiyoo searched her memory. Had she fallen asleep without being aware of it? Sometimes, when she lay in bed with her eyes closed, it felt like she was both asleep and not asleep. That night was like that, and so was tonight. According to the doctor, this happened when Jiyoo was only in a light sleep. Jiyoo regretted not asking the doctor if she could dream while only in a light sleep.

Just do something to test if you're dreaming or not. Mischievous Mouse said. *Mother's not home right now.*

Jiyoo turned her head and looked at the wall behind the bed. The pounding and the crying were only getting louder.

Doesn't it seem like it knows Mother is gone? Doesn't it seem like it's asking you to hurry?

Mischievous Mouse asked the question, then answered it.

It might be a person, not a loon.

No. Jiyoo shook her head. Who would be here but Mother and Stepfather? It could be a thief. But a thief wouldn't try to send Jiyoo a message. They would take what they wanted and run away as fast as possible.

Go over to the bed.

The good daughter inside Jiyoo, whom Mischievous Mouse hated, reminded Jiyoo of the promise she made to Mother. She told Jiyoo to jump in bed and go to sleep. She warned Jiyoo that if she broke her promise to Mother again, she would never be forgiven. She showed Jiyoo an image of her dragging her suitcase through the doors of an orphanage.

Jiyoo went over to the bed and sat down. The sounds beyond the wall continued. It was now banging on the wall in counts of three. *Thud, thud, thud... thud, thud, thud.*

I have an idea, Mischievous Mouse said as it appeared again. *Say something to the wall. If it's a loon or if this is a dream, you won't get a reply. If it is a real person, then you will get an answer. Nothing will happen if you talk to the wall. You won't be leaving the room. You won't be breaking your promise to Mother.*

This convinced Jiyoo. She worked up her courage. She cautiously knocked on the wall twice. The loon stopped crying immediately, as if to listen to the sound Jiyoo was making. Jiyoo pressed her ear against the wall and spoke to it.

"Is anyone there?"

There was a loud thud on the wall. Just once. As if to say, *Yes!*

Jiyoo took her ear from the wall in shock. Was it really a person? Or perhaps it was just a coincidence. Unable to decide, Jiyoo decided to ask again.

"Are you a person? If yes, knock once. If no, knock twice."

Thud!

Jiyoo stared in the direction of the sound. She asked her third question.

"Do you know me?"

Thud!

Jiyoo's chest was pounding. This was impossible. This had to be a dream. But she didn't want to stop the quiz. She wanted to know who this person was, this person who knew her, who cried like a loon, who was pounding on the wall in the attic.

"Then what's my name? Knock once for Jiyoo Seo and knock twice for Jiyoo Cha."

Thud!

Jiyoo jumped to her feet. She tensed the muscles in her legs as she glared at the spot in the wall the sound came from. It felt like electricity was flowing through her entire body. She could feel the blood pumping through her forehead, earlobes, throat, chest, belly button. But her mind was blank; she didn't know what question to ask next.

You dummy. You need to ask who it is. That person beyond the wall knows who you are. That means you know who they are! Call out every name you can think of.

Mischievous Mouse was right.

"I'm going to name all the people I know. If you're them, knock once. If you're not, knock twice. Or just don't knock at all. I'll start now. Father."

No sound.

"Grandma."

Still nothing.

"Auntie," Jiyoo said despite knowing it couldn't be Auntie.

Thud!

"Auntie Jane?" Jiyoo shouted.

Thud!

"Are you really Auntie Jane? My Auntie Jane?"

Thud! And then another loon-like groan. To Jiyoo, this sounded like Auntie Jane was calling her name.

Jiyoo!

Jiyoo ran to the door without thinking. But then suddenly Good Daughter stopped her.

You can't leave. You promised Mother. You said you wouldn't leave, not even if

Mother called you herself.

Jiyoo turned her head and glared at the wall. Jiyoo shouted to the wall:

"Auntie, why are you in there?"

Auntie Jane called Jiyoo again: *Thud!*

Jiyoo's feet became tied when she reached the door. She couldn't leave the room, but she also couldn't just leave Auntie Jane inside the attic. Jiyoo almost wished this was a dream, too.

It's not a dream. Mischievous Mouse said. *Do you really still think this is a dream?* Mischievous Mouse then started telling Jiyoo things she didn't want to hear. *Mother locked the attic. Auntie Jane is inside the attic. Auntie Jane can't talk. Just think about what that means.*

Jiyoo didn't need to think. She already knew the answer. Mother had locked Auntie Jane in the attic, just like she locked Jiyoo in this room. Although Jiyoo didn't know why Auntie couldn't speak, that wasn't important. The important thing was that Auntie was trapped in the attic, and Jiyoo knew where the key was. She could open it if she really wanted to.

"Wake up, little one. Wake up."

Jiyoo thought of Auntie's voice, which she had heard in her dream.

"If you have another bad dream, just call for me. Auntie's not going anywhere."

As Auntie had promised, she was always by Jiyoo's side. She had called her little one, she had woken her up from her bad dream, she had told her it was okay, she had told her not to cry, and she had come all the way to Cheongyeon to give her Dad Puppet. And yet, when she needed Jiyoo's help, Jiyoo hesitated.

Open the door and go to her. She needs you.

Jiyoo took a breath. She reached out and grabbed the handle.

*

Jiyoo was coming. She was coming like someone walking into a lion's den, quiet and cautiously.

Jane's nerves were erupting like an active volcano. Her pulse was three times faster than normal. She was panting, her throat was dry, and her head was burning like a hot iron. It felt like the thing in her mouth wasn't a duck's head but a piece of hot coal. The minute it took Jiyoo to arrive was more agonizing than the several hours of pain she'd endured.

Jane brought her knees up to her chest and rested the back of her head against the wall. She closed her eyes and counted Jiyoo's footsteps. With every step that Jiyoo took forward, Jane's throat winced with pain. She knew the conflict and fear Jiyoo had to overcome to open the door. After all, she had heard the promise Yuna forced her to make.

When Jiyoo and Yuna were in the hallway, she couldn't hear what they were saying. She knew Yuna was talking, but that was about it. Only after the two of them entered the room did their voices become clear. She could hear everything, as if the walls were made not of wood, but of honeycomb. While listening to their conversation, she gained two important pieces of information.

The first was that Jiyoo knew there was a key to open the attic. This gave Jane hope. In fact, Jane had inferred this when she saw the puppets pour out of the box Yuna mutilated with her cleaver. Jiyoo must have gotten the puppet from the attic. The other thing she heard was Jiyoo's promise not to leave the room until tomorrow morning. This put Jane into despair. Yuna was God to Jiyoo. To get to Jiyoo, she would have to break her faith.

Her probability of success was close to zero, but she had to try. Jane got busy thinking of ways to get Jiyoo to open the attic door. But there was no move that would allow Jiyoo to free Jane without putting her in danger, without Yuna finding out eventually. But there was one way of getting Jiyoo's attention—crying out like a loon.

Jane's back was flat against the wall. She had to let Jiyoo know that she was in the attic. She had to make a sound that was quiet enough that Yuna wouldn't notice. She tried her best to recreate the sound of a loon, as best as she remembered. Her mouth was blocked, but the gag actually helped her produce a howl. She scratched at the wall between howls to tell Jiyoo where she was. And sometimes she would pause to listen to what was happening downstairs. Through the incomprehensible ruckus, she was able to pick out Yuna's voice.

Honey, let's go.

She then heard the front gate opening and closing. From these two things, she guessed that Yuna had taken Eun-ho out of the house.

Downstairs was completely silent. She waited a little bit longer, but she heard no signs of movement. It was clear the two of them had gone somewhere, but she had no idea where that was. This was going to be Jane's last chance.

She could feel her pulse fluttering in her temples. Sitting against the wall, she felt her body beginning to float. Because of this, she lost all sense of self. Jane screamed as loud as she could and hit the back of her head against the wall until Jiyoo answered.

Oh, how precocious of a child Jiyoo was. The moment that Jiyoo said, "Auntie?" Jane felt her heart explode with relief. When she finally heard the door to Jiyoo's bedroom open, she almost burst into tears. Jiyoo's coming here to help her auntie wasn't just an act of kindness, it was an act of apostacy.

Jiyoo's footsteps stopped in the hallway. For a while, Jane couldn't hear anything. Jane brought her chin to her knees and tightened the muscle in her lower abdomen to stop her bladder from exploding. Jane steadied her breathing and pleaded with her body.

Please, just wait one more minute.

Jiyoo started moving again. Jane held her breath as she listened to the sounds in the hallway. The sound of keys jingling, the sound of a key entering a lock, the sound of a lock opening. The door opened. And then she heard the voice of her savior, the voice she had been waiting hours for in the dark.

"Auntie—"

Jiyoo flipped the switch and flooded the room with light. Jane winced and shut her eyes. A cautious question came her way.

"Are you really my Auntie Jane?"

Jane opened her eyes. Jiyoo was crouched in front of her. She was studying Jane's face with a fear-filled expression. Jane wasn't surprised she didn't recognize her. Jane would be covered in blood, and her face, completely swollen; the only thing that probably resembled Jiyoo's aunt was Jane's hair.

Jane wasn't sure if she should cry or smile. If nothing else, she wanted to call out to Jiyoo. She wanted to jump to her feet and give Jiyoo a hug. But all she could do was use the communication method that she and Jiyoo had made. Jane hit the wall with the back of her head.

"But Auntie, there's blood in your eyes—"

Jiyoo reached out toward Jane's face but quickly retracted her hand in shock. Jane shook her head. She looked at Jiyoo and tried to communicate with her one good eye.

No, Jiyoo. Not my eyes. My mouth, Jiyoo. My mouth.

Jiyoo's eyes turned to Jane's taped mouth. She immediately understood what Jane's eyes were trying to tell her.

"Hold on."

Jiyoo sat down in front of Jane. And with her small hands, she started to unravel the tape around Jane's mouth. It wasn't easy because the tape was wrapped all the way around the back of her head. It felt like Jiyoo was peeling off Jane's skin and hair. When the tape was completely removed, Jane lost all sensation in her face. Lastly, Jiyoo pulled the duck head out of Jane's mouth. A cough and a long stream of spit were ejected with the gag, as though she were a bottle of champagne that had just been uncorked.

Finally, she could breathe comfortably. The feeling of being drowned in a vacuum also disappeared. Jiyoo patted Jane on the back.

"Auntie, are you okay?"

"Jiyoo—" Her words were slurred like an alcoholic. "We need scissors."

Jiyoo nodded and ran out of the room. She came back with the scissors from the kitchen as fast as a gust of wind. The first thing Jane instructed her to do was cut the noose around her neck. After that, she had Jiyoo cut the ropes around her wrists and ankles.

Her body was free. Jane stretched her legs and lay down. What happened with Yuna, the noose on her neck, Jiyoo's rescuing her—everything felt like a dream. Even right now, as she lay on the cold wooden floor with her tongue hanging out of her mouth, she wasn't sure this was reality.

Jane was brought back to reality by the most realistic of problems; her bladder was sending her a message that it was about to explode. As Jane tried to get up, she fell forward, slamming her chin on the ground. She had no strength in her legs or ankles.

"Auntie, what's wrong?" Jiyoo asked as she grabbed Jane's shoulder.

Jane couldn't answer. It seemed like her bladder, which had been holding on for an entire day, would explode if she opened her mouth. So, she started doing something that she would never again do in her life. As drool dribbled from her numb lips, she used her trembling hands to pull herself to the bathroom like a seal on land. Jiyoo realized what Jane was doing and ran ahead to open the bathroom door for her.

Jane must have been sitting on the toilet for over ten minutes. As she sat there, her paralyzed muscles started to tingle back to life. When she was done relieving herself, she dragged her legs over to the sink. She turned on the faucet and cupped water into her mouth. She started out sipping small amounts at a time, and slowly changed to chugging the water like a horse. After this, she washed the blood out of her eyes and looked in the mirror.

The woman in the mirror was someone she didn't recognize. She understood why Jiyoo didn't recognize her at first. In fact, she was surprised that Jiyoo had believed her at all. She looked like a UFC fighter who had just lost by decision after five rounds of a one-sided smashing.

Her eyelid had a blood bruise and was stuck to her eyeball, her nose looked like it had been replaced with a fried dumpling, and her lips had gone from an innie to an outie. There was a rash on her cheek where the tape had been. Thankfully Jane's vision was blurry, which prevented her from getting too good of a look at herself.

Jane wiped the water from around her eyes. Only then did she see Jiyoo, who was standing behind her with a towel.

"Auntie, are you okay?" Jiyoo asked as soon as they made eye contact.

Instead of answering, Jane turned around and hugged Jiyoo. The words "thank you" came out sounding like two sobs. She wanted to leave this place with Jiyoo as soon as possible. But before that, she needed to call the cops. For that, she would need to go downstairs and find a phone.

"Your mother," Jane said as she put Jiyoo in front of her. "Do you know where she went?"

Jiyoo clamped her mouth shut and looked down at her feet. She was clearly hesitant to answer.

"Jiyoo. You must tell me. This is about your father."

Tears began welling up in Jiyoo's eyes. What Jiyoo said next didn't make sense to Jane.

"It wasn't a dream, was it? It was all real, wasn't it?"

"What dream? You mean about the loon?"

Jiyoo shook her head before bursting out in tears. This made it hard to hear what she said next.

". . . the downstairs bathroom . . . the tub was filled with blood . . . two legs . . . real legs . . . with feet . . ."

It was at this moment that Jane's worst fears were realized. Her heart sank deep into her stomach. Had Jiyoo seen it happen?

"That night . . . when my dad came . . ."

Jane pulled Jiyoo into her embrace.

"Shush, shush. It's okay. You don't need to say anymore. I understand."

But Jiyoo didn't stop. She continued as she choked on her own saliva.

"Mother told me . . . it was just a dream . . . But I know . . . It wasn't a dream . . . It didn't go away when I woke up . . . I still remember it . . ."

Jane could guess what had happened. Jiyoo had seen her father's body in the bathroom downstairs, and Yuna had brainwashed her into thinking it was just a bad dream.

"The night after that, Mother took the wheelbarrow to the Half Moon

Marsh—the one we use to feed the ducks."

Finally Jane understood the meaning of Jiyoo's recurring dream. She thought she knew why Jiyoo was so sick that she was unconscious for several days, and the reason why she was so attached to that puppet. Subconsciously, Jiyoo must have thought that when she was talking with the puppet, she was talking with her real father. And she must have believed that her father was still alive, she must have convinced herself that what she saw was just a dream.

Jiyoo's heavy crying slowly turned to a tamed whimpering. She opened her mouth several times only to close it again. But Jane had no hopes of consoling her. Nor was this a problem that could be solved by consolation. It was impossible for Jane to fathom how much pain this six-year-old girl must have been in trying to keep this horrible secret inside her. All she could do right now was wait until Jiyoo stopped crying on her own.

Thankfully, this happened sooner rather than later. Jiyoo took herself from Jane's embrace, her face covered in tears and snot. Although she was still sobbing, she was capable of asking in a clear voice:

"You want to know where Mother went, right?"

Jane nodded.

"Follow me."

Jiyoo grasped Jane's hand and led her to the bedroom window. Jane looked down at where Jiyoo was pointing. There was a single faint light moving slowly through the blizzard.

"Is that your mom?"

"Yes. I didn't see their faces, but in the wheelbarrow, there were le—there were le—there were le—"

Jane swallowed hard, forcing spit down her dry, swollen throat. She then asked something she wished had didn't have to.

"There were legs?"

Jiyoo nodded.

Jane turned her gaze to the window. The legs must belong to Eun-ho. It seemed to Jane that there was an equal probability that he was alive or dead. She could guess why Yuna was taking him to the marsh in a wheelbarrow. She definitely wasn't taking him there to play hide-and-go-seek, not in this weather.

"Is there a phone in this house? Not a cellphone, but a wired phone."

Jiyoo shook her head.

"No."

Of course there wasn't. Jane nodded. If she couldn't find her cellphone, she wouldn't be able to call the police. And what would she do if she was unable to find her car keys? Would she have to go to the marsh herself and confront Yuna?

Jane began trembling with doubt. Did she have the strength to fight Yuna in the snow when her body was in shambles? If Eun-ho was still alive, perhaps the two of them could take her. But what about Jiyoo?

"Jiyoo, can you stay here by yourself?"

"Yes."

"Don't leave this room. Not until I come back for you."

"Are you going to the Half Moon Marsh?"

"I think I must."

Jiyoo suddenly opened her eyes twice as wide.

"Then you must go along the footpath. I can show you."

Jane shook her head. "I know the way. You need to stay here. That's the only way you can help me."

"But—"

Disappointment was all over Jiyoo's face.

Jane led Jiyoo over to the bed and sat her down.

"I can't protect two people at once."

Jiyoo shook her head furiously, as though she were frustrated that her Auntie wasn't understanding her. Jiyoo looked up at Jane with pleading eyes.

"I promise I won't bother you."

"There's no time," Jane said before Jiyoo could say anymore.

"It might already be too late. If you don't let me go, then—"

Jane paused and thought for a moment. How much did Jiyoo understand about what was happening? Jane quickly realized that Jiyoo probably understood a lot more than she was giving her credit for. If she didn't, she wouldn't have freed Jane from the attic, and she wouldn't have told Jane where her Mother and Eun-ho were.

"—then the thing you're scared of will come true."

Jiyoo dropped her gaze slightly. She let go of Jane's hand, which she had been squeezing this whole time. Jane grabbed Jiyoo's shoulder and gave it a squeeze before taking her hand away.

"I'll be back as soon as I can."

When Jane got to the bedroom door, she heard Jiyoo shouting out to her from behind.

"Auntie! You'll come back with Mother, right?"

Jane turned around and looked at Jiyoo.

Jiyoo then added in a tone that sounded broken, "Try talking to her."

Jane couldn't promise Jiyoo that she would. Even if she tried talking to Yuna, there was little chance she would listen. Even so, she told Jiyoo what she wanted to hear.

"I will try."

Jane ran downstairs. She frantically searched the living room and kitchen for her phone. She eventually found a set of car keys in Yuna's bag. Judging from the emblem on them, they were probably to Yuna's BMW. But she couldn't find her cellphone. Nor could she find anyone else's phone. And all the professional-grade tools in the kitchen cabinet had disappeared—the knives, the mixer, the pots, everything.

Jane now had an answer to one of her questions. The reason why Yuna appeared here yesterday was to get rid of the evidence. Yuna must have felt that the police were on to her. Had Eun-ho also started to suspect Yuna? Was that why she was taking him to the marsh in a wheelbarrow?

Jane looked down at the keys in her hand. Was Eun-ho still alive? If he was, then there wasn't any time to go to the police. And even if he was dead, it didn't matter anyway. In the time it would take for her to come back with the police, Yuna would realize Jane was missing. And that would be dangerous for Jiyoo. It appeared she had no choice.

Jane looked for something she could use as a weapon, but there wasn't even a butter knife. She remembered the scissors in the attic, but she didn't want to go upstairs and risk having to talk to Jiyoo again. She detached the aluminum pole from the mop next to the shoe rack and ran outside in just her socks.

Thankfully, the car was parked just outside the front gate. She used her hand to dust the snow off the front and rear windshields, then got in the car. She stuck the pole between the front two seats, started the engine, buckled her seatbelt, and turned on the high beams. After backing the car up to the road, she positioned the car in the tracks of the wheelbarrow. She was now ready to go.

Jane looked down at the snow-locked wetlands. She tried to convince herself that this was a chance to cross off from her bucket list "racing through the snow in someone else's car." Jane clasped the wheel tight as she stepped on the gas.

The car shot forward with a whir. She could feel the blood and adrenaline pumping through her body. She felt dizzy, and her vision was shaking. Her head was being pushed backwards, and her butt was having trouble staying in the seat. The car bounced up and down as it jostled side to side.

And yet she wasn't hitting anything, nor was the ground as soggy as she thought it would be. Despite the ground being covered in snow, because the path was so uneven, there was enough friction to keep her wheels from sliding too much. The car barreled forward like a tank, erasing the wheelbarrow's tracks and leaving a trail of fallen reeds behind it.

Time worked differently here than in the attic. While Jane was in the attic, it felt like she was adrift on a placid lake, but now it felt like she was racing down white water rapids in a valley. Jane noticed something ahead. It didn't take long for her eyes to tell her it was the footpath that circled the Half Moon Marsh. But there was someone standing on the path.

Yuna. This was Jane's chance to finish this in one fell swoop. It wouldn't be hard. All she had to do was turn toward Yuna and keep her foot on the gas. She already had the speed, and there was just a small slope demarking the entrance to the path.

Yuna stood there motionless, as if to tell Jane that she didn't think Jane could go through with it. She was standing next to the wheelbarrow, her arms down at her sides, just staring at Jane.

And she was right. Jane couldn't do it. Leaning sideways toward the front passenger's seat, she used her whole body to turn the steering wheel to the right. The front of the car hit the side of the bank, spun at a right angle, and traced the curve of the side path as it kicked up snow and flora. Grasping the wheel and stepping on the brake, she braced herself as the car created a tsunami of snow. Debris rained down on the car, making it feel like she was inside a building scheduled for demolition.

The car came to a stop at the corner of the bank. Somehow, Jane had managed to prevent the airbags from deploying, which would have trapped her in this steaming dumpling of a car. Jane unbuckled her seatbelt, grabbed the mop, and lowered it to hide it from view.

The car's headlights illuminated the terraced rice paddies below the wetlands. Yuna was standing on the footpath, turned toward the marsh with her hands on the wheelbarrow's handles. She looked amused by Jane's theatrics, but still determined to finish what she came here to do. The light from Yuna's headlamp illuminated the frozen surface of the marsh. With barely any difference in elevation between the water and the land, the marsh looked like a vast snowfield. The wind herded snow along the surface of the marsh like a flock of sheep. Jane heard a siren in the distance. But whether it belonged to a police car or a firetruck she didn't know.

Jane got out of the car and stepped onto the footpath. She didn't call out to Yuna or yell at her to stop. Instead, she just started running toward Yuna. It didn't feel like she was getting any closer. There were only a few seconds separating her and Yuna, but for some reason it felt like Yuna was located on a planet across the solar system. Yuna calmly lifted the wheelbarrow. Jane jumped to close the remaining distance between them, like a sprinter lunging for the finish line.

Three things happened at once. Yuna raised the wheelbarrow's handles above her head. A man, who Jane assumed to be Eun-ho, slid out and fell onto the snow-covered marsh. And Jane's airborne body crashed into Yuna. As a result, all three of them ended up rolling onto the ice.

Despite having a thick layer of snow on its surface, the marsh wasn't frozen solid. As soon as Jane fell onto the ice, it let out a sharp crack and caved under her weight. Immediately, Jane fell head-first into the water. The icy water penetrated her ears, mouth, and nose, preventing her from breathing.

Despite the shallow water, the cold shock immobilized her body. It took her forever to get her feet under her and her head out of the water. But once she did, she was able to sense light out of her left eye, which was still swollen. When she turned her head, she could see the light from Yuna's headlamp shining down on her. Judging from the direction of the light, Jane realized she was now lying on her back and facing the sky. It had to be Yuna. But because she wasn't right next to Jane, she couldn't make out her image.

The BMW's headlights were also shining diagonally across the swamp, providing enough light to make out the shapes of objects. Thanks to this, she was able to find something that looked like a hole to her right. It looked like a second hole in the ice. Probably where Eun-ho had fallen.

Jane moved toward the hole. There was a good chance that Eun-ho was drugged and unconscious. Most conscious men wouldn't let themselves be loaded onto a wheelbarrow and disposed of in a marsh. Yuna must have wanted to drown him in his sleep. Jane knew there wasn't much time, but she couldn't move faster.

The bed of the marsh was covered in thick mud. Every time she put her foot down, it sunk deep into the mud, and every time she tried to lift her foot, it felt like her ankle was caught in a trap. In just two steps, she had lost both her socks. And she was slipping with every other step. Sharp rocks and shards of glass hidden in the mud cut her feet. Had the water been deeper, she would have tried swimming. The worst thing was the cold shock. Her back was shaking, and she couldn't feel her legs. And every time she took a breath, it felt like her lungs were collapsing.

At this rate, Jane wondered if she would reach Eun-ho before Christmas. And just as she thought this, her knee got caught on something. Something heavy was pressing up gently against her pants. Jane turned slowly to look down at the water. A face was floating in the dark, murky water. Its dull eyes were open and appeared to make eye contact with her.

Jane jumped in surprise. She almost screamed and ran up onto the bank. If she hadn't realized that this face belonged to the person she was looking for, she would have left him to drown.

"Eun-ho!"

Jane leaned over and put her hands under his armpits. As she lifted his body out of the water, his limp head slumped over sideways.

"Eun-ho. Are you awake?"

He didn't respond, but there was hope. He started breathing on his own as soon as she lifted his head out of the water. His breaths were loud and violent, as though he'd been holding his breath this whole time. It seemed he was aware, just unable to control his body. After all, an unconscious person wouldn't be able to hold his breath under water.

"Eun-ho, blink your eyes for me."

Eun-ho just managed to close one eye and open it back up. It was a slow, clumsy movement, but that didn't matter. What was important was that he was aware of his surroundings and could hear her. Jane put her arm under Eun-ho's right armpit and started walking toward the bank like an icebreaker in the Arctic Ocean.

It wasn't far, and Eun-ho was lighter thanks to the water, but it still took an eternity to reach the shore. The slippery mud made it feel like she was scaling a steep cliff made of loose gravel.

The difference in elevation between the bank and surface of the water was a bit more than Jane had judged. She could only lift Eun-ho's shoulders up onto the bank before he became too heavy to push. The rest of his body she could pull up when she got out of the water. But she had made a miscalculation. She had forgotten one important variable: Yuna.

Just as she put her hands on the ground and started to lift her body out of the water, something grabbed the back of her neck. Immediately, she fell backward into the water, completely defenseless. When she finally realized what was happening, she was already submerged in icy liquid. She struggled to lift her head, but something was preventing her from doing that. Yuna was sitting on top of her. Her hands were keeping Jane's head under water, and her knees were restraining Jane's shoulders. This would have been enough to suffocate Jane above land, but underwater, it was ten times worse.

Jane's mind fell into darkness. Her brain, paralyzed instantly. Only her instincts remained active, desperately flailing her arms. Jane's hand found Yuna's ankle just as she was about to run out of breath. A voice inside her head spoke to her. *Remember the day you bench-pressed your own weight. Your coach said you were the strongest girl in the gym, remember? You did it once, you can do it again.*

Jane stuck her heels into the mud, arched her back, and then lifted Yuna's ankles into the air. Yuna fell head-first over Jane's body. Her hands and knees, which had been keeping Jane's head and shoulders under water, went with her.

Jane sat up and brought her head out of the water. She coughed and spat out the water that she had swallowed. Just as she caught her breath, the same thing happened again. Yuna, who had come back to life sooner than Jane expected, grabbed Jane's hair and pulled her back into the water.

This time, however, Yuna tried to drown Jane by pulling her hair with one arm and strangling her neck with the other.

Jane couldn't believe how strong Yuna was. No matter how hard she struggled, Jane couldn't free herself from Yuna's grip. Her lungs were about to explode. And then suddenly, Jane thought she could hear her father's song in the distance.

Maria, Maria, you are my love, Maria . . .

After I sent you far away, I planted a flower . . .

Jane shuddered. She finally knew who was singing this song, and it wasn't her father. It was a song that Jane was singing to herself. It was a spell that she had cast on herself, from when she was young, until she was a grown woman. It was a warning to herself to not do anything if she wanted peace, to stand back and watch and do nothing.

This was why Jane was always being attacked by Yuna. She wanted Yuna to attack her. That was the only way to remain as her father's little princess, to do nothing and take it. The moment she stood up to Yuna, the moment she fought back, she would lose her father's trust. Her only worth as a person was as father's little princess.

Jane was no different from Yuna. Deep down, she was still that seven-year-old girl. Even now, moments away from dying, the specter of that child and her song was preventing her from truly fighting back.

Jane stopped struggling. She relaxed her body as though she had lost consciousness. She let her arms, which had been flailing, drop into the water. The only thing she moved were her fingers as she sifted through the mud for a weapon. Eventually her fingers found a sharp rock. She started counting. *One, two, three . . .*

Yuna's grip on the back of her head loosened, as did the arm around her neck. Jane waited. Waited until Yuna lifted Jane's head out of the water to check if she was alive. Jane's target was just beneath the headlamp on Yuna's head.

It happened faster than she was expecting. The light from the headlamp fell onto Jane's face. Jane opened her eyes suddenly. She lifted her arm and stabbed her target with the rock in her hand. Yuna let out a yelp as she grabbed her eye and staggered backward.

Jane stood up. She located Yuna immediately by the bright headlamp. Yuna was just four or five feet away from Jane as she held her bloody eye and cursed at Jane.

"You little cunt! You stealing bitch!"

Jane took one step toward Yuna. The song started to play again inside Jane's head.

Maria, Maria . . .

I planted a flower in my weeping heart . . .

Jane squeezed the rock in her hand. *I'm done, Dad.* She took another step toward Yuna. *I'm not your little princess anymore. I'm . . .*

Jane paused. She could hear the sirens getting closer. While fighting with Yuna, she had almost forgotten about them.

Jane turned her head to where she thought the cabin was. Red and blue lights were speeding toward them from the dark horizon. There must have been half a dozen cars. How did they know? Had Eun-ho managed to call the police before losing consciousness?

Jane turned to where she had left Eun-ho. He had managed to pull himself onto land and was now lying face down in the snow. It seemed like he had regained some of his motor skills.

Jane's gaze returned to Yuna. But she was gone. Wondering if she had simply misplaced Yuna, Jane glanced around. A dim light was moving toward the opposite shore. At first, Jane didn't understand why she was running in that direction. If she wanted to flee, she should run the other way, toward the mountain and the village. The only thing on the opposite side of the marsh was a gorge.

The gorge! It was then that it occurred to Jane. Yuna knew exactly where she was going.

Not like this. It was too easy. Jane started to cross the marsh in pursuit of Yuna. But her goal wasn't really Yuna. What she wanted was to kill the little princess inside of herself, the one that had been a prisoner to her father's love. Jane wanted to kill her once and for all, so that she would never come back.

The sirens continued to get louder. They sounded like they were ringing inside Jane's ears. The marsh was becoming brighter. But Jane didn't have any spare attention to think about what this meant. Her eyes were only focused on the light from the headlamp, and her ears filled with the song.

I watch the flowers thinking of your face.

I watch the flowers hoping for your embrace.

Maria, oh, Maria.

Just as the police cars arrived at the marsh, Yuna reached the shore. Seeing Yuna successfully lift herself onto land, Jane lunged and grabbed onto Yuna's ankles, causing Yuna to slip and fall back down the embankment.

"Let go of me!" Yuna shouted as she thrashed her legs.

"Shut up! Just shut up and die!" But Jane was really shouting at the song in her head.

As Yuna thrashed about, her heel smacked Jane in the left eye, her bad eye. Pain like lightning passed through Jane's head. It felt like her eyeball had been flattened like a *hotteok* pancake. Jane screamed out in pain. But she wasn't going to let go of Yuna's ankle. The red and blue lights were now filling the marsh.

"I said let go of me!"

Yuna continued to thrash, kicking her back legs out from behind her like a donkey.

"Freeze!" a voice called out from over a megaphone.

Without letting go of Yuna's ankle, Jane looked to her left and right. Patrol cars had surrounded the marsh.

"Both of you, freeze!" A man was shouting as he approached from their right. "I said don't move!"

Yuna's kicking suddenly stopped. She lifted her head and looked over her shoulder at Jane.

"Let go of me," she said in a low growl through her clenched teeth. "Stealing bitch."

Hidden behind a beam of yellow light, Yuna's face looked like a dark cave. Yuna really believed that Jane had stolen her life from her. This belief was eternal, binding, religious. And it was the power of this belief that had kept her going.

Jane's grip slowly started to relax. Yuna's ankle slipped out of her fingers. Jane stood up in the water and stared in silence at Yuna as she ran. Standing at the edge of the cliff, she looked like a child dressed in a black raincoat. The policeman's arms were close enough to reach her.

"Stop," he said. "It's okay. Just stop."

The policeman extended his hand. But just before he could grab her, Yuna flung herself off the side of the cliff. And just like that, the song in Jane's head stopped.

EPILOGUE

"Why did you get divorced?"

Yuna sometimes appears in Eun-ho's dreams to ask him this. He hesitates before answering.

"She told me to get out of her life."

Yuna cackles. A gust of snow scatters her laughter. Overhead, the sky sparkles with the vapor trails of falling meteors. He leans in to hear Yuna's whisper.

"That's unfortunate."

*

"Why did you do that, honey?"

Yuna invades his dreams again. Eun-ho looks for Yuna with bleary eyes. He sees a dark figure beyond the falling snow.

"You're just like my grandfather."

Yuna lowers her head and looks down at him. Her headlamp blinds him.

"Oh, but you don't know my grandfather, do you?"

The entire world is quiet. Eun-ho can't see the Half Moon Marsh yet.

"My grandfather was a famous ornithologist. But he had a stroke and lost all his dignity. He couldn't walk, he'd soil his pants, and started to slur his speech. Anyway, he would go for a walk in the marsh every morning. He would always take me with him. When we got to the Half Moon Marsh, he would tell me about the ducks. I was happiest when I was there with him. Do you know why?"

Walking uphill, Wife stops talking as though out of breath. Eun-ho tries to move his fingers without Wife noticing. He only manages to wiggle the tips of his fingers.

"Because I was suffocated at the cabin with my grandmother."

Eun-ho wanted to tell her that she could take it slow if she was out of breath.

"My grandmother used to be an elementary school teacher. And a wicked teacher at that. By the time I started living with her, she was old and retired. I was her last student. Every day, I had to follow the time schedule she set for me. I had to get up early in the morning, eat breakfast on time, and go to sleep early. I wasn't allowed to watch TV for more than an hour a day. She gave me homework and tests to do, too, and if I did poorly, she would punish me. Tell me, Eun-ho, would you be able to take that kind of treatment?"

The wheelbarrow stops. Wife waits a moment for emphasis.

"Well, *I* did. For two years. I was afraid that if I didn't, Grandma would abandon me, just like everyone else had."

Eun-ho feels the cold. His lower back shivers uncontrollably. Eun-ho's numb face is covered in ice and snow.

"You look cold. Are you okay?"

Wife's damp breath reaches his ear.

"I should have filled a thermos with some hot coffee. That would be nice, wouldn't it?"

She talks as if they are on a picnic. Eun-ho can imagine Wife grinning at him under her rain cap. But he's too afraid to open his eyes. It feels like it's been an eternity since he last loved this woman. A sob escapes between the gap in Eun-ho's lips—but a sob of pity, not fear.

"That was a nice break. Shall we keep going?"

Wife starts moving again.

"Where was I? Oh, yes. I was telling you about my grandmother."

The wheels of the wheelbarrow roll well over the snowy path. The blizzard is getting worse by the second.

"I begged my dad to take me home every time he visited the cabin. I cried and clung to him, telling him how I hated living with Grandma. But no matter how much I begged, no matter how hard I cried, no matter how stubbornly I clung to his legs, he would always pry me off with his cold, unfeeling hands. After he left, Grandma would scold me. She told me I was a dumb girl, who didn't understand what was going on. I would lash out at her in anger. You think I've got a bit of a temper, don't you? But anyone who went through what I went through would develop a temper. What she should have done was console me, not lock me in the attic whenever I let my temper show."

Wife pauses for a moment. Eun-ho tries to listen to his surroundings, but everything is dead silent. Eun-ho is beginning to feel like the police are never going to show up.

"But you know what? I resent my grandfather more. Because he said that he liked me better than her, my grandmother would lock me in that room while she slept in the master bedroom—like some fat pig. I later heard from my mom that I was there for two years because of my grandfather. He said my grandma was in good health, that I could stay there until it was time for me to start school. He said he would make me into a proper person before sending me back. When I found this out, I felt like I'd been stabbed in the back. If I'm not a person, then what am I? A beast? An insect? If I'd known this while living here, I would have pushed the old fucker into the marsh."

Wife continues to push the wheelbarrow up a steep slope. Eun-ho hears her heavy breathing.

"We're already here. I lost track of time talking about the past."

The wheelbarrow stops.

"Mr. Cha, you've arrived at your destination. Are you ready to disembark?"

*

The dream always ended just before he fell out of the wheelbarrow. When Eun-ho opened his eyes, he was lying in an oceanfront house in Aewol as sea fog engulfed the horizon. His face was still, as though he'd been crying all night. His memories brought him back one year, to that day, to the moment a single car sped into the Half Moon Marsh with its high beams on.

Wife let go of the wheelbarrow and turned to face the car. Eun-ho tried to lift his head, which was hanging out of the wheelbarrow. But he had no strength in his neck. All he could do was twist his head to see the car noisily racing toward them.

The headlights were so bright he couldn't tell who it was. All he knew was it wasn't a police car. The car wasn't slowing down, even though it must have seen Wife. It went up onto the embankment, and raced toward them as though it were going to run over Wife. But Wife didn't look like she had any intention of moving out of the way. She didn't even look surprised. She just watched the car barreling toward her with a blank stare on her face. She seemed to think that the person who flinched first would lose.

Just before the car hit her, it suddenly changed direction. The car turned at a ninety-degree angle, and slid along the snow-covered wetlands, kicking up snow until it stopped at the edge of the embankment. Finally, Eun-ho realized whose car it was. He didn't need to try to look at the license plate. It was Wife's BMW.

"There it goes again, touching my things."

As she muttered this, her voice was filled with annoyance. Eun-ho tried to remember who in Yuna's world was referred to as "it." He could only think of two people: Jane and Jiyoo.

"I guess Jiyoo betrayed me again."

Wife turned around, bent Eun-ho over, and took something out of the wheelbarrow. It was a kitchen knife.

"You wish I was dead, don't you?"

Eun-ho couldn't answer. He was too busy following the knife as Wife waved it above his head. He winced as she swung the knife at his stomach. Eun-ho opened his eyes to find that the rope on his hands and feet had been cut. He was free, but he wasn't really. His mind had already jumped out of the wheelbarrow, but his body wasn't budging. He mustered all his strength but only managed to slightly lift his head. Wife tossed the knife and ropes into the bushes then lifted the handles of the wheelbarrow.

"I've got the worst luck," Wife grumbled.

As the wheelbarrow was lifted into the air, Eun-ho started to hear sirens in the distance. But he had no time to check where they were coming from. As soon as he heard them, his body fell out of the wheelbarrow and into the marsh. As he landed, the frozen surface of the marsh gave way without much resistance. Eun-ho was sucked through the hole in the ice.

Ice water attacked his body like sharp knives. Every part of Eun-ho's body, even his sweat-filled pores, froze instantaneously. Eun-ho felt like his heart was shriveling to the size of a peanut. A frightened wild beast was rampaging inside his head.

Eun-ho knew from Jiyoo that the marsh was shallow. He also knew that he shouldn't flail. He knew he needed to hold his breath, relax, and think. The problem was that "knowing" and "doing" were two different things. Faced with death, Eun-ho's instincts took over.

His mind went blank, everything went silent, and his body went limp like a dead water plant. Icy water was entering his stomach. Images of Noah's thrashing as he suffocated flashed before Eun-ho's eyes. All he could hear was the name that Noah called in his last moments.

Dad. Dad . . .

He could also hear Yoon-hee's voice.

We can never run from the truth.

He was floating like a corpse as Yoon-hee's voice invaded his ear.

You can't run from the fact that you killed him.

Eun-ho could feel himself regaining his senses. He'd finally escaped what he'd done. He did it not to live, but to know the truth. He couldn't die like this. At least not yet.

Eun-ho started to think. If the sirens he'd heard before were police sirens, if the police were coming to look for him, how long would it take them to reach the marsh? Two minutes? Three? Five? Could he survive underwater that long? Was there no way for him to pull himself to land before then?

Then Eun-ho remember the BMW, which arrived before the sirens. If the driver was Jane as he suspected, if the sound from upstairs had been Jane, then that would mean she hadn't come here to assist Yuna. She was probably here to help Eun-ho. Just maybe she could save him. There was only one thing he could do to help her. He had to stay alive until she came for him.

Eun-ho relaxed his muscles and let his limbs drift from his body. He focused all his energy on holding his breath. A few moments later, he could feel something turning his body over. He felt his face come to the surface of water. But his lips couldn't breach. In front of his face was a layer of ice. It was thin, but not thin enough for the buoyant force of his head and body to break. He needed to try headbutting the ice, but he had no strength in his neck. His feet were scraping along the bed of the marsh, but he couldn't shift his weight and stand up. Eun-ho's lungs felt like they were about to explode. He wanted to grab at his constricting throat. If only he had the strength to move his arms.

He was rapidly losing his senses. He couldn't hear or see anything. He was losing the ability to tell between dream and reality. Before he knew it, the lake from his dream was reappearing like a phantom, and when he opened his eyes, he was still trapped beneath the ice of the Half Moon Marsh.

Because of his fading consciousness, Eun-ho hadn't been aware that he was already drifting out from under the ice. But then suddenly he felt his arm catch on something. At first, he didn't give it much thought. And when through the dull, dark surface of the water, he found those eyes, he thought at first that he was dreaming. Even as the owner of the pair of eyes pulled him out of the water, he still thought this wasn't reality. It was only much later when he heard a voice calling to him that he snapped out of it.

"Eun-ho."

It was his sister-in-law. She pulled him out of the water, but he was still in a daze. His airway opened, oxygen rushed to his decaying cells, and his skin felt as hot as though he'd been stung by a bee. But that was all; his brain was still only working at half capacity. Because of this, he didn't know what the light approaching Jane from behind meant. Only when he saw Jane being pulled back into the water by Wife's hands did he realize what was happening.

That was also the moment he heard the sirens again. They sounded much closer than when he had fallen out of the wheelbarrow. They sounded like they were near the cabin. Eun-ho dug his fingers into the embankment and started dragging his body onto land like a caterpillar. At first, he had no strength in his limbs, but with each attempt, he could feel his strength returning to him. As his muscles warmed up, they chased away a bit of the cold. He continued to listen to the sirens invading the wetlands as he pulled his body completely out of the water.

Eun-ho collapsed face first into the snow. He could see police cars entering the marsh.

He woke up two days later in the hospital. It took Jane four days to wake up. Wife, however, never woke up. She was discovered the next afternoon, at the bottom of the gorge. The snowstorm and treacherous terrain of the gorge made recovering her body difficult, so he heard.

According to Jinu, it was Min-young who called the police. Just as Eun-ho had planned, Min-young had contacted the police as soon as she got his message. The head detective sent his people to Cheongyeon, where they ran into Jinu. Jinu had gone there to look for Eun-ho, who had stopped answering his phone. Until then, because they thought Eun-ho had run away with Yuna, they hadn't considered he could be in danger. But they changed their mind when they realized that Jane had gone missing, too.

The Seodaemun Police Department had suspected Yuna from the beginning. Just before leaving for Cheongyeon, they called her into the station. That was already their second time calling her in. Yuna probably realized that the next time she saw them, they would be putting handcuffs on her. In fact, after the first time they called her, Yuna decided she needed to go to Woohyeri to get rid of the murder weapons.

But that day, Wife and Jane ran into each other at that cabin. That was the same day that Wife assaulted Jiyoo, and it was the same day that Eun-ho asked for a divorce. These had already pushed Wife to the edge of a precipice.

Locating the three of them wasn't easy. All their cellphones had lost service at different locations around Cheongyeon, not Woohyeri. Jane's phone's last signal came from a stream in Jeongin-dong, Cheongyeon; Wife's last signal came from their house in Cheongyeon; and Eun-ho's came from the outskirts of Cheongyeon. Later, the police realized that Wife must have taken Jane's phone with her back to Cheongyeon to throw off the police.

Because Eun-ho had managed to turn on his phone just before losing consciousness, the police were able to figure out they were in Woohyeri. Wife's phone had also been turned on for a short period of time in the same location. And once they realized that Jane's phone had visited the same location earlier that day, they wasted no more time.

The police found traces of Joon-young's DNA in the soil surrounding the Half Moon Marsh and on the grinder that Wife took to a junkyard. They concluded that Wife had murdered Joon-young. But she was never charged with the murders of her father or her past boyfriends. Noah's case was also left unsolved. They had no physical evidence to implicate Yuna in his death, only circumstantial evidence. And because the prime suspect was dead, the case simply went cold. Eun-ho was able to avoid charges of homicide, but his life never returned to normal.

*

Eun-ho never saw Jane again after that. All he heard was that she had taken Jiyoo and left for Russia. She probably found it unbearable to live in Korea anymore.

Eun-ho, who was labeled by the media as the "only man to survive Yuna Shin," also found it unbearable to live here anymore. As soon as the charges against him were dropped, Eun-ho quit his job and moved down to Jeju Island. It had already been a year since he moved into the house in Aewol. For the last year, he lived like a ghost. He didn't talk, he didn't work, he saw no one. The only time he went out was to sit at a café with a view of the lighthouse or walk along the beach.

Mornings in Aewol always came with sea fog. He would leave his house around dawn to take a walk along the coast. As he walked through the fog while listening to the sound of waves, his thoughts were always lingering on his dreams from the previous night.

Last night, Yuna came to him in his dreams.

"Honey, why did you marry me?"

Why indeed? Back then, he was a satellite to Yuna. Every moment of every day, he was thinking about her. He thought about her when he woke up in the morning, at stoplights on his way to work, during breaks between classes, at the convenience store to pick up a beer on his way home from work. He would sit alone in the living room and think about her laugh until she came through the front door, shining like a star. From the moment he rose in the morning, to when he lay in bed at night waiting to fall asleep, he was always thinking about her. The only solution to such an obsession was marriage.

But as payment for his decision, Eun-ho lost everything. He still suffered from doubt about whether he killed his own son. On the nights his doubt prevented him from falling asleep, he would take temazepam, the miracle drug of death that Yuna had introduced him to. High on sleeping pills, he would be taken back to the cabin in the country. When Yuna inevitably appeared to kill him, he would ask her a question.

"Are you happy now?"

And she would answer with no expression on her face, "No. I'm just unlucky."

AUTHOR'S NOTE

Midway upon the journey of our life
I found myself within a forest dark,
For the straightforward pathway had been lost.

Divine Comedy – Inferno, Dante Alighieri

This novel is a story about happiness, a story about one narcissist who tries to remove unhappy elements from her life to achieve perfect happiness.

It's common to refer to people who are obsessed with themselves as narcissists, but self-obsession is different from actual narcissistic personality disorder. The same goes for commonplace vanity, self-love, and pridefulness. All psychopaths are fundamentally narcissists, but not all narcissists are psychopaths.

Studies show that narcissists are more common than psychopaths, and this makes them more sinister. While their pride is sky-high, their egos are hollow, making them tragic figures, in some ways. And it's their charm that makes them so dangerous. People who fall for a narcissist's charm are groomed, manipulated, and eventually destroyed by a narcissist's gaslighting. Entire lives can be ruined.

This is my first time admitting this, but I've experienced this firsthand. I was gradually conditioned by this person, and when I finally got out of the relationship, I was already holding onto irreparable wounds. Narcissists have always been a topic I've wanted to tackle. And I had a hunch that such a character could only be realized in a story about happiness.

I've noticed ominous signs in current society: vanity, pridefulness, and most of all, an obsession with happiness. Of course, self-love and pride are important virtues in life. They only become vices when we delude ourselves into thinking we're special.

The individual should be respected, as no two people are alike. At the same time, we should acknowledge that—as the saying goes—if everyone is special, no one is. The moment you believe you're special is the moment you run the risk of becoming, not special, but a dangerous narcissist.

Perfect Happiness is a story born from one narcissist's obsession with happiness and a particular incident. Those who read the story all the way through will know the great lengths its main character went through for happiness. The moment you start reading, you might even have the feeling that the protagonist reminds you of someone.

Your intuition is not wrong—probably.

I want to use this space to say that this is not a true story. That "person" was only the seed of this story; the rest of the story's elements—its plot, characters, setting, narrator—are all fictitious.

And one final note: Despite this being a story about a villain, the narrator and protagonist are not the same person. In fact, the protagonist never appears front and center in the narration. I've put a zipper on her mouth and placed her behind the curtain. This was for a specific purpose. I didn't want to show the inner workings of the villain; rather, I wanted to show how one person can affect other people's happiness, how one person can destroy many lives.

Doing so was a new challenge for me. I had never tried to build a protagonist's character without also setting him or her as the narrator. So, I want to thank professional profiler Sang-hoon Bae, who was of immense assistance throughout this process. I also want to thank Professor Hyun Kook of Chonnam National University Medical School for helping me avoid fatal errors, as well as Hyeon-mi Choi of *Munhwa Ilbo* for giving me concrete and realistic advice.

We are in the pursuit of happiness. It is what makes us human and gives life meaning. But we must always remember that with the right to pursue happiness comes the responsibility to be mindful of the happiness of others.

Gwangju, June 2021
You-jeong Jeong

ABOUT THE AUTHOR

YOU-JEONG JEONG is an international bestselling author of psychological thrillers and crime fiction. She won the inaugural Segye Youth Literary Award in 2007 with her novel *My Life's Spring Camp* and the 5th Segye Ilbo Literary Award with *Shoot Me in the Heart* in 2009. Her novels *Seven Years of Darkness*, *28*, and *The Good Son* were selected as "Book of the Year" by major media outlets and bookstores, gaining widespread acclaim. Her works have been translated and published in twenty-three countries, including the U.S., UK, France, Germany, Finland, China, Japan, and Brazil.

ABOUT THE TRANSLATOR

SEAN LIN HALBERT holds an MA in Korean literature from Seoul National University. He is the recipient of the LTI Korea Aspiring Translator Award, the *Korea Times* Korean Literature Translation Award, and the GKL Translation Award. He lives in Seoul with his wife and daughter and teaches at LTI Korea Translation Academy. *Perfect Happiness* is his sixth novel in translation.

ABOUT THE PUBLISHER

Creature Publishing was founded on a passion for feminist discourse and horror's potential for social commentary and catharsis. Our definition of feminist horror, broad and inclusive, expands the scope of what horror can be and who can make it.